Together We Jump

To Bina:

Enjoy the journey.

Your friend,

Ken

To Bing:

Enjoy the Journey.

Your friend,

Together We Jump

A Journey of Love, Hope,
and Second Chances

Ken McAlpine

iUniverse, Inc.
Bloomington

To our sons Cullen and Graham,
may they know the joy of true love.
And to my wife Kathy,
who has given me that joy.

Together We Jump
A Journey of Love, Hope, and Second Chances

Copyright © 2012 by Ken McAlpine

This is a work of fiction. All of the characters, names, incidents, organizations, and dialogue in this novel are either the products of the author's imagination or are used fictitiously.

iUniverse books may be ordered through booksellers or by contacting:

iUniverse
1663 Liberty Drive
Bloomington, IN 47403
www.iuniverse.com
1-800-Authors (1-800-288-4677)

Because of the dynamic nature of the Internet, any web addresses or links contained in this book may have changed since publication and may no longer be valid. The views expressed in this work are solely those of the author and do not necessarily reflect the views of the publisher, and the publisher hereby disclaims any responsibility for them.

Any people depicted in stock imagery provided by Thinkstock are models, and such images are being used for illustrative purposes only.

Certain stock imagery © Thinkstock.

ISBN: 978-1-4759-5119-6 (sc)
ISBN: 978-1-4759-5120-2 (e)
ISBN: 978-1-4759-5121-9 (dj)

Printed in the United States of America

iUniverse rev. date: 12/13/2012

Acknowledgments

A book is not the writer's alone. Heartfelt thanks to Donna Thonis, Pat McCart-Malloy, Kathy McAlpine and Kay Mariani-Giles for their close reading of "Together We Jump". Their suggestions made it a better book. Thanks also to Linda Charvonia and Tracy McDermott for numerous services rendered, to everyone at iUniverse for the same, to Alan Bower at Author Solutions for believing in the words, and to Hank Tovar for helping to spread them.

1

My brother died on a muggy afternoon still as a pond's deeps, Florida holding its breath, stunned by the loss of a favorite son. We stood silent too, knock-kneed girls and birdcage-ribbed boys in threadbare suits, mouths slack, toes clenching the oozy bank while the Indian River ran.

That night, I knelt beside my bed. I had never prayed before. I knew I did not deserve God's ear, but I prayed anyhow, a pine knot grinding into one knee. I straightened and tilted my head back like those paintings of enraptured saints gazing up at some holy light, driving all eighty-nine pounds of my eleven-year-old frame into my throbbing kneecap. I prayed only partly for my brother. He could take care of himself, wherever he had gone after he was drawn beneath the moss-green water. Mostly I prayed feverishly for my mother, and since it is probably bad form to lie about prayers, I confess I prayed mightily for myself too. Moonlight pressing through the rusted window screen, I asked God to take me far from my doubts and the river that, until that afternoon, was our best friend.

2

On this San Francisco night, sitting in my dark study, my knees ache again, only now the ache keeps time with my hips and back, a percussionist rapping out an enthusiastic beat. If I am not vigilant, my head hangs forward, and my jaw hangs slack. On the rare occasion when I look in a mirror, I am reminded of a bulldog anxiously awaiting its owner's command. Age has a sense of humor, your sagging bits getting a jump on their journey toward the earth that will eventually claim the lot.

Today I am eighty-five. A single candle rises from the listing key lime cupcake. My baking skills have sagged too.

Outside a thick June fog crawls in from the west. I consider closing the shutters. I worry about passing children. It's late for children, but tourists forget time. Guidebooks now tout the Asian restaurants of my Inner Richmond neighborhood. I imagine the stomach of a child, already churning with cumin and cloves, performing an additional flip at the sight of a crinkled necromancer hunched over a candle.

I blow out the flame, cementing not a wish but a decision.

I touch the book and then the photograph. Both are smooth, the book because its leather binding is old, the photograph because even in this cost-cutting age, *National Geographic* uses quality stock. I let my finger rest on the photo, drawing strength from an old friend.

Do one thing every day that scares you, Eleanor Roosevelt once said.

I will see to it, Mrs. Roosevelt, that the ensuing days are well spent.

3

Abby and I married on May 14, 1942, five days before I left for the South Pacific on a troop ship ferrying the smell of diesel, vomit, and fear. The ceremony took place in a Hyannis Port yet to place itself on the world map, before the Kennedys made it a household word. We exchanged vows on a grassy knoll overlooking Quohog Beach and a ruffled Nantucket Sound. Seven people attended, including the bride and groom. I was my family's sole representative, my father declining to drive up from Florida. He wrote a single paragraph, wishing me well and thanking me for being a good son, the warmest compliment he ever ceded. My father knew war. He did not expect me to return.

Abby's parents attended our wedding, as did her older sister, Sarah, but this was easy for them, the Bremser family residing a half mile inland in the sprawling shipmaster's home that has been in their family since the first dogged young Bremser captain, barely into mutton chops, struck gold on a run to London with a hold full of fertilizer-rich Peruvian guano. "Success grounded in bird shit keeps one's head out of the clouds," my father-in-law, Godfrey Bremser, always said. Informed of my enlistment in the marines, he pumped my hand enthusiastically and said, "Hard up in a clinch, and no knife to cut the seizings," to which I bobbed my head in agreement. I later learned from Abby that this is a seaman's term for a difficult predicament. In those days, men kept their confusion to themselves.

Also present on the wedding knoll were the photographer, wrestling with his tripod in a whopping sea breeze, and the Episcopal minister, a family friend who apparently bathed in talcum powder. Abby held a bouquet of lilacs, the scent of talcum and lilac warring for supremacy. There are moments in life when you realize you are precisely where you should be, a fairy-tale alchemy of everything right. The heart defines these moments—the mind, sadly, gives up on fairy tales—recognizing them with a clarity that really does take your breath away. I stood transfixed by my impossible good fortune. The wind lifted my bride's auburn hair, exposing, in teasing snatches, a brown nape of neck. The ceremony was mercifully short. At the end, Sarah read a poem by T. S. Eliot, and though I knew the words, I barely heard them for the blood pounding past my ears on its way to points south. My bride and I were nineteen. For the first time in five months, I forgot about the war.

We spent our honeymoon night at the inn across the street from our wedding knoll. Mariner's Respite it was called, but at that juncture in our country's history, neither mariners nor anyone else had time for respite. The inn that night was empty except for the innkeepers, a doughty woman who clucked brightly at us while ordering her husband about. Our room was big enough for a bed and a bureau, one more piece of furniture than youth required. We swept aside the jumble of pillows, the force of our consummation threatening to drown us in eider. When we took up again, I began gently. Lifting Abby's hair, its weight like a handful of snow, I touched my lips to her neck, fawn-smooth and resplendent with the scent of peach and perspiration. I would later learn that Japanese men covet the nape of the neck, and Japanese women torment them by piling their hair high. We are all the same.

After our second joining, I hoped we would sleep, but Abby was never a sleeper. Squirming from my arms, she plucked two terrycloth robes from the closet.

Sliding into her robe, she stood beside the bed.

"Come now, Mr. Whithouse. Please don't tell me you plan on sleeping our life away?"

"Just a small portion," I said, but before I could roll away, Abby grabbed my shoulder.

My bride offered no explanation. We crept down the creaking steps and into the kitchen, where Abby pulled a bundle of stained newspaper from the fridge. On the verandah, she nodded toward two tin buckets. I picked them up, taking care not to bang them together. Our innkeeper had told me he was prepared for the Japanese invasion, and I had seen his shotgun behind the rack of dish towels in the kitchen.

The night was shockingly cool, as if winter had tiptoed back while we were lost beneath the sheets. It was only the heavy damp of the sea, but it seeped under my robe, raising goose pimples. Abby held the stained bundle in front of her like a greasy bouquet. Watched by a full moon, we crossed the knoll, wet grass beneath our bare feet. "I do," I said, but Abby ignored me, descending to the beach and the jetty poking into the black waters of Nantucket Sound.

The moon draped the jetty in silver. The enormous gray rocks, sectioned in some inland quarry, were nearly bright as day. Still I stepped gingerly. The rocks were separated by dark crevices several feet wide and sprinkled liberally with barnacles.

Abby walked as if strolling across carpet. When I reached the end of the jetty, she was already crouched, the newspaper spread before her. The chicken wings she had pushed about at dinner glistened. The barbecue smell made my mouth water.

"No potato salad?" I asked.

"Not unless you know how to tie it to a string."

"No sleep, no sustenance, and no knife to cut the seizings."

Abby removed two pieces of twine from her breast pocket. Deftly, she tied a chicken wing to each string.

"You'll have better luck down here, Shipmaster Whithouse."

I crouched. Just being near her was like facing into a warm breeze.

"I don't know how much more luck I can manage," I said, but Abby was already staring into the dark rift where her chicken wing had disappeared.

I followed her lead, but I ignored my string. I stared at my wife, her slender wrist making delicate bobs.

"Wisdom versus greed," she said.

Abby drew the string up. The crab spun slowly, oblivious to its change in circumstance, one claw affixed to the chicken wing, the other greedily spooning meat into its wet maw.

"Somebody's enjoying a picnic."

"Male," said Abby. "Unable to control its appetites."

Reaching behind the crab, Abby pinched its body between her thumb and forefinger and wrestled it gently from the shorn chicken wing. It went into the bucket with a mad scrabbling.

My string hung limp.

Abby raised an eyebrow.

"Female crabs," I said.

Abby returned to crabbing. Her lips were parted. Her robe had parted slightly too, milky skin dissolving into shadow. Beneath my robe, I felt myself stirring.

It was a form of greed, and it made me laugh.

"You could at least pretend to pay attention, Pogue."

"I am paying attention."

I gave my string several bobs.

"They're not frogs," said Abby.

"We suffer together, the prize just out of reach."

"Incorrigible," Abby said, and her smile made me ache all the more. Love isn't blind at all. Again happiness washed over me, real as the moonlight and the salt breeze. "Pay attention and stop daydreaming," my wife said.

I reached out slowly. Abby swatted my hand without looking up.

"Not that kind of dream," I said.

I felt a tug. I raised my string. Two crabs spun, claws striking at the chicken wing and each other.

"Dueling decapods," said Abby.

The lower crab fell from the string and scuttled into a crevice. Abby smiled.

"Crafty crustacean," she said.

I reached behind the remaining crab.

"Right in the middle, Pogue, or you'll get a good pinching."

The pinch didn't hurt much, but it startled me. The crab pinwheeled out into the night, splashing into the water.

"Acrobatic arthropod," I said.

"While we're tossing, we might as well empty the buckets too," said Abby.

"I'll do it."

I spoke quickly enough that she looked at me strangely.

"I hope you're going to be this eager every time there's a chore."

"I will love you, honor you, and wait on you all the days of my life," I said, trying to still my shaking.

The rocks on the side of the jetty were slick with algae. I inched down, settling the soles of my feet on a narrow rock. I did not look at the water. I stared at a lone fishing boat making its way beneath the stars, a red running light on its bow.

The crabs fell into the water with a basso plonk. I watched the running light until the last crab fell.

In ten minutes, both buckets were full again. I reached for them, but Abby was quicker.

"Marriage is about sharing," she said.

I could not look up.

"Please. Be careful."

I felt her eyes on me. Stepping past, she tousled my hair.

"Sweet knight. I've never seen anyone fall off this jetty."

I heard Abby's every noise. I concentrated on a crab of inordinate intellect; hoisting itself over the rim of a rift, it paused for a moment to test the night before crossing to the newspaper and snatching a chicken wing.

The splash and shout felt like a kick inside my chest. I leaped to my feet and nearly fell over Abby's robe.

My wife's smooth strokes drew her effortlessly away. She swam with her head up, her arms making ghost-white arcs over the water.

Please.

Twenty yards off the jetty, she stopped, whooped, and shouted.

"I have, however, seen lots of people jump!"

Dark and inconceivably lonely.

My throat pinched.

She swam back. Treading water just off the rocks, she released a whoosh of air.

"*God*, Pogue. *It's absolutely freezing.* Jump in and warm your wife!"

Hair plastered to her skull, she looked like a little girl. Her arms circled just below the water, and she breathed in rapid-fire huffs.

"Come *on*. No waiting for July." The dark water made her teeth impossibly white. "Don't go shy on me now. Right here," she said, slapping the surface with a palm. "It's plenty deep."

I felt lightheaded. The black water gripped my wife.

I reached out, fighting to steady my hand.

"Here. Get out."

There was something undone in my voice, but in all her huffing, Abby missed it.

"Get *in*. I'm naked, and you should be. You win."

Behind me, the newspaper rustled, crabs tearing meat from bone.

"It's too cold."

Abby spewed a fountain of water.

"That's the point! Come feel alive."

A vial broke in my chest, leaking dark stain.

"Your chance at a mermaid," Abby said, but there was defeat in her voice.

"I'm so sorry."

"I am too."

Her splashing receded. I watched my wife's ghostly figure leave the water and walk up the beach. At the top of the knoll, she broke into a run.

I gathered her robe and the buckets. The chicken wings were gone. Crumpling the newspaper, I stuffed it in a bucket.

I did not feel the barnacles.

When I slipped into bed, Abby turned away.

"Why didn't you swim?"

Keep too many secrets, and you become like a rusted padlock; the combination is at hand, but it doesn't matter.

"I was cold."

"Cold."

Moonlight threw shape-shifting shadows on the wall, a child's game. *Go on. Guess.*

"Please don't lie to me again," Abby said.

After a time, her breathing softened. I have always been an observer, gathering the moment's subtleties, cupping them as a child holds a butterfly. Now I collected my wife's gentle breaths, their rise and fall producing minute shiftings in the blanket on her shoulder, a landscape without solid foundation.

I did not need to guess. I knew the shadows. Closing my eyes did not make them go away.

4

The year is 2008. I have lived in San Francisco for fifty-five years. Both figures surprise me. Father Time performs the ultimate sleight of hand.

In structure, my three-story townhouse on Clement Street is little different from the row homes I rocked past on the train into Boston, though San Francisco's brickwork isn't gnawed by winter. Most of the year, I grow flowers in the planter outside my kitchen window. Perhaps because of this, according to the latest unsolicited real estate report in my mailbox, my modest home is worth $1.25 million. I care nothing for this obscene sum. My home is what I need, big enough for my books and small enough so that on damp evenings the heat from the fireplace rises to the bedroom. The stairs I climb each time I forget something keep me passably fit.

I also walk. My walking is confined mostly to Inner Richmond. I would like to set off for the horizon, but at eighty-five, this isn't entirely wise. Everything I need is close. Within Inner Richmond's borders are parks, affordable restaurants of every cant—Thai, Chinese, Vietnamese, Korean, Irish, English, Burmese—and tree-lined streets that make leafy music on breezy days.

After all these years, I have many acquaintances—the attentive waiters at the Singapore Malaysian Restaurant, the avuncular owner of Green Apple Books & Music, the proprietor of Heroes Club, who sells pricey Japanese action figures and always launches into wild chatter when I attempt the few Japanese phrases I still retain—but I have no friends. It both amuses and unsettles me that my insular existence is markedly similar to the one I led before I lost my heart on the train into Boston.

I have my rituals. My home is three blocks from the Singapore Malaysian Restaurant, where I go each Wednesday at noon to enjoy authentic roti and satay, though I avoid the desserts, which are heavy with coconut milk and calories. I am not fanatical about what I eat, but I am careful. I like being able to see my feet below my waist. My exercise, if a slow walk is exercise, and calorie-monitoring are not undertaken for vanity—at my age, vanity has sailed off to distant shores—but I wish to be independent for as long as possible, and this is harder if a short walk knocks you flat. Because I decline their dessert urgings and pay some small attention to my physique, my waiter friends call me Arnold. The nickname amuses me, for I possess none of Mr. Schwarzenegger's square-jawed good looks. I am a collection of discrepancies. My right ear sits lower than my left, as if it is still performing its failed ducking, a private joke I share with no one. My eyes sit low too, and my nose squats mildly flattened and askance, the result of a brief, less-than-illustrious boxing career. My torso is squat, but my arms are long. You might say I was assembled in the dark.

Many afternoons, I stroll into Green Apple Books & Music, where I browse the newest titles and sit in one of the overstuffed chairs and read, the owner's Rhodesian ridgeback padding over to insinuate himself, with a great draining of air, at my feet. The dog's name is Earl. The owner, whose name I can never remember, professes his surprise that Earl is so attached to me. It is true animals seem to trust me, but I also earn Earl's loyalty with the biscuits I slip him.

I confine most of my activity to daylight hours, though on evenings when I am feeling feisty, I drop into The Plough and the Stars for a black and tan and a draught of Irish music.

I don't confine myself entirely to Inner Richmond. San Francisco's public transportation is a marvel. In winter, I ride the bus to any number of fine museums. In summer, I attend the free

Sunday afternoon concerts in Stern Grove's lovely amphitheater of eucalyptus, redwood, and fir. I have attended these concerts for twenty years. I don't let the musical offering determine whether I go; art comes in many forms, and each should be given its chance, though I confess a recent rap performance left me puzzled. Though it's not supposed to happen, the ushers save me the last seat on the right side of the fourth row. The location accommodates my bladder and my hearing; I am nearly deaf in my right ear, and I climb over no one on my way to the john.

When the weather is pleasant, I ride the bus to the Presidio. There I walk the shaded paths with my memories, watching the syrupy tai chi practitioners, the chess players, and the young couples with their jogging strollers. If I want conversation, I find my way to Jim, who always sets up his hot dog cart with a sweeping view of Chrissy Field, the distant kite surfers skipping across the frothy bay. Hungry or not, I buy a hot dog and top it with mustard, onion, and sauerkraut. It is poor etiquette to engage a businessman in prolonged conversation without bolstering his coffers. In return, Jim relinquishes his fold-out chair. I fear he brings the cushion solely for my benefit. Between customers, we discuss world events and the stock market's unfoldings; Jim was a broker before long hours and painful returns saw him to an ulcer and a divorce. He makes a very good hot dog for someone who came to the art late. He also has a good sense of humor, and silence does not make him uncomfortable.

On the days Jim is not there, I walk up toward the Golden Gate Bridge and find an empty picnic table overlooking the bay. Some days, I read poetry. Often I just sit.

At night, I read, and then I dream. I read new books that interest me and old ones that still bewitch me. I am no literati, but I know what I like—the humor and magic of W. P. Kinsella, the thoughtful travel of Ryszard Kapuscinski and Paul Theroux, the humanity of John Steinbeck. A few years ago, I started reading children's books, which I hugely enjoy. My favorite so far is *The Polar Express*, which, like most good children's books, isn't entirely a book for children.

I keep a copy of Steinbeck's *Sweet Thursday* on my bedside table. Before I fall asleep, I take up the book and read a passage. When I finish, I switch off the lamp and try to dream of sea turtles.

5

On the bright morning following my eighty-fifth birthday, I stand on the curb staring down at the Mustang's engine. It looks like someone vomited oil.

I bought the Mustang in the summer of 1968. It is a 1967 Mustang GTA Coupe, still sporting its original factory frost turquoise. Like my townhouse, the Mustang has attained nonsensical value. Two weeks ago, I watched from my study as a man in a three-piece suit circled the Mustang. When he knocked on my door, he had his checkbook out. He offered me sixty-five thousand dollars.

I bought the Mustang for two thousand dollars from a hippy eschewing worldly possessions. In his materialistic days, he had lavished attention on the car. From hubcap to engine, the Mustang was in showroom condition; removing the shag carpet from the ceiling proved easy. These days, I drive the car once a week, a few times around the block to keep the parts moving. At least I thought I drove it once a week. Staring down at the oil-splattered engine, I try to remember the last time I pulled away from the curb.

I drive to my mechanic, the sweetish smell of burning oil issuing through the dash. I'm told it's hard to find an honest mechanic these days. I wouldn't know. Bill Gottlieb has been my mechanic since I arrived in San Francisco in 1953. In that time, neither Bill nor his garage has moved, though his garage has expanded, and Bill no longer has to bend to look under a hood, kyphosis bowing him into an apostrophe. I find myself stooping forward too; when I walk, I appear to have located something fascinating just off the end of my shoes. Bill and I share a joke. One day, when our noses touch the ground, we will audition for Cirque de Soleil.

Bill's garage is hidden in an industrial park three miles from my home. When we first met, his closet-size office was crowded with pictures of his young children. Those pictures hang on the same hooks. Somehow he has found room for their children and their grandchildren. A dozen mechanics work for Bill now, but he always examines my car himself.

Ticking in the sunshine, the car reeks of oil.

Without a word to me, Bill props up the hood. He looks at the engine. He walks around the car. He takes his time.

Bill speaks of cars as captains address ships.

"After we put out the fire, we'll have to replace her cracked gasket. Hoses too. Brake pads and belts. That's just a first take." That he cannot hide his testiness makes me smile. "We called you," he adds.

"About what?"

"Your six-month service."

"I never miss."

"You missed by three months." Bill is not a lecturer, but he takes upkeep seriously. "You should get an answering machine, Pogue."

"You're the only one who calls."

He lowers the hood with near reverence. If I ever sell the Mustang, I'll sell it to Bill. For two thousand dollars.

"Plan on driving somewhere?" he asks.

"Yes."

"How far?"

"A piece."

"Piece of what?"

"Across the country."

Bill assesses me now.

"Even you can't fix what's under my hood," I say.

"People fly."

I see my brother standing beside the Indian River, his face lit with a magic few people know.

"Flying takes you away from the world."

"It also keeps you off the freeways." Bill's finger traces a loving line along the hood. "Traveling alone?"

At our age, you are never alone.

"Are you repairing cars or running a homicide division?"

"Right." Bill straightens as best as he can. "Probably in a hurry to get going." He nods at the windshield. I keep a map of the United States on the dash.

"It's not 1980 anymore."

"I know where I'm going."

Bill almost smiles.

"Makes you a rare breed," he says.

The repairs take three hours. Bill has no waiting room, just five car ports looking out to the jumble of cars waiting their turn. I sit in a plastic lawn chair beside a silver Mercedes, its polished finish reflecting the warmth of the sun. I watch ravens come and go from a telephone wire. Heads snapping to and fro, they confer about the automotive work being performed below.

Fingertips press gently into my shoulder.

Bill says, "Don't try that behind the wheel."

I pay Bill in his office.

"She's in good shape, but I'd advise you not to push too hard," he says.

Bill's grandchildren watch from the walls. I wonder what they will do with their lives.

He is not talking about the car.

"I'll look out for the both of us."

Bill makes no reply. There comes a time when men finally know each other. There comes a time when precious time is all we have.

I see myself getting off the subway train, the frozen rubber of the closing door jarring my shoulder, the snow on the platform slick underfoot. My heart is pounding in my temples, cheering my life's one madcap impulse.

We can become mad again.

I want to see my country. I want to do my best to make things right. It will not be enough, but it will have to do.

6

Bill is right. The map is useless. I am lost before I reach Oakland's eastern edge. With a start, I realize I haven't been on the freeways in at least ten years, quite likely much longer. Nothing is familiar. I leave late to avoid rush hour, but rush hour waits for me. I have never seen so many cars, driving so close and so fast. I am swept up in a raging river. Growling trucks and silent SUVs whip past. I grip the wheel so hard a vein throbs in my neck. Sweat trickles in unfamiliar places. Eleanor Roosevelt would be proud.

My fellow drivers are unaffected. A woman passes, applying makeup.

I am looking for Highway 99. There are signs everywhere, but I'm afraid to take my eyes off the road.

I get off at an exit and pull into a gas station at the top of the ramp. It takes me three tries to pick the map up off the passenger seat. A glass-fronted cathedral, the gas station blots out the sun.

Inside, a dozen aisles stretch the length of a swimming pool. I place my map on the counter, painfully aware of my trembling hand. The boy behind the counter waits.

"Good morning. I'm looking for a map like this."

"Try the Smithsonian."

His head cocks left.

The rack rests at the end of the counter. The maps are tucked inside dusty plastic coverings. I select a map of the United States and a map of the East Coast. They are eight dollars and ninety-five cents each. I decide against a map of California. I hope the map of the United States gives a sufficient nod to California's byways.

The boy takes my money without comment.

"May I use your rest room, please?"

The key is affixed to a foot-long baton, painted bright red. I pick up the baton and my maps.

"Thank you."

"No purchases in the rest rooms."

"But I paid for them. I have my receipt."

"I don't make the rules."

I have never liked conflict, though I have seen my share.

"I suppose I can find the bathroom. May I leave them here?"

"Can't be responsible."

My bladder doesn't care.

"That's fine. I'll take my chances."

When I return, my maps are on the counter. I smile at the boy and thank him. To my surprise, he smiles back.

"They need the key."

The mother and father wear matching T-shirts, Mickey Mouse waving a wand beneath the logo *The Magic Kingdom.* The two boys wear matching shirts too. On the front, two bloodied men glare at each other. Beneath the men, in red gash marks, are the letters UFC.

The youngest boy, perhaps five, massages his crotch.

I see the key, sitting on the toilet tank.

I look at the cashier.

"I left the key in the restroom."

"The door locks automatically."

My stomach falls.

The older boy beams. His brother begins to hop about like a flea.

"Mommaaaaa! Gotta pee!"

The cashier leans forward.

"If we made the key any bigger and brighter, Grandpa, it would come with a fucking wheelbarrow and sunglasses."

Behind me, the woman says, "You must have an extra key."

"Manager's got the master. He just left for lunch."

The boy tugs at his mother's shirt.

"Nooooow!"

"I'm so sorry," I say.

The woman ignores me.

"We *can't* get into the bathroom, Zachary. The man locked the key inside."

"Grandpa *pees* himself," says the older boy. "We have to change his pants." He shoots his brother a meaningful look. "Like a baby."

Something ugly passes over the mother's face, but the older boy is focused on his brother.

"Zach's milking a cow," he says.

The husband stands behind the mother, looking uncomfortable.

"We have to do *something*," he says.

"We get twenty-minute breaks, but the manager takes as long as he wants," says the cashier.

The woman speaks slowly. "You just had to remember the key."

I am not sure if she is addressing me, but I know who is responsible.

"I'm terribly sorry. I'm afraid I've become a little forgetful."

It is not so odd to become forgetful and remember everything.

Now she looks directly at me. "We need a bathroom," she says.

The squeezing assumes an unbridled ferocity.

"No groin attacks allowed," says the older boy.

"I'll find the manager." Given my recent attempt at finding my way out of Oakland, this seems unlikely, but I have to do something. "Do you know where he eats lunch?"

"Someplace cheap."

"Might you know where?"

"If you were going on break, would you let anybody know where you were?"

"I want Skittles," says the older boy.

"Mooooooooom!"

"Stop it!" The woman yanks the little boy's arm so fiercely he staggers. Tears fill his eyes. "Jesus Christ," the woman says, but there is no regret in her face. Turning away, she stares through the plate glass as if some other world has suddenly beckoned.

There are some things worse than hurt in a child's eyes, but not many.

I remember the paper clip in my wallet. Fishing it out, I straighten one end.

"How about a magic trick?"

"Magic is fake," says the older boy doubtfully.

"Believe what your eyes show you," I say.

"Trash the door, and you pay for it," says the cashier, but I am done listening to him.

The three of us trundle down the snack aisle. When we get to the door, there is a light in both their eyes.

We should never let childhood pass too soon.

"It's a simple spell." Bending, I insert the paperclip. I pass my free hand slowly over the door knob. "The ones that matter most are the children," I chant and wiggle the clip.

The door swings open.

Both boys have forgotten why we came. I touch the younger boy's elbow.

"You can go in now."

The brother looks at me a tad fearfully.

"Maybe you should keep him company," I say.

On the way back down the aisle, the small boy takes my hand. It is without weight and impossibly warm. When we reach the counter, I pull gently free.

I look to the parents, but it's the boys' eyes I see.

"I'm sorry for the trouble I caused."

The husband says, "We're the ones who should apologize. We're a little on edge. We've seen every restroom between here and Bakersfield."

"It's fine. Enjoy the rest of your trip."

I only want to leave. I pick up my maps. The husband follows me outside.

"That was a deft bit of lock picking," he says. "Or magic."

It's as if he saw a smile once but can't quite get it right.

"My father taught me," I say. "He was good with his hands."

"I can't fix a leaky sink."

"I can't find my way out of Oakland."

"What was the spell?"

The surprising question sees me silent for a moment.

"The ones that matter most are the children. It's a Lakota Indian proverb."

"It makes sense."

The man's eyes are fixed on a camper parked in the shade. Someone sits in the front passenger seat, looking straight ahead.

"I'm sorry for my family's behavior. The boys need more discipline, but we're a little distracted right now. My wife's father has Alzheimer's. It's gotten to the point where he doesn't know us."

The man in the passenger seat thumps the heel of a hand hard against the window.

Beside me, the man says, "The child locks are on. My wife, she's not the person you saw."

Small fingers have left a perfect chocolate imprint below his collar. The rumble of traffic rises from the freeway, lodging in my throat.

"I'm sorry for your wife. Tell her forgetting isn't always a curse."

7

Most people group sea turtles into one lump. There are actually eight species of sea turtles, from the massive leatherback to the diminutive Kemp's ridley. The leatherback can reach six and a half feet and weigh 1,400 pounds. The Kemp's ridley grows to thirty inches. But size doesn't matter, for each turtle is an otherworldly assemblage of instinct focused solely on survival. Focus is a must. Leatherback, Kemp's ridley, green sea turtle, every hatchling that bursts from the sand has less than a 1 percent chance of reaching maturity. Even in the egg, they are set upon by fly larvae and fungi. Scrabbling across the sand, instants after coming into the world, they are attacked by birds, crabs, raccoons, rats, and a host of other opportunistic mammals, including man. And the sea waits, with its hungry minions. A thousand eggs are laid so that the one will survive. Yet each hatchling bursts forth as if it is the chosen one. There is always the chance. They must believe.

The miracle and the exercise in belief do not end at the water's edge. Plunging into the surf, the hatchling, no bigger than a child's hand, remains undaunted: having never seen the ocean before, the turtle swims an unerring course, first through crashing surf and then across the seas themselves, more blank and featureless than anything terra firma can conjure. How do they know what to do? Man is reduced to guessing. Scientists have learned that on entering the surf, the hatchlings orient themselves in the direction of the incoming waves. Beyond the surf, in the great Gobi expanse, they are apparently guided by an inborn sense of magnetic direction. Of late, biologists believe that, in the case of the leatherback turtle, a patch of pale skin near the eye may allow light to reach the pineal gland, which in turn may inform the turtle of changes in the length of the days, cueing migration.

Whatever their means of navigation, the turtles swim, confident and alone. Turtles do not travel in pods or packs. Each is captain of its own fate. After wobbling into the waters off the beach of their birth, they swim for years, the survivors feeding and growing, the majority struck down by sharks, disease, fishermen, drifting nets, and bits of plastic they mistake for jellyfish and ingest. It is a long list of pitfalls. Science does not know precisely where the turtles go. Tagging has revealed that a young loggerhead might swim nearly 7,000 miles, but we have never been able to fully track them as they mature to adulthood. *The lost years*, science calls them.

Biologists surmise that sea turtles require from ten to fifty years to mature and reproduce. When they are mature, on a signal we do not know, they veer in the darkness. For generations, villagers on beaches in Costa Rica, Venezuela, and Suriname claimed the same turtles returned to the beach of their birth. Science dismissed this primitive folklore. Now genetic evidence—the examination of distinctive mitochondrial DNA—suggests this is precisely what happens.

How do they find their way back to the beach of their birth? Science doesn't know. But find their way back they do, and how can you not love when science is reprimanded by folklore, when Atlantis emerges from the deeps, impossible and true? How can you not thrill to the sea turtle's magic and mystery? In a world where so much seems to be crumbling and so many are giving in, the sea turtle's dogged journey gives me hope and faith.

Though I have profound admiration for all sea turtles, it is *Dermochelys coriacea* that swims deepest in my heart. The leatherback's lineage goes back a hundred million years. Their earliest ancestors were snatched up off the sands by Tyrannosaurus Rex. Today *Dermochelys coriacea* is the largest marine reptile on our planet. The largest recorded leatherback measured eight and a half feet from nose to tail and weighed over a ton, but size is not even their most impressive trait. Leatherbacks dive to 3,200 feet, seeking the giant jellyfish that are their catnip. Their migrations circumnavigate the globe. They go where no other sea turtles can go. They have been spotted in frigid waters off Newfoundland, Norway, Chile, and New Zealand. In bone-chilling waters that would instantly kill their reptilian relatives, leatherbacks shut off the blood supply to their extremities, withdrawing inward, shepherding warmth and life. There is only one place where *Dermochelys coriacea* cannot survive. Why have you never seen a leatherback turtle in an aquarium? Placed in a tank, a leatherback will bang up against the glass again and again, bludgeoning itself to death.

8

Our father would have hated today's freeways. To him, they would have been tasteless as dust. When I was a teenager, each Sunday he would take my mother and me on a drive. Sometimes we drove north toward Daytona. Sometimes we drove south in the direction of Port St. Lucie.

Always we ambled. My father never had a destination in mind, but he always drove the coast road beside the ocean. The flickering pass of palmetto, dune, ice plant, and blue-green Atlantic soothed him. Once he was properly soothed, he would find us a seafood shanty at the edge of a quiet inlet; in those days, before the advent of marinas and chain eateries, central Florida had no shortage of these ramshackle restaurants.

Inside, out of the merciless sun, my father and mother would each order a beer. I was allowed an orange soda, and we would all dig with abandon into fried clams and catfish until our bellies hurt, and greasy napkins lay scattered across the table like sodden flower petals. After her second beer, my mother would politely excuse herself. She would return from the bathroom tidily arranged, but my father and I knew what she had been doing because her tears were as much a part of our Sunday outing as the crumpled napkins and her unsteady return. Before she sat down again, she would always look at me. It was often dim and cool inside the restaurant, the sea breeze infiltrating infinite cracks, but her standing there always made me sweat. Often she would answer my prayers and sit quickly, but sometimes she would stand for a long time with a puzzled look on her face, as if struggling to remember what it took to sit. When she did this, my father said nothing. In the beginning, I would plead in a frantic whisper—*please mother, sit down, your clams are getting cold*—flushing mightily because I didn't really give a damn if her clams got cold, but I cared greatly that the diners at nearby tables were staring at our family's queer behavior, my mother gaping like a village idiot, my father silent, my whispered pleas silent to no one. After a time, I stopped pleading. My mother sat when she was ready. Sometimes she pushed back my hair and gently kissed my forehead first. Once seated, she always smiled. "My boys," she would say, and my father would order her one last beer so that she would sleep on the drive home. It was the only time I saw her drink.

These drives temporarily restored my parents. It was also clear that my father's aimless driving was a literal act of leaving things behind. A five-year-old would have understood why my mother cried, though I now realize there were other possibilities for my mother's tears too.

We came home late. I slept in the backseat, lulled by the roller coaster passing of dunes, waking now and then to the silence of my parents, the bump of tires and my queasy stomach. In our sandy drive, my father would wake me, using my elbow like a tiller to guide me up the listing porch steps. Alcohol dissolved some of my father's reserve. Some nights he would kiss my forehead as he laid me in bed, an implant that would burn for days.

Alcohol unlocked other restraints. Once, on a late-night return, I heard my parents' muffled voices. After tiptoeing to my door, I opened it a crack and looked down the hallway. The door to their bedroom was ajar. I watched as my mother wormed violently from my father's arms. My mother disappeared from sight, but my father stood where he was, bare from the waist up, his face flushed, and then, like a shot, he was coming down the hall. I barely had time to duck into the shadows and no time to shut my door, but he passed by without a glance.

After the screen door slammed, I counted to ten to account for my earlier lapse, and then I raced to the window. My father stood upon loam and pine needle, looking up at the stars.

I was thirteen. Today an eight-year-old would probably understand what had transpired, but those were innocent times. My father struck a match. Its bright flare lit his sober face, and then he smoked, and we both fought to figure out how we might ever remedy the terrible thing that had happened to us.

Our father drove our family down to Sharpes from Pittsburgh in 1930, fleeing the Depression. I was seven. Sean was ten. We were given no warning. On a bitter cold February morning, our mother woke us in pitch darkness and helped me pack a bag. I wanted to ask what was happening, but Sean packed his own bag wordlessly, and I did not want to look scared. Finished packing, we stood outside, hands and ears stinging, stealing glances around the corner of the house, watching our father shove boxes into the back of our black Buick with sudden thrusts, like a boxer in a clinch. Our father had bought the car new, his pride and joy, but like our fortunes, the car had taken a downturn; part of the rear bumper was shorn off, and the leather top that had once glistened with lavish buffing was now dulled and cracked by Pittsburgh's winters.

Father rarely yelled at his oldest son, but on this morning he did, after Sean complained about the tight confines in the backseat. My fearless brother cried noiselessly, hate in his eyes. The sight so unnerved me, I fled into the house. In the kitchen, my mother, placing pans in a box, was crying too. I sorely wanted to join them, but I willed myself dry-eyed. Tears would make it harder to see whatever terror was steamrolling toward us, for why else would we be running away in a panic? I wanted to be clear-eyed and prepared when it arrived. It was also the rarest opportunity to best my brother.

Just before we left, my father called me over. The two of us stood beside the Buick, a loose thread of leather fluttering in the rising wind.

"Here." He handed me his gold pocket watch. "It's yours now."

This astonished me more than our leaving. Our father's father had carried the watch during the Civil War. The watch had turned back a bullet meant for his heart. Father told us the story once, providing only the bare facts. His father had carried the watch in his breast pocket, and we could see the dent where the .577 caliber Enfield bullet hit. It was as if he had told us the story a thousand times in exquisite detail, for I replayed the moment in my mind again and again, the circumstances on the smoky, screaming, blood-soaked battlefield always changing, but the end result remaining the same.

If not for the watch, we would not exist.

I stood speechless in the frozen dawn.

My father bent down to me. He was sweating. Smoky tendrils rose from the top of his head, somehow finding their way through his thick black hair.

Sean slouched only ten yards away, but our father made no secret of his words.

"Look at the time, Henry."

I looked, though we both knew I could not tell time.

"Seven-fifteen," my father said. "Time for you to become a man."

"Okay."

Father placed his hand on my shoulder, and a thrill went through me.

"It will be," he said, and he went into the house.

As I put the watch in my jacket pocket, Sean stepped up beside me.

"The only thing you'll be able to tell," he said, "is that it's ruined."

We drove to Florida without stopping, Sean and I in the backseat, box corners jabbing our ribs. There was no money for motels. Our father had already been out of work for six months. When he grew sleepy, he pulled off the road and slept at the wheel, his head thrown back at a frightening angle that made me wonder if his neck was broken.

I notched our progress with my own version of time. The big hand of the watch moved faster. I watched it move from top to bottom and then back to the top again. I counted how many downs and ups it took us to reach the butcher where our mother bought our meats (a little less than one down), and the police station (one down, half an up) where we had gone when our father put up bail for a drunken friend arrested for shouting foul words in the street. Shortly after we passed the police station, we reached a point beyond which Sean and I had never gone, but I continued my time keeping. I noted how long it took to go through our first tank of gas, how long it took our mother to ask, again, how we were, how long it took my furious massaging to remove the prickly needles from my legs. I gave up measuring how long Sean stewed silently. I knew he was stung by his crying, and devastated by the watch. I whispered to him, but he ignored me. He did not answer Mother either. Father, who was much like his eldest son, didn't bother with him.

When we crossed the border into West Virginia, I poked Sean's leg and held out the watch.

"Here," I whispered. "You hold it."

He shoved my hand so hard I nearly dropped the watch.

I opened my mouth to tell our mother, but the fierceness of his gesture was mirrored in his eyes. Easy as that, my brother reigned again.

Our father had always been a slow moving, methodical man, traits that made him a valued manager at the furniture factory in Pittsburgh. If someone had asked me then what my father was like, I would have said refrigerated syrup. He coursed through life with silent, sure implacability, though it is also true there was little sweet about him.

Driving south, it seemed a stranger took our father's place. His thumbs rubbed the steering wheel, and he kept adjusting the rearview mirror, reaching for it with a quick, jerky motion as if it were about to fall. In the middle of the night, between our mother's soft snores, I heard his rapid breathing. On the rare occasions when he left the car to relieve himself in the woods or shake off sleep, he leaped back behind the wheel, throwing gravel and dust as we jolted back onto the road.

We hardly talked. My mother hadn't even brought a book to read to us, and this scared me as much as anything. I knew we were being pursued. I wondered what my father had done. It had to be something horrible. Maybe he had robbed someone. I knew these were desperate times, and upstanding men had done exactly that. Or maybe he had lain down in bed next to another woman, because sleeping with someone you didn't know was an awful sin. The wife of my father's friend had done it, and that was why my father's friend was crying and shouting filthy words in the street. In my heart, I knew my father was incapable of such things—he held himself to a moral compass that did not twitch—but after we bailed his red-eyed friend out of jail, Father had told us that people sometimes do things that aren't at all like them, and it isn't always entirely their fault.

I kept looking in the rearview mirror, so that I would see our end before it pulled us over. I wondered if we would all go to prison since we were all running away, and if the guards would take my watch, and what kind of food they served. Just about anything sounded good.

Our mother rode silently and never questioned our father, at least not in front of us, not even when, on a midnight ribbon of road made blacker still by Virginia woods, he pulled the car off to the shoulder and ran off down the road. My heart stopped, and my eyes shot to the rearview mirror, but the world behind us was black and empty. We sat for a long time, the engine idling. Finally my mother slid behind the wheel, driving slowly down the road until our father appeared in the headlights, a dark form squatting beside the road. As soon as she saw him, my mother pulled over. Shutting off the engine and the lights, she got out of the car and walked back around to the passenger side, slipping in and shutting the door so gently I strained to hear the click. I looked at the watch. The hand swung completely around before our father got back in the car and, without a word, started driving.

As we drove south, Sean and I witnessed the impossible. Winter fell away. First the snow alongside the road dissolved, going from a thick blanket that covered the rolling fields, to ice cream dollops and patches, to brown grass. Then, nothing short of a miracle, the grass turned green again, leaves reappeared on the trees, and we could leave the window down, my brother and I inhaling the summer scent of pine with silent gusto.

In South Carolina, the smell of marsh muck wrinkling our noses, Sean leaned into me and spoke for the first time.

"Henry," he whispered. "It smells like you shit your pants."

I would have too, if he had spoken any louder, for our father had told us if he ever heard a curse word on our lips, he would cut our lips off and make us eat them like Blackbeard the pirate had done.

I did not want to be left standing lipless and alone beside the road, beside a marsh filled with poisonous creatures, but I was furious.

"You smell like horse piss," I hissed, but Sean was already looking out his window.

We ate what my mother had brought in the bag she kept at her feet; dried apples and walnuts and stewed tomatoes that swished around in our mouths like slick clams until we choked them down. My mother fixed us bread with butter; sometimes she ladled jam on too, passing it carefully across the seat. Once, when we stopped for gas, she politely asked the proprietor if we might fill our bottles with water from the station spigot. I saw how his eyes walked over her body, and the dark look that passed over my brother's face. When Sean asked if we could use the outhouse around back, I felt sick. On our return, I avoided the gas station owner's gaze, but Sean, having peed through his bedroom window, gave him a wink.

We arrived on the outskirts of Darien an hour before dark. Everywhere black men sat on the curbs of dirt sidewalks, their hands dangling. I had never given much thought to the blacks in Pittsburgh; we were raised to see them no differently than us, but these men stared unblinking as we passed, and, scarier still, the eyes of equally still children tracked us from behind grimy windows. At first my mother waved to the children, but not one of them returned a wave. Eventually she gave up.

Darien's downtown was empty. The emptiness frightened me far more. I wished for staring men and frozen-faced children, but there was no one. Buildings scrolled past, square as children's blocks, wood showing behind chipped plaster—a butcher, a hardware store, a sagging sign identifying City Hall. Every window was a black hole. I wedged the pocket watch into the crack in the seat.

Like any astute sibling, Sean sensed my fear. When our father's eyes left the rearview mirror, Sean crimped his hands into claws and sucked in his cheeks and made his eyes bulge.

"Zombies are going to eat you alive," Sean whispered. "Bloody stumps and all."

"They'll eat you too," I hissed, though I didn't really hate him that much because I saw the sweat on his upper lip.

Fog appeared as if on cue, tendrils that skidded across the Buick's black hood like skeletal fingers. Now I wished heartily for the police. I held my breath, waiting for the zombies to crash through the doors and the black windows and swarm over our car, drooling their empty-eye hunger against the glass before smashing the windshield and tearing us to pieces.

Perhaps our mother knew. She turned on the radio. Duke Ellington played "Three Little Words."

Using the music for cover, Sean leaned close, his breath Zombie-like from stewed tomatoes.

"They eat the youngest meat first."

"We're not going to die."

"If we don't die, you're still gonna have scary nightmares."

"I don't dream," I said.

It was true, and it gave me strength.

"Everybody dreams, stupid."

"I don't."

"You just don't remember," he said, and the way he said it let me know this was a stupendous failing.

When my father pulled off the road at the foot of a half-seen bridge, I nearly cried out. The fog was thickest here. Nudged by a faint breeze, it rolled over our car, a dirty tumbleweed without end.

Mother said, "William, people are desperate," but Father stepped from the car. Anxiety, not zombies, tore at my chest. I did not want him wandering about this graveyard, but I still feared Father more than the walking dead, so I kept quiet.

He opened the trunk. I heard things moving about. When he passed alongside the Buick, he held a fishing rod. I had never seen my father fish. This unexpected course of action frightened me almost as much as the specter of flesh-crazed zombies. Our mother did not look at him. When he passed, she reached forward and turned the radio back on.

Our father disappeared over the embankment. When I turned, Sean was already slipping out his door. I had no time and no choice. Our mother swayed to the music, eyes closed.

At the embankment's edge, the dirt slope fell sharply. A few steps dropped us below the fog.

It was one of the greatest shocks I had received in my short life. People lined the Altamaha River's north bank as far as I could see—black and white, men, women, and children, nearly every one of them dangling a line in the water. Some had poles, but most held hand lines. They stood elbow to elbow, looking out at the river as if waiting for the start of a show.

There appeared to be no space left on the riverbank, but an ancient black man and a boy with an enormous wart on his right cheek parted silently to make room for us. My father nodded to the man and said nothing to us. He produced a jar full of worms from inside his jacket. Where they had come from was a mystery to me. After unscrewing the lid, he smoothly skewered a worm on his hook. I felt a little better.

I tried not to stare at the wart. It thrust from the boy's cheek like a crusty volcano. I could see where his fingers had scraped away most of the rim. I wondered what it was like to carry such a thing around. He was about my age. He stared at the point where his line disappeared into the sludgy water, but the twitch of his eyes told the truth. I smiled at him, but he ignored me.

It was a relief to know we weren't going to be eaten, but some instinct kept us beside our father. Since he had snubbed me, I feigned disinterest when the wart-cheeked boy gave a short grunt of triumph, hauling a flapping fish onto the muddy bank. In a single motion, the ancient black man clasped the thrashing fish by its tail and dashed its head against the ground, the impact like a wet towel against a wall. I stared at the fish, blood pooling around its eye, and my empty stomach turned. I wondered what the fish had felt in that last instant. The wart-cheeked boy looked at me and spat in the river.

For close to an eternity, this exercise repeated itself all about us. Everyone caught fish but us. I stopped caring about the boy or the wart. A half moon, tilted like a swing, rose from the reeds on the other side of the river. We stood motionless, our line and our spirits limp. It was as if our father fished in a different river.

"Father?" Sean said, but our father did not answer.

The wart-cheeked boy gave a slight cough. This time I glared at him, making sure to focus on the wart, but he still pretended to watch the river. I wanted to slap him. Once I looked back up the slope. The fog sat thick on the embankment, but I thought I saw a shadow.

When we finally made our way back up the slope, the moon high in the sky, not one of those people, not even the children, had left. Climbing the steep bank, my feet slipping in the loose dirt, it wasn't fatigue but the soberness of the place that saw me fight back tears.

Our father returned the rod to the trunk. He started the car. I heard a soft rap. For a terrifying instant, my imaginings turned real. The zombies had come. From where I sat, I saw only the old man's withered torso and arms: the arms looked like bone strung with thin marsh grass.

Father rolled down the window. He tried to wave the man off, but the man reached through the window, placing the folded package on the dash. Turning away, he disappeared over the dark edge of the embankment.

The Buick's engine rumbled, but our father sat as if turned to stone. Our mother reached across the seat. She unwrapped the newspaper carefully. The stink of mud and blood filled the car.

Fifteen minutes down the road, our father built a fire. Our mother cooked the four crappies in a skillet, adding a clove of garlic she had miraculously plucked from the jumble of boxes. Sean and I crouched beside the fire, inhaling the heavenly aroma of cooking garlic, oblivious to the mosquitoes roiling about us like our own individual blankets. We crunched up and swallowed down everything: heads, bones, tails. To this day, those crappies remain one of the best things I have ever tasted.

We crossed into Florida sometime in the night. Morning's heat stirred me, but I dozed until furious whisperings woke me for good. I mumbled, and when I looked up, my mother and father were looking straight ahead, their heads still as flower pots. When I looked over at Sean, he looked away.

Around midmorning, we stopped at a country store. Our father turned off the engine. Our parents kept staring ahead, and then our mother leaned into our father and kissed his cheek. For another long moment, our father sat still. Then he turned.

"Henry. I need the watch."

The watch was still wedged in the seat crack. Retrieving it took an embarrassing amount of probing. My father waited.

He was gone a long time. I sorely wanted to measure it. Finally he returned, carrying several bags. Inside was flour and sugar and fresh oranges and kitchen utensils and a coffee pot and, to our joyous surprise, two peppermint candy canes.

Our father handed one to each of us even though we hadn't eaten breakfast.

"Welcome to our new home," he said.

That there were only two made me feel guilty.

Reluctantly I held mine out.

Our father turned away, but Mother looked at me as only a mother can.

"You're a sweet boy, Henry. Your father already offered me one."

I continued holding the candy cane out stiffly, my hand shaking like an acolyte struggling to put out a stubborn candle.

"Father?"

"Your father doesn't like sweets."

The store owner stood in the window, wearing a white apron. Our eyes met. He did not smile, but he gave me a small wave. I waved back, the candy cane in my hand.

I counted in my head how long it took our father to start the Buick and leave his grandfather's savior behind.

Today you won't find Sharpes on many maps—it's folded into Cocoa Beach—but the town, all six square miles of it, still exists, though half those square miles are water.

Our father rented our new home sight unseen, so he hadn't seen the bordering marsh, or the tin roofing peeling back like breaking waves, or the front porch, propped on cement blocks and listing ferociously above the loamy sand. The entire cottage tilted slightly toward the river as if it yearned to run off for a swim. Soon enough we would discover that this settling caused the clapboard walls to pull apart in places. During thunderstorms, the four of us would rip pages from Life magazine and stuff them in the cracks. Today these so-called cracker cottages sell for a fortune, but back then, only people like us rented them.

The four of us observed these deficiencies beneath a blistering midday sun. We stood in the sandy drive, swatting mosquitoes, our individual stinks wrapped about us. We stared at the dilapidated shack, and then our mother threw her arms around our whiskered father and kissed him full on the lips.

"It's like a second honeymoon," she said.

My father straightened, and then he did something I'd never seen him do before or since. With the two of us looking on, he returned my mother a kiss of her own. I think he might have kept kissing her straight through the day, but she finally pulled away, catching her breath, and when she did, even she looked at him quizzically.

His smile made him look like another man.

"April." He said our mother's name gently. "My spring."

It took us fifteen minutes to carry our worldly belongings into the shadowy front room. Sean and I stood, fairly quivering, and when father finally nodded, we crashed out the screen door and vaulted down the steps, sprinting toward the river we had sensed the moment our father stopped the car, mud and salt and the hint of decay palpable in the squatting heat.

At a flat-out run, it took five minutes to reach the Indian River. We ran through a world of violent green that alternately stroked and clawed us, and then we crashed out into the open and stopped in our tracks.

We stood, hearts still running, mouths agape, transfixed by the impossible sprawl. Water moved past in a tremendous sweep, and in the pinch-eyed distance, low lying islands rose. Sean threw a stone into the river, causing a flock of white swan-like birds to rise like a heaven-bound cloud. Both of us grasped that our lives had irrevocably changed.

We breathed in the river. Rapture fostered a momentary truce.

Sean said, "We have to change your name."

"What?"

"Henry is a sissy northern name. We're southerners now."

I wasn't sure why northern names and southern names would be any different, but I knew I should defend myself and my heritage. Henry was the name of our Civil War grandfather.

"I'm named after a hero."

"A Union hero."

"He's still a hero."

"No one cares."

"I care."

"No one *here* cares." His voice softened. "Any of the kids around here who do care, care that they lost. You tell them about our grandfather, they'll likely beat you to a stump."

I knew he was looking out for me, but I still couldn't bring myself to trade off my grandfather like a baseball card.

"Sean doesn't sound like a southern name," I said, though I had no idea what a southern name sounded like.

"Maybe not, but it's a shitload closer than Henry."

"Father's going to cut your lips off."

"Only if you tell him."

It was gloriously true. Father wasn't here. Already it was our place.

"Goddamn, you're right," I said.

The clumsy curse made us both laugh.

We stood savoring the honey taste of rebellion, watching the river flow. It seemed to me the water moved not in a single mass, but in great slabs, the edges of each slab roiling and churning as they bumped against each other. Far across the river, Merritt Island, made fuzzy by great distance, slowly became more discernible, undulating in a splotchy spread of dark and white.

"It's giant," I said. "Is the ocean on the other side of that island?"

I was humbled, but my brother was not.

"Think I can swim across it?" he asked.

In Pittsburgh, we'd never encountered anything more than a waist-deep creek. Still my brother could do anything.

"No," I said.

Sean stared at the river, as if challenging each speeding slab.

"One day I will," he said.

He turned his conqueror's stare on me.

"This is our river," he said. "It belongs to us."

I knew exactly what he meant.

"Where do you think it goes?" I asked.

I was happy he had forgotten about changing my name.

"Wherever the hell it wants."

"It's hot as shit."

Sean said, "Pogue."

The river made a sound like a gently passing wind.

"What?"

"Pogue. Your new name."

"*Pogue* is southern?"

The word felt stranger on my lips than any curse word.

When my brother didn't have an answer, he ignored the question.

"Pogue," he said. "Rhymes with rogue."

"What's a rogue?"

"Someone who does whatever the hell they want."

Even then I knew it was everything I was not, but my brother had powers I could not grasp.

"I can change just like that?"

"Just like that."

The breeze shifted. The river smell grew stronger, as if someone was shoveling up the dankest dirt from the depths of a hole.

"Pogue," I said, turning it again on my tongue. It was easier this time. "Pogue Whithouse."

Sean picked up a stick. He touched one end gently to my head, and then he threw the stick far out into the river. It bobbed on the surface for a few beats before the current swept it away.

"Good-bye, Henry," my brother said.

It was only a stick tossed in the water, but something rose inside me, a mix of triumph and hope. I turned to my brother, an outlandish curse on my tongue, but Sean was looking at the river. The curse withered, dissolved by the shadow of sadness passing across my brother's face.

I was no rogue, but from that first day, I was home. The soggy heat, the sandpaper scratch of fat leaves and poke of palmetto, the mosquitoes that ignored my pale, succulent Pittsburgh skin, they all welcomed me. Each of the elements—heat, bugs, humidity—tormented my family to varying degrees, but I was a finely tuned creature, perfectly suited to my environment. From the first day, I loved Florida passionately, and for a time, Florida loved me in return.

Our cottage had four rooms—two in the front and, down a short hall, two in the rear. The back rooms served as bedrooms, and the front room, with an adjoining closet-size kitchen, served for everything else.

Our mother worried we would hate our new home—it was roughly the size of our basement in Pittsburgh—but Sean and I worshipped it from the first creaky footfall. It was something out of *Robinson Crusoe*, wild and weathered, the perfect bowsprit for a leap into adventure.

Our bedroom window, screen bowing out like a wind-filled sail, faced the river. We couldn't see the river. It was obscured by a magnificent tangle of Longleaf pine and Turkey oak, gumbo limbo, bay cedar, and saw palmetto—exotic names worthy of Crusoe—but on nights when the wind blew from the east, from our beds we heard the river's sighs and gurglings, a magical sibling tossing restlessly in an adjacent room.

On our fourth morning, a queer jingling joined the river's mumble. Jumping out of bed, we pressed our faces to the screen.

Our father stood in the drive. Nearly falling down the porch steps, we ran to the bicycles, the last embers of a gold pocket watch.

9

In the dream, the Japanese soldiers come to me not burnt and blackened, but bearing tea. Always I sit in the same garden, each living green lovingly tended. I sit beneath a cherry blossom. Its pink petals give downy applause in the slight breeze. Music issues from somewhere. I cannot see the phonograph, but it pours forth the soulful renderings of Glenn Miller, Artie Shaw, and Louis Armstrong.

Being waited on has always made me uncomfortable, but after years of dreaming this dream, I know my protests will do no good. I give in to my hosts, marveling at the intricacies of Chaji. I admire the tea servers immensely—their attention to detail, their incomprehensible focus—for I know now, after so many nights, that they know what is coming, even as I know that this seamless ritual showcases other forms of unbending discipline.

During the tea ceremony, words are not allowed. I smile with gratitude. The servers return my smile with polite distance and return to their unfolding art. I will never know them, and they do not care to know me. Beneath their graceful effeminate surface, they are as impenetrable as stone.

I sip the tea served from the *chawan*, the simple wooden bowl. The tea lies on my tongue like honey, so sweet I try vainly to balance it there, holding its taste, but the liquid escapes inexorably like blood from a wound.

I am helpless to prevent what comes next, though I know it is coming as certain as my next breath. I sit, forever condemned a hapless witness, as shouting sunders the garden's tranquility, a rude and sudden thrust, the rape of serenity. Wherever they are in their ministrations, the servers always respond in the same fashion. Calmly folding their hands at their waists, they turn their eyes to me. They stand rigid, not a single spasm as the bullets rip through them, spitting fabric, organ, and bone. The eyes regard me without accusation. The fusillade rains through the garden like a locust swarm. The *chawan*, the *chasen* (tea whisk), and the *chashaku* (tea scoop) disappear into thin air. I sit unharmed. The bullets are not meant for me. They seek out everything we do not understand.

Always, the shooting lasts an agonizingly long time. Finally, little more than bony hangers of dangling flesh, the servers lay down on the stones, curling upon themselves like sleeping children. The smell of burning wood comes to my nostrils. Turning, I see the men in my company turning their flamethrowers on the cherry blossom. My comrades aren't men at all. Their grimy faces are contorted, and spit flies from their mouths. They scream—at the quiet sufferings of the fetal tea servers, at each other, at themselves—a hymn of hatred and despair. Always the tree burns first, leaving the blossoms miraculously suspended in the clear blue air.

Over the roar of the flamethrowers, Glenn Miller plays.

I try to dream of turtles, but the subconscious is not easily swayed.

10

I want to see my country, but I'm afraid to take my eyes off the road. My fellow Americans stomp on their accelerators as if pursued by the devil himself. From the corner of my eye, I catch snatches of Steinbeck's central valley—hypnotic irrigated fields, grassland and dun-colored hills, their dusty look mirroring the pasty gumminess in my mouth. Again, I strangle the steering wheel.

When I finally pull into the Fresno motel, I wonder if I'll be able to get out of the car. I sit in the front seat of the Mustang. The tension leaks away, but it doesn't leave. It mingles with exhaustion to produce cement weight. Few things are golden about the golden years, but they do cultivate a form of persistence. The day is done. It has left a taste in my mouth like burnt butter, but I am still here.

I am swimming stiffly, but I am swimming.

I wake in the dark, fully dressed. Over the tops of my loafers, a foggy gray eye stares at me.

On my way to the bathroom, I stagger slightly and bang hard against the TV. For an alarming moment, I'm afraid I am going to have to take up damages with the owner. But the TV is riveted to the stand. A Greyhound bus might knock it loose, but I won't.

I stand shakily in the bathroom. The towel is musty. I remove a cracked lump of toothpaste from the sink with a piece of toilet paper. Back on the edge of the bed, I read the name on the telephone. Honey Bee Motel. The plastic face of the clock radio is fogged with scratches.

Four forty-five. Perhaps too early. I don't know their habits.

Reaching for the leather satchel, I flip the latch. My fingers trace the contents: a pair of khaki pants, two balls of dress socks, two rolled undershirts, two pairs of boxers, a blue button-down shirt—formal counter to the flannel shirt I just slept in—and a fleece-lined windbreaker. My fingers glance across the cracked leather of a marine-issue shaving kit, the gritty surface of an industrial flashlight, and the cool, smooth cylinder of my stainless steel coffee thermos, bump of Swiss Army knife duct-taped to one side. Finally, my fingers touch the book's spine.

I remove the book carefully. The photograph is tucked between the cover and the first page. I lay the photo on the bed. I read a few pages, but they only make me sad.

I pick up the phone and dial the long train of numbers.

We can become mad again, Mrs. Roosevelt.

To steady myself, I count the rings. I'm about to hang up when the receiver lifts. Immediately my good ear is assaulted by violent clattering.

Silence follows.

A voice says, "Hmm."

"Hello?"

"Slimy."

"Excuse me?"

"My hands are slimy. Soap is worse than dirt." The next accounting is not entirely for me. "The phone squirted right out of my hands. It bounced off the table and hit the floor. If it's broken, I'm in trouble, but it wasn't my fault. I didn't want to wash my hands."

I am accorded a milder clack.

I wait. Outside the sky is lightening.

"That's better. I needed a towel. I could have wiped my hands on my front, but it's a new dress. If I get anything on it, my mom will really kill me. That's why I was washing my hands in the first place. The soap made the phone squirt away, *pfffffffft*, like a greased watermelon. They're still a little soapy. It could happen again." An undercurrent of hope, followed by steady breathing. "Are you selling something? If you're selling something, I have to hang up. Since you're not a computer, I have to be polite, but I still have to hang up. I'm sorry."

I feel like my thoughts are squirting away. I know she is getting ready to hang up.

"I'm not selling anything."

"If you're cleaning carpets, forget it."

"Because you have hardwood floors."

My companion absorbs surprises better than I do.

"You've been to our house," she says.

"Yes. I have."

"When?"

"It was a long time ago."

"Before Christmas?"

"Yes."

"Do I know you?"

"No."

"You might be a very good salesman."

"Trust me. I'm awful."

"You sound honest."

It depends. Are secrets lies? For once, the question doesn't depress me. In fact, I'm tempted to put the question to this cheery voice. No doubt the answer would be interesting.

"I'm Tesia."

I know this. The letters come every few months, but there hasn't been a phone call in years. Phone calls are for bad news. It's our unspoken agreement.

"Now you give *your* name."

"I'm sorry. My name is Pogue Whithouse."

"Pogue. It sounds like toad. Is it your real name?"

"Kind of. It's a nickname that stuck."

"I like it."

"Thank you."

"It's because I like toads."

I look at the photograph on my lap, hoping for strength.

"May I speak to Sarah Thompson please?"

"That's my grandma."

This will not be easy.

"I found a caterpillar yesterday. It's bright green. It looks fat, but it's hard to tell with all the fuzz. I might feed it to the bullfrogs. Bullfrogs are even better than toads. They're much bigger."

"Is your grandmother home?"

"She's eating breakfast in the kitchen. You wanna know what she's having?"

Suddenly I do.

"Sure."

"Yogurt and fruit. She loves eggs over easy, but she can't have them anymore because of the cholesterol." Co-lester-all. Proudly pronounced. "She makes eggs sometimes when Mom isn't here. When I tell her eggs are bad for her, she always says the same thing. *Life is short, and my life is shorter than most.* I don't tell Mom. Are you old?"

"Yes."

"Do you eat eggs?"

"Yes."

"Cholesterol clogs your arteries like paper in a toilet. Our toilets clog all the time. This house is super old. How old are you?"

"Eighty-five."

"That's old."

"Thank you."

"For what?"

Just like that, leaving feels right.

"For being honest. May I ask how old you are?"

"I like that you're polite."

"Thank you."

"You still have to guess."

"Eleven."

"That's silly. I'm eight. Max next door is eleven. I'm in second grade, and he's in fifth, but we're still friends. He's a good artist, and he's okay at sports, but he always forgets to zip his pants. His family has been in their house forever too."

"Does your friend Max have a grandmother named Anne Grant?"

"You knew Max's grandma?"

I see a man filled with life, a man no one could dislike. A man not unlike a child.

"I never knew her well, but I like her anyhow."

"You don't know."

Everything goes still, and my heart does the opposite. You never get used to what you know is coming.

"She froze to death. It was last winter. It was really sad. Max and his parents went away for the weekend. The girl who came to the house to watch her thought she was upstairs sleeping, but she was in the basement. She was sitting at a card table in a summer dress. The table was piled up with old newspapers. The basement doesn't have heat. The girl told Max she was sitting there like she just put down the paper."

Every soldier who came within earshot of George Grant knew he was married to Miss Massachusetts. I trained with George Grant at Parris Island, and then we went our separate ways. George did not come home from Germany. Over the years, a few of the men in his troop called on his wife. Some were good men, but Anne Grant was not interested. For some, there is only one love in a life.

"How do you know my grandmother?"

"I was married to her sister."

"Oh."

I wonder how much of this story the sprightly voice knows.

"Guess where I'm sitting."

In an instant, I have lost everything I gained.

"By the telephone?"

"No. I'm on the toilet. I'm not doing anything. We get the best reception in the bathroom." A small grunt of rising. "I'll get Sarah."

"Wait."

One more minute. It is cowardice, but I don't care.

"Is Tesia a family name?"

"No."

"It's very pretty. Like the chime of a teacup."

"It's okay, but it's too ladylike for me. Do you like animals?"

I look at the photo.

"Animals are one of my favorite things."

"Bullfrogs are my favorite. Big fat ones that gobble meal worms. My best friend, Jessica, says bullfrogs are the world's rudest eaters. Worse than her brother Nathan."

"Maybe they're just enjoying their food."

"Bullfrogs don't have to watch their manners. They can just be who they are."

"You can be yourself and have manners too."

A sigh.

"Now I know you and Sarah are friends. Sometimes I wish I lived with my dad. He barely has any rules. But now he's married to a woman who's even ruder than a bullfrog. *Guess what?*" These last words a hiss.

"What?"

"His new wife has a tattoo of a bluebird on her *butt*. Mom told me. Mom said the bluebird is a sailor's symbol for someone who is well-traveled. What's white trash?"

"Would you mind getting your grandmother, please?"

"Okay."

I listen, footfalls tapping down the hall to the kitchen. I wonder if the kitchen still smells of fresh cut flowers.

"Hello?"

Voices don't change. It is a heart-stopping deception, like expecting solid ground and stepping into space. The past rushes toward me. The ability to speak lags behind.

I can still hear.

"There's no one on the other end."

"Yes there *is*. Pogue."

My name, triumphant as cholesterol.

Sarah's words in the mouthpiece, rushed.

"Pogue? Are you there? Is everything all right?"

I rush too.

"Everything's fine. Absolutely fine. There's nothing wrong. There's nothing wrong at all."

We both know this isn't true, but the way I repeat myself idiotically makes Sarah laugh.

"You gave me a real fright," she says.

I have been the poorest of friends, a failure by every measure, but shallowness still remains beyond us.

"Why are you calling?"

I do my best to explain. I take my time. I have gone over this speech countless times, touching every detail. I manage to stick fairly closely to the words I want. I do not explain everything. I can't. I don't know myself. I am still working it out.

I finish to silence. I wonder if I have made a mistake.

"Like a walk," Sarah says slowly. "Very good. Frost's 'Acquainted with the Night.' You remember."

Her choice of poem is bittersweet. Perhaps shared chromosomes knit us tighter than we think.

"Of course I remember."

"Be sure to walk at night," she says.

"I will."

I feel the lifting again, excitement pouring like wine through my veins, producing warmth as real as inebriation.

"I confess I'm quite jealous."

I touch the bedspread.

"You'd be a lot less jealous if you could see the room I'm in."

"Describe it to me."

She is genuinely curious. This time I laugh.

"Picture a troll's tenement. The troll chain smokes, and favors paint-by-numbers art. He has his redeeming qualities. He leaves toothpaste in the sink for air freshener."

Sarah doesn't laugh. She is reserved around strangers. Perhaps that's what I've become.

"I admire what you're doing, Pogue."

Falsehood is beyond her. But the quiet way she says it bleeds away my joy.

Her next words are enunciated firmly. Robert Frost deserves the respect of clarity.

And both that morning equally lay
In leaves no step had trodden black.
Yet knowing how way leads on to way,
I doubted if I could ever come back.

I see again the falling snow, the kindness of a woman trying to make the world right. But as with any fine poetry, time has woven "The Road Not Taken" with new meanings.

Way does lead on to way. We both know this all too well.

"Rightly said, by you and Mr. Frost."

"They're still just words," she says.

If you will tell me why the fen appears impassable, I then will tell you why I think that I can get across it if I try.

"You were right, Pogue. You and I, we are one in a thousand. But I don't know if it matters."

It must. We must try to make it so.

At six-thirty, I cross the parking lot. Gray clouds have scudded in from the west, masking the sun and anointing the world in dishwater tones.

11

A few months after our arrival in Sharpes, our mother began to read to us from Pliny the Elder. She read to us in the evening before she left for the seafood restaurant where she worked nights as a dishwasher, Sean and I sitting dutifully beside her on the couch in the front room, absorbing, in our respective fashions, Pliny's *Natural History*.

My brother listened out of respect for our mother. Like our father, Sean wasn't much for books. He sat alert, but I saw his mind wandering off to the river, his slender fingers picking at the frayed cushions. I realize now my mother knew he was elsewhere. My brother was a dreamer. Words dragged him down, though, in the case of Pliny, this was ironic because few dreamed larger than the self-schooled naturalist and philosopher. As an adult, I would hear Pliny maligned for getting virtually every fact wrong, but as a boy, his words came to me not as facts but as spellbinding tales of infinite possibility in an impossibly varied world. He was no Darwin, but he bestowed an education in wonder.

My mother forgave Pliny his misperceptions because she understood his value. His words were beautiful; his wildly imagined descriptions of various natural processes were my first taste of poetry. And his curiosity was insatiable. Everything fascinated him, no matter how ugly, small, or seemingly mundane. Curiosity would kill him. He died lingering too long on Vesuvius. Hypnotized by the fiery lava tongues, the fumes choked him. Our mother did not hold this up to us as a warning. She held it up as a grail.

My father took the job his cousin had offered when he called Pittsburgh from Sharpes, hauling refuse to the trash yard his cousin owned. My father's cousin had the garbage contract for Sharpes and several neighboring towns. Even in a Great Depression, people had trash, though they threw less of it away.

The cousin quickly discovered my father's gift, and so his job became hauling and repair, for my father could take a toaster that had gone under the wheel of a truck and make it new again. The cousin sold my father a truck at a substantial discount and then dispatched him the length and breadth of Florida to hunt for discarded appliances to be fixed and resold. Within three months, my father was earning his cousin substantial returns. We were happy to have two wage earners under one lopsided roof.

Our father never sat with us during our evening readings. Sometimes he was as far away as Tampa. If he was home, he was often out in the shed applying a wrench to some mangled item. He saw reading as pointless. Boys needed skills, not words. More than once, he told our mother this, but in this matter, she ignored him. For the first time, I saw that our mother and father were very different.

Though he ignored Pliny, our father led us to miracles of our own. One afternoon, about six months after our arrival, he pulled up in front of the house with a jumble of wood in the truck bed.

"Get in," he said.

Sean and I clambered into the cab. The vinyl seat was frying-pan hot. I sat squirming next to my father. Sean took the window.

"How's your swimming?" our father asked.

"I swim like a dolphin," Sean said. "Henry," my brother still used my sissy name with our father, "is more like a tadpole."

"Tadpoles are good swimmers," my father said.

I flushed madly.

"What's the wood for?" Sean asked, changing the subject.

"You'll see," our father said, and when he turned back to the wheel, I stuck my tongue out at Sean.

We emptied the truck beside the river. There was a bundle of two by six boards in surprisingly good condition and two logs, about six inches thick and seven feet long, with the bark shaved off and the ends tapered slightly.

"Spruce floats," our father said, and Sean and I nodded knowingly, though this was news to us.

He showed us how to hammer in the three-inch nails he had patiently bent straight. I returned the first two nails to their original crooked state, but on the third try, my nail disappeared into the wood arrow true. I gave a small cheer.

Smiling at me, our father said, "Words aren't everything."

We hammered the two by sixes together, and then we fixed the expanse atop the spruce logs. For insurance, we wound rope around the front and the back of the deck, weaving it underneath with each turn so that it fixed the spruce logs tight.

When we finished, the three of us stood in silence, listening to the river voice its gurgling pleasure at the sight of our first raft.

Our father actually laughed, sharing the river's pleasure.

"What do you think?"

"It's a magic carpet," I said.

I wanted to throw my arms around our father and disown Pliny forever, but father was watching Sean.

Sean stared at the raft. Then he smiled slowly, as some private thought assembled itself in his mind.

"The river," he said, "is mine."

Our father laughed again.

"That's how I hoped it would be," he said.

We greatly improved upon this first crude design, my father driving to the big stores in Daytona and Port St. Lucie, pulling into back alleys, and wrestling the discarded refrigerator crates into the truck bed. When he returned to Sharpes, we helped him pull the crates from the truck, laying them gently in the thick grass while the other kids watched silently.

Once the crates were unloaded, he drove off. By then it was our world, and he respected that. Practice saw my brother and me to competency. We wielded the hammers, crowbars, and handsaws like extended appendages, storing them in a burlap sack hidden in a cavity between the roots of a southern red cedar just back from the river.

We had plenty of help. Sean and I alone dismantled the crates. Prying with hammer and crowbar, we carefully separated the front and back of the crate into ready-made rafts proudly sporting the Westinghouse and Sears, Roebuck and Company brand. When it came time to attach the liberally patched tire tubes that served as pontoons, everyone joined in, a dozen boys and girls and often more, spindly and sunburnt, shins stained with river mud, tongues protruding, concentrating on their assigned task, one and all aching to kick out into the river.

Like all children, we respected hierarchy. Sean always went first. It was his father who procured the materials for our magic carpets, and he was the eldest son. It was also true that no one was better at hooking a sea turtle. With my brother at the helm, his powerful legs kicking a frothy path out into the river, more often than not our raft was guaranteed a successful inaugural ride.

As an adult, I have read dozens of scientific treatises describing sea turtles as automatons, moved by primal instinct to travel the world's oceans on an unerring course, rotely following impulse and magnetic clues. But the Indian River turtles that veered toward us as we thrashed awkwardly on our raft did not operate on instinct. They vectored toward us on barnacled wings, lifting their scaly heads above the surface to crane at us with inkwell eyes and curious chuffs. When a rider lodged the blunted grappling hook under the lip of the shell just above the thick pickle neck, the short length of rope drawing taut, the turtles towed us as if they enjoyed the ride as much as we did. True, they were somewhat trapped in their course. They couldn't dive for the bottom. The inflated tubes and wide raft saw to that. Reversing course was almost as difficult. When the raft swung about, its squared edges created formidable drag. And so virtually every turtle swam as directed, swooping downriver with the current, hauling their jockey with a gusto that created a frothing wave that happily burbled and leaped at the front of the raft, water sweeping past along the planks, splashing algal taste into our whooping mouths. It wasn't like flying. It *was* flying. It was lifting away from this world. When the hook at last slid free, the raft settled into the water like disappointment.

With a wave, the rider signaled the ride's completion, and the rest of us, who had walked along the riverbank, plunged into the river and churned out in mass, returning the raft to shore with the combined thrust of a host of jerking limbs. Once ashore, we dragged the raft back upriver, using the rope to pull it through the shallows and clinging reeds, until we reached the grassy field that marked our start. And then the next hip-hopping heart took its turn.

Science claimed otherwise, but we saw clearly. The turtles thrilled to these rides as much as we did. We hooked the same turtles again and again. Here a turtle with a mossy shell mightily scarred, there a flipper with a jagged bite mark scarred white. We gave them names. Frankenstein for the turtle with the scarred shell, Captain Ahab for the shark survivor, the Iron Horse for the turtle that offered itself to our hook again and again, a reptilian Lou Gehrig who never wanted out of the game. Sitting beside the river, we talked about the turtles as if we knew them, their personalities divined by the strength of their pull, the quizzical cant of a pickle head, the indignant chuff of an exhale from a parrot-like beak. We wondered if, down in their foggy green deeps, they talked about us too.

Sean never took part in these discussions, nor did he ever call a turtle by name. He sat alone on the bank, his back to us, thinking his own thoughts. I knew he saw our talk as demeaning. To him, the turtles were from another world. To give them names and discuss them like puppies was to insult a creature beyond our pall, beyond even Pliny himself. No one enjoyed our surging rides more than Sean. In his mind, I believe, our reptilian reindeer were the stuff of dreams. I know now they allowed my brother to escape.

Like any child's world, ours hummed with competition and challenge. Several of the older boys resented that Sean went first. The boldest challenged him. He beat back their uprisings with his fists.

My brother had always been fearless. Now, entering adolescence, he fairly boiled over with reckless energy. At times, it seemed he fought constantly, not just for raft rights, but for imaginary slights suffered at school, or for the simple pleasure of the shock of knuckle on bone.

Sean was short and rail thin. His bones stuck out everywhere—a collection of doorknobs, our mother joked. As the chins of his compatriots sprouted stubble and their voices went gruff, his voice retained a childish pitch, and his cheeks kept an ivory smoothness that matched his pale skin, for it seemed the sun itself was unable to touch him. Behind his back, friend and foe called him the albino rhino. He charged into everything.

The fights took place after school on a patch of riverbank just downriver from where we launched our rafts. The clearing was roughly twice the size of a boxing ring, allowing enough room for the pugilists and a seesaw surge of shouting onlookers. Foliage palmed the clearing on three sides. The open side, fronting the river, allowed escape. When a fighter had enough, he jumped into the water, and the fight was over. This escape hatch ensured that fights were generally short and harmless; scuffs and bruises and knuckles that throbbed in the middle of the night. None of us missed how my brother's adversaries almost always started with their back to the river; the few exceptions earned themselves additional pains before they escaped. After a time, only newcomers misjudged my brother's delicate appearance. He was bull strong. In my worshipful state, I was convinced that, like the animal, the only way to stop my brother was to kill him.

I was not alone in finding his power enticing. Our riverbank crackled with sexual tension. Though we pretended to be above it, not one boy missed the first whispers of curving buttock and budding breast pushing against too-small, hand-me-down suits, promising pleasures we could only imagine. In turn, our tormenters, experiencing their own rising desires, flaunted their limited wares, pushing at straps and elastic so that we could glimpse achingly white flesh. At times, it seemed both sexes would explode with longing right where we stood.

In rare instances, things went farther. One afternoon, our rafting cancelled by pounding rain and the sizzle and cannonade of lightning and thunder, I stole down to the river just the same, for back then I loved the way the dark sky pressed cozily against the earth and the fat leaves danced joyously under the pelting drops that struck my skin with cool slaps. If it rained hard and long enough, a thin mist spread across the entire river, a smoky carpet that issued countless ghostly tendrils, and I would sit at the end of the dock and watch the vaporous risings and fallings away.

I had nearly reached the clearing when a movement made me drop to a crouch. Rising slightly, I saw my brother and Janie Clayton. I experienced a jolt of anger; they had snuck down to take the raft out on their own. But Janie Clayton did not have rafting in mind. As I watched, I was astonished to see her pull her bathing suit down to her waist and push against my brother. I had never seen skin so white. The way she moved against my brother made me forget to breathe, and when my brother stepped away, I was made absolutely certain of his powers, for though Janie Clayton was apparently far more worldly than her eleven years, my brother was three years her senior, an unbridgeable gap.

But the damage was done. For months I was haunted by the forbidden whiteness. I confess I did things alone in the woods with that vision bobbing in my head, and the knowledge that I was going to hell was only slightly worse than the knowledge that my brother possessed restraint I could never muster. My mother lauded Pliny's fiery intellectual curiosity and imaginings, but my own curious imaginings, not a matter of intellect at all, served only to produce fiery anguish that was equally unquenchable.

12

South of Fresno, along Highway 99, I stop at McDonalds for breakfast. After two hours of driving, I'm already tired. This is unsettling. Growing old is a matter of recognizing what you can and cannot do, but this is not easy, nor does it always fit into your plans. Slumped back against the seat, I stare at flies walking across the windshield. They lift off easily into the heat. Even the insect world is more nimble than me.

The restaurant is next to a gas station. They are the only two buildings for miles, cloistered tight in a vast sea of scrub and rubble. The parking lot is full. RVs rumble. Several men roughly my age walk shoebox-size dogs in a cordoned off square. I wonder what they're thinking as their companions snuffle the dirt.

The restaurant bursts with humanity. It's as if an invisible army has risen up from the desert, summoned by the claxon call of salt and fat. We stand solemnly in four lines, washed by air-conditioning and the smell of coffee and bacon. Though it is mildly disingenuous for a man who made his fortune on hot dogs to snub fast-food restaurants, for the most part, I have. The thought of entering a restaurant intent on leaving has always struck me as odd. I favor restaurants where customers linger over their coffee, and the waitress, if you show manners and a bit of wit, jokes with you and calls you "hon."

But I am a slave to black coffee, and I'm surprisingly hungry too.

Almost everyone stands silent.

A burly man behind me says, "The cows wait in the same kind of line."

When I turn, he smiles ruefully at his paunch.

"Not a whole lot of fat on you," he says, "but I'd provide my share of double cheeseburgers."

There is a commotion at the front of our line. An elderly woman and a florid-faced manager face each other at the counter. The manager says something I can't hear and gestures adamantly in our direction.

"Not an animal lover," the burly man says. "There's a surprise."

I turn to where the manager is pointing. Two short-haired dogs sit obediently beside the soda machine, terriers maybe. The man with them wears a Wonder Bread T-shirt and a Yankees ball cap that barely contains a shock of gray hair. His forearms swell powerfully. I recognize the rucksack on his back. Marine Corps issue.

Man and dogs watch the woman eagerly, their mouths open slightly.

The manager speaks sharply. I recognize petty officiousness and words intended to carry.

"I'm sorry, ma'am, but we have no alternative. I must insist your dogs wait outside. They're violating health codes."

The woman speaks loudly too, in the manner of the mildly deaf.

"I assure you, we'll all go outside as soon as I get my order. As you can see, the dogs are well behaved, and I've already ordered." Her smile is charming for being genuine. "It should be less than a minute."

The manager knows the silent throngs are watching.

"Our policy is no dogs."

"I know that now," the woman says pleasantly, "but we didn't see the sign, and I can't watch them if they're outside. They're good dogs, but they're without leashes, and everyone wanders if enough temptation is provided."

"Health codes prohibit animals inside our restaurant. Your husband needs to take them out now. We're serving food."

From another line, a man says, "Just let her order, you moron. We're all waiting."

The manager addresses the voice.

"Please. I'm just doing my job."

Someone else says, "We have jobs, and we're all going to be late for them."

"Have your husband take the dogs outside," the manager says.

"He's my son, and if I let him out of my sight, he's as apt to wander off as the dogs."

"They have to leave now. I'll remove them myself if I have to."

"Please," says the woman, but the manager is already striding down the line.

I step in front of him, surprising us both. I glance at his name tag.

"Excuse me, Douglas. If this lady will permit me, I'll watch her dogs outside while she waits for her breakfast."

I wish I had kept driving. I want it to end quickly, but the man's face tells me it's too late.

"It's not your business. The dogs are violating health policy. They've been here too long."

He turns back to the woman.

"I'm going to ask you to leave. If you refuse, I'll have to call the police."

The cashiers, the cooks, the dogs with their loose grins, everyone waits. Someone hisses.

"Please. My son has quite an appetite, and there's no place else to eat. I'll get my order, and we'll all be on my way. We won't bother you again. I promise."

She speaks calmly, but her fingers knead her coin purse.

Douglas inhales, but I cut him off.

"You're right. It's not my business, but it is yours." I say this very politely. The sign hangs above the counter, bold white letters on a red placard. "You guarantee your customers their order in sixty seconds, or the meal is free. I'll wager you've argued with this polite young lady for several minutes at the very least. Out of human decency, you should let her wait for her order. Out of human decency, the rest of us will overlook your failed policy. We all respect your difficult position."

To give the man his dignity, I look away, pretending to rummage for something in my pant pocket.

He spends the last of his authority on the teenage girl at the register.

"Get her out of here as fast as you can."

The woman watches me expectantly.

I remember I have volunteered to see her companions outside.

"May I order something for you?" she asks.

I want to flee, but I want coffee too.

"Just a cup of coffee, please."

The burly man claps me on the shoulder.

"Well done, young fellah. For a moment there, it looked like the cows ruled the food chain."

To my relief, both son and dogs follow me outside without hesitation. As I step out the door, I hear a burst of clapping. I close the door as fast as I can, wondering how I have forgotten to be invisible.

No one is outside. I find a table, a sliver of shade provided by a mummified acacia tree.

The son consults the bleached sky.

Softly he says, "That man was no leader."

"He was only trying to do his job."

"Yes, sir."

He stands straight. I realize what he is doing.

"Please, sit down."

"Yes, sir."

He sits, staring down through the table's metallic mesh.

"Policy is important." He speaks as if he is reading off the faux flagstones. "Sixty seconds is a very long time."

"What's your name?"

He sits up straight and looks directly at me.

"Lance Corporal Walter Mussing. USMC. You're an officer."

"Not anymore. My name is Pogue."

I extend my hand, but he doesn't take it.

"Sixty seconds is a long time. But dogs can't tell time."

"Lucky for them," I say and smile. He does not smile back.

"Dogs are lucky. Yes, sir."

"You don't need to call me sir."

His eyes return to the flagstones. He observes them in a friendly manner. He pokes a finger in and out of the mesh, methodically moving across the table.

"You know a man," he says. "He's your friend. You keep each other warm at night in the rain and the mud. He shares his smokes. Then he goes down next to you, his blood on your face, and you don't even call the medic. You run, and you forget him."

The dogs pant.

"It's that way for everyone," I say. "You have to try to forget."

He is too pure to see a hypocrite.

"One friend stepped on a land mine," he says. "It blew straight up through him. His head came right off, then all his insides. Like a soda you shake up. We had our time, didn't we, sir?"

"Yes, we did. Now we can relax."

"Yes, sir. I'm hungry. Here comes Mother."

The woman places an enormous bag on the table and hands me my coffee.

"I hope you like it black. I couldn't bear to be in there a second longer. That was weak of me, especially after what you did."

"Thank you. Black is just how I like it. And in case you didn't notice, I ran out too."

"I don't suppose either of us will be coming back any time soon. I appreciate what you did. Thank you."

"Anyone would have done it."

"I doubt it."

Walter and the dogs stare at the bag. The woman smiles slightly.

"I'm afraid it won't be our last visit to McDonalds, though. We're in no position to boycott."

I look for the words to take my leave, but before I find them, Walter blurts, "I love breakfast biscuits! Bacon, egg and cheese! *Lots* of cheese!" His enthusiasm takes a mild downturn. "Shouldn't eat cheese. Too much fat. Fat slows a marine down—right, Pogue?"

The woman turns her half smile on me.

"Well now. It seems Walter is already sharing his secrets with you. That's quite a compliment. Under most circumstances, he speaks to no one but me."

"Fat is okay today," Walter says. "We're on vacation. The man made us hurry."

"Everything's fine, Walter."

"Uh-huh. A little hurry is okay."

The woman unwraps the biscuits neatly, laying each one on its wrapper so that it doesn't touch the table. She puts two biscuits on the ground. The dogs gobble them before she straightens.

She places a biscuit in front of me.

"You didn't come here just for caffeine and live theater."

"Thank you."

Walter stares at his biscuits.

"Ma?"

"Go ahead, Walter."

Walter eats his three biscuits without breathing. A piece of egg drops down his front. He gulps down the orange juice. Sitting up straight, he burps and looks down at his shirt.

He gives his mother a pained smile.

"I made a mess."

Dipping a paper napkin in her water, his mother dabs gently at the stain.

"In China, it means you enjoyed your meal," she says.

"She says that every time, Pogue."

The mother displays her son's pained smile.

"I'm so preoccupied with myself I forgot my manners." She reaches across the table. Her grip is firm. "Alice Montgomery. And this, as you know, is my son, Walter."

"Pogue Whithouse."

"I want to apologize for putting you on the spot, Mr. Whithouse. There are so many rules these days. To think I narrowly missed prison time for the crime of patronizing one of America's finer dining institutions shows that life is full of surprises. As Walter said, we're on vacation." She takes in our surroundings, brown dirt radiating heat. "Not your standard Aloha Adventures package. But Walter loves the desert. We're heading for Joshua Tree."

"The Mormons said the Joshua tree pointed to heaven," says Walter. "I think Joshua Tree is better than heaven. Lots and lots of wide open spaces. No mud and rain. People climb there. Up the rock like monkeys. Sometimes they fall, but they have ropes that catch them. I want to climb when we get there, but if I eat too many biscuits, I'll break the rope."

Alice laughs. It is the laugh of a young girl at a summer carnival.

"My, oh my. When did you become so chatty?"

"He's like me, Mother."

Alice places the empty wrappers in the bag.

"What brings you to this culinary outpost, Mr. Whithouse?"

The simple version is easiest.

"I want to see my country."

"A worthy quest. May I ask why?"

"At my age, you don't get many second chances."

"Do you feel it still is your country?"

The question is like a slap. It's not what I fear most, but it does haunt me.

I think for a moment.

"I don't know," I answer. "I'm just getting started. It's too early to say."

"I admire an open mind."

"It's one of the few resources I have at my disposal. What do you think?"

I regret it before the last word leaves my mouth.

Alice stiffens.

"I'm afraid I'm no longer open-minded. I don't recognize this country anymore. If you must know, I find America apathetic, vacuous, and self-absorbed. Nothing but chatter and noise, while everything that's worth something disappears."

"Mother."

"You're right, Walter. I'm ruining this nice man's vacation." She smiles, but the carnival girl is gone. "You show us kindness, and I repay you with dour company."

"I'll give you a second chance. I've got an open mind." But there's a weight in my chest, because I wonder if she's right.

I reach for my wallet.

Alice raises a hand.

"No. Don't even think about arguing with me."

Walter's head bobs.

"Don't pay. Brothers in arms. He's a marine, Mother. An officer."

"I should go."

"No," says Alice. "You can start your quest here. Walter fought three tours in Vietnam. The first two tours, I prayed for him every day. Each time he came home, I prayed he wouldn't go back. But I raised my son to serve."

Her voice is flat, someone reading a grocery list aloud.

"Walter was the radioman for his platoon. His last tour, first day back in country, his platoon was five miles from a firefight. Orders came to call in an air strike. They were eating dinner. After three weeks of R&R, Walter was accustomed to something more filling than field rations."

"Lerps are light," Walter says.

"Occupied with everyone's leftovers, he let the apprentice radioman call in the strike. The boy gave their coordinates. Killed everybody in the platoon but Walter. Since then, Walter has been understandably concerned about eating slowly."

She carefully folds a wrapper and places it in the bag. The dogs watch, heads cocked.

"The bomb concussions did something to his brain. It wasn't how either of us expected life to go, but he's happy in his own fashion. When he was a boy, he was quick as a whip. Fifty-eight thousand boys killed in Vietnam, but I only care about one."

"Mother looks out for me. She stood her ground."

Alice looks to the desert.

"Standing your ground is overrated," she says.

13

In my favorite dream, I swim easily in green waters, just below the surface so that the sky ripples overhead, the white clouds like bed sheets in the wind. I am underwater, but the river still sings in my ears. The song is different from the one the river sings on the surface, softer, dreamier, more distant, yet infinitely more comforting. I sense something timeless, something beyond mankind's stumblings, passed to me in a whisper I cannot quite grasp, but it soothes me nonetheless. I am gripped by something that swings on the very hinges of the earth, something so large it erases any urge to conquer, to compete, to dominate, to prove, to possess, to hate, to question.

I would like to dream this dream every time, but my other dreams get in the way.

14

My life changed on a train heading into Boston. I was eighteen. I had moved to Boston to study at the American Banking Institute. Like my father, I was methodical. I also had a head for figures, enough to provide a partial scholarship. The remaining loans made it hard to sleep.

On this January morning, a snowy dawn unveiled a sump gray world, the hypnotic clack and sway of the train fractured by the screech and hiss of stops. Row homes flicked past like sooty playing cards, identical yards, ringed by chain-link fence, piled high with rusted sleds and bicycles. In 1941, Boston's suburbs were filled with Catholics. Winters were long. The need to stay warm kept the schools and churches full.

I stood watching the snow, flakes of startling whiteness that wheeled in the air as if fighting to stay off the shabby landscape. I didn't see Abby board the train. In those days, I was obsessively shy. When I wasn't staring at the snow, I fixed my eyes on the book in my hand.

Someone jostled my elbow.

"Excuse me."

The voice was a silver bell. I smelled peaches.

I was desperate to look up, but I didn't.

"It's fine," I mumbled.

The proprietor of the lovely voice and the spring-fresh smell spoke as if we were the only two people on the train, a brash violation in a realm of mutterers.

"It's these heels. They're like walking on stilts."

I was spared a rejoinder by a man offering his seat. The attractive voice thanked him. I heard the rustle of settling, and enjoyed another waft of peach.

"I don't know how women wear them. They're a sin against stability."

I don't think this was directed at me. I believe it was a general overture, in retrospect perhaps even a scientific experiment on how sullen men on commuter trains react to a discussion of women's footwear. Abby was always wondering how the world turned.

This turned to protracted silence.

It seemed rude not to respond.

"They don't look very comfortable," I said.

"How would you know? Can you see through that book?"

I had to look. There was no other option.

Abby was smiling.

"If you haven't seen it, can it be true?" she said.

When hearts are smitten, you hear of radiant smiles or eyes like dark pools or skin soft as down. What I saw was a pale scar like a slice of fingernail, hooking away from the left corner of unadorned lips. The scar extended, by a fraction, the half smile. Delicate and beautiful, it was perfect in its place. It broke my heart. I wished I had been there to wipe the pain away.

"*Physalia physalis*," said Abby. "Portuguese Man O' War. The scar," she added, unnecessarily.

The eyes were not dark pools. They were light green, tropical shallows, splashed with the sunlight of amusement.

"Siphonophores," I said.

You might think this a clever retort, but the truth is I was only able to blurt what I knew.

It is also true that a word can change your life.

The green shallows watched me intently. I wanted to swim in them.

"And they would be?"

I ached for a charming answer, but again I regurgitated the accurate one, my mind as hollowed out as my stomach.

"Pelagic colonial hydroids." I stared out at the beautiful snow, hoping for inspiration. "A voracious predator but fragile as glass."

And now the radiant smile, the uppercut that dropped me to the canvas.

"You're not reading from that book, are you? That would be cheating."

I looked at the book as if I had never seen it before. I did not mean for it to be a joke.

Abby giggled.

"Your book is about sea turtles," she said.

I wished for a train wreck. I wished the train would never stop. I wished I had woken up sick. I wished she would keep talking, that one day we'd hold hands in front of a fire, sharing memories that danced happily in the flames.

"Sea turtles eat jellyfish," Abby said, helping me along. "Some turtles even eat Portuguese Man O' War. There's always a more voracious predator."

I closed the book.

"*Dermochelys coriacea*. Leathery skinned turtle. The leatherback is the only turtle that doesn't have a rigid shell."

"You aren't cheating."

"I don't know how."

Now the full force of the smile, cheapening the radiance of every romance novel, surpassing the fires of Vesuvius. Heaven's angel, a little girl clasping a heart's desire Christmas gift.

Sixty-seven years later, I feel the heat in my face.

"How did you come to know so much about sea turtles?" Abby asked.

"They're a hobby."

In an instant, your life is made complete; in the equivalent amount of time, it is horribly undone.

The smile remained, but the eyes said I had lost.

"Sea turtles are my life's passion," Abby said.

I wanted to shout that I had lied. That I was afraid to speak on a train, that I was petrified by beautiful strangers who turned new things inside me, that I had hesitated before and lost something precious. I wanted to lift her to her feet and spill every word, the cool of the river, the hot wash of sun, the surge, the ecstasy of connection, the undercurrent of helplessness and perhaps even fear. More than anything in my short life, I did not want to lose this chance.

But of course I said nothing.

Abby gave me a final curious look and turned to the snow.

She gave me the same curious look when I stepped off the train with her.

"This isn't your stop, is it?"

The snow swirled about us.

"I've never taken a chance."

"You're sweet, but I need to go. I'm late for an appointment."

She said it kindly, but she was already half-turned.

We should embrace madness more often.

"If you scratch the shell of a leatherback," I said, "it bleeds."

You can plan and plan. Most of us do. But really, when you stop to think about it, it's happenstance that changes our lives.

15

I pull into the Desert Inn Motel at sunset, the Mustang crunching to a stop beneath a glaring neon sign, two orange cacti joining prickly limbs above a howling purple coyote. The bright colors cheer me. To the west, the last slash of day flares dark scarlet, the black sky above like a frowning eyebrow.

The motel is two miles east of Needles, along a famous, bleached, two-lane road just off Interstate 40. Beyond the asphalt, the Mojave Desert runs off in every direction.

Again my fingers uncurl from the steering wheel slowly, a shipwreck victim releasing the flotsam that saved his life. I look at the odometer. Three hundred and eighty-six miles, each one a slap in cold comfort's face. The scarlet slash on the horizon goes dark, a congratulatory wink.

The woman behind the front desk appears to have risen right out of the desert. Her face is brown as a silt-laden river, with no more room for character or wrinkles. The office is tidy. She looks up from a book, fixing me with her one good eye.

"Rooms are forty-five dollars a night. Plus tax."

She taps a blackened nail on the page beneath her hand for emphasis.

Books line the shelf behind her; a few romance novels—*Bedded at His Convenience* and *Having the Boss's Babies*—but also Graham

Greene, Louis L'Amour, and Cormac McCarthy. My heart does a small leap. The book in her hand is *The Grapes of Wrath.*

"Writing *Grapes* nearly killed Steinbeck," I say.

"Long as he paid in advance, I don't care."

I am not deterred. I know the weary look is an act. The books on the shelf erupt with Post-it notes. Post-it notes jut from the book beneath her hand. A reader who marks passages is not distant from life.

"Have you read *Sweet Thursday?*" I ask.

"I fancy Steinbeck."

I look out the window at the black road.

"The Okies traveled Route 66," I say. "You can feel the bump of history under your wheels."

"Might be your tires are underinflated."

"You've read that book before."

"Maybe so, maybe not. Plenty of people have passed through here besides the Joads, and you ain't the first to pack along an overamped imagination. Had a TV crew from UFO Hunters here two months back. Came because aliens were here. If Martians need a place to stay, they pay forty-five dollars too. The producer looked a bit like Jabba the Hut himself. He told me the aliens were on a reconnaissance mission, considerin' takin' over our planet, but they crashed instead."

"Maybe they should learn to drive first."

She scowls, but the cock of her head tells me she might be enjoying this.

A stubble-faced man enters the office, carrying a plastic ice bucket and an offended look. He holds the bucket up as if it's lighting his way.

"Ice machine don't work," he grumbles.

This scowl is genuine.

"Water comes out of the sink cold enough, Harvey. You want to drain three ice machines a day, pony up another eighty bucks and get your persnickety ass down to the Holiday Inn."

Holler-day Inn. Inn snapped off like a rifle crack.

Harvey lowers the bucket and turns his mournful eyes to the humming cooler behind the counter. The cooler is stocked with beer, wine, soda, and dark cans with lime green claw marks raking down the side.

"Room's hotter than a sauna. What's a man supposed to do?"

He says it hopefully, as if he still has a chance. I admire him for it. But Our Lady of Granite is not moved.

"Pay the last two months' rent?"

As soon as the door clacks shut, she says, "Machine's unplugged. Natural selection in action. That man's bloodline ain't long for this world. UFO types, deadbeats, and snivelers, they're all racin' to their last breath with the brains and initiative of a tuber."

She watches me for a long moment.

"I favor Hazel," she says. "Steinbeck knew real men. Almost none around anymore. Nothin' but blowhards, connivers, finger pointers, and whiners. Hazel had his faults, but he owned up to them and did what he could. He might have blown his chances, but he didn't blame anyone when he did."

Lack of ice is not the problem in my room.

I call the front desk from the bathroom. The phone is cordless.

"You can't figure out the ice machine either? The hell's that drummin'?"

"The faucet handle came off in my hand. I can't turn the water off."

"Christ almighty. I should have taken the job as an heiress."

The receiver goes dead. I stand listening to the thrumming water. Waste bothers me. I decide to fetch the tool box from the Mustang's trunk.

As I reach for the doorknob, someone knocks.

I open the door to a man bearing an easy smile and a tan satchel, the kind doctors carried in the days of house calls. He's wearing checkered Bermuda shorts and a long-sleeve denim shirt, and he looks comfortable in them both.

"Esmeralda says you're in here dismantling your room." He waits. "I'll admit it's rare for a repairman to show up so quickly."

"Come in."

"Thanks." He extends his free hand. "Chet McCreary. I'm also your neighbor across the way."

I like this man already.

"Still an impressive response time."

"Thins the excuses."

He goes into the bathroom. I stand undecided, and then I sit on the edge of the bed. It's a small bathroom.

A mirror hangs above the dresser off the end of the bed. If I sit on the far right side of the bed, I can see into the bathroom. I watch Chet place the satchel on the floor. He withdraws a wrench, several clean washcloths, and a radio. He tinkers with the coat hanger antennae. Suddenly Joseph Haydn battles for supremacy with the faucet.

Pounding water and tile give Chet's voice a warbling echo.

"I hope you don't mind. Music makes repairs go easier."

In my excitement, I'm afraid I shout.

"Haydn is a joyous relief."

I have a cabinet of records I play in the evening. I have not listened to radio for years. I tried the Mustang's radio several times since leaving San Francisco, but the music was mostly screaming noise. As I said, I try to keep an open mind, but it seems unwise to listen to music that might turn me deaf in both ears. I had no luck with talk radio either. I am no prude, but the hosts cursed and ranted, insulting their callers and using language I haven't heard in a long time. In return, the callers revealed shockingly intimate details about their lives.

Chet smiles at me in the mirror.

"Feel free to stand in the doorway. I have no objection to a little conversation or advice."

I go to the doorway. With the wrench, Chet gives the handle a twist. In the sudden quiet, even Haydn almost sounds like a wail.

"Whoops," Chet says.

He turns the radio down. The faucet handle is the old-fashioned kind, porcelain and shaped like a ship's wheel. Chet turns it upside down and looks at it.

"Stripped. You're stronger than you look. Actually, I suspect the culprit was the guy who stayed here last night, bodybuilder heading to a contest in LA. Puffed up like a blowfish. Steroids would be my humble guess. You don't see many forty-year-olds with acne. He went room to room arm wrestling folks for money. Made the odds just tempting enough—five dollars if he won, twenty if he lost. Foolish enough to take synthetic hormones, but smart enough to play on primal supremacy."

Chet takes another long look at the stripped handle.

"Had I let things be, this sink probably wouldn't be ruined," he says. "But I can't stand unfair odds."

He wipes the stem dry with a rag and then carefully taps the base with the wrench. He looks at the handle again.

I am being played.

I lean back out of the doorway.

"I guess I'll go watch a little TV."

"You've spent some time around storytellers. Fine, I'll tell you the rest, but only because I don't want to see you beg."

Friendship has crept up on us, simple as that.

"Thank you for sparing my dignity," I say.

Chet salutes me with the wrench, and returns to work.

"As you probably know, proposing a contest of strength among males is no gamble," he says. "Pretty much every man on the premises lost five bucks. Here's the thing. Most of the folks here can't afford to lose anything. So I introduced Captain America to Javier and made a proposal. Captain America puts up everything he's already won. If he beats Javier, I triple his winnings. If he loses, he pays each of his opponents ten dollars and leaves without a word." He nods in the direction of the front office. "All this is between you and me. If Esmeralda finds out there was gambling on the premises, we'll be nursing our wounds for months. She interprets the Lord's word literally, and she's got the devil's temper."

Chet gives the stem another tap and nods approval.

"Don't seem to be any other leaks. I should be done in a few minutes."

He rummages in the satchel. Producing another handle, he examines its threads carefully. Rachmaninov plays the piano.

It is wonderful being played.

"What happened?" I ask.

"Your faucet was broken. Don't you remember?"

"I'm not so far away from coming back to haunt you."

"Point taken." He smoothes his shirt sleeves. The cuffs are wet. "Captain America accepts my offer. Appealing odds, plus I show him a photo of Javier. The man's thinner than bamboo. And, of course, there's the challenge to primal supremacy. Unfair, I suppose. Not many steroid abusers capable of turning the other cheek. So I fetch Javier, and Captain America's smirking, and everyone gathers around the table, and there's a few smirks there too."

Chet fits the new handle on the stem. His elbow swings in and out.

"See, we all know something Captain America doesn't. Javier's worked twelve-hour shifts at the meat-packing plant for nearly a year now. Pound for pound, if there's a stronger man, I don't want to meet him. Javier's no showman. As soon as I tap their knuckles, he jerks Captain America's arm to the table. Game over. Captain America gets a humbling surprise, everyone gets their money back plus a little extra, and Javier makes more in three seconds than he makes in a week."

"Most men aren't brave enough to bet on themselves."

I say it because it's the truth, and it bleeds a little joy from the moment.

"Javier would never bet on himself either. He's as avid a member of the Lord's flock as Esmeralda. I placed his bets for him. I'm not normally a gambling man, but I'd taken enough of a disliking to Captain America to make a side wager with him myself. A tithe for our country's miserable immigration policy. I gave the money to Javier. Not entirely a happy ending, though. 'Roid rage is responsible for this sink."

Chet turns the handle on and off a few times.

"Good to go," he says. "The last of Captain America."

Chet carefully places everything but the radio back in the satchel and zips it up. He picks up the radio, playing Handel now, and gives me a wink.

"Don't go tearing anything else off the hinges, okay?"

Suddenly I am desperate for company. I speak before my natural inclinations stop me.

"Do you have plans this evening?"

He taps the pager on his belt.

"Not yet."

I feel as awkward as I sound.

"Would you like to share some conversation, say in an hour?"

He doesn't pause, and I am grateful.

"Happy to pass the time." He shakes my hand again. His fingernails are clean and neatly trimmed.

I remember.

"I'm Pogue Whithouse."

"Well then, Mr. Whithouse, since it's already clear we both have impeccable taste in music and a fine sense of humor, I'll be back in an hour. Adjusting for traffic."

"Would you bring the radio?"

"I'll throw in an extra chair too. This establishment has its five-star points, but an excess of furniture is not one of them. We can sit outside. The nights cool off nicely."

"Hence the long sleeves."

Chet glances at his cuffs.

"I've always been the sort who likes to prepare ahead of time," he says.

It's dinnertime, but I'm not hungry. These days, I eat almost nothing. I know I should remedy this. I fix a cup of coffee and pass a little time watching the news. All of the news is from Los Angeles, as if nothing of merit happens outside the borders of Southern California's bloated megalopolis. Quickly dispensing with a gang shooting, water shortages, and a financial meltdown at City Hall, the news team devotes the remainder of the newscast to an actor's arrest for drunk driving. I recognize the man, but I forget his name as soon as they say it. The actor, flanked by two stone-faced men who are either his attorneys or his bodyguards, reads a prepared statement claiming he is not guilty. He asks America's justice system for the fair shake every citizen deserves. When he finishes, men and women shout questions and brandish microphones as if they are being attacked by bees, but the actor walks away. The anchor promises me they will stay abreast of the story.

I miss Walter Cronkite.

I walk to the front office. A boy of about ten has taken Our Lady of Granite's place. He is watching a small television on the counter.

I hesitate.

"I can sell beer," he says, without taking his eyes off the screen.

In the State of California, employees seventeen and younger can sell beer if they are directly supervised by someone who is twenty-one or older. I am familiar with many arcane laws that will never affect me, or, in some instances, anyone else. Did you know that in Alabama it is illegal to carry an ice-cream cone in your back pocket? It's a silly hobby, but I find it interesting the lengths man goes to in regulating himself.

I don't like buying beer from a child, but I don't want to ask the boy to bring out his supervisor. I suspect both of us would pay.

"May I have a six-pack of Heineken, please?"

The boy slips off his stool. A skinny, brown arm hefts the six-pack up on the counter.

"How did you know I was buying beer?"

"Everyone buys beer at night." His eyes are back on the TV. Cars crash. This is followed by shouting and gunfire. "Eleven dollars and fifty cents."

"That's steep for one six-pack."

He doesn't flinch.

"You picked the most expensive beer."

I don't want to encourage such tactics.

"Should I ask your mother if that's the price?"

I say it kindly. I was in business myself.

His eyes leave the TV with studied slowness. He makes a show of carefully turning each bottle until he finds the one with the last bit of sticker.

He pulls the bottle from the carrier and casually thumbs away the last evidence. "Nine dollars and fifty cents. If that's too rich, you can drive into town."

You want to drain three ice machines a day, pony up another eighty bucks, and get your ass to the Holiday Inn.

I put the money on the counter. Every businessman deserves a margin of profit.

"Thank you," I say, but he has returned to the gunfire.

Chet knocks right on the hour. He's brought a card table too. He sets the table and the plastic lawn chairs in the empty parking spot in front of the room next to mine.

"Ethan Allen, eat your heart out," he says, settling my chair in the gravel. "No better place than the desert for stars. Your neighbor is in Blythe visiting his grandson. He won't be back until the day after tomorrow."

Across the lot, other tables are already outside; at nine o'clock, the evening still holds heat, a tropical beach after nightfall. Our neighbors hold court in shadowy groups. Lanterns glow; coolers rest beside chairs. There are thirty rooms, ten in each wing. Every door but one is open.

Chet declines a beer. He has brought a bag of pretzels and a six-pack of Diet Pepsi.

After popping the top, he holds up his Pepsi.

"Welcome to the neighborhood. For better or for worse, most everybody here knows each other. We're not really a motel for visitors. Most of the residents have been here at least six months; a few of us have been here far too long. Thirty dollars a day is way cheaper than what you'll pay for an apartment, and Esmeralda, despite her guff, allows for some leniency in the matter of rent." He shrugs apologetically. "Esmeralda charges transients a higher tariff."

Turning his smile toward the black road and scrub beyond, he says, "Someone once called us an invisible American subculture. From here, though, it's America that's invisible. And that's how most of us like it."

A crackling Bach lauds the stars. I tip my beer.

"The music in your neighborhood is second to none."

Chet gives the antenna a slight tap, and the crackling stops.

"It's getting hard to find classical stations these days, but there are enough codgers out here in the desert to allow classical music a final stand. The station is right here in Needles. The whole enterprise is run by a seventy-five-year-old manager and a young Berkeley grad with a master's in Jazz History. It's a real grassroots operation. Advertising dollars are hard to come by, so music lovers from miles around give what they can. On the first of each month, the station manager goes on the air and reads the month's list of donors, whether they gave fifty dollars or fifteen cents. I ask for anonymity." He gives a rueful smile. "My wife hated classical music. She said it made me old before my time."

Chet's shoulder-length brown hair is bleached by the sun. His goatee is neatly trimmed. Neither sport any sign of gray. I am no longer the gauge of age I once was, but of this I am sure.

"I'd say you've got a few years left before AARP kicks down your door."

"That would be the immaturity's shine. On some fronts, my wife wanted me older before my time. Pleasing her became quite a conundrum. But enough about me. Jazz is far more interesting."

I'm afraid I fairly leap at the conversation. No doubt my eagerness is clear, but I no longer care. Sitting beneath the stars, cupped by night and murmuring strangers, I have left the riverbank. I am out among the spinning slabs of water. I remember the intoxication.

Chet doesn't ask why an eighty-five-year-old man throws himself at a stranger like a child embracing a favorite aunt. He doesn't ask where I've come from or where I'm headed. We discuss classical music, books, man's inclinations, good and bad.

A slight wind rises. Chet wears jeans and the same denim shirt he wore when he made the repairs. I'm glad I put on my windbreaker.

We talk quietly. Occasionally a car passes on the black road.

"Not exactly the promised land the Okies hoped for," Chet says. "People say there are all kinds of layers in *The Grapes of Wrath*, but what I like most is the simple story of how the Okies just kept going. I admire that sort of perseverance and optimism, though I can't say I've always mirrored it in my own life."

A man who keeps secrets admires even the slightest revealing.

"The Okies suffered plenty of doubts," I say. "Don't be too hard on yourself."

"I suppose they did, but they didn't let those doubts stop them." Chet's eyes wander over the other tables. "Plenty of folks in this country still see us as the world's superpower, and maybe in terms of unmanned aerial drones and sheer military weight we are, but underneath all the technology, I don't think we have the resolve of our forefathers, the simple pigheaded toughness of forging on. Modern life's softened our will. Even Steinbeck persevered. I read that when he finally wrote the last passage in *Grapes*, he shouted with joy. It must feel pretty good to fill your life with something so magnificent."

I am familiar with the story of *Grapes*'s completion; a friend, staying at Steinbeck's house in Los Gatos, California, waking at three in the morning to the author's shouts, his opus made whole by the perfect ending. But I don't interrupt. It is pleasant listening to Chet's soft voice, telling the story of a man certain he had gotten things just right.

A dust devil spins in the road before veering off into the desert.

"They risked everything," says Chet. "Drove west with bald tires and rope belts and hollow stomachs and hearts filled with hope. Even when their first look at California was this, they refused to turn back."

I see again the stores of the Depression, empty shelves holding a scattering of routine items suddenly made extravagant. To a child, it was incomprehensible. It was only a candy bar. Why couldn't we afford it? Today's supermarket shelves groan with largesse, and I can afford any of it. This is equally incomprehensible.

"Few people understood the Okies back then," Chet continues, "but I'd wager even fewer would understand their resolve now."

I know who he is chastising.

"I get the feeling you've lived right."

Chet pretends not to hear. This is an act of kindness, as I will see. Across the gravel lot, blue light winks on and off behind a dark window.

"It's a brave new world," Chet says. "Not all of us can adjust to it."

A small shadow leaves the office, tailed by a dog. The boy is carrying a bag. I see it as he passes beneath the neon coyote. Boy and dog cross the road and dissolve into the desert.

"He seems like a fellow who can take care of himself," I say.

Chet chuckles.

"You bought beer from him."

"Yes."

"Jake turned ten last month, marking his tenth year as a natural-born businessman. Though some might call it price gouging."

"Price gouging isn't a felony unless it's a civil emergency. I talked him down a little, but I suspect he still turned a profit."

"If it makes you feel any better, he puts most of his profits toward a good cause." Chet stares at the spot where the boy and the dog evaporated from the earth. If I were an alien, this is where I'd land. "You wouldn't know he's inclined to good causes," Chet says, "but trust me; he's got some soft spots."

I think of the mocking cashier at the gas station.

"Today's young don't seem very young to me," I say. "They seem tired and bored and maybe even a little mean." I am surprised by my honesty and my bitterness. "I'm not passing final judgment, but I've already had some memorable first impressions."

"Some shining examples out there, no doubt," Chet says, "but I think they're still young; it's just a version of youth we don't recognize. No more barn dances and inkwell pigtail dipping. There are times I feel sorry for them, but then I remind myself that maybe it's just my way of seeing that makes me feel sorry for them. Nostalgia clouds the truth."

I am nearly overcome by the urge to tell this man everything, spread my plan out beneath the stars in all its blind hope and sentimental foolishness. I know he'll listen. He might even understand. He won't judge. He might help.

But when I look across the table, I see a stranger tapping his fingers to jazz. His life is not my life. Discounting ghosts, I am alone on this journey.

In this seesaw of emotions, I recognize the tingle of inebriation. I am also reminded of beer's secondary effects.

When I return, the radio is silent. I can't hide my disappointment.

Chet pops another Pepsi.

"They go off the air at ten. They claim it's financial, but I'm pretty sure Jazz History has a girlfriend, and the manager can't stay up past nine. Not everyone has your stamina."

There is a burst of applause. A man moves quickly down the walkway toward us. As he passes each table, the gathered cheer, causing him to move faster still. He passes in and out of light like an old picture show.

"Robin Hood," says Chet.

Drawing near our table, the man slows and hesitates.

"Good evening, Javier."

The man stops in a shadow. The light from my window slants down on ruined cowboy boots.

The words are slow and perfect.

"Good evening, Mr. Chet."

"Your work week is finished?"

"Yes."

"Thankfully, your employer's wife is a God-fearing woman, or you'd be working Sundays too."

Perhaps the mention of God causes the man to take off his baseball cap. When he steps into the light, I see he is indeed reed thin. Broken nails pinch the bill of the Dodger's cap.

A smell, mildly sweet and vaguely familiar, lingers in the air.

Chet pulls the last Pepsi from the plastic rings.

"Please," he says. "You're just in time for a drink."

"I cannot."

"No need to stay, but you must accept the drink or I will take it as an insult."

"It is your final one."

"This is America. There is always more."

Javier takes the can.

"Thank you."

"This is Mr. Whithouse."

I begin to stand, but Javier spares me, stepping forward and holding out his hand.

"It is my pleasure to meet you, sir."

The hand is too heavy to belong to this man. It feels like a bag of gravel.

"The pleasure is mine," I say.

"I like your cap," says Chet. "Blue suits you."

"I purchased it today. The sun is becoming quite hot."

"Hotter than the Dodgers," says Chet. "I told Mr. Whithouse about your contest of strength."

Javier looks at his boots.

"Luck only."

"Luck for everyone here. Please, take the soda to your room. I know you are tired."

"Thank you, Mr. Chet."

Javier turns to me.

"Good evening, Mr. Whithouse."

He bows slightly. The motion chills me. He is gone before I can recover.

I am surprised by my reaction, but then I tally the three empty cans on the table and the one in my hand.

"I've had too much to drink."

"I'll see to it that you don't get pulled over."

Javier opens the only closed door. The room stays dark.

Alcohol makes me nosier than I'd like.

"Is he going to turn the lights on?"

"He prefers the dark."

Chet watches the dark window.

"Javier doesn't speak unless I force him to," he says. "His English embarrasses him. Javier places considerable demands on himself. I speak passable Spanish, but he has asked me to address him in English. He understands pretty much everything, and his speaking will catch up soon enough. Sometimes he reverts to Spanish. Last night when he sat down at the table to arm wrestle, the only thing he said to me was, *'Que si pierdo?'* Captain America turned to me and said, 'Tell this wetback I'll rip off his arm and FedEx it back to Tijuana.' Javier didn't blink."

"I don't speak Spanish," I say, embarrassed.

"It means *'What if I lose?'*"

In the distance, the lights of Needles waver.

"Javier's job is gut snatcher. Eleven hours a day, he pulls the insides from butchered hogs."

"Does he have a family?"

"He did. Javier is Mixtec. He came up through Altar with his wife and ten-year-old daughter. Altar is a town of thieves and dope addicts that serves as a staging area for honest men and women before they make their run across the border. Javier gave his life savings, one thousand dollars cash, to a guide who didn't know any more than he did. They bought black plastic trash bags for three dollars each. The guide told them the bags would foil the heat-seeking sensors the border patrol has on the other side of La Linea."

I watch the wavering lights.

"Crossing the border has gotten a lot worse with the drug wars. The *burreros*, the guys who haul the marijuana and cocaine for the drug cartels, cross the border too, and they're not averse to picking up a little extra cash by attacking migrants. In the dark, their guide wandered off, or maybe he knew what was coming. Less than a mile from the Arizona border, Javier and his family were jumped by two *burreros*. All I know is that Javier's wife and daughter were killed, along with one of the *burreros*. The other man got away. Javier made a stretcher with the trash bags and some branches from a mesquite tree. He dragged his wife and daughter to the border. He left them in front of a remote control camera. Everyone in Mexico knows that in America the dead are not left to rot."

Chet finishes the Pepsi, crushing the can in a single squeeze.

"It took awhile for Javier to tell me the rest of the story. The dead man had bags of cocaine taped up and down his body. Javier didn't take any, but it's a good bet the next folks by did. He's been here fifteen months now. He leaves before dawn and comes home after dark. It's a big country, but there's no way of knowing if it's big enough."

Across the way, someone laughs.

"He has an altar out there. He leaves his wife and daughter offerings: flowers, candles, thrift-store dolls. Everyone here thinks he leaves his lights off to save money. Gringos think Mexicans are cheap. No one knows this, but Esmeralda doesn't charge him for the room, only for utilities. She doesn't know about the *burreros* or the altar. She thinks he's saving money so he can bring his family here. Jake and I are the only ones who know his story."

Chet places the crumpled can in the paper bag.

"They come across the border in droves. Some say it's the biggest story of our lives. A biblical exodus. We don't care. They're different from us, even stranger than Okies." Touching two fingertips to his temple, he tips them in the direction of the dark window. *"La esperanza muere al ultimo."*

A gust sends the bag leaping for the edge of the table. Chet lunges, slender fingers pinching the bag.

The bumps on his forearm are pale red like ancient mumps.

Chet sits back slowly. He doesn't push the sleeve back down.

He smiles his neighborly smile.

"You have some familiarity with medicine," he says.

"I fought in World War II."

"Morphine has peacetime applications."

I make a motion of dismissal, but Chet shakes his head. I wish with all my heart that Mozart still filled the night with beauty.

"I was a physician. An ugly divorce and emergency room stress saw me to methamphetamines. I knew better, but it didn't matter. I'm clean for the moment, but it takes some doing to stay that way, and I don't know how I'll go. We can't all be Okies."

He draws down the sleeve, buttoning the cuff.

"Things move too quickly for some of us these days," he says. "Some nights I sit out here until dawn. When the moon makes for the horizon, it's not hard to imagine it's running away."

He gives me a half smile.

"What did Jake charge you for the beer?"

"Nine dollars and fifty cents."

"He must have liked you."

I hear an angry buzzing. Chet plucks the pager from his belt.

"Esmeralda. I'm required in surgery."

He gathers up the radio and his lawn chair.

"I'll get the table later. I'd encourage you to stay out here. It's a beautiful night."

I want to tell him I understand, but that would be a lie.

"I really enjoyed our conversation," I say.

"I did too."

He means it, I know, just as he meant to page himself.

I leave at dawn. The note is tucked under the wiper. The handwriting is atrocious. Once a doctor, always a doctor.

Good company is as precious as good music. Safe travels. Your friend, Chet.

I drive, scrub and dirt scrolling past. The desert looks different to me now. I think of death beneath sunny skies. I wonder where the border patrol buries the bodies they find.

Two miles down the road, I pull off on the shoulder. Dust settles slowly in the first light.

When I walk back into the office, I'm surprised to see the boy behind the counter.

"You work the early shift too?"

"Mom's eating breakfast."

Gunfire pops from the TV.

"You'd think they'd be out of bullets by now," I say.

"It's a DVD."

I'm not here to win him over. I put the envelope on the counter.

"You paid your bill."

"I underpaid for the beer."

His face remains impassive, though I see, for an instant, that he holds his breath. That's all. Children are the consummate keepers of secrets.

Pulling back out on the road, I search the desert, but I see nothing.

I was a good negotiator in my day. In the end, it earned me wealth I don't care for. I also know you ruin a man by giving him too much.

There is enough in the envelope to buy a nice offering, with a little left over for something on the side.

16

It was overcast the first time I met Sarah. We met on Quohog Beach. I had a week's leave. I had come to Hyannis to meet Abby's family. In six hours, we would have lunch together for the first time. In a month, Abby and I would marry. A week later, I would go to war. Things were happening fast.

I waited for dawn at the water's edge, my bare feet sinking slowly into the wet sand. The sun rose with equal deliberation. It was as if we were connected, two cautious children on a great seesaw. Dark clouds scudded along the horizon, a storm moving southwest.

The sun, blood orange, wrenched free of Nantucket Sound. Back then, even the sunrise rang with war.

"Sweet is the breath of morn. I already know you'll fit right in. We're a long line of poor sleepers."

I had not yet learned to listen with all my might. I would have jumped, but I was buried to the shins.

Sarah stepped up beside me.

"The first is a quote from Milton's 'Paradise Lost.' The second is a family curse, but it allows for moments like this."

Abby's sister was only two years older than me, but dark eyes, coal-black eyebrows, and a slightly outthrust chin collaborated to make her look older, sterner, and not a little intimidating. She was also tall. My first encounter with my future sister-in-law brought to mind a schoolboy cowering at his desk. I half expected her to rap my knuckles.

I'd hoped to be alone. Disappointment and surprise turned me stiff and absurdly formal.

"Good morning," I said. "I hope you're well."

"It is, and I am. Thank you. Sarah," she said. Her hand was surprisingly light. She stood easily, as if we met here each morning.

"Henry Whithouse. Everyone calls me Pogue."

"Odd to meet someone you know you'll be friends with for the rest of your life."

She smiled, and her severity fell away.

"We don't have much time," she said. "Fifteen minutes at most."

As if waiting stage left, the first puffs of wind stepped forward on cue, ferrying salt and spring cool.

Sarah inhaled deeply, like someone savoring their favorite meal.

"If memory has a taste, mine is salty," she said. "I love storms. They have more personality."

At last I managed to form an opinion.

"I think dawn is my favorite time of day."

"It allows more time for deciding."

Even then Sarah saw into the future.

My sister-in-law still towered over me. I looked down. Instead of sinking, her feet flattened out like pale snowshoes.

"Plank feet and skillet hands. My sister got the perfect parts, leaving me a bit of a platypus."

It was true. Where Abby was subtle curves, her sister was jarring angles, with flat hips and wide shoulders. Had she been a farmer's wife in the Westerns I devoured as a boy, the writer would have called her rawboned. The flaring planes of her physique were accentuated by her height.

"Do you sail?"

A scattering of sailboats rocked at anchor, their ivory sides reflecting the rising sun. The smallest boats swung slowly, nudged by the freshening breeze.

We saw sailboats in Sharpes, on the Indian River and the nearby Atlantic, but owning one was beyond us.

"No," I said. "But it looks like fun."

And now I saw there would be no pulling the wool over my sister-in-law's eyes.

"Sailboats are an extravagance not afforded everyone," she said. "Abby and I took lessons right in this sound, probably on one of those boats. Abby was ten, and I was twelve when we started. She was better from the first trim. Like everything else, a natural from the get go. Once we mastered the basics, our father started us racing. If I had a nickel for every time your bride raced by me, I'd be standing on a beach in Monaco. She has a gift. She can find wind where there isn't any and steal it all for herself. Our father favored her for it."

I began an apologetic murmuring.

Sarah stopped me with a small laugh.

"Kind of you, but it didn't bother me at all. I'm quite proud of my sister. Eventually she walloped all the boys too, and that *did* bother people, notably the yachtie fathers. Not everyone welcomes the idea of girls sailing. Boys should be boys, and girls should watch boys be boys. To this day, there are a few bruised yachtsmen who won't speak to our father. But if father is anything, it's insistent. And he insists on us doing our best, which, in Abby's case, was more than enough. When she won the summer's end regatta, we celebrated by smoking one of my father's cigars behind these very dunes. We were both violently ill. She was even better at that."

The wind batted us in gusts. Out over the sound, rain threw shadow veils. Small waves sprinted to the beach, running up over one another.

To my astonishment, I said, "I had a brother like Abby."

"A gifted sibling leaves marks good and bad."

A gust rocked us.

"You have a gift," I said.

The sober eyebrows rose.

"Pray tell."

I looked at the sheets of rain and consulted my watch.

"Thirteen minutes. I'd say we've got about two minutes left."

The eyebrows remained raised.

"It would be pathetic if you tried to ingratiate yourself into this family."

"Nothing of the sort," I said.

"Good. Save your wooing for my sister."

Unannounced, comfort had slipped between us.

The approaching rain reminded me of the squalls that marched across Florida's beaches. I leaned into the wind.

"No sailing off now," said Sarah. "You're expected at lunch."

"I'm looking forward to it."

"I'm sure you aren't."

We stood quiet.

"I picked a poem to read at your wedding," Sarah said. "Abby doesn't read much poetry, but she loves this poem. Do you read poetry?"

I thought of my mother and Pliny the Elder.

"I love to read, but I haven't read much poetry."

"Poems aren't for everybody. Sometimes they help me make sense of things. You should see the poem too."

"I already approve."

Sarah smiled.

"Look before you judge. And stop wooing. Now tell me the truth. How badly does lunch scare you?"

If I could go back again, I would be honest more often. The truth opens doors.

"I am scared witless."

I did not know real fear yet.

"Good, but you shouldn't be. You've already talked to my father."

"Only on the telephone."

I had called from Florida to ask for Abby's hand in marriage. Quaintly old-fashioned now, but de rigueur in my day. My father sat next to me as I asked, reading the newspaper and tapping his foot.

"Abby chose you. There are no other hurdles."

Sarah played with a strand of hair.

"I suppose I can help a little. Mother baked a blueberry pie. She picked the blueberries yesterday. A nod to their freshness will win you points. The scallops are a family recipe. The orange-butter sauce was passed down from our great grandmother. Spill it down your front, and you'll not only carelessly squander a family tradition, you'll carry the stain forever."

Friendship flung its jaunty leg over the wall built by an introverted boy who was anything but a rogue.

I laughed.

"Blueberry pie. Orange-butter sauce. A bad case of nerves. Would it set me back if I wore a bib?"

"If you let mother spoon feed you, it will cement your victory. She always wanted a boy."

That afternoon, after my discerning palate swept my future mother-in-law off her feet, I found an envelope in my suit jacket pocket.

Alone in my room at Mariner's Landing, I read T. S. Eliot's "A Dedication to My Wife." I read the poem a dozen times, my eyes walking slowly over each word. Parts of the poem were foreign to me; I didn't yet have a wife. But other words seemed released from a vein that pulsed in the most private chambers of my heart.

My first brush with poetry was a startling success.

17

It was mostly green sea turtles and loggerheads that appeared in the Indian River at the beginning of May, arriving on the Atlantic barrier islands to lay their eggs. Through summer and into fall, their shells broke the river's surface like mossy gumdrops, and when we settled the plastic hook in the crook of a shell, we stepped through a portal into their world.

We all sensed this with absolute clarity, knew it as well as we knew our own face, felt it in our hammering heartbeat, in the turtle's surgings, in the green water rushing past, though in all our riverbank talks, no one ever found the words for the serene pulse that mocked the frantic, tinny beatings of our own hearts. It was never articulated, but we knew the same spell bewitched us all. Plowing through the water, you felt of the moment and far beyond it, ushered by something so old it swung on the very hinges of the earth.

No ride was mundane, but most assumed a pattern. On a good ride, a turtle might carry raft and rider two hundred yards at the pace of a brisk walk—those of us striding along the river bank knew this, though to the rider it felt far faster—before the rushing water pried the hook loose. There was a small matter of skill. If you relaxed on the raft, the hook stood a better chance of staying lodged. If you squirmed about, the hook often slipped free. Those of us keeping pace along the riverbank engaged in our version of trifecta—skill of rider, speed of turtle, hand of fate—wagering on the length of the ride. We had no money to wager, but wagers were made. Loss forced Janie Clayton to produce her training bra—she had just come from an aunt's funeral—her deft twistings to free the undergarment surprising everyone but me. Miscalculation saw Matty Simpson stand rooted at the end of the dock beneath a shrieking storm of gulls, the rest of us howling and throwing bread crumbs from a safe distance. He might have drowned in bird shit had Sean not put an end to it. Seventy yards, one hundred yards, one hundred and fifty; these distances were within our accounting.

And then one July afternoon, the world turned on its head. From the middle of the river, Sean waved, and we watched dumbfounded as the raft performed a surge we had never seen, the front riding up on a frothy boil big as a mattress. We broke into a jog along the bank, gesturing madly at the water pluming up in small, curved fountains on either side of the raft. We jogged until a brick wall we had never encountered blocked our way, and my brother rode out of sight and into legend.

We stood panting, our noses pressed against brick. Janie Clayton spat, "God damn Yankee"—no one but a northerner would wall their home off from the river—but this show of bravado was only a cover for the unsettling we all felt.

Cowed by what we had seen, we walked silently back upriver to the comfort of our grassy sward.

After a time, Matty Simpson asked where the Indian River ended. Someone wondered aloud if Sean had drowned, and when they all turned their downcast eyes to me, I managed a passable laugh. My own bravado wasn't entirely an act. Experience had shown me my brother was invincible, though I kept this to myself, realizing that giving this voice would make me look both worshipful and stupid.

When Sean did return, carrying only a length of frayed rope, there was a peculiar light in his eyes, and we all knew he had moved beyond us.

Whenever any of us returned from a ride, we promptly regaled the gathered with every dip and bob. After his rides, my brother never said a word. I knew it was his way of distancing himself from us and strengthening his grip on the throne. Kicking the raft back to shore, he helped haul it upstream, and before the next launch, he was the one who rechecked the knots and hitchings. But then he would turn his brown back to us. Sitting cross-legged, vertebrae curved like a straining bow, he would watch the river. His snubbing infuriated me. I knew it was his way of showing he was better, even if he was. I felt the snub's sting like no one else, for I was his flesh and blood.

On this momentous day, there was no raft to prepare, but the fact there would be no more rides that day did not bother us because my brother sat in the grass and began to talk, and we gathered silently about him. He told us how ancient Roman scribes described sea turtles as great bird-like beasts, so powerful they sometimes flew from the water. He told us that some claimed the Red Sea contained turtles so big people used their shells as sailboats. He told us earaches could be cured with a mix of turtle's blood and woman's milk. The prospect of securing the latter sent a jolt through us all.

I recognized the words of Pliny the Elder, but I was still transfixed, for my brother spoke with a rapture I had never heard. By now, I knew Pliny was often wrong, but this didn't matter, for my brother had moved beyond this world. He spoke of impossible magic. The older kids recognized this, but how could any of us doubt magic's existence after witnessing his ride?

The sun sank low. Goose pimples rose. The river breezes sang. Misty stars appeared. My brother did not stop talking until the first angry parents arrived. Spell broken, those who weren't escorted off by the ear sprinted for home.

Sean stayed, so I stayed too. We sat together at the end of the dock, our feet swinging above the black surface, listening to the suck of water moving up and down the pilings.

I kept quiet. Even as a child, I knew you learned nothing by talking. But I was resentful too. Even our turtles had anointed my brother the chosen one.

I sat on a pot boiling with questions.

"Henry, can you keep a secret?"

The sound of my birth name surprised me.

"Sure," I said, though I wasn't sure at all.

Sean dug into the pocket of his cutoffs.

"Look."

I lifted the object carefully from his palm. The jade was cool and light. The carving was only two inches long, but the artist had crafted a faultless replica. The sea turtle hung from the leather lanyard by a small gold ring.

Sean held out his hand. I didn't want to give it back, but I had no choice.

He held up the lanyard. The turtle spun slowly before us, as if trying to bore its way down to the water.

"It's a Lakota Indian talisman," Sean said softly. "They believed the turtle was brave and wise."

I didn't care about its history.

"Where did you get it?"

"Cotton gave it to me."

Cotton was an old fisherman who had succumbed to drink. His drinking had cost him his skills and then his boat. He spent his days sitting on the stoop of the fish packing plant, bumming cigarettes from the packers when they stepped outside for a smoke. We all made fun of him. Once at recess, I used an umbrella to render my classmates hypoxic with a drunken imitation of Cotton casting for cigarettes. I knew it was wrong even as I did it, but it was rare and heady stuff having a laughing audience.

Mother had told us to stay away from him, but none of this mattered now.

"How do you know what the Lakota believe?" I asked.

"Cotton told me."

It surprised me that a drunk would know anything, but I didn't want to seem ignorant. Maybe alcohol let you see things sober people couldn't. There had to be a reason people drank it. Sean had once gotten me to take a sip of Father's whisky. It tasted like turpentine and burned the back of my eyeballs.

"Why did Cotton give it to you?"

"We understand each other."

"What the hell does that mean?"

I didn't even hear my curse.

"He knows I don't make fun of him."

Sean knew it would sting.

"How does he know that?"

"He knows a lot more than you think."

My brother's smugness irritated me.

"What makes you an expert about what Cotton knows?"

"We're friends."

I stewed for as long as I could, and then I asked again.

"How did he get it?"

"A Lakota Indian gave it to him."

"In Sharpes?"

"In South Dakota, stupid."

"I hate you."

We both knew I didn't mean it. Still, I spat forcefully into the water, punctuating my utterance.

We watched our swinging feet.

"I'm friends with Cotton because he taught me how to fight. I steal cigarettes for him too. Come at them like you're going to kill them."

"Dad's going to kill you."

Sean did not look at me.

"Cotton also knows how to keep a secret," my brother said pointedly.

Greed is fiercer than curiosity or pride. Sean held the charm in his open palm. It shone in the moonlight. It might have belonged to a Lakota Indian or it might have fallen from the stars.

"When did he give it to you?"

"Last week. Our secret, right?"

"Okay."

He wanted to tell me something else, I could tell by the way his legs swung faster, but I didn't ask. He had to pay a little.

"Henry?"

I tried to count to ten, but I only made it to six.

"What?"

"Today was the first day I wore it."

The thought settled raft-like between us. Beneath our feet, baitfish scattered, a brief silver squall in the dark.

"Do you think that's why you got the ride? Is it special?"

I didn't want to use the word magic. Magic was for children.

"I don't know," Sean said.

When our father came, Sean was talking about Pliny again, facts even I hadn't remembered, and I wasn't mad anymore because my brother had shared his secret with me. We were still on the dock, backs to the riverbank, but I had turned slightly to lean against a piling. I saw our father walking across the dark field. I wished him away. For a big man, our father walked lightly. Sean, still talking, did not hear him step up behind us.

Our father stood still. Several minutes passed.

I coughed.

Looking over our heads at the dark river, our father said, "Who told you those things?"

"Pliny," my brother said without turning around.

Night made my father's voice deeper.

"Is that the book your mother reads from?"

"Yes, sir."

"I'm glad you met the man."

That night in bed, I wanted to talk about our father's strange behavior, but Sean said, "It was a leatherback, Pogue."

I sat up so quickly my head swam. Moonlight fell across my brother's bed. Sean sat with his back against the wall, swinging the Lakota talisman above the sheets.

I realized with a start that no one had asked about the turtle.

He stared at the swinging talisman, as if hypnotizing himself.

"It never slowed down. It didn't even know I was there. I could have ridden forever. It swam like a rifle shot and a leaf in a breeze."

It wasn't something my brother would say, but maybe my brother's afternoon with Pliny had been contagious. I didn't care. I was transfixed by the jade figure cutting through the moonlight. I now believed utterly in its magic.

"It was the biggest thing I've ever seen. Its head was the size of a pumpkin." My brother spoke as if he were just realizing these things himself. "Its shell went right into its neck. The hook caught on a flipper. I don't know how, but it did. The force of the water kept it there."

I knew now with absolute certainty that my brother had gone to a place I would never see. His bold spirit linked him even to the animals. He was something I would never be. It was dark, but I looked away, embarrassed by my envy.

A drawer opened and closed.

"Pogue?"

"Yeah."

"The rope didn't break. I cut it."

I concentrated on the moon, the one constant in an unraveling world.

"I was afraid it was going to pull me under. The raft, me, everything."

From that day on, I never pretended to know anyone, and so it came as less of a shock when one humid evening a few weeks later, kicking up stones along a dirt track meandering into the brush, I looked up and saw our father's pickup, his broad-shouldered form in the cab. I started to call out, but the queerness of the situation made me hesitate, and as I stood there, my father laughed and leaned across the seat of the cab and kissed a woman who wasn't our mother.

I recognized the woman. She worked as a clerk at the post office. I saw her every Friday afternoon when I went with my father to pick up our mail. My father and the woman barely exchanged a word across the counter, but now in the falling dusk, they put their heads together, and the fact that this woman was not my mother was made clear when my father laughed again, the evening ringing with a boyish timbre I did not recognize.

Hunkered in itchy bramble, I was too frightened to be angry. It was as if the hard earth had been yanked from beneath me, for until that moment, I had known there was one woman for every man, two pieces that complete a jigsaw puzzle.

I walked home and went to bed, pretending I was sick. The next morning, I woke with a fever. I recognized it as just punishment for a secret I had already decided to keep.

18

Six months after I returned from the war, on a day nearly identical to the one on which we met, Abby came home on the train.

I met her at the apartment door, taking her coat and swollen briefcase, March cold elbowing its way in like an unwelcome guest. I felt much the same.

Abby surprised me by smiling wide.

"Pack your bag, Pogue. We're leaving this disgusting weather behind."

In those days, I often felt like a sleepwalker. It was hard to explain, this disconnect. My fellow servicemen understood, but no one else did: not Abby, not her family, not the psychologists I never went to see. If I had put it in a sentence, I would say this. It was like watching your own life from far away, a play seen from the cheapest seats, with one eye always on the wings, where, at any moment, something terrible might vault from the shadows.

"How?"

This time my wife did not dissolve into anger.

"Most people fly, silly."

We still stood in the hallway. She took the briefcase back. Rummaging in a side pocket, she produced an envelope. She waved it lightly under my nose like smelling salts.

"Two tickets to St. Croix," she said, and I saw the trepidation in her eyes.

I had no job. Abby worked as a research assistant for a Harvard biologist named Angus Quinlan. Angus Quinlan was in his seventies, globally recognized for his research on sea turtles, locally recognized for severe agoraphobia, a fondness for Irish whisky, and an inability to part with a dollar. Abby did most of his work, securing his grants, traveling to research outposts on various Caribbean islands to notch his observations, now and again even driving him home when whisky got the better of him. Her passion and painstaking meticulousness earned Angus Quinlan even more renown. In return, Abby earned a pittance.

I hated myself as I said it.

"We can't afford it."

My wife's smile faltered.

"I know you're trying, Pogue. I know I've been hard on you. It will be good for both of us." She retrieved the full smile. "We can afford it. It's a long-term loan from Sarah."

Sarah worked in the admissions office at Boston College and took night classes toward a master's degree in English Literature. She came by the apartment every Tuesday at noon on her lunch break. When Abby was home, they sat at the kitchen table conferring quietly, for in those days, our apartment possessed the air of a funeral home. Often, when I wandered in, the conversation stopped. When Abby was away, Sarah and I sat at the table and read poetry aloud. When Sarah read, I looked out the window, watching the world go about its business. When I read, I tried to ignore Sarah watching me.

It's funny how one's view of money changes. On that snowy evening, it stained everything.

"We can't afford to pay her back," I said.

I watched from my seat in the mezzanine, a haggard man in baggy wool trousers and a lovely, young woman wearing a square-shouldered jacket and fading hope. I wanted to shout at the man in wool trousers. He left a foul taste in my mouth.

Abby said, "We can't afford not to go." She rose up and kissed me on the lips. "Please. I have faith in us. I have faith in you."

I stood in the cold foyer, my heart racing, the touch of her lips still warm, watching her hurry down the hall. That mankind falls so easily in and out of love is a blessing and curse.

Two afternoons later, we stepped down to a coralline airstrip, the sun like a torch. A sharp ammonia smell rode on the heat.

"Guano," Abby said happily. "Foundation of all things Bremser."

For most of the flight, we had sat strained and quiet, but stepping onto the St. Croix tarmac transformed my wife. She grew happier with each step. She knew the customs officials, the luggage handlers, and the taxi drivers queued up out front, and when our taxi circled a roundabout, the policeman directing traffic gave a dignified salute, which Abby returned with a laugh.

It made me happy to see my wife like this.

"You should run for president," I said.

Abby gave my arm a squeeze.

"It's a small island, inhabited by gracious people."

We stayed in Christiansted for two days. During the day, we walked narrow alleys among cheery yellow and blue buildings, calypso music cavorting from open doorways. As we strolled, the islanders waved to each other and to us. Abby did not know them all, but she knew many of them. They spoke with us in the easy fashion of people comfortable in their own skin, and we smiled back like a honeymoon couple. But when night came, Abby and I moved about our hotel room like boats skirting each other's wake, at last kissing awkwardly and slipping into bed. Back turned to me, I saw my wife's shoulders, young and silken-smooth, already assuming a golden hue.

Changing climates did not change my circumstances. I lay awake watching the ceiling fan gallop, listening to Abby's luxuriant breaths. I prayed for sleep. I prayed not to sleep. The fan made indifferent circles.

On the third morning, we packed and took a cab to the northwestern end of the island. The Seuss buildings of Christiansted fell behind, replaced by jungle sagging beneath its own weight, and above the jungle, green hills dotted with trees and white scraps of cloud. Bumping along the dirt road, we passed apathetic goats and scurrying chickens, and women cooking over open fires. Children shouted and chased after us, laughing.

We passed a series of bays, each with its own white-cusp beach, dilapidated dock, and anchored pirogues. The brightly painted boats, piled with nets, swayed empty. In the shade of palms, fishermen sat on crates, drinking beer and playing cards.

Silence was our enemy. I wanted to change things with all my heart.

"Why isn't anyone fishing?"

"It's Sunday," said Abby. "The European influence and a good excuse to play cards."

Here and there, we passed overgrown ruins, stone buildings split by roots and nearly swallowed by jungle. Our driver recited the names of the sugar plantations. Morningstar. Solitude. Upper Love. He smiled as he spoke each whimsical name, but their sun-splashed decay made me sad, for I saw families in ruin.

"The English, Irish, Spanish, and French, one at a time done in by the heat and the lassitude," said Abby, the two of us sticking to the backseat as another crumbling cairn scrolled past. "I suppose you could say it's a very patient place that doesn't care much for time, or us. A fitting nesting ground for a creature that witnessed the demise of the dinosaurs." She smiled at me. "Your turtles."

I took her hand.

"I believe these particular turtles are yours."

"Ours." Abby looked past me to the blue water. "You've never seen nesting like this, Pogue. The numbers are astonishing. A sanctuary of creation."

We swerved around a man walking naked in the middle of the road. Our driver honked and shouted, "Oy! Isaac!" But the man continued to smile at his feet.

Our driver shook his head.

"Ohhhh, his mother will not be happy."

"Is he all right?" I asked.

"Better than most, and crazier than most."

"Should we stop?"

"Only his mother can turn him about. She is accustomed to it."

"Does he do it often?"

The driver grinned at me in the rearview mirror.

"He escapes as often as he can."

We rode silently past another group of men playing cards in the shade.

I leaned close to Abby.

"I'm sorry," I said.

"For what?"

"For being so practical."

"You were only doing what you always do."

"Impersonating Ebenezer Scrooge?"

"No," said Abby, squeezing my hand. "Looking out for us."

And what is it that I can control?

Three boys in their underwear watched us pass.

"Apparently I overpacked," I said, waving to them.

Out past the fringing reef, the water was nearly purple. Islands rose in the distance, pale blue in the bright sun.

"I don't think I'll miss Boston," I said.

"You'll love the cottage, Pogue. It's on a hill, with an otherworldly view of the sea."

"Have you stayed there before?"

"No." A tick of hesitation, then lightly, "It's a wee bit grand for a researcher's budget."

A belt drew tight around my chest.

"Well, we're not researchers, are we?" I said, smiling. "How did you find it?"

"A friend told me about it. Another researcher. I've passed it dozens of times on my way to the nesting beach. Greens and hawksbills come ashore on this side of the island." She looked right in my eyes. "Leatherbacks too. The great returning."

When I kissed her, she pressed back. Even as we kissed, I tried to remember the last time we had done this. There was a stranger in the front seat, and I didn't care.

"Well," said Abby, breaking away and looking down at her hands.

Five minutes later, the driver stopped.

"Cane Bay. End of the road unless you are a goat."

The driver pulled our suitcases from the trunk, got back in the cab, swung around, and caromed back toward Christiansted, spilling black smoke into the silence. We stood in the middle of the road.

Reconnaissance is a habit that never leaves. Cane Bay's arc of beach was longer than the others we had passed, a mile of beach between two rocky thumbs of grass-topped bluff. Twenty yards from where we stood, the macadam ended, its jagged foot crumbling to a sand footpath. Palms lined the foreshore, brown and green coconuts at their base. Tiny emerald waves lapped at the bright sand.

I looked up the hill. The cottage sat in a clearing, the jungle hacked back so that only luxuriant grass held sway. The cottage was blue with white plantation shutters, topped by a tin roof that flared in the sun. A verandah wrapped three sides. Reflexively, I noted the distance from the cottage to the jungle.

"It's incredible," I said, though it wasn't what I was thinking.

"You haven't even *seen* it, Pogue."

"I already know it's perfect."

My wife wore a pleased expression like a child holding out an anointed art work, but a part of me whispered, *We are alone.*

A mountain rose behind the cottage, dark green and rounded.

"Mount Eagle," said Abby. "One thousand, one hundred and sixty-five feet. St. Croix's highest spot."

"I didn't pack my pitons."

Abby laughed.

"Good. We'll stay by the sea." Her hands began to dance. "You won't believe the life here, Pogue. We've done hatchling counts on this beach and a few of the beaches nearby. The numbers are incredible. And I've heard there are beaches on the far side of the island that make these beaches look like the Gobi Desert. I'm hoping we can hike there, if you don't mind."

Her embarrassed smile made me want to hug her.

"Apparently, we *are* researchers."

"Only part time. I promise."

"One stipulation."

"Anything."

"Fraternizing is allowed."

Two fingers touched my heart and then circled a nipple.

"It was part of my research proposal."

A polite cough interrupted us.

"Traffic is sparse, but it is still wise to avoid the midday sun."

The man stood so straight I knew he had never slouched. Smooth skin and a sinewy frame made his age indeterminate, but white curls, knitted tight to his scalp, provided a hint.

I had no idea where he had come from. It unnerved me slightly.

"I apologize for interrupting." He extended a hand, big and rough as a paddle. "Calvin Isaacs, at your service. You are Mr. Whithouse. It is a distinct honor to meet you, sir."

He was probably older than my father.

"Please. Just call me Pogue."

"Mr. Pogue," he said, gently releasing my hand. "Welcome back to Cane Bay, Mrs. Whithouse." Our estranged circumstances made the name sound odd. "An equivalent pleasure to see you again."

"The pleasure is always mine, Calvin."

Abby turned to me.

"Calvin is here to help us. He's ..."

"Usually I help the researchers," Calvin said to me, "but in this case, I come with the cottage. Not quite a butler, not quite a handyman, not quite a useful cook. And," he bent to pick up our suitcases, "a poor excuse for a bellman. But we are each an assemblage of many things."

I tried to take a bag, but Calvin gripped the handle firmly.

"When I vacation in America, you will carry my bags, Mr. Pogue."

Calvin strode up the incline as if there wasn't one. Placing the bags in the shade of the verandah, he went to each of the plantation windows, flicking off the rusted hooks and folding the shutters back with soft clacks.

"First we welcome the sea breeze. Then we welcome you."

The interior of the cottage was immaculate. It smelled of varnished wood and lemons. A bowl of sliced lemons rested on the glass coffee table in the sitting room. Another sat on the waist-high kitchen counter. The counter, ironwood polished to showroom sheen, separated the sitting room from the small kitchen.

A short hallway, its windows looking to the sea, ran back to the master bedroom. I followed Calvin past framed pencil sketches of tropical birds.

"Mostly birders stay here," said Calvin. "They are even more absorbed than lovers. They walk down the middle of the road with binoculars glued to their faces. Oh yes, it is an attention-getting matter to round a bend and find one's windshield filled with an octogenarian."

The entire rear of the cottage was our bedroom. The room was dominated by a four-poster bed, made hazy by mosquito netting.

Calvin placed the bags on a footlocker at the end of the bed.

"The mosquito is our national bird, but they are only particularly troublesome in the evening around sunset. We are not the only species that celebrates cocktail hour."

Back on the verandah, a breeze had come up. The grass ran up the hill in rivers.

"A steady breeze is a good omen," Calvin said. "Practical benefit too. The mosquitoes are now heading to visit my relatives on the east side of the island."

The three of us stood looking out at the Caribbean Sea, robin's egg blue to the horizon. A single dark hummock interrupted the Serengeti expanse.

"There you see St. Thomas, a ship upon the sea, some forty miles distant," Calvin said. "Truth be told, that is not far enough for me. Now that I am old, I prefer a life of seclusion."

Touching a finger to his forehead, he started down the steps.

"But I am not so old to forget the young enjoy seclusion too."

Twenty minutes later, Abby came out to the verandah wearing a T-shirt that fell just short of her knees. Masks and snorkels dangled from my wife's hand.

I stared at the book in my hand.

"I'm not falling for *that* again," Abby said, waving a mask in the air. "Time for a fish count. You've already got your suit on."

"I'm enjoying the breeze. I'll make us gin and tonics. We already have lemons."

How is it that a grown woman can look like a little girl informed that Christmas is canceled?

"You'll be glad you went. You won't believe the sea life here. We might even see a turtle. Please?"

Don't ever lie to me again.

Closing the book, I stood.

"No book is that good," I said.

The way Abby jumped for my elbow wrenched my heart. Yanking me down the steps, masks clacking in her other hand, she spoke in a rush.

"You've never seen so many fish. It's like genesis itself, a biblical flood! It's crazy. And," she squeezed my elbow, "there really is a good chance of turtles. I didn't make it up. The hawksbills keep their distance, but the juvenile greens swim right up and bump your face plate. The local kids feed them fish bits."

Some species of sea turtles change their diet as they age. Green sea turtles are mainly carnivorous as hatchlings and juveniles, and then they slowly shift to a herbivorous diet. The mouth cavity and throat of the great leatherback is lined with spine-like projections called papillae that are pointed backward to help them swallow the soft jellyfish that are their catnip.

Abby released my elbow and walked faster. Already I felt my breaths turning shallow. I concentrated on the grass, soft beneath my feet, and the supple flex and lengthenings of my wife's firm legs.

A half-ton leatherback eats its weight in jellyfish in a single day. A single lion's mane jellyfish, a leatherback favorite, is as big as a trash can lid and weighs ten pounds or more.

None of it was working. At the road's edge, I dropped into a sprinter's crouch and uncurled. I heard Abby laughing. I kept running. As soon as I passed her, I closed my eyes. The shallows were bath warm. I staggered but kept my footing. When I finally came to a stop and opened my eyes, tourmaline water circled my chest. I could feel it drawing out, beckoning.

Abby finned toward me, kicking smoothly with her head up, holding my mask and fins above the surface.

"You'll need these, Jessie Owens."

Her own mask pinched her nose, turning her voice nasal. Handing me my mask and fins, she gestured to where the water went from green to deep blue.

"That's the edge of the reef. Follow me."

I kicked out on my back, Mount Eagle and a circling frigate bird jostling in my face plate. Once I glanced over my shoulder, scanning the blue expanse for the dark prong of Abby's snorkel. I reached for familiar tricks, trying to make each breath slower than the last. The water cooled. I counted out ten kicks and ten more. Rolling over onto my stomach, I forced my eyes wide.

Indigo blue crashed against my face plate. My throat seized. Beams of sunlight spun down, fuzzily dissolving into the bottomless blue.

What is it like when the stars wink out and your lungs scream for air?

I felt the familiar rush of claustrophobic panic. I inhaled, but the snorkel seemed to have closed itself to only the thinnest shred of air. Not quite pain this shallow drawing, but terrifying.

I knew what to do. I was only five months removed from war. I descended into the familiar refrain. *Nowhere but here. Slow the heart. Focus completely. You are all you can control.*

I kicked.

When I opened my eyes again, I was back over the reef. Thirty feet below, a school of bright yellow fish wove like a river through a kaleidoscopic explosion of sea fans and corals. The fish looked like flowers bestowed the gift of flight. I felt the sway of passing waves. My good ear filled with the crackle of countless life forms gnawing on the reef.

Raising my head, I looked for Abby. She was thirty yards away, still at the outer edge of the reef, finning easily.

It was better in the clear shallows and better still on the beach. I sat in the sand, fighting to calm my breathing.

When Abby finally sat down beside me, she squeezed my knee with wrinkled fingers.

"Incredible," she said.

She pulled the T-shirt over her head, balling it in her lap.

"It was," I said.

"See any turtles?"

"No."

"Me neither."

"My legs started cramping. I'm a little out of shape."

Abby looked out to the reef.

"It worries me a little," she said.

"That your husband's getting soft?"

"That there weren't any turtles."

The breeze had died. The last of the whitecaps disappeared before our eyes.

"This reef used to be completely untouched. They fish here a little now, but I've been told the fishermen still fish mostly off Christiansted and a few of the other bays we passed on the way here." She absently touched an ankle. The fin strap had left a raw mark. "Did you see that school of fairy basslets?"

"Which ones were they?"

"The enormous school that looked like a cloud of blue and orange sparks. Right along the edge of the reef."

"They were beautiful."

"They're one of my favorites."

Abby stretched her legs out and put her mask in her lap. Moistening a fingertip, she dabbed at grains of sand on the inside of the mask.

"Turtles are usually here this time of year," she said.

We both heard the steady popping at the same time. In the distance, a bright yellow fishing pirogue made its way around the southern headland, churning through the water like a banana. The popping grew louder as it moved in toward the reef. Two men were in the boat. When they reached the reef, the man in the stern cut the engine. They bent as one, hands working out of sight. They threw the net together.

The man in the bow bent again. When he stood, he had a baseball bat in his hands. Balanced on the bow, he swung the bat in a home run arc. Their laughter carried across the water.

Abby stood. She didn't brush the sand off her legs.

"I'm cold," she said.

Halfway up the hill, a delicious smell of frying seasonings greeted us. Calvin was at the stove, stirring something smoky in a skillet. A radio played Kay Kyser's "He Wears a Pair of Silver Wings."

Two open beers rested on the counter. Calvin spoke, but the radio was loud, and I was poorly positioned. Four men stand in a clearing. In the instant before the artillery shell detonates overhead, one man crouches to tune a radio dial. When he rises, his companions are shredded by shrapnel, and he is deaf in his right ear.

Calvin's mouth moved again, and I shook my head.

He turned off the radio.

"I'm sorry, Mr. Pogue. Music is a lifelong vice, and strangely, it gets softer as I get older." He circled the fork in the pan. "When the last of these conch fritters have attained the proper burnish, I'll bring them to the porch. For now, take your drinks and make yourselves comfortable. St. Croix's version of afternoon tea, and as you know, Miss Abby's favorite dish."

We ate with the plates in our laps, their heat on our thighs. Music filtered out from the kitchen, interspersed by banging pans.

"They're delicious," I said.

Abby did not look up from her plate.

"They're one of Calvin's specialties."

"I didn't know conch fritters are your favorite dish."

"We don't talk much."

Reaching out, I put a hand on her knee.

"Tell me something about you."

She looked up, her face stone.

"Does that seem fair?"

Calvin left grouper fillets for dinner. I fried them, adding the spices Calvin used on the conch. It began to rain. The grouper's sizzling melded with the drumming rain.

The rain chased away the mosquitoes. After dinner, we sat on the verandah, liquid darkness making soothing noise about us. There were no lights anywhere.

"I liked the fish," Abby said, without much feeling.

I tried a smile.

"I'll pass your compliments on to Calvin. I just turned on the burner."

A notebook rested on the arm of Abby's chair.

"Working?"

"I made some notes while you were cooking. I'm worried. We should have seen at least a few turtles."

"A good scientist draws no conclusions from a single observation."

It was her expression.

"Duly noted," she said.

You rarely think such things, but looking at my wife, damp T-shirt pressed against her firm body, it occurred to me that she was two months short of twenty-two. So much ahead.

Remembering now makes it hard to breathe.

Placing my plate on the arm of the chair, I stood. When I put my lips to Abby's ear, her hands made a small jump, but she did not move.

"Let's go for a walk."

"It's *pouring*, Pogue."

I kept my lips where they were. Commanding yourself to be impulsive is as good as being impulsive if no one knows.

"It's warm rain. I haven't forgotten."

"Forgotten what?"

"That we're young."

Smiling made her ear lift.

"Back in a minute," I said.

"Where are you going?"

"There's wine in the fridge."

When I came back, the note was wedged in the screen door.

I like to play hide and seek.

She was standing in the middle of the beach, hands awkward at her sides. Her nakedness made her bones more pronounced.

I felt her hollows and corners as she stepped into me.

"I wanted you to find me," she said.

We stood awkwardly, trying to couple, and then we went to the sand. Entry was like a warm drowning. The only sound was the rain. I felt the sand grate against my elbows, but when I tried to shift Abby to her side, she locked her thighs tight against me. We pushed into each other, the soles of her feet stroking my calves. Water ran down her cheeks like tears. It was quick. The weeks of waiting saw to that. About us, the sand leaped in small droplets.

Afterward, we sat with our bare hips touching. The rain made talk impossible. We passed the wine, watching the rain stipple the black sea.

After a time, Abby took my hand and led me up the hill. We made love beneath the mosquito netting. We tasted of salt and wine, and sand chafed between us. My hands went shyly to familiar places. The rain had stopped. This time, I heard my wife's sighs.

When we finished, Abby rested her head on my chest, her hair made impossibly soft by the rain.

"It's like telling each other secrets," she said.

"Thank you for bringing us here."

"Nesting areas are the best place to meet females."

Abby's breaths touched my skin like warm petals. Beyond the netting, mosquitoes whined frustration. The cottage made tiny settlings, as if it were lying down to sleep.

Abby ran a fingertip along the length of my arm.

"Our limbs are the same," she said.

The wine was creeping up on me. I managed a sleepy mumble. "The same?"

"The same as a sea turtle's." The fingertip made a series of pleasant, tingling loops. "Our limb bones are longer. Theirs have shortened, and what would have been wrists and ankles have flattened. And their fingers are very long. But otherwise, flipper and arm are the same."

I floated in my good dreams.

"I wish we could swim like they do," I said.

The fingertip stopped.

"Do you?"

My drowsy inebriation vanished. I waited, hoping for a redirection, a turtle banking in the deeps. *La esperanza muere al ultimo.* Hope is the last thing to die.

"What happened?" Abby said softly.

"To what?" I asked, though I knew.

"To the boy who swam with turtles. To the man I thought I married. To the truth. Why are you afraid of the water?"

"I went snorkeling this afternoon."

The fingertip left my forearm. We stared up into the circus big top of netting.

"Maybe if I was a better wife, I'd let you have all your secrets," Abby said, the words like a slow bleeding. "I try. I don't ask you about the war. I don't ask you what makes you shout out at night. I don't ask you what you think when you sit in the kitchen in the middle of the night. I don't even ask you how long it might take you to come back to this world. I want to help you with all those things. I want to help you with all my heart. But I've tried to wait until you ask."

Try sometime to distinguish between a sigh of hurt and a sigh of pleasure.

"But the swimming is a lie that's been between us since we met. I can't let that one go. I've really tried to forget. I tried tonight. But the lie was right there the whole time. Every second."

There are moments when you can save yourself, when the right word, the honest confession, can turn you back onto the road to redemption. Sometimes you even see these moments as they arrive. But you can read these words and know they are true, just as you can see these moments in your own life and still ignore them. Just as you will see, as the years pass, and you grow old, how you will relive these moments again and again, returned to like carrion to something never quite dead.

But in that moment, in the waiting and the cottage settlings, secrets still reigned supreme.

"Why are you afraid of the water, Pogue?"

The mosquitoes droned.

My wife turned away again.

"There were no fairy basslets," she said.

The following morning, I rose in darkness and went out to the verandah. I read with a flashlight, and then I turned the flashlight off. I did not see the horizon's first tincture of orange or the sun pull itself from the sea.

The screen door creaked.

Abby walked to the edge of the verandah. She stood with her back to me, looking toward St. Thomas.

"Sarah's poets?" she said.

"Yes."

I started to close the book.

"I'd like to hear one."

"Anything in particular?"

I didn't mean for it to sound hurtful, but it did.

Abby didn't look at me.

"Read a poem you like," she said.

I found the poem I wanted.

I have been one acquainted with the night.
I have walked out in the rain—and back in the rain.
I have outwalked the furthest city light.

I have looked down the saddest city lane.
I have passed by the watchman on his beat
And dropped my eyes, unwilling to explain ...

When I finished, Abby was quiet.

"Who wrote that?"

"Robert Frost. It's called 'Acquainted with the Night.'"

"It's beautiful and sad."

"It is."

"I would have liked to walk with Mr. Frost. He sounds lonely."

A mother and father who died when he was a boy, a family history of mental illness, four of his own children already dead: Frost's night *is* depression.

"He was. He was also honest."

The morning light walked up the grass and wrapped itself about my wife.

Abby turned.

"I know you're trying, Pogue."

I saw her slick nakedness, her awkward hands, standing on the dark beach exposed to chance. There are braver things, but not many.

"We're both trying," I said.

"Make me a promise."

"Yes."

In that instant, my tower of secrets tottered.

"Promise you'll read me poetry."

"Whenever you ask."

"Promise I won't have to ask."

Love has been described as many things, by wordsmiths far greater than me. But often I envision love as a sea surging to and fro, those caught in its surges reaching out to each other, fingertips glancing, before falling away again.

Robert Frost is long dead now, buried in the Old Bennington Cemetery in Bennington, Vermont. In the end, he reached some understanding of love and life. His epitaph reads: *I had a lover's quarrel with the world.*

19

Calvin was like the sea breeze that stirred to life with Swiss watch precision midmorning. He arrived at the cottage twice a day. At seven in the morning, he brought a platter of fresh fruit, moist-bright slices of papaya and pineapple, and always two mangoes. At four in the afternoon, he returned with more fruit and a string of fresh fish. In the morning, after some brief banter, he left. But in the afternoon, he stayed, filleting the fish in our kitchen, deftly extricating bone from soft flesh with the fishing knife that dangled at his side. Before he began filleting, I would fix him a gin and tonic. Each time I poured the gin, he admonished me.

"Not too heavy-handed now, Mr. Pogue. I enjoy reaching out to this world with ten fingers."

I enjoyed Calvin's company. I sat on the barstool at the counter while Calvin prepared the fish and talked of the happenings in his village. It was a small village, thirty residents with comings and goings, but there was always drama. As Calvin put it, "The human pageant does not require volume."

Abby did not join us. I asked, but she politely declined. I believed she did not want to intrude on what was for me a rare friendship. Other than Sarah and her weekly visits, I had no friends in Boston. While Calvin held court in the kitchen, Abby walked the beach or read research papers on the verandah. I tried to convince Calvin to stay for dinner, but once the fish was seasoned and the fruit diced, he left, always demurring with the same response.

"Old age is a stain on the bud of youth."

On our fifth night, I woke from a sound sleep to a steady rapping on the screen door. I looked at my watch. I hurried to the door. It is never good news at two in the morning.

Calvin's gaunt silhouette stood outside the screen.

"Good news," he said.

He smiled at my foolish look.

"The turtles," he said. "They are here."

The three of us walked south along the beach. The night smelled of salt and plumeria. Where the bay ended, we followed a dirt track wending steeply up the side of the headland. Abby walked so quickly, Calvin and I had to trot to keep up.

On the opposite side of the headland, the path descended to another bay. The beach was smaller than Cane Bay, the seas much rougher; the beach faced more west, into the brunt of approaching weather. The swell was rising. Plumed breakers crashed on the outer reef, making white zippers in the darkness. Settling as they crossed the deep lagoon, the waves reformed again in the shallows, dashing against the beach with appreciable power.

More than thirty turtles had already plowed up the sandy beach, hawksbills and greens, leaving signature tank tread tracks in their wake. Most of the turtles stopped short of the tangle of sea grape and stumpy palms marking the jungle's edge, though some had bulldozed right on up and over the slight rise to a thin patch of sand beyond. The turtles dug their nests with their back flippers, flinging sand like naughty children. At the water's edge, more dark forms appeared in the jumble of frothing white.

With a cry of joy, Abby ran to the water to meet them. Calvin and I watched her. She plunged into the foamy rush, pirouetting and spreading her arms to the stars.

Again I fell in love. I made no attempt to hide my pride.

"Passion is a gift," I said.

Calvin spoke in the darkness beside me.

"There is a man who lives in our village. He is already in middle age, but his mother still looks after him. Whenever he can, he slips away and walks naked along the road, wearing only a smile. He covets nothing. He harms no one. He only smiles and walks. Long ago, I asked him why he does this. He said the sun feels good against his skin. Many in our village consider him daft, but I am not among them."

"Isaac," I said.

Calvin laughed softly.

"That is so."

"We saw him," I said.

"I am not surprised. He is a man who indulges his fancies as often as he can."

Bowling ball shadows moved in the faces of the moonlit waves, a lumbering D-day invasion summoning life, not death. The waves made rifle crack explosions, dashing the turtles against the beach. How they kept coming, I don't know. Tumbling in the whitewash, they found their footing, grinding up the beach with lumbering aplomb.

The beach filled with turtles. Two enormous females collided, one determined to nest, the other determined to return to the water. For a minute, they pushed against each other. Finally, with a slight grinding, the smaller turtle rode up and over the back of its larger compatriot, surmounting yet another obstacle.

Abby hopped about in the waves' rush, pausing now and again to scrawl in the notebook she held at chin level. All around her, the ocean expunged dinosaur gumballs.

"Some might consider your wife daft."

Suddenly I was immeasurably happy. I laughed.

"I wish it was contagious."

"Recognition is the first dance step."

I should be dancing beside my wife.

"You see this as joy and life," Calvin said.

"Yes."

I confess I was distracted by my wife.

"We both know the world is not such a simple place," Calvin said.

The soberness in his voice made me want to walk away.

"Miss Abby told me why you are here."

My joy leaked away. I watched Abby, but I felt Calvin's eyes on me.

"We were removed from the war here," Calvin said, "but today, no place is wholly removed from the world. We are grateful to you and your fellow soldiers for serving our cause. If brave men do not come forward, cowards will rule this world."

I tried not to sound angry, but I am afraid I failed.

"I'm no braver than you are. You would have done the same thing."

"I cannot say how I would have behaved."

This was true.

A wave twice the size of its fellows threw itself forward. Its leading edge, a liquid sledgehammer, exploded directly on the back of an unfortunate turtle. The turtle disappeared. I scanned the milky turmoil until I spotted a flipper waving above the soupy broth like a swimmer in distress. The broth receded, struggling turtle in its clasp. It sucked the turtle back into the pounding shore break where a second enormous wave picked up the dark round outline and threw it forward again.

"For some, it is quite a fight," said Calvin.

He gave his polite cough.

"Mr. Pogue?"

"Yes."

"It may not be my place, but I would like to say something."

I had been happy. Calvin had let the darkness in. I fought it, but it was too late. Already I heard the immeasurably sad echo of Glenn Miller.

In those days, I thought war had taught me everything I would ever need to know about sorrow.

"It's not your place," I said, and I walked down to the unfair sea.

Had I listened, I wonder if it would have changed things.

Abby ran to me. I caught her in my arms, and she kissed me hard on the mouth. Her breath was hot.

"I told you," she said, pulling away. "The world made right."

Her face possessed an ethereal flush. The moon turned highlights in her hair. I had never seen her look lovelier.

"You're otherworldly. An angel in her place."

Abby laughed.

"All these female hormones are going to your head."

"My head?"

"Our heads."

We walked to where Calvin sat on a pale piece of driftwood. He stood before we reached him. He did not look at me.

Abby said, "Thank you, Calvin."

"It is not my doing."

My wife was blind to Calvin's sobriety. She laughed again.

"I don't care who's responsible. There must be *two hundred* of them. *They have to crawl over each other.* Beautiful. No. Far better than beautiful. Eden. You are an enlightened people," she said, but Calvin was already walking away.

Walking back to the cottage in the half light of false dawn, Abby said, "I've heard there's a beach on the windward side where turtles come ashore. I'd like to see it."

Calvin walked with his head down. It had been a wearying night for an old man.

He shook his head slowly.

"It is nearly two hours distant, and the going is very rough. Near the end, there is only the barest trace of trail. It is very treacherous. Before it descends to the beach, it runs along the edge of a high cliff that falls straight down to the rocks. Hard rains have loosened the cliff edge. It is not uncommon for people to fall to their death, and they are villagers familiar with the trail."

"I know how to walk."

Calvin had made a mistake, but he was unperturbed.

"The turtles that come to that beach are no different from the ones tonight, Miss Abby."

"Every turtle is different."

Wisely, Calvin made no reply. When we reached the foot of the hill leading up to the cottage, he left us without a word.

At the cottage, I boiled tea. Abby sat on the porch, scratching furiously in her notebook.

I placed the mug on the arm of her chair.

"A touch of cinnamon, just the way you like it," I said.

"Thank you."

Abby kept writing. I sat beside her. The jungle usually woke with a cacophonous shriek, but on this morning, it was strangely silent. My wife's breaths were lullaby soft and steady. I thought, *I want to listen to this for the rest of my life.*

Finally Abby closed the notebook and put it in her lap. In doing so, her elbow nearly swept the mug off the arm of the chair.

"You made tea?"

"Lukewarm tea."

"I'm sorry. I must have been distracted."

"It's possible."

"You're not angry?"

"That you snubbed my tea?"

"Not the tea. The deceit. That I brought you here on a working holiday."

"It's the perfect deception," I said. "Sea turtles are a passion."

Abby ran her hands over the worn leather covering as if summoning a genie.

"You could *feel* it. A beginning without end. The fresh start of new life, but the turnings of something almost as old as the earth." She quieted. "I felt like I was the one giving birth."

There was an uncomfortable silence.

"You dance beautifully," I said.

Abby smiled into her mug.

"I'm afraid I got carried away. Decidedly unprofessional. Professor Quinlan would be appalled."

"Your version of Irish whisky."

"You're sweet. And what is your Irish whisky?"

"Your happiness."

She took my hand. Turning it over, she kissed my palm.

Love surged forward. I wished I could hold it forever.

"Of all the turtles, the leatherback has the largest heart," she said.

She sipped the tea. Her eyebrows lifted.

"Cinnamon?"

When I laughed, she gave me a curious smile.

The following night, I woke to faint scratching. I willed the creature away, but nature is persistent. The scratching continued, annoyingly impudent, followed by the softest cough.

This time, Calvin did not smile. Putting a finger to his lips, he motioned me outside. I followed him out onto the cool grass.

His mysterious behavior annoyed me.

"What are you doing?"

"I will take you to the beach Miss Abby asked about, Mr. Pogue."

"But it's a two-hour hike."

"It is an easy walk. Forty minutes at most."

I was angry again.

"Why did you lie? What do you think you're doing?"

"You will see."

"Wait here," I said brusquely.

"Only you."

When I turned back to him, he had a look I knew. The sorrow spilled into his slumping shoulders, a familiar defeat that sent a chill through me.

"Why?" I asked.

"An offering of gratitude."

"You don't owe me anything."

"It is important you see this."

I might still have ignored him had I not recognized, in this stranger's voice, the absolute certainty of my wife.

"I can't leave her alone."

This time Calvin spoke brusquely.

"We both know she can manage for herself. We'll return before she wakes."

At first we followed the previous night's path, silver and easy to see beneath the full moon. Then, at a point with no discernible markings, Calvin turned and disappeared behind a wall of green. Even in the full moon's light, the opening was nearly invisible. It appeared slowly before my eyes, shoulder wide and slightly less than head high. Calvin's rustlings were already receding quickly.

I took a deep breath and plunged in. I might as well have been diving into water, for it was instantly black. Panic throttled me, squeezing my lungs and freezing my limbs. I forced myself forward. I felt the familiar tingling in my fingertips. The buzzing galloped up my spine, slamming into my brain, a dash of icy water. My eyes adjusted, absorbing the familiar fat leaves groping like hands, the latticework of branch, creeper, and vine, the thin gray scar of path. Again the dripping, from everywhere and nowhere, and behind that, perhaps the lightest whisper of fabric. My forearms tensed, though I held nothing.

Calvin appeared, coming back for me, his blackness gray in this dark.

"The path is steep, but it is short. No more than five hundred yards. Then we come to a clearing, and we are almost there," he said, and he was gone.

Wet leaves slid past me; threads of webbing adhered to my face. All around me, the darkness made muted, unrecognizable noises. My memory assembled them into mocking calls and whispered threats.

There was no danger, but my brain continued its lies. My body listened, tensing to bestow or receive the thrust. My foolish imagination made me curse. I cursed Calvin for bringing me. I cursed myself for coming. I cursed the webbing and the leaves that slapped at me like sponges.

Then the jungle was gone. I paused in the clearing to gather my wits and still my breathing before walking along the edge of the bluff and down the short path to the beach.

The beach shone silver in the moonlight, imbued with the near light of day. I stood at one end of a tight cove, an arc of sixty yards at most, with a dark buttress of headland at each end. Nothing moved. Mounds rose from the sand. Some were small. More were taller than a man. *Driftwood*, my brain said protectively, but driftwood is not so delicately sculpted.

There were dozens of piles. I walked among them.

When Calvin finally stepped up beside me, he spoke in a hushed voice like a man inside a great cathedral. He did not look at me.

"In their innocence, they keep coming. The living crawl over the dead. The greediest poachers kill them before they even lay their eggs. That is a pointless exercise, for the eggs earn us money, but blood turns some men crazy. We kill them with machetes and baseball bats. A turtle takes a long time to die. Even after their throats are slit and their shells are smashed, the females continue up the beach, laying their eggs in pools of blood."

The moon's light gave the bone piles a ghostly glow.

"The males swim just beyond the waves. On calm nights, we hear them surface. They make a sound like a great sigh. The scientists tell us the males are waiting to mate with the females when they return to sea, but I sometimes wonder if they surface for another reason. The dying females make no noise we can hear, but I wonder if the males know their pain."

Bones are beyond answering.

"We are not enlightened, Mr. Pogue. We are stupid and greedy. There are two sides to Eden."

When I slipped into bed, Abby said, "You were gone for three hours. Where were you?"

My heart raced again.

"Walking."

"Walking?"

"On the beach. I couldn't sleep. I had another dream."

The bed shifted.

"Oh, Pogue." Fingertips caressed my temple. I felt dirty. I lay on my back looking up into the netting. I could not look at my wife. "I'm sorry," she said. "I wish I knew what it was like."

"It's not always bad. Sometimes I just need to think."

"Our friend Mr. Frost."

"Yes."

Outside, the jungle croaked and clicked, the noises of the eaters and the eaten. The circles slowed. Fingers slid down my temple, bumping past my cheek.

"I'd walk with you," Abby mumbled, and she was asleep.

I listened to the jungle. It began to rain.

Robert Frost was not the only poet who walked the night alone.

And down by the brimming river
I heard a lover sing
Under the arch of the railway;
'Love has no ending.

'I'll love you, dear, I'll love you
Till China and Africa meet,
And the river jumps over the mountain
And the salmon sing in the street ...'

I tried to push away the passionate crowings of W. H. Auden's naïve young lover, silenced all too quickly by the inevitable, but each word rose in my ears, as real as the drops of rain.

The glacier knocks in the cupboard,
The desert sighs in the bed,
And the crack in the teacup opens
A lane to the land of the dead.

Is it better to crow happily, blind to the cracks and the graveyard lanes? Or is it better to see both sides of Eden? I can't say. I only know what my own life has shown me and the mistakes I may or may not have made.

But I can say this. We can decide to quit, or we can decide to continue on.

20

The summer Sean turned fourteen, he fought a college boy. We all knew the boy. He had grown up in Sharpes. Thick in the chest and thin on reason, he had bullied most of us since grade school. His father was born dirt poor, but he had turned hard work and a nose for advertising into enough wealth to send his only child off to a fancy northern college. Apparently he spent most of his first year in the gymnasium, for he returned to us with an additional coating of muscle and arms that bulged like Popeye's. Most of the girls forgot his stupidity and mooned over him. Their stupidity irritated us all.

Through July, he rode the turtles with us, going to the front of the line whenever the mood moved him. No one had the courage to stop him. Sean appeared blind to this brazen violation of our code, though we all recognized it as an indirect challenge to my brother.

Finally a direct challenge came. News of the fight blitzkrieged through Sharpes. By the time the fight started, at high noon—we were not without drama—on a white, bright Saturday, nearly forty kids crowded the field. There were faces we had never seen. The new faces took their place at the back of the ring.

When the boy took off his shirt, a hush fell. The muscles in his arms and chest moved, slithering over each other as if each vying for attention. He walked around the grassy ring slowly, preening like a rooster.

Everyone watched his posturing, but I watched my brother, for this unbridled confidence was something new. Sean observed the bully's strutting poker-faced. His expression did not change when the boy stopped with his back to the woods.

From the back of the crowd, someone shouted, "Smash him!" and the fight began.

Both fighters moved cautiously at first, throwing probing punches, the soggy ground squelching protest beneath twisting feet. The bully began baiting my brother, calling Sean a pansy and a queer, telling him he liked dicks in his mouth. Several girls laughed, a high-pitched, nervous yelp. My brother said nothing. He squelched in a silent, tightening circle.

I kept staring at my brother's face, but now I had a different intent. He once told me that even the best fighters telegraphed an oncoming punch with a flick of the eyes, but nothing moved when Sean stepped close, so quickly that, for a frozen instant, the two stood like dance partners, the tall, surprised man-child and the short, pale boy bringing his fist up.

It was a punch like nothing we had seen. Fist on bone made a sound like a dropped plank. The bully's head snapped back. Blood gushed from his nose, and he sat down hard. Some of the kids gave a halfhearted cheer, but I stayed silent. Sean did not approve of cheering. Looking at the felled bully, I felt a wash of relief. As the boy preened, I had seen the sweat on my brother's upper lip, and the world had canted slightly.

Now all was right again.

But when I looked to my brother, my heart fell, for there was an expression on his face I could not quite place. There was twisted fury and an emperor's defiance, but there was something more, something I am fairly certain only I saw, the faintest tint of sadness, and something else I couldn't quite recognize, something that tugged at me and made me want to run to my brother's side.

My brother's assailant stood. In the stunned silence, Matty Simpson cried out. Looking back now, I hear the strangeness of the cry, a warning, but a warning suddenly strangled, as if the shouter had changed allegiances in mid-cry. Everyone's eyes went to the fishing knife.

Sean just barely jerked his head in time. The bully's swipe removed the upper corner of his left ear. Blood flowed from the wound, cherry red in the sun.

My brother stood for a moment, his hands dangling at his sides. Everyone screamed at him to defend himself, and even his assailant was momentarily puzzled, and when the bully finally went to strike again, I closed my eyes and said a quick prayer, but not for my brother, for I had seen the terrifying blankness in his eyes, and I knew his hands were already rising. I heard the impact and a great whooshing exhale.

When I opened my eyes, my brother was straddling the bully's chest. The boy jerked beneath my brother. My brother bent forward and whispered in his ear, and the boy went slack. My brother sat up. Blood from his ear fell to the boy's face and chest.

The boy remained still as Sean placed his palm firmly against the boy's forehead. He knew what was coming—they were working together—though the boy panted madly. When Sean inserted the knife in the boy's mouth, some of the kids cried out, and someone began praying to God, though we all knew God was gone from this place. My brother moved the knife carefully. The turnings produced terrible screams. The year before, our school bus had run over a neighborhood dog; the boy's screams were the dog's screams as it went under the wheels.

Blood ran down the boy's cheeks, and his hands tore at the muddy grass.

When Sean finished, he stood. Coiled tightly, the boy did not react to the first prod. Sean nudged him again with his foot. The boy crawled to the riverbank. At the river's edge, he rose to his knees and stood. He wiped his mouth, but the blood kept coming. When he spoke, the blood at the corners of his mouth bubbled.

"It's not done," he said.

My brother stared at him as if committing his handiwork to memory, and then he nodded slightly.

The boy waded into the river until it lifted him off his feet. He floated for a moment, and then the river carried him away.

As soon as the boy drifted out of sight, everyone left, shaky-limbed older kids ushering crying children.

Sean walked along the river to the dock. I followed.

My brother stood at the end of the dock, swaying slightly. I stepped up beside him. A bruise was purpling around his right eye. The blood from his ear had darkened and slowed. He took off his shirt. Leaning out, he dipped a corner of the shirt in the river. The dripping shirt made the same splattering sound as blood on flesh.

He pressed the damp shirt against his ear, leaning into it slightly as if it were whispering secrets.

The bloody knife hung loose in his other hand.

I was afraid for him, and afraid of him.

"Sean." I whispered his name, half hoping he wouldn't hear me. "Are you okay?"

"Yes."

"He cut off a piece of your ear."

"That was a surprise."

"Does it hurt?"

"A little."

"Were you afraid?"

He spoke to the river.

"At first. But now it feels good."

He was not the victor lording his power over me. He stared at the river. Something in his expression made me feel sorry for him.

"One day you'll swim across," I said.

"No, I won't."

Sean held the knife up, turning it slowly. I saw now that the handle was monogrammed, the letters HDH etched in gold cursive. I tried to remember the bully's name, but for the life of me, I couldn't. I wanted to puke. The world spun slowly like the river eddies.

"Jerk," I said. "Asshole."

"Maybe," my brother said. "You never really know people."

My brother didn't look like the winner at all. He looked bloodied and beaten. I saw now what I had failed to recognize as Sean stood waiting for his opponent to recover from the punch. The hopelessness in his eyes scared me more than any of the day's events.

I spoke my wish.

"It feels like a dream."

"It's not," Sean said. "It's the way things are."

The words were not a rebuke; they came soft and slow, flowing like the river and the blood.

"Are you okay, Henry?"

The question stunned me almost as much as the love on my brother's face.

"I guess so."

"Good."

He dropped the knife in the river.

"I didn't know teeth were so damn big," he said.

I looked down at the hand where the knife had been. I had never seen a full tooth. I was shocked by the length of the bloody root. It made a long scimitar curve beneath the tooth. I couldn't imagine the pain involved in uprooting such a thing.

In two great heaves, I puked breakfast into the river.

Sean took the shirt from his ear. Folding it precisely, he used a clean section to wipe my mouth. Then he dropped the tooth and the shirt in the river.

"To life's twists and turns," he said.

Turn a human tooth upside down, and it looks like a fang.

21

There are two places I want to see on my journey. One of them is the Grand Canyon.

From Williams, Arizona, I follow US Highway 89 north toward Tuba City. As I drive, clouds form a dark velour ceiling, and thunder rumbles. The air quivers with imminent violence.

An hour outside of Grand Canyon Village, the skies split open. In seconds, I am ensconced in a waterfall. My heart jolts as I pull the car to the side of the road.

I leave the engine and the wipers on. The wipers toss off no water I can see. The roof of the Mustang vibrates, and thunder bangs in my chest. The air inside the car feels thick and hard to breathe. I pick the photo up off the center console and hold it against the steering wheel. With the rainwater pouring down behind it, I half expect it to swim out of my hand.

Cars slosh past. No one stops. Why would they? Staring at the puddled windshield, I run through the short list of people who know me. Parents, childhood friends, fellow soldiers, business associates, my wife, my brother, they are gone; chip, chip, chip, the years pass, and the meaningful things that hold your world upright fall away until finally you find yourself beside the road, as invisible as last week's trash.

I put the photo down. Maybe the windshield puddles more. I press my hands against my lap.

Mrs. Roosevelt, it is turning out to be a real humdinger of a day.

I reach the South Rim and Grand Canyon Village just after nightfall. The rain has scrubbed the sky clean. The stars are impossibly bright.

There are no rooms anywhere. A senior hostel convention has booked anything with a roof. I stand hopefully in a half-dozen lobbies while desk clerks peck at keyboards and shake their heads. At the El Tovar Lodge, a sign behind the reception desk tells me Albert Einstein once stayed here. My mother revered Einstein almost as much as Pliny. *Remember, Pogue, what Mr. Einstein tells us. The most beautiful experience we can have is the mysterious.*

I'll bet Einstein didn't need a reservation. The mystery is where I'll sleep.

The El Tovar is my last chance. The concierge looks up from his keyboard, mouth puckered.

"It would have been best to plan," he says.

I am bone-weary and a trifle frightened. This makes me less the person I want to be.

"I have seen the value of plans," I say, already embarrassed by my anger.

I am halfway to the door before I realize a boy is walking beside me.

"Sir," he says, "you can camp."

I keep walking. If I stop, I'll lay down in the foyer.

"I don't have a tent."

His smile makes me forget the rude concierge.

"You don't need a tent. This place rents trailers. They're nothing fancy, but they're comfortable. It's not exactly close, about thirty miles back down the road, but it's an easy drive. Here."

I stop to take the envelope.

"They're directions," he says, "and the phone number in case you need it. I'm not sure when the owner goes to bed."

I want to hug him.

"Thank you."

He holds the door open.

I reach into my pocket.

He shakes his head.

"Only hotel guests can tip," he says.

It is not the campground of travel brochures. Even in the dark, I can see there isn't one single tree. There's even less grass. The narrow road winding to the campground office passes bathrooms breathing chlorine and not-quite-masked waste. RVs sit on cement pads, their generators thrumming. Arranged in precise rows, they look like a stout strike force that will never get off the ground. It's just past ten, and almost all the RVs are dark.

The office is a windowless cinderblock bunker with two brown doors. The slit beneath the left-hand door is dark, but there is light beneath the right-hand door. When I knock, there is an abrupt shout, which I have to accept as a welcome.

The room is the size of a modest walk-in closet. A woman and a metal desk are wedged inside. The woman ignores me. She forks canned sausages to a small dog, stabbing vindictively at the tiny sausages with a toothpick and depositing them on a tea saucer on the floor. The dog, barely the size of a child's fist, is milky-eyed. Still it zeroes in on each sausage like a sniper's sight, downing them lustily and then sitting back on its haunches and yipping expectantly.

The woman resembles the toothpicks, only topped with a cotton candy beehive of hair. When she bends to the dog, I see her spotted scalp. She chews one of her sausages doggedly, staring with a mixture of jealousy and affection at the dog's frenzied gobblings.

I watch this communal meal for what I consider to be a proper time.

"I'd like to rent a trailer please."

The woman remains bent to her forking.

"I can't remember the last time I went at anything with such vigor. Age hasn't slowed you one bit, has it, Elvira? Thirty-five dollars a night. You're more patient than most. You got sheets?"

"No."

"County health department requires sheets. Don't sell sheets. Do sell sleeping bags, though."

"May I buy a sleeping bag?"

The woman sits up. The dog nudges the empty saucer with its nose. The woman clucks lovingly.

"No more now. Sorry, darlin', but I'm savin' you a world beater of a stomach ache."

She looks at me for the first time. All the love is gone.

"Camp store closed at seven."

"I don't have any place else to go."

"I understand." Her smile reveals gums, endowed, in places, with teeth. "Don't waste any money on beauty magazines anymore. After hours' sales cost more."

"I understand."

I am bestowed additional gum.

"I like a customer with some business sense."

Standing, she bangs her palm angrily against an empty peg on the wall.

"Damn that girl. Sonny! Sonny! Girl, I know you can hear me."

A girl slouches out of the night. Since there isn't room for three people, she leans against the doorjamb. She wears a wool cap pulled down just above her eyes and a fine-boned prettiness. Her dark purple lipstick shines.

"The hell you got on your lips? Varnish?"

"Orchidazzle."

"Looks like a welt, and you look like a tramp. Where's the key to the camp store?"

The girl walks to a series of pegs on the opposite wall. With a bored movement, she lifts a lanyard with a key on the end. She goes back to the doorway. Slouching again, she swings the lanyard back and forth.

"You reorganized. Remember?"

"Don't you sass me."

The girl remains quiet.

"You talk too much," the woman says.

The girl nods at me.

"He's handsome."

"He's short, and long in the tooth."

"Last I looked, your sweet sixteen wasn't around the bend."

"Bein' sixteen only makes you an ignorant smart-mouth. Bein' nineteen gives the smart-mouth more practice."

The dog whines.

"That dog should be dead of clogged arteries," the girl says.

"Elvira eats whatever the hell she wants, and I do too."

"You're going to put this gentleman off with your schoolgirl charm."

"I should spank your bottom."

"Now you're really pouring it on."

I can't get a word in. One starts before the other finishes.

"You need something else in your life besides a ratty dog."

"I choose my own company. It's one of the few pleasures of old age."

"You like that dog because it's the only thing in this county that's older than you."

Their words hold no malice. They banter like dockworkers.

"A gentleman like this would do you good."

It's uncomfortable being discussed while standing in the room.

The girl still swings the key to and fro.

"Hypnotizin' me won't change my mind," says the woman.

"It might restore your eyesight."

"You like him so much, you run away with him. Leave me and Elvira in peace. He's no prize, but two minutes tells me he's a decided improvement on the trash you call boyfriends. At least he knows how to stay quiet. Probably can hold his liquor too."

The old woman steps forward. With surprising alacrity, she snatches the lanyard from the girl.

"You could put those fast hands to use."

"I never imagined a girl would be so fresh to her grandma."

Just like that, both women smile. The girl's smile reveals a line of tiny silver rings, three on the upper lip and three on the bottom. They shine in the fluorescent light.

The grandmother brushes past me and out into the night, the dog trotting behind her.

As I pass, the girl whispers, "She likes you. She doesn't open the store for everybody."

"I'm grateful for the special treatment."

Rolling off the door jamb, she says, "I believe you are."

The paint on the camp store door is peeling off in long strips.

"Why don't you charm one of your Picassos into paintin' this door?" the woman says, inserting the key.

The camp store is slightly bigger than the office. Shelves line the walls from floor to ceiling, goods tidily arranged. The lower shelves hold shrink-wrapped firewood and canned food, including beans, soup, and sliced peaches. T-shirts, brightly colored foam noodles, and dive masks and snorkels in plastic bags rest on the upper shelves. A ceramic Jesus stands on the highest shelf, arms spread to the merchandise. No less than five signs warn against refunds and shoplifting.

The sleeping bags are in a metal bin. The woman unlocks the padlock securing the top.

"Help yourself. No refunds."

There are no prices on anything, including the sleeping bags.

The girl slouches in a new doorway.

"How much are the sleeping bags?" I ask.

"Fifty-three dollars."

"That's expensive."

"After hours' price. You can sleep standin' up and pay forty dollars when we open in the morning. Where the hell did you get those shoes?"

I falter in the face of this odd negotiating tactic.

Behind me, the girl says, "Bought them last week. Nice huh? Bought the shoes, stole the blouse."

The woman crosses herself and dips her head toward Jesus.

"Stealin' is a sin."

"Today's prices can be a sin," I say.

The girl laughs. Her grandmother turns from Jesus to me.

"That so? You condone stealing?"

"No. But stealing comes in many forms."

"You callin' me a thief?"

"I prefer profiteer."

"Fancy word for thief."

"One's more business-like."

"It's a question of supply and demand. And who might be the one demanding?"

"Atta' girl, Grandma."

"Pogue Whithouse."

"I'll say one thing for you, Mr. Whithouse. You've lost a few inches, but you still got your wits and a little starch. Most people would have paid their fifty-three bucks and slinked off by now."

The girl gives a small whoop.

"Turn it on, girl!"

"Zip your orchid lips. Forty-three dollars, if you don't keep us standing here any longer."

"She's romancing you, Pogue. I've never seen her drop her price. Ever."

For some reason, it pleases me to hear my name spoken by pierced lips.

The woman growls, "Your generation has no concept of romance."

"Speaking of romance ..."

With a last glint of rings, the girl slides into the night.

Her grandmother actually seems to deflate, as if part of her left too. She looks past me.

"I don't know how much longer I can hang on. She was sweet when she was little, took her grandma's instructions like a little soldier. Now she gives me fits. I'm afraid she's doing more than flirting with the boys, but there's only so much policing I can do. Plus, she's nineteen, and as you can see, nearly a woman."

Back in the office, I settle my bill, seventy-three dollars for a sleeping bag and a trailer to put it in.

When she smiles, I see a glint of the girl.

"Sonny's right. You're a trim fellah. I like that. Not much of it left in this country of everything. You should see the folks who come in here—fat parents and fatter kids, waddlin' like ducks, guppy eyes lookin' around for somethin'. Sloth, greed, and stupidity are draggin' our country down."

She points a finger at me.

"Don't you misread me. Much as my granddaughter would like it, I'm not wooin' you. I'm jus' tellin' you I appreciate your attention to discipline."

"And I appreciate your flexible business practices."

"Then we understand each other."

Reaching into a drawer, she pulls out a key. She hands it to me and claps her hands together.

"Never eat too much or stay too long. Lot forty-three's got a bit more privacy. Now if you'll excuse us, Elivira and I are settling down for a little *American Idol*. I confess, I do have a thing for Simon. The good life's turnin' him chubby-cheeked, but he's still a man who speaks his mind." She smiles up at me. "You don't need to worry about me sneakin' into your trailer tonight. At my stage of the game, fantasy is more pleasin', and easier."

I drive slowly through the serpentine maze of trailers. Finally, the marker I'm looking for appears in the headlights.

The trailer has a sink, an oven, and a microwave. The bed is bigger than I expected, though its foot rests right at the bathroom door. This chlorine smell is laced with raspberry.

I spread the sleeping bag on the bed and lay down. I look at my watch. Eleven o'clock. Fatigue and depression are banished, and I am young again. For longer than I care to remember, I have woken to precisely the same thing. Tomorrow, I will wake to one of the world's greatest natural wonders. I am wracked with a childish jolt of adventure. It is impossibly delicious. I lie in the raspberry smell, savoring the thrill. I am out in the ocean, riding the currents.

I can't sleep. I pull on my khaki pants and slip the windbreaker over my head.

As soon as I step outside, I know I've made the right decision. The RVs are big and ugly and parked on dirty rubble, but they rest beneath a wide desert sky.

The air is crisp, and the half moon throws gauzy light. Unfortunately, the RVs cast dark shadows, and the road is rutted. I walk cautiously, shuffling my feet. I imagine a misstep, the liquid turn of an ankle. Some of the youth leaves my step. Why do the years turn your thinking to pessimism?

I spy a campfire. As I draw closer, a tent glows like an alien toadstool. Dark forms ring the fire. Keeping my head down, I speed my shuffling.

"Pogue!"

A shadow approaches. I don't recognize her at first. The knit cap is gone. Her face is framed by luxuriant black hair that falls to the middle of her back. Even at this distance, it reflects the firelight.

"Aren't you the night owl?" Sonny leans close and purses her lips. "Like this one? It's called Boy Magnet."

Flickering shadows hide the color but not the full lips.

"I don't think you need it." I am smitten. It is the honest and embarrassing truth. "You are a beautiful young lady."

This is also the truth, and it feels fine to say it. This, too, you can do at eighty-five. Few women take you seriously.

Sonny's smile makes me understand why her grandmother worries.

"You're sweet. I knew it when I saw you. My grandmother did too, but she's a hard read unless you know her." She hesitates for a moment, deciding something. "Out looking for a better trailer?"

"I couldn't sleep. It's a beautiful night."

"Hey listen, come on over and sit with us." Already her warm hand is on my arm, guiding me over the shadows. "I could do with some intelligent company for a change."

"I'd better not," I say, but she doesn't let go. Afterward, I don't blame her. She was just a bored girl, looking for a little fun. She didn't know how things would go.

"Just for a little while," she says.

The fire's glare blinds me. I blink furiously at the ground. When I raise my eyes, I count six boys, all sprawled in low lawn chairs.

"Hold on," says Sonny.

I hear a brief scraping, and then the warm hand turns me by the elbow.

"Sit here. Guest of honor."

Sonny helps me sit. I know I can't get up. Gravel pokes my backside.

"This is Mr. Whithouse. The man I was talking about."

She accentuates *man*. No one says anything. Across from me, one of the boys reaches out and draws something to his chair. Sonny sits effortlessly beside me. She squeezes my elbow again, and this time it makes me flush. I'm glad it's dark.

"Comfortable?"

"I'm fine, thank you, Sonny."

The boys' faces are oddly pale for kids who live in the desert. They are dressed identically, blue jeans and, except for one boy, white T-shirts. The T-shirts are tight. Muscles sculpt the cotton. Sloth and greed have not reached this campfire.

Four boys have crew cuts. A fifth has shaved his head. It glistens like a slick toadstool. The bald boy sports a goatee, its end cut to a sharp point. With a sinking heart, I recognize his boots.

I can't see what the sixth boy looks like. He sits slightly back from the circle, and he's wearing a black sweatshirt with the hood up. The sweatshirt is baggy, but it doesn't hide his broad shoulders. Like the others, he's nearly laying down in his chair, long legs stretching to just short of the fire.

A deep voice issues from the hood.

"Come on, Sonny."

"Come on, what?"

There is a long silence.

"Whatever," says the hooded boy.

Sonny wears jeans. Her T-shirt is tight too. I know her grandmother would not approve of the fact she has neglected to wear a bra. In the wool cap, she looked boyish. Firelight in her hair, she looks like Snow White among trolls.

Crumpled beer cans are strewn beside every chair. Blackened cans rest in the fire.

A boy holds up a hand-rolled cigarette, waving it slowly back and forth. The sweet smell lingers in the air. He stares at me and says, "Ganja." With a spluttering laugh, he passes the marijuana cigarette to a stocky boy to his left.

I am not taken aback. In the sixties, it was hard to tell the marijuana clouds from the fog rolling off the bay.

Sonny says, "Do you mind?"

I am responsible for no one.

"It's not my business."

The staring boy releases a cloud of smoke.

"Fucking right."

"Clean up your mouth, Ansel. I know it's an adjustment, but there's a gentleman here now."

Sonny's look is right out of her grandmother's book. Several boys shift in their seats. Someone coughs. I see the young hippies with their drugs and their confusion, struggling to grasp the world.

The hooded boy remains still.

Ansel taps his middle finger to his forehead in salute, but his silence announces his defeat.

Sonny smiles at me, wide and winsome.

"Every one of them wants me. That's one reason they're afraid of me."

Leaning forward, she plucks a beer from the nearest six-pack. Popping it open, she hands it to me. I would not drink in front of children, but my mouth feels as if it's coated in sawdust.

"Thank you."

The stocky boy holds the joint out to me. Everyone laughs.

The shaved boy says, "Bein' old is bein' stoned."

Sonny ignores this boy, but I already know I must watch him. His eyes dart back and forth as if they are following their own private tennis match. His hands, one on each knee, drum out a beat only he can hear. His fidgeting reminds me of a punished dog, afraid of the whip, but ready to leap as soon as the punisher turns.

"How's the trailer?" Sonny asks.

"It's perfect. All the comforts of home."

"Some are better than others. You got the pick of the litter. It's the only rental with a microwave and a TV."

"A senile citizen without his own fucking RV?"

The high-pitched laugh ends abruptly.

"You've got shit for brains and ADD spooned on top of that," Sonny says. "A first-rate queer."

The boy stares at the fire. The smile comes slowly, as if finding its place on his face. I know the smile. The night takes on an added chill.

The boy rests his chin on his knees.

"I could show you different," he says dreamily.

I speak to the boy beside me.

"What's that tattoo on your hand?"

I nod at the tattoo, a shaven-headed man on a cross.

"Two-tone," answers Sonny.

"What does that mean?"

"Down for black and white."

I have no idea what she is saying. This is clear to her.

"He opposes the delusion of racism," Sonny says. "America isn't a white man's country anymore."

She stares at the shaved boy, but he is looking into the fire.

"Fucking cows," he says. "They're all afraid. Awake and afraid. Listening to every word."

He stands so suddenly his chair tips over. The movement is lithe and mindless.

Cupping his hands, he speaks loudly in a whiny voice.

"What are we going to do, Ernest? Those crazy drug addicts are going to break down our door and rape me and kill you. They're crack babies. They've got no conscience. I read about it in *Reader's Digest*."

Someone sniggers. Lead fills my stomach. Sonny's hand settles on my arm. I don't know why.

The boy turns to me. He is half crouched. His hands drum his knees.

"Middle America, shitting its pants. Afraid we'll go off. Crazy fucking tweakers."

He is talking fast.

Swooping down on the settlers, the Indians screamed so they could not hear their own fear.

"Please stop."

He looks at me with genuine curiosity.

"Why?"

The boy is not right, and for this I am sorry, but I have seen boys his age holding their entrails. I am angry, but not so angry that I don't see that anger is the sickness.

"You should stop shouting because you're right. They are listening, and they are afraid. But you should also stop because you're rude and ignorant, and no one should have to listen to your language."

"Don't."

I hardly hear Sonny. I know I can't take my eyes off the boy now. I also know I can't get out of my chair.

The boy spikes an empty can with his boot heel. Lifting boot and can, he deftly flings the can into the fire. Sparks fly up to the stars.

"You a priest?"

Priests have God. And different memories.

I work to control my anger.

"No. I just prefer a world that's civil."

The eyes no longer jerk about. They zero in on me.

"Are you afraid?"

"Yes. Everyone is afraid."

"That so?"

"Everyone who is honest with themselves."

He studies my face.

"How old are you, old man?"

"Eighty-five."

"You recognize my boots."

"Yes."

"They're the real deal. Not some fucking knockoff. You like them?"

"Not at all."

"There's a surprise. Check it out."

He lifts one boot sole and then the other. On the bottom of each sole is a number, printed in white. Twenty-three on the right foot, sixteen on the left.

"Don't bother guessing," he says. "W is the twenty-third letter. P is the sixteenth. White power."

Now I feel sick.

"Hitler was a tweaker and a queer."

The hooded boy says this so softly we all lean forward.

The shaven boy shoots him a menacing look and giggles. It's like watching two different people. He spits in the fire and giggles again.

"Fucking wigger," he says.

Sonny says nothing. I realize now these boys don't know each other. Everyone has shifted forward in their chairs. Only the hooded boy continues to lounge, but I see that his feet are now planted.

The stars watch this eternal game.

Sadness, dark and heavy, snuffs out my anger.

"I knew a man, he's dead now, but he was young when I met him, only a few years older than all of you. He had a five-year-old daughter. His wife was already dead, killed by a bomb in Poland. He didn't know it yet. He was in the South Pacific, trying to stay alive so he could see his family again."

The shaved boy says, "Pay attention, class," but everyone is.

I could leave now. What good can this do? But I think of the couples lying dry-mouthed in darkness, straining to hear over their pounding hearts.

"Hitler's soldiers found the man's daughter. She was living in the street. They put her in a basement prison cell, eight feet by eight feet, with one barred window at street level. German soldiers would stop on the sidewalk and urinate through the bars."

A log settles. The hooded boy's feet are no longer planted firmly. Once a watchful child, always a watchful child.

"Three families shared the cell. After two years, my friend's daughter was the only one left. My friend survived the war. He found his daughter. He wrote me a letter. Afraid for her sanity, he told me the very first thing he asked her was what she remembered most. She said, 'At night, the sky was filled with stars.'"

I am looking directly into the boy's face. I have no idea how I got out of the chair.

"Now you have a story to go with your boots."

I walk quickly and carelessly. Immediately I am lost. The RVs all look the same. I walk to a wood post. Eighty-four. This would help if I hadn't forgotten the number of my site. The stars mock me.

"Hey," says Sonny. She stands quietly. "This way. It's not far."

It isn't.

In front of my trailer, she says, "Was that story true?"

I am drained.

"Yes."

"I'm sorry."

"It's fine."

"No, it isn't. I was wrong. It was just a game, and then it wasn't. It was totally my fault."

And this sets you apart from the rest of us?

"Apology accepted."

She scuffs a tennis shoe through the dirt. She doesn't look like a tramp. She looks like a little girl.

"Are you going to the canyon tomorrow?" she asks.

"Yes."

"May I come with you?"

"I don't know." I just want to sleep. "I'm leaving early."

"What's early?"

"Six."

"I'll be ready."

I step up to my door and turn the handle. I hope we're done.

"Why were you so polite? They were rude to you."

I grip the handle.

"Every man must be allowed his dignity."

"Every asshole should get what they deserve."

I turn. A nineteen-year-old girl stands below me, but it's the German soldiers I see, urinating through the bars in great slashing arcs. After the soldiers left, the mothers got on their knees and scrubbed the floor, carefully parceling precious water from their rations.

"Why are you and your friends so angry?"

Sonny's face turns hard.

"Why are you so naïve?" she says.

We are all naïve, until life tells us otherwise.

One night, as Sean and I lay in our beds, a pickup crunched to a halt in our drive. A man stepped out. Immediately, the screen door clacked.

Sean and I knelt on his bed, looking out the window. Our father and the man stood beside the truck.

"Matty's father," said Sean, and when I looked at him, I saw sadness and moonlight.

"Sean?"

"It's okay," he said, though we both knew it wasn't.

Matty's father did all the talking. Both men wore stained coveralls; for a moment, I wondered if they slept in them. They both stood rigid, hands buried in their pockets. At one point, my father turned and walked abruptly to the edge of the woods. When he returned, his head hung down like a dog waiting for a blow. This frightened me even more than seeing him sitting beside the midnight road.

Sean laughed softly.

"Looks like I should have cut his tongue out too."

"It's Matty who blabbed," I said. "You need to get out of here."

Sean watched the two men.

"Maybe. But where would I go?"

I frantically searched for an answer, some miraculous plan that would save my brother, but already the truck door had slammed and the engine started up, headlights cutting the dark woods, and

I could see my father striding for the porch, though strangely his head still hung down.

The bedsprings squeaked.

"You should leave."

At first, I thought I'd spoken. Before I had time to heed Sean's advice, the door opened. Our father stepped in, closing the door behind him.

Sean stood in the middle of the room. Our father said nothing. Stepping forward, he struck Sean in the face with his fist. My brother fell to his knees. He made no sound. In the darkness, his kneeling form swayed slightly, our father's bulk looming over him.

To my horror, my father struck him again.

His voice was hoarse.

"You are not my son."

After he left, I tried to help Sean up, but he pushed me away. I saw his face in the moonlight. It scared me that he smiled at nothing, the smile almost like love.

"Get up. Dad might come back."

"He won't."

I could not look at my brother, but I knew he was still smiling. Our father had knocked something loose in his head.

I felt like I was going to puke again.

"Please," I said.

"I belong here."

"You're scaring me."

I started crying, but I didn't care because my brother just knelt there, unafraid. For a moment, I hated him again, hated him for being so different from me. He was kneeling, but I was the one who was weak.

He held out his hand.

"I'm sorry I scared you," he said, and I helped him to his feet.

Late that night, we heard hammering. When we went to the shed the next morning, Sean's bicycle was ruined.

22

My brother and I fought once, two months before he died. I was crouched near the shed, gently tapping the lid of a glass jar with a hammer. Lid and jar were not originally paired; I was making the lid fit. The jar held my current pride and joy, a crayfish snake, sleek and glossy brown as a minister's polished shoes.

Sean spoke behind me.

"That won't keep him in."

I hesitated. In those days, I was incessantly plagued with doubt, and no one instilled that doubt more effectively than my brother.

"It will."

"Nope. He's good as gone."

"Shut up. You don't know everything."

"I know you're gonna' lose that snake, stupid ass."

I knew it had nothing to do with me. Sean pushed against me as he pushed against everything. I would have just ignored him. But when he placed his foot against my rump and gave an upward nudge, I wasn't ready. I fell forward. The jar slipped from my hand and broke. The crayfish snake shot off into the thick grass.

I don't recall what happened next, and Sean never told me, but my unbridled rage gave me unforeseen strength. After a flurry of scuffling, we fell to the ground, and, by some miracle, I was straddling Sean's chest.

I crushed my knees together. Sean actually wheezed.

Still he found his voice.

"Now what? You don't even know what do to. Get off me, chicken shit, before you get hurt."

Tremors wracked my body.

"I hate you."

At times, children are seers. My brother produced his conqueror's grin.

"You don't even know that."

I felt my arm lift. It wobbled over my head, oddly weighted.

Not all the victory left my brother's eyes.

"Put it down, chicken shit."

I stared down at my brother. Blood oozed from a cut on his cheek. His eyes passed over my face, and then they widened.

"Shit," I think he said, but I couldn't be sure because the entire world spun crazily, and somehow I was on my feet, one foot to be exact. I didn't fall, for my father still clamped my wrist. Pain shot through my arm.

My father yanked me around. He didn't hit me with his fist. He struck me with an open hand, but it was more than enough.

Crumpling to the ground, I curled into a ball. I began to cry. My father stood over me, face twisted into a person I did not know. He took a step back. I had the wild thought he was going to kick me.

"Father," said Sean. "It's my fault."

My father stood shaking, balanced on something only he could feel. A moan issued from his lips.

"Mother Mary," he said, and his boot kicked the ground near my head, and something spun off across the gravel.

When I opened my eyes, my father was gone.

Sean helped me up.

I stood before him, bent like a monk, holding my wrist, convulsed in sobs.

When I finally got my breath, I stuttered, "Was he going to kick me?"

Very slowly, my brother said, "I don't know."

I realize now he was answering my question and one of his own, for when I looked at him, he was looking away, his eyes fixed on the dusty hammer, a thoughtful expression on his face.

It is pitch black in the trailer, but I don't turn on any lights. Holding my hand in front of me, I shuffle to the bed and sit. I am old, but I am not naïve. Their language, their haircuts, and their tattoos were strange to me, but I knew the boys.

Often I have wondered how my brother would have fared in the world, had he lived. In the years immediately after he died, I was often furious. Death, I thought, had cheated him of so much.

Now I am not so sure. Some of the boys around the campfire were like my brother. They would butt up against the glass until it shattered, or the glass won.

Either way, the end is the same.

23

O ddly, I dream a different dream. I am on a boat. The engine is failing. I hear it knocking below deck. At first, it knocks sporadically. Then the knocking turns insistent and loud, prelude to the rupture of machine innards.

I sit up with a start. Someone is banging on the door of the trailer. I reach for my watch. Six-fifteen.

Sonny stands in the ashen dawn, a stained brown bag in one hand, a steaming Styrofoam cup in the other. She lifts one and then the other.

"Blueberry muffins. Coffee, if you drink it. Best to get a move on. The early bird gets parking. I know people, but I'm not a miracle worker."

We eat the muffins as we drive. Dawn recedes quickly, shadows racing into the folded hills where the sun finds them and burns them away.

The blueberries are sweet, the strong coffee a perfect counter.

"Thank you for breakfast and the wake-up call. How did you know I like black coffee?"

Sonny is wearing the knit cap, the waterfall of hair tucked inside. Today's T-shirt is baggy. A skateboarder flies across the front, leaving script behind. Powell Peralta, it says.

"Every old person drinks their coffee black."

"You don't drink coffee?"

"Caffeine's bad for you."

Sonny's window is down. Morning chill whirls through the car, rouging her cheeks. The cold feels good. Distant bluffs morph from gold to brown.

"Does your grandmother know where you are?"

"She trusts me. I'm nineteen, and I trust you."

"Did you tell her you were going with me?"

"God, yeeeessss. You already sound like my grandfather, and the two of you haven't even dated." She drops her head back so that her Adam's apple looks out the windshield. "What was on the roof?"

"Carpet."

"You put carpet on the roof?"

"I didn't. The original owner did."

"What? He thought he could stretch out on the ceiling?"

I see the hippy, stoned and unshowered, blinking at me slowly. Harmless ancestor to last night's hate monger.

"It's possible."

Sonny takes a bite of muffin.

Mouth half full, she says, "Sometimes I hate this place. Other times, there's no place more beautiful. Grandma was born here. I live with her because my parents are children. Divorced children. Mom lives in Huntington Beach with a television writer. Dad moved back to South Carolina. He was a shrimper before he met my mom. The desert is no place for a shrimper."

"I'm sorry."

"I'm not. I don't think they ever understood each other, and my mom's a slut. And in case you're worried, I'm not."

She smiles, and the rings are revealed. I wonder how those rings will feel one day when she kisses a child's cheek.

She holds the muffin wrapper out the window, letting the wind rake away the crumbs. Scoured clean, she folds the wrapper neatly, tucks it inside a paper napkin, and puts it back in the bag.

"Keep a tidy ship, my father used to say. He really tried to make things work, but my mom was way more than he could handle. They divorced when I was seven. She couldn't keep her hands off men. After my dad left, she could bring them home. I'd lie in bed scared to death. I thought they were hurting each other. I suppose they might have been."

She takes my wrapper and gives it the same scouring before placing it in the bag.

"Most of those boys are like my mom. They've got no control. So I control them. That much I learned from my mom." She plucks an errant blueberry from her lap and pops it in her mouth. "My father really loved my mother. He's asked me to come live with him, but I don't want to. He's too sad. It's not bad with Grandma. She's cuckoo about that stupid dog, but other than that, she's all right. I know you didn't like my T-shirt."

I start to speak, but Sonny waves me off.

"You can't lie. Some people are so honest, they're transparent. I don't know how people like you make it. You remind me of my father. That's why I'm here with you. I don't ride off with anyone. My father is a gentleman. He's really smart too. He plays the piano and reads Shakespeare and Charles Dickens. Mom always told him he was born in the wrong century. After he left, I found poems he'd written my mother. They were beautiful. My mother hid them under her mattress. Weird, huh, screwing one man on top of another man's love poems?"

Abruptly she throws something in the air. It takes me a beat to realize she has only lifted her hand.

She examines the ring on her finger, a blue stone set on a thin silver band.

"Agostinho gave it to me. What do you think? He said it's expensive, but I don't think it is." She tries to sound nonchalant. "Know anything about rings?"

"Which boy was Agostinho?" I ask, though I'm pretty sure I already know.

"The one inside the hood. He's kind of in charge."

"In charge of what?"

"Us. Our gang."

She turns her arm over. The tattoo on her forearm is the same shaven-headed man on a cross.

"I got it when I went to Vegas with Agostinho. We stayed at the Bellagio and ate at this fancy French restaurant called Cirque. That was a kick. All these pasty high rollers and snooty waiters pretending to be French, and us. We ordered their best champagne. Agostinho paid cash. The other guys call him Aggro. He likes that. But I call him Agostinho because I like the sound. It's exotic. Aggro sounds stupid and classless. In case you didn't know, he's as black as his sweatshirt."

He'd kept his hands in the pockets of his sweatshirt.

Sonny grins.

"Those white-power jerk offs never knew either. Dumb, dumber, and dumbest."

I try on these ideas slowly.

"They were a racist gang?"

Sonny laughs with genuine merriment. She raps her knuckles against her forehead.

"Helloooo? He didn't shave his head so we could admire his acne. You're sweet, but you need to live on this planet. Aryan Nations. White Aryan Resistance. Nazi Low Riders. The Church of the Creator. Boneheads. You called them the Ku Klux Klan. Fancy names for the same white trash."

A small voice rings in my ear. *What's white trash?* And so we continue, each generation building on the sad foundations of the last.

I don't want to hear more, but at the same time, I do. It's like driving past an accident.

"Okay," continues Sonny, "pay attention, class. Tweakers are speed addicts. Speed, meth, crank, crystal, ice, it's all the same. Whatever you call it, it jacks you up, makes you feel real powerful, like you'll live forever. Sometimes it makes you real paranoid. Like Mr. Bobble Head last night."

"Why did you go to their campsite?"

"They had pot and beer, and in case you haven't noticed, this place isn't exactly overflowing with fascinating things to do. Most of the guys just wanted to fight. I thought it would be more fun to see how stupid they were. Agostinho thought so too. It was our idea to hide him under the hood. Great minds think alike." Her voice assumes a deep professorial tone. "I digress. Wigger. Short for white nigger. Short for a white person who tries to be black. As in, I almost fell over when that tweaker called Agostinho a wigger."

I recall Agostinho's retort. *Hitler was a tweaker and a queer.* He knew his history.

Sonny considers the napkin turning in her hands.

"I guess Agostinho isn't really a nigger. At least not an American nigger. His family is from Angola. He's named after a famous Angolan poet."

"Agostinho Neto."

Sonny jerks. She stares at me.

"That's the poet's name?"

"Yes. Agostinho Neto was jailed by the Portuguese for rebellion. Later he became the first president of independent Angola."

I leave out the part about Amnesty International pressuring the Portuguese to free him from jail and then, when he was prime minister, pleading with him to free the enemies he had jailed.

Here in prison
rage contained in my breast
I patiently wait …

Poets can be tyrants, and tyrants, poets. We are no oil and water mix.

"Jesus," Sonny says. "I can't believe it. Dad would have known that."

Bugs click against the windshield.

"I visited my dad last summer. He's back to shrimping. He works all the time, but when I visited, he stopped so we could spend time together. It was weird, though. When we talked, he didn't look at me. He didn't say so, but I knew why. He'd never seen me with breasts. I'm pretty sure it freaked him out. I'm pretty sure he hasn't been with a woman since my mom, either. He lives in the middle of nowhere, and everyone's his cousin. He's got this big house on the edge of the marsh, all squeaking wood and crumbling porches. His family's owned the land forever. He promised to take me fishing, but he never did. At night, he'd play the piano, these really sad songs. I was supposed to stay for two weeks, but I left after five days. It depressed me to think that Mom might have been right. I think he would have been happier if he was born a hundred years ago. A traveling bard, she called him, when they were getting along."

A long strand of hair frees itself from the knit cap. Sonny pulls it down across the bridge of her nose and looks at it cross-eyed.

"He still sends me birthday cards, but that's about it. I hear that piano sometimes, and the frogs croaking like crazy. Do you have a family?"

I've been expecting this question.

"No."

"Married?"

I try the easy way first.

"No."

She cocks her head and gives me a coquettish look.

"Man as handsome as you?"

We are twenty minutes from the canyon. Already the sun throws merciless light on everything.

Maybe a keeper of secrets can change.

"I was married. My wife died."

I haven't said this out loud in years. There is no epiphany. Saying it proves the same as thinking about it. Instantly all my organs are scooped out, leaving my heart to wander lost through a black hollow. Loss is never lost.

"I'm sorry. You don't have to tell me anything else."

"You don't have to be sorry. It was a long time ago."

"I doubt that matters."

I drive, dusty-mouthed and flaky-skinned, a cadaver behind the wheel.

"Where are you going?" Sonny asks.

"To the Grand Canyon."

"I know. *After* that."

"Home."

I focus on the road.

"Great," Sonny says. "Why is it no one lets anyone in? It's weird and sad. Here I am seeing Agostinho, and I have to find out from you who he's named after. Now I'm trying to be your friend, and you won't even tell me where you're going. It's not like I'm going to follow you."

I'm not even sure where home is.

"I'm driving to Florida."

"Florida. That's better, though not exactly specific."

Leaning forward, she traces her finger over the dashboard. She works carefully, the tip of her tongue running over the rings.

When she finishes, she sits back.

"Agostinho is a scary fighter. I saw him almost beat this guy to death with a pipe. The guy was twice his size, but Agostinho broke him. Being named after a poet is romantic. My boyfriend keeps secrets. My father doesn't talk. You don't tell me anything. Maybe you're a hit man."

"If I was, I'd drive a car with a bigger trunk."

"If you had a bigger trunk, you'd just fill it with more khaki pants."

You don't have to pull a trigger to kill someone.

"What are we going do when we get to the canyon?"

Live in the past.

"I just want to look around."

"Original. Maybe you could throw everyone for a loop and buy a paper weight at the gift shop."

The road assumes a serious upward cant. Blue sky fills the windshield. The sun coming off the dashboard hurts my eyes.

"What did you draw?" I ask.

"Nuh-uh. You get your secrets, I get mine. And I know you're too cautious to lean over and look."

"I'll look when we get there."

"You'll forget."

Leaning forward, she makes another quick trace.

"You've got money," she says.

"Enough."

"Enough so you don't care."

"Enough so I don't care."

"That must be nice."

We are on top of a butte. Desert runs away from the road, drops away into space, and then runs off again.

"Want to know how I knew you were rich?"

I smile.

"Want to know how I know you're going to tell me whether I ask or not?"

"Very funny. You didn't care about the sleeping bag. You didn't ask about the price of the trailer. Everyone who stays at the park tries to bargain Grandma down on everything. Which, as you might imagine, is wasted effort. How much would you have paid for the bag if Grandma hadn't gone all sweet on you?"

"Not much more than I paid."

She clucks approvingly.

"Good. I want you to be rich, but not stupid. What did you do to make so much money?"

"I sold hot dogs."

She falls against the door.

"You're *shitting* me."

Her surprise is so genuine it makes me laugh.

"I am not. Deceiving you."

"You are my father. Where did you sell hot dogs?"

"In Boston, at first."

"You had a hot dog restaurant? Like a Weinerschnitzel?"

"I sold them from a cart first. Along the Charles River." *Beacon Hill, the gold domed Massachusetts State House, Back Bay, East Cambridge, Kendall Square, MIT. The lovely song of water.* "I expanded from there."

"You must have sold a shitload of hot dogs."

"Enough."

Just for fun, I let silence settle. For this, I receive a malevolent look.

"And?"

"One cart led to another. I expanded into other cities on the East Coast. New York, Philadelphia, Washington. Pretty soon, I had a lot of carts and a lot of business."

And what good did it do anybody? It's a sad fact that most of us labor for a lifetime before seeing the true value of our work.

Sonny's face is pinched in thought. Suddenly she brightens.

"Maybe I had one of your hot dogs! Grandma took me to Boston when I was five. We rode the subway. I still remember it. It was so cool being underground. The lights from inside the train flickered against the walls of the tunnel like an old movie. When we walked up the stairs, there was this guy selling hot dogs and these humongous pretzels. If they were your hot dogs, they were the best hot dogs I ever had. I ate three of them." She laughs. "I gobbled them down faster than Elvira. Grandma had a hot dog too, only hers was smothered with this disgusting stringy stuff."

"Sauerkraut."

"Yeah. Her breath smelled terrible for the rest of the day. I like my hot dogs straight up. Hot dog, bun, ketchup." She scrutinizes me. "I still don't get it."

"People like hot dogs, and I sold them for a long time."

"No. Why hot dogs?"

I see myself walking up the subway stairs, the For Sale sign swinging beneath the cart's cheery yellow umbrella, the letters perfectly penned, alternating red, white, and blue, a sketch of an American flag in one corner. The vendor's name was Dan. He was my father's age. I watched him carefully make hot dogs for a young mother and a little boy, the boy hopping up and down like he was at the top of the stairs on Christmas morning. Funny how a career decision is cemented.

I paid Dan one hundred and fifty dollars for everything. He gave me a discount because I was a serviceman. When I told Abby that night, she left the kitchen table without a word.

"Fate," I say, hating myself and the word. *Fate, chance, happenstance, providence, luck, doom.* If you don't fight the currents, you are swept up by them, and there is only one person to blame.

"Did your hot dog stands have a name?"

"Dan's Delectable Dogs for a while. Then I changed them to Sweet Thursday."

"Sweet Thursday Hot Dogs?"

"Just Sweet Thursday."

"What kind of name is that?"

The day after Lousy Wednesday. The laughter after the tears. Changing a company's name nine years in is not something they recommend in business school, but I was the widowed CEO, and there you have it.

"It has nothing to do with hot dogs," Sonny says. "It doesn't even *mention* hot dogs."

It doesn't mention the need to get up and push on either.

"We added a relish sweetener. I thought it had a nice ring."

This is partly true.

I have fallen several pegs on Sonny's intelligence meter.

"You're lucky you sold any hot dogs," she says.

"Luck plays a role in everything."

"Maybe you should have been a priest instead. You stopped them from fighting, you know. Agostinho would have kicked that white tweaker's punk ass."

She looks out at the desert.

"I like that in a man. My dad couldn't even stand up to my mom."

When we arrive at the South Rim at seven-fifteen, the parking lot is nearly full. Winnebagos swing about in the bright sun, working to insinuate themselves into the last spaces.

"Welcome to Disneyland," Sonny says. "There's our spot."

She points to an area cordoned off with yellow caution tape. Behind the tape are two dozen empty spaces.

"It's closed," I say.

"Not to us, Papa Pessimist."

I nudge the Mustang up to the tape. A boy steps from the booth. He wears a green Park Service uniform and an exasperated expression.

"This lot is closed," he says.

Sonny says, "Who put you in charge of the Grand Canyon, Jimmy?"

The boy dips his head to the window and peers past me.

"Fuck, Sonny."

Sonny pats my leg.

"He's handicapped."

"He looks fine to me."

"He's not. You ever hear of Sweet Thursday?"

"No."

"See?"

"You never make any sense," Jimmy says.

He walks to the back of the car.

"There's no sticker," he says when he returns.

"He's too proud," says Sonny. "Are you going to make him get out of the car and prove it?"

"Shit, Sonny, you've always been a pain in the ass."

"Love you too."

The boy's face disappears. The tape lifts.

As we drive past, Sonny looks at me and says loudly, "Another spurned suitor."

The parking spot edges right up to an overlook. Before I get out, Sonny says, "Give it a little limp. And let me know if they're showing anything different."

I'm glad she's staying in the car. I walk to the overlook, fighting to breathe. I place both hands on the railing and stare hard to the east.

Final good-byes are a strange thing. They're something you don't envision until a certain age, and even then, the stack of farewells does nothing to make the individual good-byes any less strange. Say it out loud. *I will never be here again.* Some good-byes are small. Some are not. Both are equally final.

I grip the railing. Trivialities flood over me. Clarence Dutton, geologist and fancier of Eastern ways, who, in 1880, named the staggering butte of Vishnu Temple, still rising high above the Colorado River like a stubby thumb. John Wesley Powell, one-armed Civil War major and leader of the first descent of the Colorado River. *We are now ready to start on our way down the Great Unknown ... What falls there are, we know not; what rocks beset the channel, we know not; what walls rise over the river, we know not.*

Intertwined in a single sleeping bag, Abby and I had watched the first sliver of sun etch the top of the sheer canyon walls. The light came upon the eastern buttes slowly, transforming them, one at a time, into pink layer cakes. As the sun rose, pink slid down both butte and canyon wall, pushing shadow to defeat. At last, the sun touched our cheeks with its tepid kiss.

I find Vishnu Temple. Stubby thumb, yes, but stubby thumb of incomprehensible age and mass. An updraft ferries Clarence Dutton's words to me as clearly as if he has spoken them. *It must call forth an expression of wonder and delight from the most apathetic beholder.*

A delicious chill runs through me, like a kiss everywhere. I may be saying good-bye, but the canyon will remain indescribably beautiful in morning light.

To each, our own expression of wonder and delight. I carry my smile back to the Mustang.

I rap on the window.

"Behold the magnificent day."

Sonny opens her eyes slowly.

"What's up with you?" she says, rolling down the window. "You look like the village idiot."

"It's still my country." She is smooth cheeked and fresh. How can she understand? "May I buy you breakfast?"

"You're handicapped. The restaurant is a half mile from here."

I perform a passable jig.

"Nature heals."

She winks at me.

"I'll have some of whatever you're on."

The restaurant sits just back from the canyon rim, affording a neck-cricking view of sky and sandstone. We sit on the patio under a blue umbrella, buffered from the elements by spotty Plexiglas. We eat pancakes and hash browns on cafeteria trays. The ponytailed server behind the counter—Mike Havasupai, his name tag read—scooped out identical portions. The hash browns are oversalted, and the pancakes taste like the desert.

The patio and indoor restaurant are filled, but it is nearly silent. Most of the diners are elderly couples. They do not look at the canyon or each other. They stare at their plates, forks moving slowly up and down.

My elation is draining away. Even Sonny is subdued.

"It's like eating in a cemetery," she says.

I speak mostly to bolster my own spirits.

"Do you know the story of Bill Beer and John Daggett?"

"Why not Bill Beer and John Joint?"

I ignore this.

"They did an amazing thing," I say.

Sonny stabs a piece of pancake and leaves it to marinate in a syrup puddle.

"Survived this meal?"

"They went down the Colorado River. Two hundred and eighty miles. Rapids and all, from Lees Ferry to Lake Mead. In the spring of 1955. Swimming."

Carried by the waters.

It boosts my spirits to see this still impresses.

"They started on Easter Sunday," I continue. "They towed their supplies behind them in army-surplus rubber boxes. They wore wool long johns with thin rubber suits over the top. The water temperature the day they went in was fifty-one degrees."

Like every story, this one has another side, but for the moment, I see only their wild bravado. Even after all these years, it still fills me with hope and joy. When I first heard what Beer and Daggett planned to do—their attempt was national news—I cheered their insane foolishness from behind my practical desk.

"How long did it take?"

"Twenty-six days. They were national heroes."

Sonny's face screws with contempt.

"You couldn't do that now. You can't spit in the river without getting a float permit."

The Plexiglas bends the rocks so they appear to be craning forward to hear our conversation.

Softly I say, "*We felt infinitesimal. It was hardly important whether we continued or quit, whether we lived or died. We were intruders who meant nothing.* Beer said that. Plenty of people thought they were crazy. Saner words were never spoken."

"What did they do when they finished?"

I hear the girl's question and taste the paste of uncooked batter on the roof of my mouth, but I stand beside Beer and Daggett on that Easter morning, the river running before them, meager supplies at their side, no doubt questioning their sanity, wondering what hardships were around the bend. Entirely possible that Beer also felt the gnawings of fear, though I have always wondered if Daggett felt fear too. So many things go unanswered. But if you were to ask me, I would say Daggett's heart entertained many emotions, but fear was not among them.

"Pogue?"

I look at this girl who knows my name.

"Sorry," I say. "Daydreaming."

"What did they do when they finished?"

"I don't remember."

It disappoints me.

"Probably went on *Good Morning, America*," Sonny says.

Walking back to the car, we pass another overlook. Something catches my eye. Sonny continues on, but I walk to the railing. To one side, barely visible, a thin trail drops steeply between the pines before switchbacking out of sight.

Behind me, I hear conversation and metal tapping on metal. Four backpackers—two boys and two girls—walk past me and start down the trail. Above their taut legs, frame packs bulge, and water bottles and cameras dangle from swinging straps. One of the boys says something to the closest girl. Her pretty laugh rings in the canyon silence. Like straws into quicksand, they drop from sight.

It was Beer and Daggett's river and mine too, and now it belongs to a new generation who, if they are lucky, will hear its song.

Good-bye.

Sonny is waiting in the car.

"You left it unlocked," she says as I lower myself cautiously behind the wheel. "Not too bright with all the lowlifes around here. See enough?"

"Yes."

"Sometimes I don't get it."

"Get what?"

"What people see."

"It's one of the most inspirational sights in the world."

"I know that," Sonny says. "I'm not talking about the tourons. There are people who live here who come here every day and sit and stare out at the same thing. I'd go nuts."

"They're old."

Sonny grins.

"You advance to the next round," she says.

As we roll past the attendant's booth, Sonny uncorks a show-stopping smile. The boy smiles back, but he looks quickly away. I feel for him. Few of us are swaggering fighters.

"He seems like a nice young man," I say when we are out of ear shot.

"Too nice."

"I would hope that's not possible."

She looks at me wearily.

"Jimmy was in our gang, but we kicked him out. He wouldn't cord me in."

"I don't understand."

"*Initiation.* They corded me in. All of them together, they beat me up. I took the punches. Not a word. They ripped my shirt off. I knew they'd do that, so I wore a sports bra. Even Agostinho looked disappointed. My right eye turned purple. Like a rose."

I was wrong. This world did not belong to me.

"You let them?"

"It's just a game. Jimmy didn't want to play, so we kicked him out. After that, they knew I could handle mine. Jimmy's sweet, but he's gutless."

I think of the old people—my people—eating their silent breakfast without looking at the world around them.

Sonny leans her head against the window and closes her eyes.

"Don't you fall asleep," she says.

At the trailer, I pack my things. The Mustang's seats are coated with a film of dust. I find paper towels under the sink. I wipe the seats, back and front.

I remember as I shut the front passenger door. I open it and lean in. The sun through the windshield makes the dashboard dust sparkle. Two hearts are traced, their edges overlapping.

24

A bby and I visited the Grand Canyon thirteen months after I returned from the war, in October of 1946. The visit was part of my continuing therapy—our therapy now—though neither of us acknowledged this. We had psychiatrists back then, but in those days, you first tried to help yourself, and if you were lucky and had someone who loved you, they tried to help too. Today it seems that people go to the therapist like they go to the grocery store. I don't know if this is right or wrong. It is certainly good for the therapists.

Taking a trip was Abby's idea. I suggested the Grand Canyon. At that point, I favored wide open spaces.

We drove from Boston. Early October rewarded us with the weather of dreams—crisp, clear nights and cool days with puffy white clouds that cavorted like happy sheep.

In those days, almost all visitors to the canyon hiked the Bright Angel and Kaibab trails down to the Colorado River or bumped down astraddle mules. I wanted us to be alone, away from mule droppings and man. We parked and walked, military-issue packs on our backs, to the canyon rim. The Grandview Trail was a barely perceptible notch on the canyon's edge. After five minutes of descent, we were alone.

We made our way down the steep trail to Horseshoe Mesa, Abby stopping often to gaze out at the chasm of space and stone and the vast buttes pronging into the sky—Newberry Butte, Krishna Shrine, Solomon Temple. Her frequent stops frustrated me. In those days, movement was another salve; impatience saw me hike faster still. Soon I left her alone.

I reached the mesa just past noon; Abby arrived twenty minutes later. Waiting for her, I set up our camp and fixed sandwiches for lunch. After lunch, we slipped on light packs and hiked a little way down from the mesa. There we stumbled on a small grove of cottonwood trees, blooming like magical flowers among the walls of rock. The grove was cool and shady. A spring trickled from an opening in the rock, forming a small pool. As we stepped into the grove, a frog halted its croaking. I was glad to be in the shade, for now I saw that Abby was pale, her brow beaded with sweat. I had seen enough heat exhaustion to know the signs. I found her a spot in the deepest shade, and she stretched out, propped against a cool slab of rock. Wetting my handkerchief, I placed it behind her neck and fed her orange slices until she fell asleep.

Within this cool oasis, I sat and watched my wife, her own form as much a testament to something beyond us as the monolithic rock. Fluttering leaf shadows played across her unguarded face, and I fell in love with her yet again. She twitched as she slept. Leaning forward, I gently kissed her forehead. I might have dozed too, for the next thing I knew, our oasis resonated with triumphant frog croaks, and Abby was watching me.

"Thank you," she said. "I guess the heat was a little much for me."

I took the handkerchief from my lap.

"It's hot," I said, "and I walk too fast."

I held the handkerchief beneath a thread of water issuing from a crack in the rock. Moss grew at the opening where the water flowed. While the handkerchief dampened, I traced a finger along its spongy softness.

Abby said, "Nature perseveres."

When I turned, she was looking into the pool.

"Thank you for looking out for me," she said.

"There's a good chance it was my fault in the first place."

"You can't control everything."

About us, the eons breathed agreement.

Crouching beside Abby, I dabbed the handkerchief against her throat. I touched her cheek with my finger. Her skin was soft and cool as the moss.

"Nature doesn't quit, does it?"

"No," said Abby.

We both understood. It wasn't nature that concerned us.

"If I was moss," I said, "this is where I'd grow. Do you know why?"

Abby smiled faintly.

"Because every other spot for miles around is a blast furnace?"

"Because you're here."

Her smile softened. In retrospect, perhaps she was preparing me, though, of course, even she couldn't have known what waited for us.

"And when I leave?"

"I'd come too," I said.

"You wouldn't last five minutes if you were moss."

"It would be worth it."

Abby watched me for a long time.

"It would be easier if we both just stayed here," she said.

I saw the fissure the first time we hiked to the western edge of Horseshoe Mesa to watch the sunset. Watching the sunset became part of our routine. During the day, we explored, hiking further down into the canyon to Tonto Platform and Hance Creek, but we always returned to the mesa well before day's end. We would hike the ten minutes from camp to the mesa's rim, sitting quietly as the shadows ran down the vast walls like blunt fingers, the canyon deeps rouged and purpled, and slowly stars and a scrim of moon appeared.

That first evening, we got a late start, the setting sun already throwing long shadows so that Abby, leading the way across the gently rolling mesa, missed the turret slash in the towering thumb of rock.

There was only one route to our sunset lookout. The second day, I tried to dawdle until the shadows came again, but Abby wanted to go, and when her shout rang back down the trail, I knew what she had found. I stopped in my tracks, and for a moment, the canyon itself seemed to close in around me.

By the time I reached the fissure, only Abby's backpack remained.

Her joyous shouts echoed from the dark slash.

"Pogue! The narrow part's only about six feet long! Take your pack off and slide through on your back. Once you get in, it opens up. It's huge! God, Pogue. It's like a fairytale!"

I could have stayed where I was. Abby would have been fine. But for reasons I did not yet understand, I could not leave my wife alone inside the earth. I must be honest. I see now it wasn't heroic chivalry but compulsion. At twenty-five, I was already programmed, my actions little different from those of a sea turtle blindly following the earth's magnetic vortices.

I stood in the light taking deep breaths.

I pushed my backpack through the opening first, forcing it as far as my arms would extend. I squirmed through the fissure on my back, rock nearly scraping the tip of my nose. The world rang with Abby's happy shouts.

When I stood, Abby panned the flashlight over me and laughed.

"God, Pogue. You're one sweaty mess."

The flashlight beam whipped away.

"Look."

Abby moved the beam slowly, first over the dimpled ceiling twenty feet overhead and then across the cave floor in front of us. Overhead and underfoot, the rocks were puddled and folded as if we had just arrived at the tail end of a tremendous melting.

Breathe evenly, but make no sound. Wait. Let panic settle into something that might be corralled, wrapped tight until a time when you can break down and sob. Move forward. There is no other choice.

There was a soldier in my platoon who, before he squeezed into the opening, always touched the playing card tucked in his helmet band. Jack DeSeno from Philly. The Jack of Diamonds. Diamonds are indestructible. Jack was not.

Abby whispered, "Beautiful, isn't it?"

Illuminated by the fuzzy glow of flashlight, my wife walked as if in a trance, her slow footfalls stirring miniature mushroom clouds of fine dust. The flashlight beam swept across geologic madness. Here something resembling coral heads. There, thick sheets, iron-stained, resting atop each other like slabs of bacon. At the far end of the cavern, an entire limestone wall of folded drapes that would never be moved by a breeze.

She swung around, blinding me for a moment.

"Sorry," she giggled. She reached for my hand. "Come on. It keeps going."

I knew I couldn't stop her, but I tried anyhow.

"We should go back."

Abby panned the flashlight beam over the frozen curtains.

"Why?" she said, barely listening.

"We only have one flashlight."

Abby laughed.

"And you, my knight in shining armor, have at least one extra set of batteries in your pack. Probably two. Am I right?"

"One."

"I promise not to drop the flashlight."

"We have to be out before dark."

"Stop being silly." Abby was already walking, flashlight trained on a door-size opening at the far end of the cavern. "It can't get any darker in here."

Yes it can.

We passed through the second opening, Abby in the lead. This passage was just broader than my shoulders; the ceiling nearly touched our heads. The floor sloped down gently. I knew what was going to happen, the way you feel the cool of an approaching thunderstorm on your skin. I tried to pretend that we were strolling through a cavernous art gallery, finding our way by flashlight while somewhere in the building electricians worked to repair the short circuit.

Slowly the walls began to press in, a great lung deflating. Games failed me. Abby grunted. Ten yards ahead of me, my wife's backlit form assumed a catcher's crouch. She moved ahead in a duck waddle, the flashlight beam playing over the encroaching ceiling. I waited for the shadow patches to begin moving.

"We need to go back."

"Just a little farther." My wife's voice was a reverential whisper. "It's like our own secret world. Aren't you curious where it goes?"

I knew she didn't expect an answer. I couldn't muster one. We were both on our hands and knees now, Abby carefully moving the flashlight along in front of her. The passage echoed with our labored breathing.

"There's an opening up ahead," she said.

And now the coin toss. Life or death.

Two months after I returned from the war, the phone rang in our apartment. It was one of the men in my platoon. He was in Boston. He wanted to take us to dinner that evening. Abby was at work. I told him I was sick. Quarantined with measles. Never had it as a kid and was being punished with a double dose of it now. There were a few more calls. I made similar excuses. After that, the calls stopped.

Abby disappeared through the opening. Her voice drifted back.

"You won't believe this."

She shone the light back toward me so I could see where the ragged opening fell away. I crawled through, dropping my hands and then my feet to the cave floor.

I stood. Cool licked my face. *Death.*

The cavern was huge. Head thrown back, Abby played the flashlight along the ceiling and down the wall.

"Our cathedral," she said, and flicked the flashlight off.

I lunged. My hand found her wrist in the dark and yanked. Abby cried out in pain and surprise. Wrenching the flashlight from her other hand, my thumb swept the smooth surface and pressed the switch.

Only when the beam illuminated my wife, bent over and holding her wrist, did I realize what I had done.

"Jesus," she sobbed. "What's the matter with you?"

She pressed her wrist against her chest and rocked back and forth. My heart broke.

"Abby."

The forgotten flashlight swayed in my hand, sending crazy shadows swinging along the cavern floor. I felt sick.

Gingerly, Abby moved her arm away from her body and looked at her wrist.

"I think it's broken."

"I'm so sorry."

I wanted desperately to say more, but all I could do was reach for her.

She shoved my hand away.

"Stay away from me. Turn off the flashlight."

I did. There were a few whimpers and then quiet. Water dripped.

In the dark, my wife said, "We have too many secrets."

That night, we slept apart. At first light, we packed up camp, speaking only when it was necessary.

Abby hiked slowly as we climbed out of the canyon. This time, I waited, keeping a distance, but always keeping her in sight. I knew she wanted to be left alone.

Cresting the canyon rim, she brushed past me without a word. Only when she slipped into the car did she cry. I reached for her again, but this time I stopped myself, frozen by her animal glare.

Abby bent forward, her wrist the purple shadow of our sunsets.

"I'll get you to a doctor."

The way she jerked her head back and forth poured despair into my heart.

"It's not my wrist, goddamn it." Her tears dropped to the floor. "I did it for us. I did it for you. I tried."

She rocked. Her body trembled. My world crumbled.

"Tell me what to do," I said.

"Nothing. I'm afraid of heights."

I no longer consider myself a careful observer of the world. It is foolish to think you see anything clearly.

25

During the war, Abby wrote once a week, though the letters did not arrive on Peleliu quite so punctually, the United States Marines consumed with matters more immediate than mail. In the letters, Abby professed her love, but mostly she spoke of everyday matters. She wrote of cold snaps, neighborhood doings, and her ongoing battle with the radiator, which, running counter to her scientific intuition, possessed a mind of its own. The war sorely reduced the frequency of her research trips, though one long trip to St. Croix saw her letters stop for three weeks. The next letter I received was apologetic and, even for Abby, unusually long on research details.

Stranded at Harvard, she turned her powers of observation on her fellow academics, none of whom were more entertaining than Professor Aiden Quinlan, whose love of drink had taken him firmly in hand. This kept Abby busy. Apparently the professor now celebrated both scientific advance and setback with a tumbler or three. Often Abby delivered him home, though, in pleasant weather and at Mrs. Quinlan's request, she left him slouched and snoring against his front door. One spring night, without Abby as a tender, the good professor made it as far as the flagpole outside the chancellor's office. The following morning, undergraduates were treated to the sight of a dozing professor naked from the waist down, yellow-moon boxers snapping crisply in the breeze.

In the beginning, these stories made me smile, but soon all amusement left the world. Finally there came a time when I read one of Abby's letters and recalled nothing of what I had just read.

Initially, I served my country as assistant to the platoon leader for E Company, Second Battalion, First Marines. My papers, secure in some distant filing cabinet, declared me aide-de-camp. This was my official position when I arrived on Peleliu, though eventually I became something far more practical.

Life is a tug of war between how we would like things to be and how they are. War is the same, magnified horribly. When we arrived on Peleliu, our commanders predicted the battle for control of the once-obscure island, five square miles in all, would last several days. It raged for nearly two months. For those of us tangled in the rage, it seemed to last far longer.

In this tropical purgatory, men on both sides did and suffered unspeakable things. Men scooped up their intestines, bright yellows and reds steaming in the dirt. Men disappeared without a trace; one moment whole, the next gone, not a fingernail left. The heat was brutal and relentless. Tongues swelled. Lips cracked, blistered, and bled. A soldier in our unit had a bullet crease his lips. It took the medic ten minutes to find the furrow.

Limestone made burying difficult. Marines were placed in body bags or covered with ponchos. The Japanese dead bloated and burst in the sun. Blowflies feasted on the dead and formed clouds around the living, humming like bees. At night, when the trade winds died, the smell of rotting flesh was suffocating, and the Japanese slid invisibly along the perimeter of our camp, finding opportunity to add more fuel to the stench. One ghost bayoneted seven soldiers in ten days. He stole right into camp. We knew it was the same man because he placed a Mickey Mantle card in each victim's hand.

There was no respite. The shockwaves of 1,000-pound bombs or the night rustle of animal or man, each drove a needle tip into our nerve endings. One afternoon, our platoon leader walked along our perimeter as if someone had just told him to fetch a loaf of bread from the corner store. Men screamed at him to get down, but he strolled until the sniper's bullet removed the left side of his head.

Five days later, his successor stepped on a land mine inside the perimeter we had camped in for two months. Fearing other mines, we only watched. For a terribly long time, he gathered up his limbs and organs like playing cards.

In this fashion, I rose rapidly through the company rank, advanced by attrition and my transformation into something that both terrified and, I must be honest, thrilled me. While bomb bursts and quiet rustlings saw strong-willed men offer themselves up to snipers, I turned calm and detached. I have since read this is a common reaction to all manner of calamity, though many people become so calm they are, in effect, giving up. Passengers sat in deck chairs as the *Titanic* sank; office workers sat at their desks as the Twin Towers crumbled.

I did not sit passively. The din of war still rocked me, but slowly war's silent face became my friend. I told no one this, but my superiors saw it, for I was the one sent to scout alone through the dripping jungle, and eventually I was the one who waited beyond the perimeter for the bayonet ghost, the nights so black I wasn't even certain of his existence when, after eight nights of waiting, I finally felt his weight on the end of my bayonet and heard a baby's gurgle. He had one Mantle card left and three Stan Musials at the ready. I placed them neatly, two in the palm of each hand.

For the next three nights, there was no human movement on our perimeter. Our platoon leader, who had not yet taken his ill-fated walk, foolishly perceived this as our enemy's psychological collapse. Hoping to keep our enemy demoralized, each night I was sent into the jungle. I was ordered not to shoot. Pricking away at the pricks, he called it.

My actions earned me notoriety among the men, but I was never proud of what I did. I did it then because killing is what war requires, though now this does nothing to ease my conscience. The killing itself always made my stomach turn, for a bayonet plunged into flesh is not a prick at all. Even as these men took their last bloodied breaths, I knew I would carry the memory of their weight in my shoulders for the rest of my life.

But the waiting and the silence became a drug. Crouched in blackness, part of my mind remained hypervigilant, while the other slid through a reel of pleasant daydreams. I sat on a crate in the restaurant kitchen, watching my mother wash dishes. I sat beside Sean on the sunbaked dock, the two of us quiet, soothed by the Indian River's lullaby swirl. My jungle forays restored me. I returned to camp with a spring in my step and a light in my eyes. One dawn, as I slipped back across the perimeter, a man who knew me looked up from his rations and said, "You're a gook." The other men watched me, saying nothing. I imagined I was Cotton, a man no one knew or understood. My nighttime reconnoiters ended when, with three weeks of fighting and the horrors of mop up still ahead of us, I assumed leadership of our unit.

Sarah mailed poems. Her letters did not come often, and when they did, the letter was always short: a few paragraphs of news and then the chosen poem. I knew she did not want to overstep her bounds and outdo her sister.

I read those first poems over and over, the words of Yeats, Wordsworth, and John Donne briefly taking me away to a different place. This surprised me, for I had little interest in poetry before, but as I sat sweat-soaked and bone-numb, their words stirred memories and thoughts I didn't know I had. Sarah did not pick poems that spoke of pale moons, lost loves, and lake water lapping. The poems she chose said things so that her letters didn't have to. The poets seemed to know the place I knew. Wrote Yeats,

And what rough beast, its hour come at last,
Slouches towards Bethlehem to be born?

In the beginning, I was just like everyone else, an anonymous and frightened grunt. I made friends, and they chided me for getting letters from two women. They reminded me that bigamy was a crime, and it would be God's good joke if I survived the war to go home to prison.

By the time I became platoon leader, such camaraderie had withered like salted grapes. But the men followed my orders, and

I followed the orders of my superiors in kind, though the orders I received were often senseless, assaults to seize patches of earth of no value, victory, by either side, measured in actual yards of blood-soaked ground. Yard by yard, forward and back, we drove the Japanese into the interior of the island, bestowing and absorbing death, killing promise before it had barely begun. That man considers such things triumph still unnerves me.

When the war officially ended, the Japanese we hadn't killed disappeared into the now famous rabbit warren of caves they had dug in preparation for just such a retreat in the coral rock ridges of Umurbrogol Mountain. Their commanders preached not optimism but realism. Subterranean lairs filled with Japanese soldiers ordered to fight to the death, Peleliu, in yet another instance of military nonsense, was declared secured. I have since read that the Japanese dug upward of six hundred caves to make their last stand. I don't know how many they dug, but they were everywhere, each silent opening breathing the same horrible question.

Our duty turned to extermination, rooting out these holdouts in the last place war had sent them, claustrophobic caverns where dust rose and hovered, and startled cockroaches scuttled by the hundreds so that it seemed as if the cave walls were moving.

Caves close to the surface were dealt with simply; we burned the occupants alive. If a passage was too long for flame throwers but wide enough for a barrel of gasoline, the barrel was lowered through the passage and exploded with a rain of bullets. We called it ant killing. This made it easier for some of the men, though most didn't care.

Some caves were too deep for flame throwers and their tunnels too long for barrels. These were reached by a single man crawling through a passage often less than shoulder-wide, forcing the crawler to squirm forward with his arms in front of him like Superman, only Superman didn't cry, silently waiting for a bayonet to pierce his skull. Many of these deep caves were empty, but some were not. It was a soul-crushing game of roulette.

This flushing rotated among units. It also rotated among the smallest men, for the slight Japanese had dug their tunnels accordingly. I was small, but I was the platoon leader. Ferreting out was not meant for me, and for a time, I followed these orders. Men pushed into the openings, cursing their ancestors' genes.

One morning, we found an opening deep in the jungle. I knew whose turn it was, a freckle-faced farm boy from Des Moines, a good boy, quiet and quick to take orders.

When I turned, Henry Gaines stood, slouched and sickly. He straightened slightly. I wondered if he was trying to make himself look taller.

"Sir," he said, "permission to speak."

"Please."

"Sir. Gunnery Sergeant Lutz is going instead. We agreed to trade places."

Standing a few feet behind Gaines, Lutz looked even sicker.

The heat made it difficult to think. The hole at my feet was like a living thing, its stale breath licking my boots. I had a bad feeling about this hole, but in war, there are so many bad feelings, you almost stop listening.

"You agree with this, Mr. Lutz?"

This was an idiot's question, but Lutz answered as if it wasn't.

"We arranged it, sir."

"Fine then," I said, though we all knew it wasn't fine at all.

Lutz disappeared into the opening, his rifle, bayonet affixed, leading the way. In different circumstances, it might be amusing to watch a grown man's boot soles scrabble and scuff for purchase in the opening of a hole, but on Peleliu, it was nauseating.

For fifteen minutes, we marinated in familiar throat-clutching silence. I confess I drifted, distracted by a rising anger I couldn't place.

In war, you hear every kind of screaming, but we had never heard anything like this. One man began running in circles. Several fired rounds into the trees. Lutz's screams kept coming. The moments between the screams were worse, for we heard his pleas clearly. No one responded. He was not calling for us.

Finally the screaming stopped. I knew there was something I should do, but for the first time, I was at a loss. Someone ran past me. Falling to his knees, the freckle-faced farm boy clawed at the opening.

I fought for his name.

"Henry," I said. "Step aside."

He kept digging. A soldier stepped forward and pulled Gaines to his feet. His mouth jerked opened and closed like a fish dropped on a dock.

"I heard breathing," said the soldier who had pulled Gaines up, and then the hole exploded in a rain of dirt and squealing.

The boar stood quivering in the sun, coarse hair smeared from snout to shoulder in blood. Something pink dropped from a tusk. More gore clung to the animal's forelocks and hooves. Man and animal stood stupefied. Then someone screamed, "Fry the motherfucker!" and the world erupted in flame.

That evening, I asked Henry Gaines to come to my tent.

He stood, holding his carbine.

"Henry."

"Sir."

"You may stand down. We're finished for today."

"Yes, sir."

He stood as he was, the tears rolling down his face.

"We played poker," he said.

I looked down quickly, pretending to brush something from my pants, but I knew, in the brief moment our eyes met, that he had seen my thoughts. I also knew he had never cheated before.

"Henry. You need to hear me and understand."

"Yes."

I looked at him, but he did not see me. His eyes had gone somewhere else.

"Henry, you're a fine man. Even the finest men make mistakes."

"If we confess our sins, He is faithful and just to forgive us our sins and to cleanse us from all unrighteousness."

We both heard the verse, but I knew only one word rang in Henry Gaines's ears.

"This is a terrible place," I said. "You cannot hold yourself accountable for things beyond your control. Do you understand?"

"Yes."

Standing there, sickness in his eyes, Henry Gaines looked like a small boy. I wondered if, on a blue Iowa afternoon, that same face had looked up from a skinned knee, the blood just starting to bubble, and shouted across the farm yard, calling, as Lutz had, for the one person who mattered.

The next morning, a soldier came running, and I knew I had made an irreparable mistake. I ran to where the men stood. Henry Gaines stood away and alone. His eyes were sleepy, but when I pushed through the circle of men, he blinked and straightened. Pulling the pin turned the morning bright, and stickiness appeared in the trees.

That night I walked into the sea. I walked in up to my knees, tepid water flooding my boots. The ocean's surface sparkled beneath a full moon.

Sickness made me weak. There was no connection between the world as it was and the world as man tried to sculpt it, no explanation for a terrified animal, intestines gummed to its tusks, screaming its own screams as flames peeled hair and flesh away, no explanation for the fact that tomorrow we would turn the same horror on our fellow man.

I stood for a long time, feeling the warm breeze and the surprising weight of the loosely bound pages in my hand, and then I turned and walked back to camp.

While the sea breeze whispered, I wrote Henry Gaines's parents. I told them their son died bravely. I told them they had raised a fine young man, that I saw this every day, and that they should be proud. I told them there was nothing that could have been done. I told them the island was littered with live armament. I told them that so many things were beyond our control.

I sealed the letter and sat staring at my hands. I wondered how often poets lied. I wondered why I couldn't drop their words into the water.

26

On the eastern edge of Albuquerque, I find a pay phone. I don't know exactly why I do it, but I do. Maybe I am trying to be more impulsive. It is getting late. I should be looking for a motel.

The phone is outside a convenience store. I experience a momentary setback when I find a pop top jammed in the coin slot. I pry it out with my Swiss Army knife. Someone has scratched a crude sketch of male genitalia on the phone's metal face plate.

I find the number in my wallet. I dial quickly, before I can stop myself.

"Hello."

I hear the excitement in my voice.

"Hi, Tesia. It's Pogue." I pause. "Remember? Pogue the toad."

"I remember. I'll get Sarah."

As if she is reading from a script.

"Wait. I called to talk to you."

I hear breathing.

"I saw the Grand Canyon. I met a friend. She reminded me of you. She had lots of gumption."

Gumption? What am I doing? The word disappeared with Indian Head nickels and spats. I see my vague reflection in the metallic plating, already a ghost. I am a fool. This phone call is self-indulgence of the worst kind. Why would an eight-year-old want to talk to an old man she hardly knows? But I can't hang up on a child.

Inside the store, fluorescent lighting bleaches the customers' faces. They look like cadavers. I was a boy on a riverbank once.

"Have you found any more fat, green caterpillars?"

"That was a long time ago."

I am hanging by a fingernail.

"Should I call back another time?"

"I'm glad you called now."

"Is something wrong?"

"I'm worried."

When you realize the world is not about you, it often rights itself.

"What's wrong?"

"We're doing a play in school. It's called 'Vacation to Mars.' We're just rehearsing right now, but we've got *problems*. We visit all the planets. Different kids have different planets. Most of the planets are working fine, but we're having a real problem with Jupiter. Two special-ed kids are doing Jupiter. They try real hard, but John can't read the cue cards, and Pearl gets mixed up." A clearing cough, and then song like a breeze riffling a grove of cottonwoods. "This is not our vay-caaaay-tion. They made a mistake and sent us to the wrong des-tin-aaaaytion."

"You have a beautiful voice."

It is possible that women are focused from birth.

"Sometimes Pearl says *constipation* instead of vacation. If she says constipation during the play, the sixth graders will start hooting. They're real butts."

"Which planet are you?"

"I'm not a planet. I'm Ariel. She's one of the two kids going on the vacation. I have lots of funny lines, but it won't matter if everyone is already laughing."

"I'll bet once Pearl and John practice enough, they'll be great."

"Maybe. It sounds like something's broken."

It takes me a moment.

"They're quarters. I'm dropping them in the phone."

She crows.

"Like in old movies!"

I am glad I called.

"Hold on."

I drop three quarters. I add a dime and three nickels for good measure. They do make a merry ching.

"We have rollover minutes," says Tesia. "Why aren't you using your cell phone?"

I understand why I'm the one prying the pop top from the coin slot.

"I don't have a cell phone."

"Even Mrs. Dunsmire has a cell phone."

"Who is Mrs. Dunsmire?"

"The librarian. She smells like our carpet. It's rain damaged. Everyone has a cell phone."

"I could be from Mars."

The sound of giggling is sweetest of all.

"Does anyone else know?"

"That I'm from Mars?"

"No. That you don't have a cell phone."

"It's a secret. No one knows but you."

I smile. Inside the store, a man looks away.

"What do you look like?" Tesia asks.

"Why?"

"We have a secret, so now we're friends."

"I'm short, and my hair is white. I've got bushy eyebrows that are white too. And I have a crooked nose. Like a boxer who lost a fight."

"You sound like a hobbit. I love hobbits. I know all about them. My favorite is Peregrin Took. He's the youngest hobbit, but that's not why I like him. I like him because he gets in tons of trouble, and he's a loyal friend."

"I'm more like Bilbo Baggins."

The right words do open a heart.

"Bilbo's my second favorite! There's only a little bit of him in *The Lord of the Rings*, and he's really old and kind of crotchety, but it's okay because in *The Hobbit* he's young and super funny, and he becomes really brave, though it takes him a little time. Frodo is the same way. Sarah says Bilbo and Frodo are like all of us. There's more to them than there seems."

Something warm steals over me, and I am transported.

"Sarah reads to you," I say.

"Every night before bed. She does amazing voices. They're really funny. She says it's her Tookish side. Can I tell you a secret?"

"We're friends."

"I'm not at all like Frodo and Bilbo. I make Sarah skip the really scary parts. Like the giant spiders in Mirkwood. I'm really scared of spiders. All hairy and quiet, with big pinchers." Her voice is smaller. "It scares me thinking about them."

"Frodo and Bilbo were scared. Even Gandalf was scared, and he was a powerful wizard."

"Maybe it would be better if I let her read me the part about the spiders."

A journey. I am fairly floating.

"I'm afraid of spiders too," I say. "You don't have to read that part until you're ready."

"I guess. I asked Sarah about you. She said you were going for a walk, but I know you're driving. Frodo and Sam walked all the way to Mordor in bare feet. It's funny you're short, because Sarah's tall. She used to be really tall, but old people shrink. I wonder what happens if you start off short."

"You just disappear. Like Frodo and Bilbo."

"That's the evil ring."

Greed, temptation, power, domination—not at all beyond the ken of children.

"There's a picture of Sarah on our fireplace mantle. It's my favorite. She's wearing a brown dress, and her hair is standing up all funny in the wind, and she's laughing. Sarah says everybody has one special picture of themselves where they look on the outside how they'd always like to feel on the inside. She says that's her picture. She thinks she looked like a skinny scarecrow when she was young, but I think she looked like a tall princess."

Plank feet and skillet hands.

"What time did you put your children to bed?"

"I didn't have any children."

"I go to bed at eight."

I don't miss the pregnant pause. I add two hours to my watch.

"Now we're both in trouble?"

"You're funny. Don't worry. Mom probably thinks I'm in the bathroom doing a really good job with my teeth."

"You'd better go do that."

"If I was your daughter, what time would you make me go to bed?"

"Eight o'clock."

For a moment, I wonder if she is gone.

"I'm glad you saw the Grand Canyon. Good night, Bilbo."

"Good night, Peregrin Took."

"Call me tomorrow."

The dial tone drones, but I keep the phone to my ear. I watch a boy through the glass. He might be two years older than Tesia. He stands alone in front of a rack of candy. It worries me that his parents have gone off down another aisle.

He puts a candy bar in his pocket. Stepping out of the store, he looks at me. He stands there as if he doesn't have a care in the world, and then he steps around the corner.

That night, I can't sleep. Laying in the dark, I try to resurrect the Grand Canyon's majesty, but my mind wanders its own path. I see the Nazi soldiers, laughing and pissing through the bars. Calvin's poachers hack at turtles whose throats already spurt blood on the sand, and the shoplifting boy slouches, mockery in his eyes. I wish him away, but Yeats whispers again in my ear.

The blood-dimmed tide is loosed, and everywhere
The ceremony of innocence is drowned;
The best lack all conviction, while the worst
Are full of passionate intensity.

I stand in the jungle again, the faces of my men tight with rage and revenge, and when I give the order, the flame throwers roar so that only now do I hear the screams of the losers of war.

I am a member of the race of man. When Sean pried loose the bully's tooth, something inside me cheered.

27

I wanted to see my country, and most of what I see is the same. Between the open spaces—and I am grateful to see that in the west there are still open spaces—are pea-in-a-pod exits, gas and fast food with silent patrons and employees. Cities announce themselves first with sprawling suburbs and pyramidal shopping marts, Home Depots, Targets, and Coscos rising from the earth with the sameness of some gargantuan crop, as if a mercantile Johnny Appleseed has loped across the land. In the suburbs and the cities, I am clasped again in a vehicular torrent, and though I am sure each driver laughs and loves, behind the wheel they are stone-faced gladiators. Twice, merging onto the freeway, I am nearly forced off the road.

From Albuquerque, Interstate 25 winds south through Las Cruces and then across the border and into Texas. Just past Las Cruces, Interstate 25 becomes Interstate 10. After another fifteen miles, I stop at a rest area, hoping a stretch might ease the pain in my back. I stand beside a man in shiny, black leather cowboy boots. The two of us share a meager patch of shade while consulting a map pocked with colorful pushpins designating assorted Texas attractions.

The World's Largest Muleshoe, Jackrabbit, and Killer Bee are separated by equally vast distances.

"Maybe everything *is* bigger in Texas," I say.

The man spits on the hard ground.

"Three words," he says. "Stupid tourist bullshit."

I search the pushpins, but even the Toilet Seat Museum doesn't cheer me. I wonder if I am seeing my country as it is. Perhaps we have bartered away our spirit and our land.

I spend the night in Van Horn. Twenty dollars buys me a room that looks as if it may just last the night. The World's Largest Cracks crisscross the ceiling. Everything is chained down, even the buckshot-riddled garbage can outside the motel office, as if the World's Largest Vacuum Cleaner is about to pass by.

When I wake, my back still throbs. The coffeemaker produces a bitter liquid even I am forced to pour down the sink. I shave in front of a metal sheet that isn't much for reflection. When I lean close, hoping for a better view, the metal has a familiar smell, tart and antiseptic, I can't quite place. When it finally comes to me, I drop the razor and hold tight to the sink.

The morgue.

Memory can be a physical blow.

I breathe in, breathe out.

I wag a shaking finger at my blurry countenance.

"They're only spiders, Bilbo."

The first hand-painted sign appears east of Saragosa, a plywood square affixed to a stake hammered in sorely off canter.

Feast Your Lecherous Eyes on Adam and Eve's Original Sin. Count 'Em. Only one hundred and seventeen lickety-split miles.

The world is rendered mysterious again.

Ten minutes later, the next sign appears. *What's Longer than Your Tally-Whacker and Gets Plenty More Respect?* Ten more minutes and *Sex Sells, Don't It?* The signs sprout from the desert like anorexic shrubs with vertigo. In contrast, the block lettering looks like a stamp. I watch the odometer. The signs are precisely thirteen miles apart. When the next sign whizzes past, I give its creator an appreciative salute.

Just short of Ozona, a sign the size of a truck panel rests against two convenient boulders.

Don't Turn off Ahead, but You'll Regret it Forever.

I made my decision 117 miles ago. The dirt track is barely wide enough for the Mustang. It meanders among appreciable chuckholes and hedgehog and pincushion cacti. There is only one track, but after ten minutes, I wonder if I am lost. No surprise, a sign appears.

Used to Be the Main Highway, But it Ain't Anymore. This too Shall Pass. 3 Scant Miles Betwixt You and God's Miracle.

For ten more minutes, nothing but desert wavers, and then a low-slung wood building, slouching in embarrassment, wavers amid it. I stop near a hitching post and shut off the Mustang. From where I sit, I can see the underside of the porch roof, sagging in like a fallen soufflé. Three of the four front windows are boarded shut. The fourth is half covered with a Hefty bag that pops in the wind. A sun-bleached two by four hangs straight down from the porch rafters, swinging slightly on its rusty chain. Touching an ear to my shoulder, I read the sign. *Uncle Ray's Rattlesnake Farm. Safer In Here Than it is Out There.*

It's abandoned, and I am a fool. The wind whistles through something. As if summoned by this cue, a man kicks open the screen door, nearly sending it off the hinges. Nimbly vaulting three porch steps, he lands in a sunny puff of dust. He doesn't linger.

A hand thrusts through the window and bobs in front of my face.

"Been a long while since anyone rode in here on a Mustang. Uncle Ray. Proprietor and ladies' man."

"Pogue Whithouse."

No face appears. I shake the hand.

"Not bein' rude. Only bend when I have to."

The hand jerks back. I step slowly from the car.

Uncle Ray beams.

"Well now, a man who understands the need to conserve. Apologies for that stretch of jarrin' road. Invested all my capital in roadside advertising, and our county officials have spent all my tax dollars on liquor and whores."

"The signs were a sound investment," I say. "Not your conventional sales pitch."

"Appreciate that. Might have been Poet Laureate if I hadn't gone into snakes. It's all about advertising. Walmart never shuts up. Get their mailers twice a week, no small accomplishment with a mailing address like this. Doubt I'll drive 200 miles for a juicer, but they're willin' to chance it. I like an optimist, even if it's Walmart. Keep on pluggin', and you never know."

Reaching out, he runs two fingers tenderly along the Mustang's hood.

"Nineteen sixty-seven would've been a good year if the hippies hadn't ruined it. You ain't a free-love dope smoker, I hope." He is walking away, waving a hand in the air. "Don't matter, don't matter. Those of us with experience need to keep an open mind." He turns back. "You comin'? Standin' there stoned on the wacky weed?"

Mounting the stairs, he nods at the dangling sign. It spins slowly like a bored drill bit.

"Youth is responsible for the annoying cant of signage. But the guts of the operation, by God, they still shine. Sure you've been around the block enough to know appearances are deceiving. Pick any presidential election for starters."

I finally get a good look at him in the porch shade. He is rail-thin and pigeon-chested. Tufts of gray sprout above the collar of a clean white undershirt. He wears baggy jeans. An enormous tan Stetson is jammed low on his head, the outsize hat made larger by the fact that its wearer is little bigger than a leprechaun. His skin is sun-bleached gray.

We stand in a hum of gunslinger quiet. We are sizing each other up. We both know it. Even two steps from a death rattle, men still do it.

Uncle Ray screws up his face.

"Shit. Sorry 'bout the hippy thing. You look like an upstandin' fellah. Celebrated my seventy-eighth last week, but I'm bettin' you've got a few years on me. Folks these days don't know or appreciate the past, though when you're livin' it, you don't realize you're history at all. I'm bettin' you were in the war. Served your country, and I'm grateful to you for that. Simpler times then. Folks didn't question our wars, and we usually had them in a place we could pronounce."

A screwdriver sits on a windowsill. Picking it up, Uncle Ray regards it sourly. It disappears in the chasm of a jean pocket.

"Damn sign came loose three nights ago. Wind here blows everything to hell and back around. Told the boy to fix it. Never seen a lazier generation. No doubt disrepair ain't helpin' the influx of customers."

"If you can't maintain your storefront, who's to say the inside isn't crawling with loosed rattlers?"

It's a feeler, but Uncle Ray ignores it.

"Precisely. Likely, I should be huntin' for a reliable partner. For now, though, I suppose I got to stand on the porch railing and fix the sign myself. My balance ain't what it used to be. If I fall, my worthless excuse for a grandson will sell this entire empire before I hit the ground. Won't extend hisself much for my funeral either, not if it means spendin' more than two nickels and gettin' out of bed before noon."

He springs away, calling back over his shoulder.

"Case you're concerned, snakes are out the back in pits. Ain't lost a snake yet. A real herpetological Alcatraz."

We step through the front door, walking through musty dimness past empty shelves and scattered boxes, some open, some not. Postcards spill across a smeary glass counter, next to several collapsing piles of T-shirts and a half-dozen dusty prescription bottles, the labels scratched off.

"Needs a woman's touch," says Uncle Ray. "'Course the touch comes with a tongue."

We clack through a screen door in the back. The short respite of shadow makes the sun's assault even brighter.

"Thought you Hollywood types always wore sunglasses. Don't sell shades, but if you're achin' for a snakeskin handkerchief to wipe yer brow, I'll open the register when we're done. Today's your lucky day. It's"—he glances at his watch—"Thursday. No deliveries on Thursday. Uncle Ray himself will give you a personal tour of his serpentine kingdom."

We're in a dusty courtyard. There may have been flowers once, but the planters are dry and cracked as the ground under our feet. In the center of the courtyard, waist-high adobe walls make three brown circles. They could be wells, only they yawn a little too wide.

We walk to the nearest ring and look down. The inner wall is smooth as ice. At the bottom of the pit, at least fifty rattlers lay immobile on a pad of white bright cement.

Uncle Ray pats the wall as if it were a child's head.

"Dug these pits by hand myself back in livelier days. Thirty feet deep, forty feet wide. Ground around here fights you off like a virgin. Can't grow nothin' 'cept bitterness and rattlers." He tugs his hat brim down. "You're lucky the tour buses just left."

This jaunty leprechaun makes me smile. I'm glad his establishment isn't marked with a pushpin, though it should be.

"Digging these pits is quite a feat."

"I've told a few lies in my day, but that ain't one of 'em."

I see how he fights down his pride, and I like him even more.

"The World's Largest Muleshoe doesn't have a snowball's chance against this," I say.

"Damn right. You stopped at the Paisano Pete Rest Stop. Texas's got a shitload of pushpins, don't it?" He cackles. "Few years back, stopped there myself to pass water. That map screamed free advertising. Bad timin', though. Two minutes after I stopped, Texas trooper swings in. Caught me with a pocket fulla pushpins. Uncle Ray's Rattlesnake Farm, ground zero for Texas entertainment. No ticket, though. Sweet talked him into letting me pick up dog dirt for the rest of the afternoon."

The rattlesnakes in the sun are still as stone. I see more tucked in the myriad crevices of a pile of rocks in the middle of the pad. The other two rings are bigger.

"How many rattlesnakes do you have?"

"Three hundred. Maybe three-fifty. Been awhile since I've been in the mood for countin'."

"The great state of Texas is committing the world's largest oversight."

Uncle Ray cocks his head.

"Might be able to find room in my public relations department for a sharp tack like you."

"What do you do between visitors?"

"Got no TV or magazines. Helps us avoid the world's trash and sin. None of them video games either, though my grandson never stops whinin'. Read a book now and then. Got plenty of chores and an equal number of snakes. Nature's own entertainment. Never a dull moment. Wondrous creatures, as much a part of God's world as we are. Adam and Eve were dead wrong. Too addled with matters of the flesh to think straight. Sometimes I sit and watch 'em for hours."

"It's just the two of you?"

"Yep. More than enough."

"What does your grandson do?"

Uncle Ray's face goes sour.

"Ain't you been listenin'? He doesn't do shit." The Stetson shakes rapidly back and forth. "My apologies. It's the boy that irks me, not you." He nods toward a filmy window. Behind the film, I see the outline of a pulled shade.

"He occupies himself with sleepin' and tormentin' his grandpa. When he ain't avoidin' chores, he reads." Quick as a snake strike, Uncle Ray's voice loses its angry rasp. "Never seen a boy read like that. Bookmobile comes by here twice a week. Engine ain't stopped tickin' afore Jimmy's got hisself an armload fulla books. Reads 'em all before the next trip out. Man name of Kiowa Jackson runs the bookmobile. Drives 150 miles just to bring books for Jimmy. Kiowa says he's investin' in Jimmy. Says Jimmy's gonna' be the next president." Uncle Ray's eyes narrow. "Though from what I've seen, you don't need much education to get that job. Look. You can ask my grandson all about his life yourself, but I'll tell you now he ain't talkin' to no one until he fixes the sign out front."

Perhaps it's the vibration of our voices, but several of the rattlers have started moving, crawling sluggishly over their fellows. A moat of water circles the cement.

"Water's just for looks and the comfort of the clientele. Rattlesnakes swim like fucking mermaids. I modeled the pits after pictures of cobra pits in Malayshee-a. Cobras sport in the water too. Seen pictures of 'em swimmin' with their head up, hood flared like a sail. Majestic. Snakes fancy a good coolin' swim. Had a woman once from Boston, annoyin' bitch, kept insistin' rattlesnakes didn't swim. Just wouldn't let up. Forced me to excuse myself. Came back and tossed an M80 into the pit. Two hundred rattlers swimmin' like goddamn Olympians. She was probably just frustrated. Her husband was a runt. Sure bet the smallest snake was three times the size of his pecker."

The heat off the cement made the snakes' geometric patterns blur and wobble.

"What kind of rattlers are these?"

"Swimmin' ones. We got the sidewinder or massasauga, Latin name *Sistrurus catenatus consors*, and the ground rattlesnake, *Sistrurus nziliarius*, found all over our great state. We got the green rattlesnake, *Crotalus molossus*, inhabits the valley of the Rio Grande, and the plains rattlesnake, *Crotalus confluentus*, lives in the northwestern counties, not to mention the diamond rattlesnake, the banded rattlesnake, and the Texas rattlesnake. Reckon them herpetologists ran out of names by the time they got around to that last one."

Uncle Ray is staring into the pit. His face loosens.

"Amazing creatures. God's greatest design. Even been in the news of late. Know why?"

I realize I haven't looked at a newspaper in three days. At home, I read the newspaper front to back every day. The young make news; the old stay abreast of it. I also enjoy the newspaper for the occasional odd item.

I remember.

"Horse trainers are using rattlesnake poison to help horses win races," I say.

Uncle Ray wheels, spittle flying from his mouth.

"Great Gawd almighty!" He actually reaches out for me. For an unnerving moment, I think he might kiss me. "A customer of grace *and* intelligence! It's my lucky day! I'll tell you the truth, I'm tired as shit of the same moronic questions." Pinching his face, he whines, "'Uncle Raaaaay, how quick can a rattler kill you? Uncle Raaaaay, you ever been bit? Uncle Raaaaaay, you ever eat rattlesnake stew? Uncle Raaaaay, how many gallons you got in that hat?'" He spits hard. "Shit. It's enough to make you give up hope and throw yourself in the pit."

His wide smile reveals tobacco-stained teeth.

"Rattlesnake poison is horse racing's secret weapon. Course if you California hippies are readin' about it, maybe it's not a secret anymore." His eyes actually swing around the courtyard, and his voice lowers a notch. "I'll let you in on somethin' the reporters don't know. Used to send the venom I milked to labs for snakebite antidote. Now it goes to a chemist in San Antonio who doesn't give a rat's ass about antidotes. He turns the venom into tablets or powder, dilutes it some, he tells me. Frankly, I don't care if he mounts it on a lollipop stick. I get paid three times what I used to for an ounce of venom. Now that's privileged information, understand? The trainers, they mix this magic potion with the horse's feed. Lot of race horses suffer from breaking blood vessels. Finishes a fine horse, lickety-split. When the animal's racing, the blood going through its lungs gets thicker, and sometimes the walls of the blood vessels give way. The venom thins the blood so it goes swooshin' through the lungs; less chance of the walls collapsing. Me and that San Antonio chemist, we got ourselves a booming market in England."

Uncle Ray slaps his jeans, sending up a small cloud of dust.

"I'm part of a global conglomerate. Tablets and powder go in vials from San Antonio to a pharmacist in London. The pharmacist sells it to the trainers. Hear he calls the stuff Crodalus Horridus. Called him once. Could hear him soilin' his pants from 8,000 miles away." He produces a worried expression and a surprisingly good Cockney accent. "'Can't let word of this out. *Quite* improper. My clients are quite powerful. Reputations would be ruined. Must keep it all very hush-hush.'" Uncle Ray spits into the water and wipes his mouth with his sleeve. "Quite. People are way more interesting when they're havin' the shit scared out of 'em."

We walk to the farthest pit. It's the biggest, but it houses two dozen snakes at most. A metal pole leans against the outer wall.

Uncle Ray gazes down.

"I almost forgot to ask. You like snakes?"

Dog-eared books and snakes in pungent jars, lovingly brushed of ants and washed in the sink when our mother wasn't looking. In our bedroom, Sean and I would unscrew the lids again and again, never put off by the putrid smell, never tiring of the satin feel and the saurian set of jaw. Alongside Sharpe's rivers and creeks, we saw their living counterparts, rat snakes, crayfish snakes, and indigos, glossy, ethereal creatures, moving smooth as nightfall.

Uncle Ray nods.

"'Nuff not said. Tell you what. You ain't my average customer. Good listener, for one, which is something I don't see much anymore. Initiative too. I got to be honest, not so many people wander this far off the beaten track anymore." Some starch leaves him. Then he fires up the brilliant amperage of smile. "Shit. Why not? I'm offerin' up a rare opportunity. Care to take a spin in the pit?"

A rope ladder drapes over this wall. It stops two feet above the water.

"Got to do a little backward hop at the end, but I'll clear you a spot first." He takes off his Stetson and places it carefully on the ground. Age spots pepper his bald head. "Need my peripheral vision."

In one smooth motion, Uncle Ray grabs the pole and swings a leg nimbly over the wall. The enclosure makes his voice echo as he clambers down the wood rungs.

"Best snake stick there is. High-grade titanium. Light and quick. The modern world ain't all bullshit and waste."

He says something else, but I don't catch it. It is Sarah's voice I hear, the radiator making its pings and pocks in the background.

'O plunge your hands in water
Plunge them in up to the wrist;
Stare, stare in the basin
And wonder what you've missed.

Another walk, this one with W. H. Auden.

Pushing off the wall, Uncle Ray drops nimbly to the pad, sweeping away the closest rattlers with the stick. Now there is plenty of movement. The rattlers coil instantly, castanet tickings rupturing the hot silence.

Uncle Ray waves the stick overhead.

"Come on in! The water's fine."

Across the pad, the remaining snakes begin to move. Instincts pricked by the ruckus, a few take up their own angry warning.

Uncle Ray shouts, "What do you call a snake who works for the government? A civil serpent! Har! Hitch up you skirt! I don't plan on spendin' the night down here."

Good-bye.

I slide up on the wall butt first and slowly swing my legs around to the ladder. Climbing down is harder than Uncle Ray made it look. My arms strain. The ladder and my knuckles bang against the wall. When I reach the bottom, my knuckles are scraped, and my forearms burn.

"Just a little hop," says Uncle Ray. "I got you a fine space cleared."

Somehow I push back. The jarring sends a flare of pain into my hips. I grunt.

"We ain't got the springs we once had," Uncle Ray says. His eyes are on the rattlers. His bald head glints in the sun. "Goooooood fellahs, goooooooood fellahs. Beautiful, ain't they?"

They are. My heart pounds from exertion and anxiety, and excitement too. The rattlers wind about each other in a muscled ballet.

"Magnificent."

I whisper, for I am in the presence of something extraordinary. The rattlers chatter their agreement.

"Teddy Roosevelt said it best," Uncle Ray says. "Life is best inside the ring."

The stick has a small hook at the end. Uncle Ray swings the hook slowly to and fro above the triangular heads of the closest rattlers, piled tight and rattling furiously.

"I was down here milkin' just yesterday, but they never seem to get used to me. That one seems particularly perturbed."

As if on cue, the thickest rattler strikes. Uncle Ray steps aside so quickly I am only barely aware of the movement. With a wet sack sound, a three-quarter length of rattler lands where he just stood.

Coiling quickly, the snake strikes again. Now the head is pinned beneath the hook, the body lashing furiously.

"Never show the same hand twice," says Uncle Ray quietly. "Lost a step or two, ain't you, old fellah?"

Crouching, Uncle Ray reaches out with his free hand, gripping the snake firmly just behind the head. Dropping the stick, he deftly pins the lashing body with his other hand. He appears to have forgotten the other buzzing snakes. The pit reverberates. It is almost like applause.

"Up you go," Uncle Ray says.

He stands, panting slightly.

"Dubya is one heavy fucker. Texas rattlesnake. He's been with me a long time. Named him Dubya because he's always strikin' out blind."

The rattler is draped between his hands, a convulsing wreath, snow-white underside glistening in the sun. Beneath the scales, muscles sweep like ripples across a pond.

"Venters are what the underside scales are called. Hypnotic, ain't it? Easy to see how Adam and Eve were duped. Here's how you tell male from female."

He turns the snake slightly. In the same instant, it convulses and extends.

Somehow it is now affixed to his wrist.

"Well, shit," says Uncle Ray.

The rattler dangles from his wrist like a loopy walking stick. He regards it curiously before reaching out and pinching the head. Jaws forced loose, the snake falls to the ground. Immediately, it takes up its buzzing.

"There's a surprise," he says and sits down cross-legged. He turns his arm over. He is not even watching the snake. "Bull's eye. Right on the artery." He looks up at me, his lips drawn tight. "What's the best thing about deadly snakes? They got poisonality."

A familiar tingling courses through my limbs.

The fat rattler buzzes, two hands away from a Levi'd knee. Uncle Ray watches the snake now, his words even.

"Venom's odorless. Put a little on your lips, and it tingles. You'll need to deal quickly with this fellow. Two strikes and I'm out." His eyes tilt down to the right. The snake stick is four inches from his right hand. "Nice and gradual now."

I hear my breath, slow and steady. Conducting a five count in my mind, I lower slowly to one knee. It's hotter, like peering into an open oven. The rattler's buzzing is deafening. Snakes sense heat and movement. I remember.

My heart throbs in my fingertips.

I can see Uncle Ray out of the corner of my eye. He is still as a gargoyle, spittle in one corner of his mouth.

He speaks softly, not quite a whisper.

"When it comes to snakes, most people can't sort out their feelings. Hatred and attraction. Vilification and desire. Same thing with murderers. Goethe said, 'I have never heard of a crime which I could not imagine committing myself.' Knew a woman once, kept rattlers as pets. Swore when she caressed them, they arched their backs like cats. Relationship ended in fatal termination."

I feel the familiar sensations, floating dreamily but every sense on alert, waiting for the right moment.

I lean forward. The rattler's cadence does not change. The sides of the triangular head look swollen, a man with a ferocious tooth infection.

The titanium is cool and light in my hand. I bring my arm back slowly, the stick just off the ground. The snake ignores me. I rise in increments. If my knees cry out, I don't feel them.

"Performed like a surgeon," says Uncle Ray dully. "Next up, you'll need to pin him on the first poke. I ain't feelin' like myself. Old boy gave me a good pumpin'."

The triangular head sways.

"Ain't you pretty," says Uncle Ray, and he leans forward to caress the snake.

I swing as the rattler strikes. The impact tears at my shoulder. The rattlesnake slides across the cement, writhing crazily for purchase.

Uncle Ray hops up.

"You ought to take that swing on the senior tour," he says, swatting the dust off the seat of his jeans.

My body shakes. This is a new sensation, separate from the tingling focus. Across the pit, the buzzing crescendos as the sliding rattler comes to an abrupt stop amid his annoyed brethren.

Pulling the ladder out so I can reach it, Uncle Ray says, "Heroes first."

Adrenalin sees me effortlessly up the ladder. Back on solid ground, I search for anger, but all I find at first is exhaustion.

I lean the snake stick against the wall.

"That was quite a parlor trick," I say.

Uncle Ray displays all his teeth.

"Somethin' very special. Knew from the get-go you weren't my average customer. Milked old Dubya just before you arrived. Some racehorse will be damn chipper, and so am I."

He is sweating. He wipes his brow with the back of his hand. Settling the Stetson on his head, he says, "I would apologize, but I think you understand. Done flirtin' and fightin', men our age need any excitement we can get. No point in livin' otherwise. Truth is America ain't much interested in rattlesnake farms anymore. So I got to up the ante to keep things interestin'. Yours was a fine performance. Even better than I expected."

I feel my own grin pulling at my face. This surprises me almost as much as Uncle Ray's parlor trick.

"I should throw you back into the pit," I say.

Uncle Ray cackles.

"An irregular way of showing gratitude for what most would see as a priceless memory."

He walks me back through the dusty store. Passing the counter, he scoops up one of the prescription bottles. He gives it a brief shake and drops it in his pocket.

"Constipation. Embarrasses me a little, so I scrape off the sticker."

We shake hands beside the Mustang.

"My brother loved snakes," I say.

It's as if someone else spoke. I look away, but I know Uncle Ray's eyes are on me.

"I'll bet he was something special."

I turn to him. It is possible to find kindness in the hardest faces.

"He lived more than most."

"It would have been a privilege to show him around," says Uncle Ray.

The dry smell of baked earth rises between us.

I tip an imaginary Stetson.

"To a man who confers irregular entertainment from start to finish."

"Quite," he says in a perfect Cockney accent.

The grin vanishes. Maybe it's the light, but he looks pale.

"You and me," he says, "we got to make hay while the sun shines." Boot heels turn crisply in the dust. "We can see the horizon."

I stop for gas fifteen miles down the highway. The pumps hide under a tin covering, but the covering provides only the visual portion of shade.

I am suddenly hungrier than I've been in months. The inside of the station is just big enough to stand in. A rack of snacks presses against the wall. Beside it, a cooler houses nothing but beer.

I pick up three bags of pretzels. The man slouched on the stool is wearing mirror shades so that I can see my loopy grin.

"You're havin' a fine day," he says.

"I stopped at Uncle Ray's."

He sits up a little straighter.

"No kiddin'. Havin' a visitor must have startled the shit out of him."

"I'd say he's pretty hard to spook."

"You're right about that. That's one crazy old coot. Been alone in the desert two centuries too long."

"He's got a grandson," I say, though I already know it's not true. I've seen the man's name tag.

Kiowa Jackson pushes his glasses up on top of his head, but not before I see my smile fade.

"Grandson? Ain't nothin' there but him and those rattlers. The two of them grow more alike every year. He's been bitten so many times, he's part rattler himself. He's not stupid, though. Keeps bottles of antivenin handy in case a particularly potent rattler crawls into his bed. Not all the snakes around here are confined to pits."

"Do you know him well?"

"Well enough to look in on him twice a week. Bet he told you his story about the London pharmacist."

"He did."

"Gotta love that accent. Plenty of time to work on it. Medical facilities do their own milking these days. He hasn't been in those pits for ten years."

28

Sarah visited our apartment once a week after I returned from the war. She came on Tuesdays, during her lunch break. She worked in the Boston College admissions office. She brought lunch for both of us—bologna sandwiches usually, but sometimes homemade tuna casserole or mushroom quiche. I had been home two months when she first came to the apartment unannounced. I knew Abby had asked her to look in on me. As she did with everything, Sarah took the job seriously.

We ate at the Formica table in the kitchen, the rusted legs always flaking, the plastic seats always cold. We talked while we ate, about Boston College, or the latest city workers strike, or a recent snowfall.

When we finished, I cleaned up, and Sarah took out a book of poems. When I returned to the table, we read poetry out loud. I didn't tell Sarah that poetry had been ruined for me. I did not want to be ungrateful. I knew she was trying to help in the best way she knew. When I read, I knew she watched me. The poems, I thought, were therapeutic for her.

We took turns reading. Sarah chose the poems before she came, torn paper bits jutting from the pages like ragged shark fins. When she read a passage that moved her, she would fall silent. In the silences, the rattling refrigerator and the knocking radiator shouted at each other. I read my poems without stopping.

At night, Sarah attended Boston College as a student, taking courses toward a graduate degree in English Literature. When we began our Tuesday lunches, the week after New Year 1946, she was wrestling with James Joyce. The professor worshipped the Irish writer. Sarah found Joyce baffling.

"Doesn't the professor explain what Joyce means?" I asked.

Bologna smell hovered between us. Outside, the scentless snow fell past the kitchen window. When the wind gusted, the snow waved like a curtain.

"I'm not sure he can," Sarah said. "When I ask him a question, he smiles in a very professorial fashion and says, 'Keep reaching, and you'll see.'" The angular shoulders hopped. "Probably only Joyce knows for certain. I read that Joyce's wife once asked him why he didn't write something people could read."

"You won't know an honest critic until you get married," I said without thinking, and we both stared out at the snow.

One month into our readings, I opened my designated page to William Butler Yeats's "When You Are Old."

When you are old and grey and full of sleep,
And nodding by the fire, take down this book,
And slowly read, and dream of the soft look
Your eyes had once, and of their shadows deep;

How many loved your moments of glad grace,
And loved your beauty with love false or true,
But one man loved the pilgrim soul in you,
And loved the sorrows of your changing face;

The words were like slaps. I faltered and lost my place.

And bending down beside the glowing bars,
Murmur, a little sadly, how Love fled
And paced upon the mountains overhead
And hid his face amid a crowd of stars.

I felt a hand on my arm.

"It will work," Sarah said.

Falling snow darkened the kitchen and made it seem smaller.

"I want it to work," I said.

"Sometimes wanting isn't enough."

Anger rose like steam through a pipe.

"What does that mean?"

Like Abby, Sarah's face was fine-boned and delicate, the kind of face you wanted to cup in your hands for fear of it breaking. Pale skin added to this fragile air. She brought to mind a tea setting. The women in my life have proved far stronger than the men, but back then, I was still naïve on many fronts.

I knew my anger hurt her, just as I knew I was the tea setting, precariously poised.

"It means wanting isn't the same thing as trying. I want you to try, Pogue."

It was our business, Abby's and mine. But the snow fell like a veil of privacy, and something in me was loosed.

"I want to try, but it's complicated," I said.

"You can make it simple."

It's not just the war. It's an unbending father. It's a brokenhearted mother. It's a brother kicking out into the middle of the river. It is silent Sunday drives, ferrying three crippling versions of loss and haunting questions.

Sarah sat back and folded her hands in her lap. The dark eyes were intent, but the face was smoothed with kindness.

"Try with me. Just say what you feel. Don't worry about getting it right. We'll work together to get it right. Nothing leaves this kitchen. Not even Abby knows. I promise."

I did want to try. I tried to think of words that weren't melodramatic. I addressed the war. It was our immediate problem, and the trouble people recognized.

"I'm afraid to sleep at night. I have dreams. So I come into the kitchen and sit at this table, but I don't turn on the light. I sit in the dark, and I try to think of how I can explain things to Abby. But it's always the same. They can't be explained, at least not in a way that she would understand."

Oh, and one more thing. It's an entire crypt of secrets, sealed tight.

"Why wouldn't she understand?"

Again, just the war.

"The things that happened, they were from another place. But they changed everything in this place."

"Try me," Sarah said.

"When I got back, the first time I went into a bathroom, I just stood and stared."

To her credit, she didn't bother to guess.

"I'd never seen anything so white," I said. "I don't know how long I stood there. We were in a restaurant. Abby sent a waiter to look for me."

I looked down at the open book. There was a photograph of Yeats, taken in 1885. He was young and bookish. I wondered what words he would have chosen to describe the end of Lance Corporal Henry Gaines.

It was as clear as the poet looking up at me. With the war ended, Abby's research trips had resumed. She had returned from St. Croix just three days earlier, buoyant with new discoveries. In a matter of hours, the joy seeped out of her like air from an old balloon. I drained her. Nature was exciting. Nature had a plan. I was silent and drifting without purpose, waiting to be saved by a man with a hot dog cart.

It is hard to properly gauge the importance of things against the weight of a dead man in your hands, but in the end, this was simple.

"I'm not good for Abby."

"You're wrong. You're what my sister needs."

She spoke so fiercely I looked up in surprise.

Perhaps embarrassment made her next words softer.

"When you were gone, Abby and I read the papers first thing every morning, every article, every word. We read every news report about the war, and we read them again and again. One day, I stopped by to see her. We were sitting at this table. I started telling her about an article I'd read that morning, reciting it almost verbatim, and she picked it up at the next word. She would have finished it if we hadn't both started crying." The fierceness was back. "Every day, Pogue. She lived her version of the war every day. It wasn't what you saw, we know that, but it hurt her too. She's trying, Pogue, but she's not perfect. She needs to know you care. Just simple little things, things that let her know you're trying. It's a bleak place to be, trying alone."

This I knew.

"It can make people do desperate things," she said. "*You* have to understand too, and you have to let her know."

Reaching out, I took her hand. It surprised us both. Her fingers were rough.

"You're the only friend I have." Her hand lay inert. The radiator knocked. "I'm grateful for your help."

"I have my own motives. She's the only sister I have."

She gently freed her hand and stood.

"You're the best thing for Abby. You're like poetry. You explain things for her."

"I'm no poet."

"You're no Yeats, but you are a poet."

There was a fondness on her face I had never seen. It made her look vulnerable, all sternness stripped away. I imagined a little girl gazing up at Godfrey Bremser.

Quietly, she said, "If you scratch the shell of a leatherback, it bleeds."

An ambulance passed, siren blaring. For a moment, I was lost. When I looked at Sarah, she was stern again.

"Regret is the sharpest thorn," she said.

After she left, I went to the refrigerator. Pouring myself a glass of milk, I returned to the table.

Sarah had forgotten the book. I sipped the milk, absently fingering the ragged shark fins. Five. We had read four poems.

The poet was anonymous, but he had known the thrall of love. Only experience allows such things to be put to words.

I have since seen this poem many times. It's often included in collections of love poems alongside the heated professions of Byron, Shakespeare, and Shelley, for unlike sea turtles, we need words before we mate. Even after countless readings, the poet's passion blazes undiminished in my ears, though on that first winter morning, the newness of the blaze created its own wind too, a wind run through with fresh hope.

> *When the breeze inflates your two robes of silk*
> *you look like a Goddess enveloped in clouds.*
>
> *When you pass, the flowers of the mulberry tree*
> *drink in your perfume. When you carry the lilacs*
> *that you have gathered, they tremble with joy.*
>
> *Bands of gold encircle your ankles, stones of blue*
> *gleam in your girdle. A bird of jade has made its*
> *nest in your hair. The roses of your cheeks mirror*
> *themselves in the great pearls of your collar.*
>
> *When you look at me I see the great river Yuen flowing.*
> *When you speak to me I hear the music of the*
> *wind among the pines of my own country.*
>
> *When a horseman meets you at dusk he thinks*
> *it is already dawn, and brutally he brings his*
> *horse to a standstill.*
>
> *When a beggar beholds you, he forgets his*
> *hunger.*

I watched the snow fall, and then I got up and put on my coat. It took three hours, but I found what I was looking for.

When Abby came home, the lilacs were on the kitchen table. We had no vases, so I arranged them in a pickle jar. A single shark fin protruded from the book.

Abby was tired. I saw it the second she stepped in the door. I kissed her cold cheek and followed her into the kitchen, where she placed her satchel, its tan leather sides swollen by research papers and books, on one of the chairs.

She sat in the other chair, turning the pickle jar slowly. Her face was still brown from the sun, but when she looked at me, I saw dark rings under her eyes.

"Sarah," she said.

I said nothing. I already knew the dark rings would win.

"We can't afford fresh lilacs in January. Where did you get them?"

"Mahoney's. They gave me a serviceman's discount."

I regretted the admission before it left my mouth.

"How did you get there?"

"I walked."

She looked out the window. The dusting of snow on her coat hadn't started to melt.

"We can't afford extravagance," she said. "I thought you were practical."

"Not always."

"Well in this case, you needed to be." She pushed the pickle jar back to the middle of the table, squaring it with both hands so the front of the jar faced her. "I appreciate what you did, but we need to work on bigger things."

Sometimes it's impossible to know where to stand.

Abby nudged the book with a finger.

"You had lunch and read poetry, and then you went for a long walk."

It embarrassed me, but I still very much wanted to try.

"Yes. We also talked about us."

"You could take classes. Finish the business degree you started before the war. You used to think that was important."

"You're right," I said.

Abby tapped the paper marker.

"Are the poems good?"

The lilacs erupted from the pickle jar as if greeting a summer day.

"Some of them are beautiful."

My wife's face was bare as the snow. She pushed the book away.

"Poetry isn't life," she said.

That night when I came into the kitchen, I turned on the light. The pickle jar was in the drying rack. The lilacs were in the trash under the sink.

I sat at the table. Opening the book, I read the poem on the page. It was W. H. Auden's "As I Walked Out One Evening." Sarah had read it slowly the week before, giving me time to absorb Auden's truths. When Sarah finished, she said nothing. She pushed the book across the table so I could take my turn. But I had not missed the changes on her face as she read, passing tics, not quite sadness, not quite fear, something more subtle and difficult to discern, in retrospect the hardest emotion of all for youth to recognize.

I removed one lilac from the trash and laid it on the table.

For the first time in my life, I looked closely at a lilac. At our wedding, I had been distracted. I had noticed the lilacs, but I had not really seen them.

Their leaves are shaped like hearts.

On a Tuesday three months later, Sarah flew into the apartment. She stood in the foyer gasping for air, and then she threw her arms up in the air and cheered. It was so out of character it made me laugh.

"I met someone who likes plank feet," she said.

In the kitchen, Sarah told me about Benjamin. He was an engineer, born and raised in Philadelphia until a new job brought him to Boston. He was funny and smart and had hair that was curly and soft as a baby's. He loved poetry and literature, and he was equally baffled by James Joyce. He was taking the same course Sarah had taken. They met when he came to the admissions office with an enrollment question.

Sarah laughed. It was a sound like a bird in spring.

"Can you imagine taking Joyce for no reason?" she said.

We ate peanut butter and jelly sandwiches. I was happy for Sarah, and I told her so, but after she left, I sat quietly. Through the half-open window, I heard the shouts of children playing. I realized it was the first warm day of spring, but I realized something else too. We had read no poetry.

I knew it was time to move forward. Just as I knew I would never read poetry with anyone again.

29

You feel Galveston Bay before you see it, an invisible wall, moist and cool. I pass the port, massive cranes and container ships vaulting into the sky, poised to carry on the world's commerce. A magazine writer once described me as a captain of commerce, a ridiculous bit of hyperbole. Now I know that though I labored mightily at its feet, commerce never really interested me at all.

Galveston's industry falls away. I drive along an empty two-lane road paralleling the bay. Dunes undulate alongside the road, seductively smooth. A scattering of thready clouds nap in blue sky. The Mustang's tires hum happily.

The sandy parking lot appears as a gap in the dunes. I park and step out into the sunshine. The morning is crisp, more like fall than early summer. Someone has dropped a brown lunch bag. The boy who might be the owner is sprinting toward a boardwalk that arcs up over the dunes, his backpack open. It is too late for a rescue. Screeching gulls rise and fall above the bag, tearing it to pieces. The lottery winner flies off with an entire donut.

Three school buses are parked in the lot. A banner is draped across the side of one of the buses, a bed sheet adorned with colorful splotches, which, on closer inspection, become fish. Blue and yellow letters proclaim *Sea Camp Rocks!* There are children's handprints too. The handprints scratch at my memory, but I can't recall what I should remember.

I follow the jumble of footprints to the boardwalk. The wood is worn and redolent with the smell of creosote. Two feet wide, it barely holds its own in the sands, Homer's raft upon the sea. Even on this still morning, tiny rivers of sand spill across the wood. That nature is always in motion adds spring to my step.

At the end of the walkway, backpacks and piles of clothing rest in tidy circles in the white sand. The beach swarms with children. This turns me springier still.

A boy greets me. He might be six. He's already been for a swim; a sandy towel is draped around his chicken-wing shoulders.

"Got sea snot in my nose. It burns."

He regards me, a finger working dexterously inside a nostril.

"That's the salt," I say.

"Yeah." The finger switches nostrils. "You someone's grandpa?"

"No."

He falls in slow step beside me.

"What are you doing here?"

"I stopped to see the water."

"We're here with Sea Camp."

"That's wonderful. I saw your banner. It's a really good painting."

"I drew the angel fish."

"The angel fish was my favorite."

He nods as if he already knew this.

I totter through the sand. He appears to glide above it.

"We're learning about sea turtles."

My heart skips.

My escort executes a fierce snort. He consults the stringy mucus in his hand.

"I wonder how they get the sea snot out of their noses," he says.

"They actually get rid of salt through their eyes. They cry tears."

"You can't pick your nose with a flipper."

I smile down at him.

"You would be a good scientist."

"How come?"

"Scientists look at things and think about how they might work."

"Why are your eyebrows so thick?"

"They're actually caterpillars."

"No, they're not. Caterpillars can crawl away."

"See for yourself and decide. You're already a scientist."

I lean down. He takes a good look. I wonder for a moment if he is going to reach up and give me a good yank.

Instead he reaches to take my hand.

"You're hairy," he says. "The sea snot was on my other hand."

I wonder if anyone is looking, a strange man holding a boy's hand, but everyone seems preoccupied with their own business.

"I'm Alec," he says, swinging our hands.

"I'm Pogue."

"My mom carries Kleenex."

I pull out my handkerchief. Alec takes it and gives another hearty blow.

He holds the handkerchief out.

"Keep it," I say. "It's a present."

I see now that the children are divided into groups. It doesn't seem possible that so many bodies arrived in three buses. Halfway down the beach, one group squirms toward the dunes on their stomachs. A teenage boy walks between the squirming forms, shouting.

"They're turtles. That's Counselor Mark. I was a turtle until I got saltwater up my nose."

Drawing close, I see that Mark wears a white T-shirt adorned with the same logo on the banner. All around him, children bump resolutely forward on their forearms.

Grinning, he shouts, "Remember, no hands! Pull with your forearms and elbows!" He picks up a shell and throws it toward a driftwood log thirty yards up the beach. "That's where you're going to nest."

The squirming mass moans as one, but they continue bumping forward.

"Army crawl!" Mark shouts. "When you get to the driftwood, start digging!"

"You should try it," says Alec. "It's super hard."

"Did you start in the water?"

"That's how I got sea snot."

The first children reach the driftwood. Mark trots over to them.

"Sea turtles don't have hands, so how do they dig a hole? With their elbows!"

Another communal groan rises from the beach. Several children rise to their knees to dig.

"Hey, guys! You're a sea turtle. A sea turtle is too heavy to lift herself off her stomach. If your elbows don't work, dig with your feet. You need a hole three feet deep."

Alec has tugged us close enough to discern individual complaints.

"Owwwwww."

"No way I'm going to dig three feet!"

"How much *loooonger*?"

"I'm glad I'm with you," Alec says.

"One more minute of digging!" Counselor Mark smiles at me. "But remember, sea turtles can spend three hours just digging."

Frog-smooth legs sweep futilely at the sand. The beach reverberates with expulsions and grunts. Mark consults his watch. Finally he claps his hands.

"Done!"

As one, the children go limp in the sand. A few sit up, casting sad eyes on their slight indentation in the sand.

"Okay! Next step! We'll pretend you actually dug a hole three feet deep. Now we're going to pretend to lay a hundred eggs in the hole."

"Pooping out eggs," says Alec.

Most of the children look at each other, hoping for direction. A few perform desultory frog kicks.

Mark claps his hands.

"All done! Now you need to fill in the hole, crawl back to the water, and swim all day!"

Not one body moves.

Mark grins.

"How does it feel to be a sea turtle?"

"Tiiiiiired."

"Who does all this work?"

"The girls!"

"That's right. And what do the male turtles do?"

"They stay in the ocean!"

Alec says, "Men don't lay eggs."

Counselor Mark is serious about education.

"Biologists need to find the eggs after the turtles cover them up so they can take them someplace safe where the raccoons can't eat them," he says. "How do you think the biologists find the eggs under the sand?"

"With an egg detector?"

"I've got sand in my butt."

"The biologists on this beach get help from Ridley. Ridley is a dog. A terrier with a nose for turtle eggs. First they trained him to find dog treats in the sand. Then he learned to find turtle eggs on top of the sand. Now he can find eggs buried three feet deep."

I am probably the only one who hears this last tidbit, for the entire group is chattering as one.

Mark turns to me.

"Lots of them have dogs," he says. "They like turtles, but they love dogs."

Some children love turtles.

"Turtles aren't much for chasing balls," I say. "What kind of turtles nest here?"

"Kemp's ridley. It's actually a real success story. They used to be the most critically endangered of the seven sea turtle species. Eight years ago, they only found six nests along all the beaches in Texas. Last year, they counted 128 nests, and there were probably a lot they didn't find."

He really cares. I like him even more.

"Thank you for teaching them," I say. "You're very good at it."

"Thanks. I'm not sure how much they'll remember, other than the work."

"You'd be surprised."

I look down. My hand dangles empty.

When I look back at Mark, he is no longer smiling.

"They've been around for four million years, but we nearly wiped them out," he says, sounding mildly puzzled.

I buy a dozen steamed clams and return to the same beach an hour before sunset. Since this morning, someone has squared four stakes in the sand, stringing them together with caution tape. One end flutters loose. I tie it again, carefully avoiding the sand between the stakes. Abby once told me of a beach in Mexico where tens of thousands of Kemp's ridleys came ashore, an incomprehensible armada of life. One hundred and twenty eight nests does not seem like cause for great celebration.

I sit beside the nest, the caution tape performing faint snaps in the lukewarm offshore breeze. Small waves beat against the now empty beach. Looping forward, their crests leave wispy trails in the air. There is no sign of the morning's frenzy. The beach has been smoothed by the wind. In the waning light, the water assumes a bruised blue.

The briny smell of clams rises from the box. There's a partition for rice and a small salad too. The box warms my lap. Somehow I have managed to misplace the plastic fork and knife. I eat with my fingers and listen to the waves.

One night, Sean woke me. It was early July, our second summer in Sharpes.

"Get up, Pogue."

Rising on an elbow, I looked at the clock on the dresser between our beds.

"It's the middle of the night."

"You can tell time. Get up."

My brother had defeated the college bully. He had ridden the enormous leatherback. He possessed the talisman. Janie Clayton had taken her top off for him. I no longer questioned him. We pushed out the screen and slipped out the window.

Sean rode my bicycle to the beach. I sat on the handlebars. It was five miles. I was glad I had put on my windbreaker. The bridge across the Indian River arched steeply, but my brother pedaled effortlessly. Below us, through the grill work, gulls slept on rusted iron beams. Far below them, the dark river moved.

The beach was as black as the river; the sand cold beneath our feet.

Talking was difficult on the bike. Now I said, "I hope Mom and Dad don't find out."

Sean didn't look at me. His eyes swept the beach.

"Mom would understand."

"What are we doing?"

He sat down.

"Waiting."

The stars on the horizon winked fuzzily like coins at the bottom of a river. I watched the waves break, fizzing lines of white in the darkness. My eyes winked too.

Sean shook me roughly.

"It's happening," he said.

I clambered groggily to my feet.

"It's dark," I mumbled. "What am I supposed to see?"

"*Look*, Pogue."

The hatchlings spilled from the nests, perfect elliptical stones erupting from the sand. They moved forward in small thrusts, comical but efficient progress, their perfect flippers tossing tiny bits of sand.

When I finally remembered to breathe, I released my breath quietly, as if my noise would alter their plan.

"How did you know?" I whispered.

"Cotton told me."

"Cotton?"

"You dumb *and* deaf?"

"How did he know?"

"Ask him."

But I didn't really care about Cotton or reasons. Standing beside my brother, watching the scuttling turtles, my heart soared. It was a luminous sight, the tiny humped backs bobbing toward the low slash of sea. It was birth and hope. I didn't see it in those terms then, but some instinct inside me thrilled to the glory of the moment, the world continuing on. I wondered what the ocean looked like to the hatchlings as they scrabbled over the sand. It must have looked like all there was in the world.

There are times in your life where you find yourself in the one place you want to be.

"I wish Mom could see this."

"Shit!" said Sean.

I turned, frightened. That same instant, I heard the wing beats and the first raucous cry.

The gulls fell on the turtles with cheerful savagery, plucking them up by flipper, head, and shell. As the gulls rose, the turtles dangled from their beaks like dark amulets, flippers swimming through the air. Sean was running, yelling, and swinging wildly at the gulls rising easily out of reach. After he ran on, the gulls fell to the sand behind him.

I ran too, swinging haplessly. The first hatchlings reached the water, and I shouted at the gulls with both hatred and triumph, and then I saw how the waves pushed the little shells back; before the wave even receded, the gulls fell on them. I ran into the water. I was crying and screaming, made furious by futility. Wings beat about my ears. I felt a sharp pain on the top of my head.

In the end, not one hatchling made it to the sea. The gulls wheeled off. The waves hissed and sighed.

Sean panted beside me, fists still clenched.

"Fucking Pliny should have seen *that*," he said.

Four weeks later, on a still August afternoon, my brother again waved his arms wildly over his head, this time from the middle of the Indian River. He waved only briefly, and then he disappeared. His body was never recovered, but a local trapper killed the alligator. At least he claimed it was the same gator. He brought the reptile to our house two days later, dragging it behind his pickup, its snout tied to the trailer hitch by twenty feet of rope so that when he first turned up our drive, I thought the alligator was performing a death roll behind the truck.

My father ran out of the house. I heard him shouting at the trapper, but my mother was already right behind him. In an instant, the anger of the men evaporated. They stood mute in the bright sun as my mother screamed and kicked the carcass, the sound like a baseball bat striking a sack of sand. Finally my father pulled her away. I watched from our bedroom window, limbs frozen, paralyzed by the greatest mistake of my life.

That evening, a doctor I had never seen came to our house. I was sitting on the porch steps when he arrived. He touched my head gently as he stepped past.

After he left, my father came out and sat beside me. He sat for a long time, but he said nothing. Finally he stood and went back inside.

That night, I pushed out the screen and crawled out the window, spied only by a crescent moon hanging like a fish hook in the sky.

When I returned, the lights were on in the front of the house. Sweating and dirty, I slid back through the window. I crept to the bedroom door and slipped into the hallway. Why I did this, I don't know, but I tiptoed down the hallway, staying close to the wall. Leaning out slightly, I glimpsed my parents, sitting still and silent in the front room. In the lamplight, their faces shone like wax dummies. For the first time, I saw them for what they really were, flesh and blood vessels, wed to the same rutted path as everyone else.

Just before I reached my bedroom door, I heard a chair scrape.

"God," said my father, and then I heard the rapid beat of footsteps, and I only just shut the bedroom door behind me as he passed, his shuddering gasps like a child's, and then their bedroom door slammed, and I heard the sound of things falling and then breaking glass.

Somehow I slept, my sleep shot through with sweet smells. The torment woke me just before dawn. I went into the kitchen to get a glass of milk.

When I turned on the light, my father stood blinking, dish rag in his hand. The counters were covered in white. It looked as if someone had opened a hundred-pound bag of flour with a chainsaw.

"What happened?" I asked, though I didn't want to know.

"Your mother was baking."

Because he looked away from what he did not want me to see, I saw it immediately.

The pie rested alone on a shelf above the stove, in the only spot that wasn't covered in baking aftermath.

I did not have to ask the flavor—the evidence was everywhere—but for some reason, my father felt obliged to tell me.

"Key lime," he said.

"Is Mom okay?"

"No."

I poured the milk as quickly as possible, using a dirty glass in the sink. I waited for my father to admonish me, but he had returned to his mopping and his own demons.

My mother served the pie at dinner that night, carefully cutting a piece for my father and me. We ate it in silence, the pie like glue on the roof of my mouth, and said nothing when we finished, for my mother had gone to her room.

The next night when my mother went to serve the pie again, it was gone, nothing but the pie tin, scraped clean.

"I finished it at lunch," my father said.

"You must have liked it," my mother said.

"I liked it very much."

My mother smiled.

"Like father, like son," she said, and my father looked away.

That night, I had the first dream of my life. I dreamt I was in a bakery, with shelf upon shelf of pies. I was starving. I shoved the pies into my mouth as fast as I could, but no matter how many I ate, I was still hungry. My father was in the bakery too, but I did not ask him for help. I knew he hated sweet things.

The last of the clams gripped in coagulating butter, I rise from the sand. In the twilight, I take off my shoes, setting them side by side. I lay my folded trousers and shirt on top of them.

I stand at the water's edge in my boxers. When I step forward, the Gulf waters swirl about my ankles. The air is cool, but the water is warm, as if the sun, lowering itself into the Gulf, is transferring its fire to the water.

My first strokes are jerky, my body struggling to recall ancient motions. I swim with my head up. The small of my back clenches. Terror presses its heavy head against my chest.

I am lucky; beyond the small waves, the water is sheet smooth. I force my face into the water. The world goes to shadow, and salt stings my eyes, but the pressure on my back eases, and my crawl becomes less a progression of clumsy thrusts and more of a unified stroking. I focus on kicking hard. My legs burn, and the burning quickly leaps to my lungs. Lifting my head, I note the red sun hovering mere inches above the horizon, but I am only dimly aware of its presence. What I see are hatchlings tumbling forward, my mother, hunched before a towering pile of pots and pans, my father gazing out a window, quietly thinking his own thoughts. We have no choice but to forge ahead.

The water goes dark. I did not account for the sun setting so fast.

I keep swimming. Eighty-five strokes, but it is no game. I count the strokes off, throwing each arm forward like a punch, striking the dark water with equal parts fury and fear. Once, swimming was as thoughtless as breathing. I slipped seamlessly through a medium that was barely there. Now every molecule of that medium fights me, refusing to release my arms, drawing my legs down, forcing itself rudely into my mouth. I fight back, kicking harder. It is foolish, I know it. I cannot afford such wasted energy. An inferno rages in my chest. Eighty-five strokes is too many. I have lived too long. I feel the water gripping me, pulling me down.

When I reach my goal, I stop so suddenly inertia swings my legs under me. My head goes under too. Clawing furiously, I thrust my head above the surface. I hear someone gasping. Salt burns my throat. I roll onto my back and kick.

I don't drown. Settling into a scissors kick, I jerk back to shore like an overturned frog.

I spend ten minutes wandering the beach in my boxers, shaking uncontrollably, until I finally locate the dark heap of my clothes. If not for the glow of the Styrofoam box, I wouldn't have found them at all.

I am still shaking when I slip into bed in a motel room that smells of raspberry air freshener.

Again the Japanese serve me tea, but this time, I am not alone. I sit at the table where I always sit, but this time, Counselor Mark joins me. Other linen-topped tables rest in the courtyard too. With horror, I see they are occupied by children. Alec waves soberly.

I try to stand, but Mark gives me a knowing smile and places his hand firmly on my forearm. When the marines start shooting, the bullets don't touch us.

He nods approvingly as the dying children crawl slowly past our table on their stomachs.

"A sea turtle has no hands," he says.

Terror wakes me. I don't want to go back to sleep. I am shaky and nauseous. I turn on the bedside light and rummage through the satchel.

I read for a time, but words don't distract me. Putting the book down, I pick up the photograph. I don't know why I look at it—I am familiar with its every detail—but sitting, propped up against the pillows, it feels good in my hand.

It occurs to me, for the countless time, that the *National Geographic* photographer has done a remarkable job. The leatherback hatchling swims through the Caribbean shallows, taking first tiny flight above a field of white sand. Its eyes are dark and unreadable, but its scaly head thrusts resolutely forward in the green shallows, the ravenous cries of the gulls already forgotten. The turquoise waters clasping its tiny form are clear and lovely, but at the far edges of the photograph, the waters drift into shadow.

Now that I have seen into the shadows, I admire the leatherback even more.

30

A week after Sean died, my father sent me to the store. My father must have thought that keeping me busy was the best thing, though he didn't need to ask me. I did my chores and Sean's chores too, and when I finished, my father assigned me tasks no sane person would do, like picking the weeds that sprouted along the perimeter of our dirt yard. It took me two full days. I pulled every last weed, sweating in the hot sun, and I had started moving into the jungled foliage when my father came out and gently raised me to my feet. He led me inside and served me cold lemonade. It must have been my father's plan, because during the day, my mother sat in the living room staring at nothing.

On this particular afternoon, my father sent me to the store for a ten-pound bag of flour, for every evening, on some invisible signal, my mother woke from her stupor with a start and fell furiously to baking. On this day, she already had four pies lined neatly on various shelves and windowsills, but my father knew what she needed.

Leaving the store, the bag hauling down on my arms, I passed two men I didn't know sitting in chairs outside the door. They'd been playing dice, but they were taking a break.

"Still cain't shake it," one said as I passed.

I slowed.

"Shake what?" said his friend.

"That gator attack."

The world went black. I stopped on the sidewalk, trying to feel my feet. I was now twenty yards away, but my hearing was sharp then.

"Cain't imagine," the first man said, "takin' you down, black as midnight, spinnin' and twistin' and turnin' in a hurricane of bubbles. Musta been terrifyin', bein' shook like a rag doll, knowin' what it is, maybe wishin' you didn't know, maybe feelin' pain, maybe not, but knowin' for sure you're a goner. Don't know what's worse."

"What d'ya mean?"

"Dyin' or drownin'. Had a cousin whose boy nearly drowned. Boy couldn't swim a lick, but he jumped off the dock anyhow. Went straight to the bottom." The man picked up a dice, turning it slowly between his thumb and forefinger. "Asked the boy about it a few months later."

I yearned with all my heart to walk away, but I might as well have stood in a bucket of cement.

"Yeah?"

"Said he stood upright on the bottom in the muck, like you and I would stand in the street, and just looked up. Said at first it was only a little uncomfortable cuz he'd gulped a big mouthful of air. Said he sipped that air in his mouth slow as he could, but pretty soon, it felt like someone had worked their fist into his throat, and the burnin' that started up was terrible. Said if he could have, he would have torn his own chest apart to finish it quicker. But you know what scared him the most?"

The storyteller put the dice back on the table, pausing a dramatic beat.

"He said bein' down there felt like bein' in the loneliest place in the world. He said lookin' up into the dark water was like all the light had gone out of the stars. That boy, he didn't have a third-grade education, but he sounded like Walt Whitman. Gave me the willies."

Only then did I realize I was staring at the men guppy-eyed. I kept staring as the storyteller fixed his eyes on me.

"Strange and unsettlin'," the storyteller said to his companion. "Most boys are dumb as stumps, as God is our witness."

I threw up right there, splattering the sidewalk with key lime pie. I was running before I finished. Only when spots started dancing before my eyes did I realize I was holding my breath.

When I came home, my mother was sleeping. She had never slept during the day before, not even after the nights she worked, but back then, I did not attribute it to the pills.

My father had pulled a second chair onto the porch. He sat, tapping the arm of his chair with a broken fingernail.

"Sit down, Henry."

I lowered myself reluctantly into the empty chair.

"We need to talk about something," he said.

I wondered what he wanted to talk about. I had recounted the details to my father, though not to my mother. The two of us sitting on my bed, I told him how Sean, gripping the raft, had kicked his way out to the middle of the river, how the bright sun smashing down on the water had nearly erased the shadow passing off the end of the dock so that I was unsure how, in my confusion and doubt, I had said nothing, his meek and indecisive son. I said what I could, and then I cried, great sobs that made me want to double over, but I sat up straight for I wanted the full impact of the blows I knew I deserved, for I had killed my brother.

My father let me cry. When the worst of it had passed, he took me in his arms and pressed his lips to my ear.

"Some things," he said, "are beyond us."

Sitting on the porch, his voice was hushed again.

"Henry, the trapper asked if I wanted him to cut the gator open."

Something inside me lurched.

My father sat very still. His palms rested flat on the arms of the chair, but I saw how the hand closest to me shook, the faintest quiver in the blunt fingers. My father looked out toward the river that had changed our lives, and then he turned to me.

The heat made a ticking in my head.

I felt my father wanted me to speak, but I was afraid that merely opening my mouth would see me sick again.

His fingers were tapping now. He looked away again, but I did not. I stared at his profile. In that moment, it seemed he had aged a hundred years. His mouth was slack so that the skin under his jaw sagged, the bristly hairs there gray, and on his cheek a quarter-inch purplish line ended in a latticework scattering of veins like dead branches in the finest reaches of a tree.

His voice shook.

"I told him not to, Henry. I couldn't bear it."

A mosquito settled on my father's cheek. It fed without interruption.

The two of us sat silent, neither one brave enough to face the truth.

Softly, my father said, "He was just a boy."

31

"You didn't call."

I see the banner with its small handprints. I remember what escaped me. *Call me tomorrow.*

I sit on the edge of the bed, my muscles aching. I wonder how it might be if we were allowed to give just one mistake back.

"I'm so sorry. I've gotten forgetful."

"It would be easy if you had a cell phone. You can use it any time. You wouldn't have to find quarters."

"I don't know how to use a cell phone. I'd need someone to teach me."

"Sometimes you have to do things for yourself."

Now a new voice.

"No more lectures for you, Mr. Whithouse."

"Hello, Sarah." I try to sound cheery, but hurt is easily transferable. "Is that a lifetime guarantee?"

"We know you're traveling. It's nice of you to call *any time.*"

A faint protest. Then, louder, "Nuh-uh."

"You certainly *will,* young lady," says Sarah. "Where are you?"

"Galveston."

"Is everything all right?"

"Everything's fine."

"You sound tired."

I went swimming. I swam a little farther than the length of a community pool, and I almost drowned. Twelve hours later, I feel like I've just gone fifteen rounds.

"Maybe a little road weary and disappointed in myself. I didn't know it was possible to forget so many things."

"You've never remembered to be easier on yourself. I'm sorry Tesia was impolite. She's not *usually* like that."

Again, a brief storm of hissed protest. The vision of a young girl, chin thrust forward with righteous indignity, restores some of my spirit.

"I deserve a lecture. I didn't keep my promise. I need to be told."

"Whatever the case, I know one stubborn young lady who needs to learn how to forgive *and* apologize. She's not really upset with you anyhow."

"Yes, I *am*," this time clear as a bell. I know she leaned into the phone, and this makes me smile all the more.

"I'll give you the phone if you apologize and promise to behave. She's upset about something else."

"What is it?"

As if we talk every day.

"She has bullfrogs in her class."

"I know," I say.

"You do?"

The surprise is so genuine I laugh.

"We've shared a few things."

"Is that so? And how many times have you called, Mr. Whithouse?"

I do not have to remember.

"Three."

"Well, that's a surprise to *one* of us."

"I like talking to her. She reminds me why I'm alive."

The truth of it startles me. Distance hums between us.

"Please don't be so difficult."

"What?"

"I'm sorry, Pogue. Hold on a moment. You need to come here, young lady." Footsteps. "Would you like to tell him?" A curt reply. "I don't see why in the world he likes talking to you."

"Mrs. Huber's bullfrogs died," Sarah says to me.

"How?"

"Mrs. Huber keeps the aquarium on a table. The legs sit in coffee cans filled with water." Sarah's voice softens a notch. "Someone let the cans go dry. Ants. When Mrs. Huber came in in the morning, it was too late."

I see the bullfrogs with nowhere to go, the ants having their way. It is not hard to imagine.

"So we're sad for the moment."

This outbreak is noisy and prolonged.

Sarah lets it play itself out and then says, "Everyone's heart heals eventually."

I hear Tesia clearly.

"Not mine."

So young and so right.

She is on the phone.

"I get to class early. I saw them first. Mrs. Huber hadn't even noticed. They were just sitting still like everything was normal. I could see them opening their mouths. Only they were black."

"I'm so sorry."

"The ants ate out their *eyes,* and they were still just sitting there."

"I'm sure that after a while they didn't feel anything."

"Mrs. Huber said that too. I don't believe it. How can you be alive and not feel anything?"

I can't find any bookstore in the small towns I drive through. At a gas station in Patterson, Louisiana, I stop and ask to borrow a phone book. I write down the library's address.

The library sits, enfolded by enormous oaks, beside a lake. The largest oak arcs over the wood shingle roof like a curious giant. Its limbs are as big around as a cask. Several picnic tables rest close to the lake.

The library is small and empty, except for the young librarian. She is around twenty by my guess. She wears a kelly green cardigan sweater over a white button-down shirt. Thick glasses round her eyes slightly. I wonder if she was hired on the spot.

As soon as I step inside, I know why she's wearing the sweater. It's meat-locker cold.

"I'm sorry," she says, when I reach the counter. "The thermostat's stuck."

"I like the cold. I've seen enough hot days, though I don't think I've seen a more magnificent oak."

When she smiles, the glasses slip down her nose. Beneath the failing eyes rest perfect white teeth.

She nudges the glasses up.

"It's close to three hundred years old." The smile fades a little. "The tree people think it's dying, though. They're planning on cutting it down. Otherwise we'll have bigger problems than a thermostat."

Death is what concerns me. When I explain what I need, the young librarian beams.

"That's sweet. I have the perfect book for you." Round eyes peer at the computer screen while her fingers peck at the keyboard. "And surprise, it's in. People around here aren't much for reading. Aisle four is the children's section."

There are only four aisles. I find the book quickly, but when I return to the counter, things don't go as I hope.

"You're lucky you came when you did. I was just about to close. Library card?"

"I don't have one. At least not for this library."

"Do you live in St. Mary Parish?"

"No. I'm traveling."

"Oh." She actually hunches down into the collar of her shirt. "I'm *really* sorry. We don't let books out without a local library card."

I stand in the arctic cold, lost. The young librarian is a quick thinker.

"There's a bookstore on Ash Street. I bet they carry it. They're open an hour later than we are. Until seven." She jots the number on a piece of paper with an apologetic smile. "It's a small town, and a smaller literary world. You can call from here. I won't even shush you."

I look toward the door. I see only a water fountain and a foldout chair beside it.

"Is there a pay phone?"

Rummaging in her purse, the girl produces a cell phone.

"I'll call for you. The owner has a terrific selection of children's books. I'll have her put it aside." She taps out the number with the same keyboard efficiency, smiling at me. "Mrs. Warner was my second-grade teacher. The mystery writer John D. MacDonald had a theory that there were ten thousand people in the south, and if you knew one of them, you knew them all. I wish I'd known him, but he died three years before I was born. Travis McGee was quiet, but he could take care of himself."

I knew John D. MacDonald as well as I knew his South, but she is on the phone, a purple nail tapping the counter.

She hangs up, frowning.

"Maybe she had early dinner plans. The truth is she closes and opens when she chooses. We don't have any of the big chains here. Folks won't allow it. We're firm in our stances but short in our conveniences. I'm really sorry."

"It's fine. There's always tomorrow."

No, there isn't. Not at my age, not at any age.

The book sits on the counter. She places a hand gently on the cover.

"I'll put it back."

"Thank you."

I am passing the water fountain when she calls out.

"Sir?" Touched with eagerness, her smile is even prettier. "I have an idea."

Patiently, she shows me how to make a call.

The picnic table rests beneath one of the smaller oaks. Before I sit, I run my hand over the ancient trunk. A finger catches on a piece of bark protruding like an errant shingle. It breaks off easily, falling to the ground at my feet. Nothing is entirely strong and solid, nothing entirely weak and fragile.

I sit on the wood bench, the phone in front of me. We stare at each other, one modern apparatus, one not so. I review what the librarian told me. My fingers fumble over the tiny buttons, but somehow the call goes through.

Sarah answers.

"I hope you're not calling to make amends, Mr. Whithouse. That's someone else's job, and she's upstairs getting ready for bed. Bedtime matters to *some* of us."

I explain my purpose.

"Bedtime can wait," says Sarah.

"Thank you. I promise it won't take long."

"Take all the time you like."

The lake is covered with whitecaps. The wind is strong enough to make the smaller limbs creak.

"Hi, Pogue! That's weird. I was brushing my teeth. One hundred strokes, up and down, and don't forget the gums. It takes a long time, so I was thinking of you. And now you're here."

"I was wondering if I might read you a bedtime story."

"You sound funny."

"I'm a little nervous."

"Why?"

"I've never read a story before."

"It's easy. Just read like you normally do in your head, only say it out loud. Sarah does funny voices, but since it's your first time, you can just read."

"Thank you."

"Wait a minute." A long scraping, followed by the sound of muffled blows. "Dusty cushions. You don't listen to a bedtime story standing up. It's an ottoman. My legs are hanging over the end, but that's okay. They didn't used to, but I'm taller."

Suddenly I am paralyzed. It is not my business or my child. I haven't even read the story. What if it's not right?

"So," Tesia says, "you start at the beginning."

I push the doubters out of my head.

The Tenth Good Thing About Barney. My cat Barney died this Friday. I was very sad. My mother said we could have a funeral for him, and I should think of ten good things about Barney so I could tell them ...

I am self-conscious at first, but the story is so good that I forget myself. When I finish, I sit silently. Along the shore of the lake, wavelets jostle the *Spartina* and glasswort.

Tesia speaks slowly.

"The bullfrogs were really ugly, but they were very patient, and they never ever asked anyone to hurry. And they always let us pick them up, even though some of us were rough. And they were quiet, except when they were hungry. And they were ruder than Jessica's brother, Nathan. How many is that?"

I count.

"Four," I say.

"Is it good to be rude?"

"It is if you're a bullfrog."

"Good," she says. "You can help."

"They did what they wanted, but they didn't hurt anyone."

"Five."

I look at the oak. It swims slightly. *I know ten good things.*

"We need five more," Tesia says.

"Maybe it's better if you think of the rest. By tomorrow you could easily think of five more."

"*Five thousand* more. But it hurts a little to remember."

"You don't want to forget."

"I guess not. It's a sad story, but it makes you smile too."

Many things are so.

"I know another good thing," Tesia says. "You called."

When I return the book and the phone, the librarian leans toward me.

"You might want to use our rest room."

I do have to use the rest room, though how she knows is a mystery. Washing my hands, I glance in the mirror. I wet a paper towel and dab my face.

She is standing at the front door when I come out. She flicks the lights off when I reach her side.

"It was a good day to be a librarian," she says.

"Thank you for seeing to my appearance."

She holds the door open for me.

"The pen is mighty," she says.

I walk her to her car.

"I'm grateful for what you did. I'm sorry if I kept you."

"I hope your friend liked the book."

"She liked it a lot. I think it helped. It helped me."

She gives me a blinding smile. Again my heart trips. Youth does not realize how breathtaking it is.

"A good children's book really isn't for children at all," she says. "I'm sorry I'm such a stickler for rules."

She traces the ground with the edge of a sandal. Her feet are big; the toes splay out like sausages. The toenails are pale blue. The big toenail has a yellow sun in the middle.

"I painted them Friday night," she says. "Boys around here prefer girls who don't act like librarians."

"You're not a librarian. You're a swan."

She blushes. It is not a creeping blush. It covers her whole face in an instant.

"You've been reading too many children's books," she says.

I shut her door and step back. Behind the wheel, she pulls the sweater over her head. It catches her glasses and they fall off. Extricating herself from the sweater, she looks up at me. Beneath tousled hair, her eyes remain bashful and pleased, and I see what she doesn't yet realize.

Patterson's only book store is closed, but the florist is still open. A boy sits on a bar stool watching me fill out the paper work. He has curly hair, braces, and chipped fingernails. Outside, the sky rumbles.

"Sorry for all the forms," he says.

"Rules are rules."

"Yes, sir, they are." He lifts his eyes to the rumbling and smiles. "I hope you have rain gear."

"I've got an umbrella."

"You might need a slicker. Around here, the rain comes in sideways. You can get a good deal at the army-navy surplus store just down the street."

I watch him.

"Have you ever read *The Tenth Good Thing About Barney*?"

He looks down at his hands.

"I don't read that much."

"What do you like to do?"

"I'm okay at fixing things."

"How old are you?"

"Nineteen."

John D. MacDonald died in 1986.

"You should go to the library," I say. "Ask about the thermostat."

That night it rains. The boy is right. It comes in sideways, hard as the winning run to home plate.

Restlessness rattles inside me. I go to the window and raise the shade. Water streams down the glass. Thunder rumbles, long and distant, a melancholy sound. Putting my palms against the glass, I feel its tremors.

Stare, stare in the basin.

I have not witnessed a rollicking good thunderstorm—the sort that cracks with broken-limb violence and rolls inside your chest in a molasses wave—in fifty years. Fifty years. It doesn't sound possible. Thunder cannonades in somber acknowledgment.

I should be tired. I arrived at the motel after ten, driving three hours from Patterson to Biloxi in a deluge, leaning forward the whole time, the Mustang's wipers swiping frantically at the curtain of water.

It is now half past midnight, but the air's hum has flicked away fatigue. Another thunder clap buzzes the glass, its wild energy leaping into my palms. I lean into the glass with my eyes closed, remembering strange things. Our first look at the river. Hammering the crates together. Janie Clayton's milky white skin. Abby dancing beside the sea.

The motel is two miles from the Mississippi Sound. I drive along the empty boulevard fronting the water. The antebellum mansions are dark, their eyes closed to the rain-lashed sound.

I park the Mustang beside the seawall and sit for a moment in my starchy new raincoat. Not one car appears. The umbrella rests on the passenger seat.

I shrug out of the raincoat. Pushing the door open, I step into the rain. In seconds, my hair and caterpillar eyebrows are doused flat. The rain is warm, and I remember. My feet carry me to the center of the boulevard; heel-toe-heel-toe, I walk the centerline. A voice warns that each step takes me farther from the Mustang. I tell the voice I will not count footsteps. Distance does not concern the young. I may say this out loud.

Raindrops leap prettily on the yellow stripes. Thunder booms merriment above the dark mansions.

I angle back toward the seawall, feeling again the magnetic draw of a great body of water. The seawall rises to my waist. I run my hand along its top, rough cement catching my fingertips.

Someone has placed an empty milk crate beside the wall. I step up gingerly, balancing for a moment. Palms flat, I place a knee on the sea wall and push. Kneeling on the sea wall, I totter precariously, and then slightly, and then not at all. Commanding myself to stand, I push myself to my feet.

Twenty feet below, the beach has nearly eroded away. Black water reaches almost to the seawall. Twenty yards to my left, a dock pokes into the sound. Light posts line the dock. They are replicas of the cast-iron light posts of the thirties, my life now nostalgic decoration. In their diffuse light, Sabots and Boston Whalers swing at their moorings, provided just enough slack to swing with a circling wind. The people who live here know the water.

You'll fall and break your neck. The world is in bed; no one will find you. Even if you don't fall, you'll catch your death of cold. You only have one change of clothes. You only have one life to lead.

The gusting wind pushes against my chest, and rain slaps at my face. I lift my arms slowly, making jerky adjustments like a doddering pilot, until they are raised above my head. Far out in the sound, lightning forks, a bright crack in night's curtain. I stick out my tongue, tasting the salty rain. Water fills my shoes.

I have walked out in the rain—and back in the rain.

I continue, speaking the words aloud. I do not just read them. The rest of the world is sleeping. Mr. Frost's is a lonely poem, but who says joy cannot be found alone?

Lightning tears again at the world's fabric. I am no rogue, but I am the captain of my course.

I sleep until ten. Before I leave Biloxi, I make a stop.

I drive east, the sky, scrubbed clean by rain, a robin's egg blue, the box on the seat beside me.

32

Our mother died three months after Sean. She had been sick for a year, but she used the grief that consumed our house to hide her cancer from my father and me. Only when she asked my father to take her to the hospital did we realize something was wrong.

On the night she died, the world roiled. Outside the hospital room, rain lashed down, and palmettos jumped as if trying to uproot themselves. My mother had slipped in and out of consciousness for two days, the cancer in her brain conducting the last of its black murder. The doctor called our home just after dinner. My father picked up the phone as if it were poisonous, his own face a skull as he listened.

At the last, my mother seemed to rebound. She looked us both over and gave a slow, luxuriant smile like a cat stretching.

"My boys," she said.

I felt as if my neck were welded in place. My mother already looked like the skeleton she would become. I was hypnotized by the transformation. My twelfth birthday was a month away. Beside me, my father made a choking noise. Things moved inside me, looking for a way out.

I thought of how my mother had driven slowly down the road, waiting for my father as he sat out in the darkness. That was my definition of love.

"I'm thirsty, William," my mother said.

I heard the sliding of curtains as my father pulled them aside. Then it was quiet.

"My Henry," my mother said, and then she gave me a mischievous wink. "The Lord won't hold it against me."

I could not imagine any sin she may have committed. At times, I had hated her for it.

"Henry. Don't be hard on your father."

"He'll get the water quick, Mom," I said, though I didn't believe it.

She smiled again. Smiling drew her skin tighter, making her look more like a cadaver.

"So much, so young," she said. "You are my strong son."

I saw my father stumbling through the hallways that smelled of floor polish and rubbing alcohol, a child himself, looking for a nurse. I knew I would have no birthday. My disappointment made me feel dirty.

"I know," she said.

A chill washed through me. I wondered if death made you clairvoyant.

"Know what, Mom?"

Her eyes were shining as they held mine. How could she still love me, after what I had done to her firstborn son?

"Your father's friend," she said. "The other woman."

It made no sense.

"Okay," I said.

"Good. I'm glad we agree." She looked to the door, and then she answered my question. "Confronting your father would have made things worse for all of us. I still love him. He is a good man. I want him to be happy. It's the best you can get from life." I concentrated on my feet, but I knew she was watching me. "And the best you can offer."

I did not understand. My mother knew this.

"You will love," she said.

I started crying. I touched her hand. It was cold as my lunchbox.

"I love you," I said.

"You will love others."

I heard footsteps.

"Henry."

"Yes, Mom."

"You can change things. Be there for your father."

The door opened. My father came to the side of the bed. I looked up at him, but he just stood there, holding the paper cup, and then it slipped through his hands and fell to the floor.

The next night, sitting on the end of the dock watching the black water make its tiny eddies, I heard voices that were not the voices of accusation in my head. I pushed into the piling. A full moon shone overhead, but the river created its own darkness. I was fairly certain I couldn't be seen.

Turning carefully, I saw two figures walking across the silver field. My father walked a few paces ahead, his head bowed forward like a priest coming down the aisle. Mrs. Cooper walked behind him, making no attempt to catch up. She spoke, but I couldn't hear what she said. As I watched, my father fell to his knees. Mrs. Cooper took two quick steps and wrapped my father in her arms. They stayed like that, Mrs. Cooper pressing my father's face against her waist, the two of them swaying together in the night.

The day after our mother's funeral, my father and I went to the grocery store. He walked the aisles so slowly that eventually I left him to get what we needed.

I found him at the front of the store, looking at the notices on the community corkboard. Dozens of messages were scrawled on index cards and torn scraps of paper, thumbtacked to the cork with equal haphazardness, but my father and I saw just one.

Book Fair. Saturday, Noon until Four. E.P. Foster Library. Readers Needed, Please.

My father said, "Just like her to add *please*." His eyes did not leave the card. "I wish I'd listened to her read."

"It wouldn't have changed you."
I don't know how I knew it with such certainty.
My father looked down at me.
"You're right, Henry."

My mother was wrong. There are some things you cannot change. When Matty Simpson's father pulled up to our house that night, I knew why he had come. Two weeks earlier, hunting for snakes in a bramble thicket near the river, I heard Sean's hushed voice. In the ensuing silence, I crept closer. Sean and Matty stood close, and when my brother leaned forward and kissed Matty Simpson awkwardly and delicately on the mouth, I understood in an instant my brother's violence and imperial aloofness.

Certainty, fidelity
On the stroke of midnight pass
Like the vibrations of a bell

W. H. Auden called his poem "Lullaby," but in these words, of course, there is no lullaby at all.

33

My spontaneous night takes its toll. I make it as far as Myrtle Grove, less than three hours of driving. The Mustang's wheels thump over the roadside shoulder warning bumps four times. The fifth time, I find myself half off the road.

In the motel room, I turn on the television. I don't want to sleep at three in the afternoon; I'll wake in the middle of the night.

I'm in Florida now. I feel the change as surely as a sea breeze starting up. This is childish imagination, I know. Florida's soil is no different from the Alabama soil I left just minutes ago, but there is no denying the constriction in my throat and chest, the insidious clench of accusation. I recognize this familiar tormenter, but he is exponentially stronger now. I have crossed into the land of my worst sins. I do not want to be alone with myself at 2:00 a.m.

Giant is on the TV, James Dean and Elizabeth Taylor together again. I saw the movie on opening night in 1956. I didn't like it. James Dean reminded me of everything I was not. This version is in color. I don't think James Dean would like it.

Memory is the unreliable porter; one moment, carrying nothing, the next ferrying frightening clarity. I see the theater as clearly as if I were sitting in it, the soft abrading of the velour seats, the gargoyles on the balconies, and, on the ceiling, an enormous painting of a Buddhist prayer wheel, because this was San Francisco, and Flower Power was just around the corner. A woman sat beside me. Not once during the entire movie did I look at her directly, but I can still tell you her cheeks were sun burnished, and she smelled pleasantly of ginger, and when our forearms brushed, her skin was smooth and shockingly warm. On her opposite side, a man fidgeted constantly. No ginger here. I smell pine, the ubiquitous cleanser of choice.

Adarene Clinch: "Why, Luz, everybody in this county knows you'd rather herd cattle than make love."

Luz Benedict: "Well, there's one thing you got to say for cattle ... boy, you put your brand on one of them, you're gonna know where it's at!"

I try to concentrate on the movie, but my mind keeps returning to the woman. We laughed at the same moments, and when we first brushed, she whispered a soft apology. Late in the movie when our forearms touched, neither of us pulled away. Through her skin I felt her rapid breaths.

I wonder where this woman went when she left the theater, how her life proceeded with the fidgeting man beside her, if indeed he had been her husband, for I never looked at her ring finger.

I suppose what happened was simple, for who hasn't felt the charge of a stranger? Sea turtles mate indiscriminately. Sean told me this, and I didn't forget; random unions are the sort of thing a young boy retains. Sex without romance sees to the continuation of the species. We might follow the sea turtles' lead but for all the complications, tearing off our clothes, and seeing to our species success in elevators, car seats, and secluded park glens.

I had one wanton tryst in my life, electric and real. One morning by the river, Janie Clayton wordlessly took my hand and led me into the bramble. The other kids hadn't arrived. Her bony fingers burned a grove into mine.

She did not pull down her top—I was not my brother—but she kissed me so hard our teeth clacked. Her mouth was so warm I wanted to crawl inside. I would have stood there looping tongues for the rest of my life. I believe she may have felt something too, for when she finally pulled away, we both gasped.

She looked at me, puzzled. Then she smoothed her bathing suit and stepped out of the bramble.

I turn off the TV. Outside, Florida's glare assaults my eyes. Across the street, a monstrous building is going up. A crane sits idle. Men move about the scaffolding. A draped banner proclaims a new mall.

I rummage through the Mustang. I can't find the box. For a queasy moment, I wonder if I left it in the store.

I find it under the passenger seat. I sit in the car and open the box. I've already forgotten most of what the sales girl told me. Wisely, she did advise I get big buttons. I punch them. In my excitement, I'm not sure exactly which buttons I press.

The phone rings loudly. In my panic, I nearly close it shut. Across the street, a drill whines.

"Hello."

It's more of a question.

"Pogue?"

Tesia's voice is loud too. I'm still holding the phone slightly in front of me. It looks like a clamshell. I'm afraid if I put it to my ear, I'll hang up on her.

I bow toward the phone.

"Guess where I am," I say.

"On a runway?"

"No."

"I want you to be in Hyannis."

Who tells us we should hide our feelings? I smile at the clamshell.

"Sarah told you."

"Yep. We're reading *The Hobbit* again. I asked her to. I asked her to read the part about the spiders twice."

"That was brave."

"They're still scary."

"But you faced them."

"I guess. She said you were on a journey too."

"I am."

"Are you in Wyoming?"

"Wyoming?"

"We just learned about Wyoming in school. Real cowboys live there. If you say it slow, it sounds like a question."

"You're right. But no, not Wyoming."

"Too bad. If you were in Wyoming, you could see a rodeo."

I remember that the cell phone has a battery. I wonder how long it lasts.

The drill quits, and a truck starts up.

"I'm in Florida. They have real cowboys in Florida. They used to call them Crackers."

"That's a weird name for a cowboy. Cowboy Crackers. It sounds like a snack."

"Some people say they called them that because of the cracking noise their bullwhips made when they herded cattle." I know now that portions of our conversations make their way to Sarah. "Some people don't use the word anymore because they think it's rude."

"How come it's rude?"

I should explain to your Lordship what is meant by Crackers; a name they have got from being great boasters; they are a lawless set of rascals ...

Sean had been forced to read the passage, a letter to the Earl of Dartmouth, aloud in history class. Having discovered it, it became his mantra. He repeated it often, rolling *a lawless set of rascals* on his tongue as an aficionado rolls a cigar. He often did it to irritate me. *Cotton and me, we're a lawless set of rascals.* I was not a member.

Our family had known Crackers. They were good people. Cracker seemed tame set beside the language I'd heard on the radio.

"Some people think Cracker means the person is poor and uneducated."

"Like white trash?"

I remember the new girlfriend.

"You're supposed to be guessing where I am."

"In Florida. You said so."

I am actually holding my breath. I release it as quietly as I can.

"And?"

"You're sitting outside. You bought a cell phone like I told you."

For some reason, I am still watching myself in the rearview mirror. My deflated face nearly makes me laugh.

"You must be a detective."

"You're on speaker phone. I heard the truck."

I stare down at the phone. It stares right back.

Tesia says, "I knew you'd do it. Sarah said you'd never buy a cell phone."

Now I do laugh.

"She did, did she?"

"She said you'd use a pay phone until the only place to call from was a museum, and then you'd charm the security guard into letting you use the one there."

I smile at the dashboard. I remember Sonny's hearts, etched in the dust.

"Well, be sure to tell her, very politely, that she was wrong."

"I will."

"Politely."

"You said that."

"There's one more surprise," I say.

"What?"

"You'll have to wait until tomorrow, or maybe the next day."

"Good."

"Good?"

"It's good you're full of surprises."

The next morning when I turn on the phone, it buzzes angrily. I flip it open. The instructions are on the screen. Technology has considered consumers like me.

I press the appropriate buttons and listen to the message, Tesia describing the bright yellow truck, and how the deliveryman smelled like dirty laundry, and that the vase was on her bedside table, and that I should always leave my phone on in case there is an emergency call like this one.

And then Sarah telling me how Tesia carried the flowers up the stairs herself, clasped so close that her mother held her elbow since she couldn't see past the end of her nose, and how a lady never forgets her first roses. She pauses, so that at first I think she is finished, and then she speaks slowly, so that someone else might think she is struggling to remember.

Not I, not anyone else can travel that road for you.

When I close the phone, I again speak out loud.

Long have you timidly waded, holding a plank by the shore,
Now I will tell you to be a bold swimmer,
*   To jump off in the midst of the sea, and rise again and nod to me and shout,*
*   and laughingly dash with your hair*

I remember a time when I did such a thing, and the memory is bittersweet, but that is life.

I suppose an old man who recites Walt Whitman is still just an old man, but it feels like something more.

Sarah didn't ask why there were ten roses. Tesia, I knew, had explained it to her.

34

I found the letters, three stacks bound loosely with twine, on a bitter afternoon—February 12, 1953—the ice on the trees so thick that our peaceful Newton, Massachusetts, neighborhood echoed with the rifle shots of snapping branches.

It was the fourth day of a fierce cold snap. I had spent the morning cutting up fallen limbs. It could have waited. The air made my lungs ache, and my fingers stung, the worn work gloves doing little to protect them, but the work felt good. The bite of the handsaw, the burning in my forearms that forced me to switch hands, made me realize how much I disliked spending time on the telephone ushering along the advance of a hot dog empire.

At one point, I looked across the street to see Mr. Ryan mincily negotiating his way along his snowy walkway. He returned my wave with an ungainly salute, picked up the paper, and hustled cautiously inside.

Like most of our neighbors, Mr. Ryan was retired, former chief financial officer at a company I could never seem to remember. In the silence of the fairytale ice world, their oak door clicked shut, but I knew they were still watching me. I had seen Mrs. Ryan several times, standing at the edge of the sitting room curtain. I imagined the conversation taking place inside. *Crazy fool has been out there all morning, sawing like Paul Bunyan. He could buy his own tree-trimming company. That's what happens when you make so much money young. You get strange.*

The thought made me smile. Like many truths, this one was simple. Labor felt good. When I finished cutting up the limbs and stacking them beside the house, I crossed the street and shoveled the Ryan's walkway.

More limbs would fall during the night. With Abby not yet home from Harvard, I searched the house for better gloves. I knew they were somewhere. Abby had bought them for me as a housewarming gift, sturdy leather with the smell of a baseball glove.

The letters were in a backpack I had never seen. The backpack was wedged behind two suitcases in the recesses of a closet in a guestroom still littered with boxes we had yet to unpack. I was already discovering the upshot of success: the house was so big I hadn't yet discovered this closet. There was no reason the gloves would be in this closet, but since I had already poked my head in, I stooped and shuffled to the closet's dark and mildly musty rear. Poking above the suitcases, the small loop of rucksack strap materialized slowly.

I read the letters in the den. There were forty-one. The letters were written over eighteen months. The first letter was penned four months after I returned from the war. They had met nearly a year earlier, but the letters told me their relationship was only professional at first. No doubt there were sparks, but Abby was married, and, at that point, I had done nothing to drive her away. As soon as I read the first two, I knew there were an equal number of letters responding in kind.

The letters smelled faintly of peaches. They were bound with fresh twine.

When I finally lifted my eyes from the final letter's last line, I saw that, beyond the puddle of lamplight, the house was dark.

It's funny what comes to us during the turning points in our lives. When the front door opened, I was thinking of Calvin. I had already returned each letter to its envelope, stacking them again, patting them into place like a blackjack dealer, my wife's smell on my hands.

I heard the jingle, Abby hanging the car keys on the hook by the door. I heard her call my name and make a joke about not paying our electric bill, but I did not answer. What is there to say? We hear these stories again and again—infidelity is as old as time—but they are never more than stories, recountings that make us a little sad for the participants and thankful it's not us.

A ship's clock rested on the desk, a gift from Godfrey Bremser. It kept perfect time, but I was not interested in ship's clocks, so I had paid little attention to it. For some reason, I now found it fascinating. I saw that it was set in a wood casing that opened like a compass. When I moved the casing slowly, the light from the desk lamp crept across the clock face like dawn across the water. I pushed it until it butted up against the stack of letters.

She stood in the doorway. The light in the hall behind her made it difficult to see her face.

In the barest whisper, she said, "If you scratch a leatherback's shell, it bleeds."

It felt as if the air was gone from the room. I gripped the captain's clock, like an old man steadying himself after a long climb up a flight of stairs.

"Sea turtles mate indiscriminately," I said.

I heard the jingling like a departing sleigh. Our house was new, but our cars were still old. The car started, hiccoughed to a stop, started again, and was gone. I sat, wrapped in the ticking of the captain's clock.

The phone rang an hour later. The roads were as icy as the trees. I did not need to read the police report to know she was driving fast.

When I pulled up behind the row of police cars, their lights throwing blue and red into the black woods, the car was being towed away. I watched through the windshield as it passed, the sprawling hood of the forty-six Buick crushed all the way to the backseat.

I carry a flashlight in the glove box. Once a marine, always a marine. A policeman, even younger than me, escorted me past the flares. I trained the flashlight on the gnawed oak and the stained ice at its base.

The stain rose from the ice and lodged in my heart.

The young policeman stared into the woods.

"I'm sorry," he said.

"It's not your fault." I fought to distinguish the proper steps. "My wife?"

"They took her."

He still looked into the woods.

My mind marched methodically like a ship's clock.

"To the morgue."

"Yes, sir."

A radio crackled. I stared at the unrelenting oak. The flares made their barbecue sizzle.

"You should always try," I said.

At the morgue, I acquiesced to requests made by somber voices. People watched me out of the corner of their eyes. I signed papers in a glass-walled office entombed in formaldehyde smell. Through the glass, I saw an older man wearing a fresh white smock. When I finished signing, everyone left the room. Only then did the chief coroner come in to see me.

When at last I opened the door to our home, the lamp in the den still battled the forces of darkness with its valiant puddle of light. I stood in the doorway looking toward the lamp, measuring the distance of opportunity lost.

I burned the letters in the kitchen sink. The ashes swirled on top of the water, fighting to the last before disappearing down the drain. Through the kitchen window, gray dawn backlit our own oaks, towering firm above the clean snow.

Only when I bent to drop the twine in the trash did it come to me. I knew now what Calvin had wanted to say on the beach of bones. The letters were mailed from St. Croix. I wondered what Calvin thought of the man who had disappointed Abby and the researcher who so obviously loved her.

Abby was buried in the Bremser family plot in Wellfleet two weeks after the accident. She made the request in her will. On odd fronts, she was a planner. I hadn't looked at her will—I was thirty years old—but when I did, there it was.

I had made up my mind. Standing beside the grave, I absently heard the Episcopal minister's murmurings. The minister who married us had died. I had spoken with the new minister the day before the funeral in his overheated office, making the arrangement we would keep between ourselves for the next thirty-five years. The minister had not been surprised. He was young, perhaps three years older than me, but the requirements of his vocation had already taught him something of humankind's myriad impulses.

Standing in the cold cemetery, the world still with snow and ice, I thought of all the times I had waited. Waiting for the zombies to tear us limb from limb. Waiting in itchy bramble for the woman in the truck to become my mother. Waiting on the dock as Sean kicked out into the river. Waiting as the woman I loved turned the key a second time. Waiting beside a grave.

When the service ended, I waited. Everyone drifted away until a last figure remained. She stood beneath a solitary pine. I closed my eyes, smelling talcum powder and the sea, and then I walked to Sarah.

We stood for a moment, looking at a changed horizon.

"It's why you came to lunch," I said.

"Yes."

Far below us, a sea of trees spread supplicating limbs to the sky.

"I bought lilacs."

"I know."

"She threw them away."

"She knew you were trying."

"You knew everything," I said.

"Almost."

"You could have told me. Instead of useless poems."

I heard the slight inhale. I was glad it stung.

"I'm so sorry, Henry. She was my sister. She told me in confidence."

Our breath made dreamy clouds. I had intended to be angry, but suddenly I was only exhausted and hazily confused. It was not unlike the moments between battles.

"You knew from the beginning?"

"Nearly."

"Did it bother you, sitting there?"

"Yes."

Fresh tears followed the lines left by their predecessors. At the foot of the hill, the black limousines sent exhaust into the air. I imagined the faces watching us behind the tinted windows. *How sad. They must be heartbroken.*

"Henry, I didn't know what to do. She was my sister."

I wondered if repeating it was like some chant to ward off evil spirits.

She sniffled.

"Do you feel betrayed?" she asked.

"I don't feel much of anything."

Each letter had been marked with the day, month, and time. Researchers are sticklers for annotation. I wanted to know for certain.

"How long did they write?"

Write. Such a harmless euphemism.

"Eighteen months."

"Thank you," I said.

"I never lied to you. Ever."

"Silence is a lie."

Her face twisted, but she did not turn away.

"You need to know. She never betrayed you, Henry."

"What does that mean?"

"It didn't go beyond writing. A few stolen kisses. My sister, your wife, respected marriage."

"A strange way to show it."

"It sounds wrong now, I know, but I did it to protect you. I didn't want to see you hurt. I thought keeping quiet would save you pain. I thought you would never know. I knew Abby would end it."

This stopped us.

The wind rose. Scraping across the snow-laden boughs, it sent sparkling tendrils drifting down between us. From somewhere came a rumbling like distant thunder.

The letters had made it clear, but we are resolute in our desire to embrace hurt wholly.

"Did you ask her if she loved him?"

"Yes."

"And her answer?"

"Yes."

I waited.

"It wasn't an affair, Henry, at least not as a man would envision it. He was an escape. Women need to be needed."

I had simply proceeded. When chance handed me a hot dog cart, I did what I had always done, accepted my circumstances and adapted to them. I had worked hard in the cold apartment. I had continued working hard at the desk in the big, new house I did not know. I had woken to my wife and gone to bed with my wife, but I had forgotten the girl who had seen me undertake the one rash exercise of my life.

I stared out across the rows of headstones. Only in death does life finally organize itself.

"Would you have done it?"

The rumbling was louder, but neither of us looked toward it.

"I don't know," Sarah said. "Sometimes all people want is to be happy for a moment."

She stepped close, quickly touching my cheek with a gloved finger.

"Don't think less of yourself, Henry. Distance is like poetry, always beautiful. Up close, life intervenes."

"I'm leaving."

She breathed out a stream of vapor.

"One day you'll say something that surprises me. Where?"

"Somewhere out west. I'm not sure."

She knew this was a lie.

"Will you call me when you're settled?"

"Yes."

She saw this lie too.

"Do you remember when we met on the beach?" she asked.

"Yes."

"I was afraid of you."

"That's hard to believe."

"It's true. Anyone my sister chose had to be beyond this world's pall."

"You both proved to be a poor judge of character."

Something passed across Sarah's face, disappearing the instant it rose, a shooting star without a trail.

"The accident wasn't your fault, Henry."

"I'll be the judge of that."

"You can't be the judge of everything. I pray one day you'll understand that." The rumbling was almost on us. "I can't stand here anymore," she said.

We looked down the hill at the steaming limousines.

"You don't need anything?" I asked.

She shook her head slowly. I recognized it as good-bye.

She took small steps down the icy slope, the cautious sister, plank feet and awkward angles. A door opened. Benjamin's curly hair appeared just above the roof line. He was slightly bowlegged; when he came around the front of the limousine, he moved with a fast crab-like walk. He reached Sarah before she was halfway down the hill. Taking her elbow, he led her down the hill.

I watched him open her door. Sarah did not look up. After she ducked in, Benjamin looked toward me and waved. I waved back.

Watching the limousines pull away, I wondered what their life would be like. Everyone wants happiness, but everyone has secrets.

The rumbling was close. I heard rattlings and grindings too.

I closed my eyes, but it was not Abby I saw. Nine months earlier, John Daggett and Bill Beer had swum down the Colorado River. Many of the reporters had questioned their sanity. I could not explain

Beer's reasoning, but I now understood why John Daggett had plunged without hesitation into the icy waters on Easter morning.

For some, there is no hope of resurrection.

When I opened my eyes, the backhoe was beside the grave, pushing frozen dirt over my wife and our unborn child.

I said the second prayer of my life—for John Daggett, for my parents, for everyone who will lose a child. Then I walked down the hill without any thought of falling.

35

I follow Florida's western edge through Pensacola and Panama City, the humidity gathering in my pores. Past Tallahassee, I turn south on US Route 19, joining the long-haul truckers.

My plan is to drive south until I come to Highway 40, taking that artery across Florida to the Atlantic side, a point just south of Daytona Beach. From there, it is a short drive south to Sharpes.

Passing through Chiefland, memories settle about me. I fight them at first. I can't succumb to every sentimental whim. I pass chockablock outlet stores and a Walmart Supercenter, its vast parking lot full, as if all Levy County has unanimously reached the decision to shop. I see the sign for Highway 40. My shoulders tighten, my body's reaction to indecision, and then I watch the exit for Highway 40 pass.

I imagine myself banking, veering gracefully, only instead of soaring through dark waters, Florida smashes against my windshield with unapologetic heat and glare.

I tip my coffee to the rearview mirror.

"Lawless rascal."

A year after our arrival in Florida, our parents surprised us with a trip to Sanibel Island. As our father carefully wedged mother's suitcases in the trunk—excitement always saw her over-pack—my brother and I realized why, for several months now, our father had worked late into the night and why, when his cousin sent him as far south as Fort Lauderdale, he went without complaint. Our mother told us our father felt badly about taking us from Pittsburgh, as if this was some great secret, and when she told us we were going to Sanibel, putting Pliny down on the sheets and giving us a little girl's happy smile, Sean leaped from his bed with an Indian whoop. I became so breathless my mother thought my asthma had returned.

Sanibel was everything Sean and I had hoped for. There were great blue herons picking their fussy way along every waterline, manatees that rolled and chuffed in the calm waters like bloated logs, and, alongside Sanibel, the sable palmed islands of Captiva and Cayo Costa with their white sand beaches whose grains, so much finer than the coarse Atlantic beaches, passed like satin through our toes.

Best of all, for four days, everything changed. We ate together. We did not count each penny. Our father and mother took walks. One evening, they walked along the beach fronting the iron rise of Sanibel Lighthouse. We spied on them as they walked hand in hand. At first, Sean and I whispered and giggled and pushed each other so that we must have made an elephant's noise behind the wall of sea grape and palms, but soon we grew quiet. It was strange seeing them together. After a time, Sean turned wordlessly for the cottage, and I followed him.

Back then, we arrived on Sanibel via a wood bridge just high enough above Pine Island Sound to dangle a little too much fishing line. Now a skyway bridge arcs high over the water, a phalanx of toll booths at its foot. The attendant takes my money without pausing in her phone conversation, and when I fumble with the change for a fraction too long, the driver behind me leans on his horn.

Causeway Boulevard is lined with tourist shops and seafood restaurants with names like Captain Ahab's and Barnacle Phil's, and Periwinkle Way and Sanibel-Captiva Road are choked with similar establishments, but when I park the Mustang in the shade of an Australian pine and take off my shoes, the sand is still satin, and a shell tossed into the silken gulf waters still makes the cloud reflections jiggle.

There are no hotel rooms available on Sanibel, a national needlepoint convention is in full swing, but this time I know what to do. At Dinkin's Bay Marina, a fishing guide gives me directions to a place the tourists don't know.

I spend the night at Jug Creek Cottages on Pine Island. I sit on the screened porch until midnight, listening to the night breeze palm the lullaby of insect and frog, and, from the adjacent creek, the occasional splash of a hungry fish.

In the morning, I wake famished. The Jug Creek owner recommends Waterman's Galley, carefully writing out the directions and a reminder to order the biscuits with gravy.

But somewhere I make a wrong turn and so find myself driving down an arrow-straight road bordered on both sides by bleached pasture and cedar rail fence. It's not quite nine, but already oven heat spills through my window. The Mustang's wheels hum a drowsy song, and then the humming turns to unearthly screaming, and before I know what I am doing, I have yanked the Mustang off the road and thrown open the door.

I do not recall clambering across the ditch or climbing over the fence, though I do feel a jolt as my left knee strikes something unrelenting. The ensuing pain sees me stagger slightly as I run across the field. The screams are terrible, but they are no longer unearthly, for I have heard them before, pure screams of animal terror.

I must be a fine sight, staggering at a half run across the pasture, but the cowboy does not get to enjoy it, absorbed as he is with quirting the horse. The horse's screams must drown out my shouts, for the man is astonished when I push between him and the horse. I know he does not mean for it to happen, but there is no stopping the forward motion of his arm. I catch the quirt full in the face.

Hot pain explodes in my head. I sit down hard. The sunbaked ground sends more pain up my spine. In his astonishment, the cowboy drops the reins. I sense the rising horse as a cloud moving across the sun.

Something strikes my shoulder with the force of a blacksmith's hammer. I am suffocating, but the screaming blessedly stops.

When I wake, I am on my back in bed. This is a puzzle. I remember no bland lobby, no desk clerk, no fickle room key, though my entire body throbs with a long day's driving. A ceiling fan turns slowly, circulating the smell not of pine but of sage. I make a note to congratulate the proprietor on his fresh approach.

The bed is firm. Even half-conscious, I feel the stretch of sheets drawn crisp by military cornering. I'm wearing pajamas, smooth and cool as the sheets, and my mouth is gritty. These are also puzzles.

Only when a hand, rough and dry, settles on my forearm, and a strange voice speaks, do I recall the screaming horse.

"How are you feeling, brave knight?"

I start to turn toward the voice; a current of pain lasers down my right side. I stay on my back, panting and staring hard at the fan.

"Whoooaaaaa now. Best to stay as you are for the moment."

I let the pain recede.

"The horse?" I ask.

"Fine. Already been tended to by the vet."

"The cowboy?"

"Dismissed. He was a new hand and a good actor. I sorely misjudged his character." A chair scrapes, the voice softening. "I can't tell you how sorry I am, you having to pay for my poor judgment."

Again I hear the sound of fish breaking the surface. The hand on my forehead possesses heavenly cool. I try to turn, but both hands press firmly.

"You're either stubborn or groggier than I think. You need to stay still. I've got you in a makeshift sling, but I'm no doctor. I just cleaned you up a bit. You had an acre of sod in your mouth. The doctor will be here this afternoon, soon as he's done with his office hours. Not many doctors make house calls these days, but around here, we're lucky to have one who does. I'd appreciate you lying still until he arrives."

More faint splashing; cool this time against my neck.

"You've got a mild fever. Your body fighting all the stress I've seen you to."

I want to apologize, but already I've forgotten precisely what happened. I must mumble something, because a quiet laugh issues from the bottom of a well.

"Plenty of time to sort things out," the voice says.

I do not dream, and for this, I am grateful.

I wake to the cool hand on my forehead. I recognize now that the hand holds a damp towel.

My mouth still feels as if I've just finished grazing in a field cut close to the dirt.

"Still more turf in there than I'd like," says the familiar voice, "but I didn't want to move your head too much. No need to be concerned, though. You're a fidgety sleeper. I've been watching, and everything works."

Gratitude washes over me, so strong I'm afraid I might cry. I count to ten.

"Thank you."

"I don't believe you have much to thank me for. I should thank you for being indestructible, though not quite able to leap tall fences at a single bound."

I remember. Smiling hurts.

"I'm pretty sure your knee's just bruised," the woman says. "Again, just a lay opinion."

"Where am I?"

"That I can tell you. You're reclining on the back porch of the Akers family ranch." A faint tinkling. "Now you don't need to know everything right off the bat. I suspect you'd like a drink."

A whirring raises me slowly. The ceiling fan drifts back behind my head. A dim room replaces it, dark wood everywhere except for French doors set with sparkling clear glass. Through the French doors, an equally spotless kitchen is illuminated by muted track lights.

"How does that feel?"

"Fine."

"Good."

The owner of the voice is behind me. The tinkling grows louder as the glass passes my good ear. Cool touches my lips.

"Spit out the first round. As I said, you've still got a square foot of topsoil in there."

The glass tilts, allowing just the right amount of water to swim in my parched mouth. A ceramic washing bowl, its edge chipped, appears in front of me.

"Don't lean out too far."

I spit gently.

The woman laughs.

"No cause to be so decorous. This isn't Cotillion."

After several spits, I am allowed a swallow. It is the finest water I've ever tasted. Spitting has tired me. I sink back into the pillow. The wash basin and the ice water settle somewhere with respective clinks.

"I suppose we should become acquainted, though truth is after what happened, I'm a little embarrassed to show my face."

A woman appears at the foot of the bed. Small and wiry, she stands as if at attention, her military mien countered by a dusty and sorely faded denim jacket. Her hair, cut in a short bob, is thick as a snow bank and equally white.

"Opal Akers," she says. "In his youth, my father was an incorrigible wanderer. Among other locales, he wandered among the opal mines of South Australia. Said when he saw my eyes, he knew what to name me. Our family tree flowers little indecision."

I see now her eyes are a curious gray.

"Opals come in all colors, but my father didn't know it then. The only mine he knew produced light opals, crystal, white, and gray." She waves a hand. "That's far too much about me. As I said, you're on the back verandah. The nearest hospital is an hour and forty minutes away. I thought transporting you there would be an uncomfortable affair. Far as I can tell, you suffer nothing life-threatening. You took a glancing quirt across the face and a solid kick in the shoulder. Our misanthrope cowboy had at least enough conscience to bring you in.

My guess is your shoulder is bruised. Possibly the scapula is cracked. But we'll leave the diagnosis to a professional."

"You sound like a professional."

When I try a broad smile, spots dance in my eyes.

"We aren't built much different from animals," Opal says. She holds the glass to my lips.

"Thank you, Opal."

"You're a polite old codger. How do you feel?"

"Comfortable. As long as I don't move."

"Good. I can see you're the rare patient who listens. I own this ranch. The horse that kicked you is mine, if you can own an animal. Regardless, I am responsible. We're both lucky the horse didn't trample you."

The world is returning.

"My car."

"Parked outside in the drive. The cowboy drove it over with you in it. Had him clean it up after we got you settled. His last working act on the premises. It's getting harder and harder to find good hands. Not many folks are trustworthy, and the few who are don't tend to stay long. Everyone's on the move these days, hurrying to something."

I let my eyes roam the verandah I can see. Pine floor, peppered by worn throw rugs. Several end tables, more tree stump than table, their tops polished to a sheen. A coffee table with neatly fanned magazines. The ceiling beams are thicker than a man. I know this place.

"The beams are one piece," says Opal. "Solid oak. My great-grandfather built this verandah as a birthday present for his wife. In those days, cool was a prized commodity too. He positioned the porch so it catches every breath of breeze. Not that cattle ranchers spent much time sitting."

"Florida Crackers," I say.

The laugh is a pleasant tinkling, not unlike the ice cubes.

"Yes indeed."

A chorus of barks erupts outside. Closer by, a bird sets up a ferocious squawking.

"That would be your doctor activating the alarm system. As you'll soon see, animals are my vice. I've got more horses than any one person needs. The dog's an Australian shepherd. The squawking belongs to a very intelligent cockatiel who blew in here on the wings of Hurricane Andrew. Given his colorful Spanish, I'd say he last resided with an unsavory crowd in Miami before the winds of change brought him to me."

"Michael Sandoval is your doctor." She starts for the door and turns. "He'll ask, so I suppose we'll need a name to attach those manners to."

"Pogue Whithouse."

The squawking abruptly stops.

"Doctor Sandoval is at the door. That bird has an eerie genius for character. Possibly a result of his previous life. I named him Einstein. Not very original."

"I like him already."

"The question is will he like you? Now if you'll excuse me, I'll fetch the doctor."

"I'll wait here."

"Let's not start a contest with Einstein."

The doctor is a boy. It shouldn't be a shock, but it is. He has sandy hair and a shy manner, but his hands press firmly, and the pressure eases before I grunt. Still the pain rests like a simmering burn along my upper back. My jaw aches too. The boy manipulates my jaw and shoulder gently.

I don't see Opal. I wonder if she is in the room.

I answer the doctor's questions as best as I can. At first it's easy, but with shocking quickness, it exhausts me. The young doctor touches my hand.

"That's all from me," he says. He waves toward the kitchen. "Mrs. Akers is big on privacy."

I hear footsteps and the now familiar tinkling of ice. Opal carries a tray with three glasses of lemonade and a sweating pitcher.

Placing the tray on the end table beside my bed, she says, "I thought you might be thirsty, Michael. And this young fellow drinks, well, like a horse."

"Thank you, Mrs. Akers. I'm always thirsty when it comes to your homemade lemonade."

"In this heat, bleach would taste good," says Opal, but I see her flush. "How is our patient?"

"Nothing broken, though the contusion on his scapula is severe. You'll need to keep him fairly still for at least a few days. Keep him hydrated too. Wise to have the blinds pulled. That will save him additional headache. Other than that, Mrs. Akers, a square meal or two when he's in the mood," the boy grins at me, "and soon enough he'll be up and running."

"It's a good man who comes to the aid of an animal," Opals says, embarrassing me.

"You would know, Mrs. Akers." A zipper opens. "A little something for the pain if he needs it."

"Thank you for coming so quickly, Michael."

"It's my pleasure, Mrs. Akers." In the silence, the rattle of the vial being placed on a table. "You've made some nice changes."

"I like to stay busy."

"I'd prescribe bed rest for you now and again if I thought you'd listen." A slight change of tone, from professional to deferential. "May I ask how you've been, Mrs. Akers?"

"You may. I miss Conrad, but that's to be expected."

"He was a fine gentleman, Mrs. Akers. It was an honor to have known him."

"I was the luckiest woman. And what about you, Michael? You can't play doctor twenty-four hours a day. Has anyone stolen away with your heart?"

It's the boy's turn to flush.

"Doctoring keeps me pretty busy."

"Don't let it. You've grown into a winsome boy. You could have your pick of any girl in any county, though Lee County would be convenient."

I don't have to look to know the boy is staring at his feet.

"I'll try to remember that, Mrs. Akers."

"Do that, for your own good. Don't make life work. And how is your mother?"

"About the same."

"She's in good hands."

A latch clicking shut.

"Call me if anything changes, Mrs. Akers. I can see myself out. Thanks for the lemonade."

"My pleasure. Michael?"

"Yes, ma'am?"

"You don't have to keep dropping in to see me."

"I enjoy it."

"That's a fine lie." The protest is cut off by a motion I don't see. "I'm talking to you as your mother's best friend. Don't spend so much time around old widows. It's your time now."

After a few minutes, a car starts in the distance.

"Not a peep out of that bird." Opal smiles. "Einstein knows his stuff."

Waking in the dark, I shift. The pain makes me gasp.

A lamp clicks on. Opal sits on a couch fronted by the coffee table.

"Good evening and good timing." The smell of sage has been replaced by something heavenly. "I hope you like tomato bisque."

Steam rises from the bowl on the tray. My stomach switches to high alert. I had been heading for breakfast, starving.

"I love tomato bisque."

"Let your taste buds be the judge of that." Opal rises from the couch and moves to the bed. "Relax as best you can." The buzzing stops when I am just short of upright. She settles the short-legged tray above my lap. "Careful. I don't fancy calling Michael back for first-degree burns."

"Here's hoping he's unavailable."

Lamplight turns features softer. Opal's smile spreads like syrup across a plate.

"You're a listener."

Next to the soup, there's a plate with two rolls and two slabs of butter.

"Sourdough, baked soft. Real butter because time's short and it tastes better." She rubs her hands together. "Now, tell me what you'd like to drink. There's water, milk, orange juice, and eggnog. Eggnog is one of my better vices."

"Water, please."

Opal goes to the kitchen. She has raised the porch shades. The darkness outside is complete, the night that descends on country places. On the other side of the French doors, I see Opal open the door of a stainless steel refrigerator.

She has shifted the bed, allowing me a slightly different view. Something enormous hunkers just beyond the lamplight. It takes me a long moment to collect what I see. The massive trunk rises from the floor, its girth barely narrowing as it vaults up through the ceiling.

I fight to breathe. Sometimes it is not hard to imagine what it is like to drown. I look away into the night.

"It's a family heirloom," says Opal, returning from the kitchen.

I find enough breath.

"It's beautiful," I lie.

There are few things like a pleased woman's smile. I try to let it sweep me back into the present, but it doesn't work.

"I thought you might like it," Opal says. *"He who owns a veteran Bur Oak owns more than a tree. He owns an historical library.* My great grandfather would have liked Aldo Leopold. He couldn't bring himself to cut the tree down. His ancestors have been forever grateful. Sometimes my father would just stand quietly and run his hand along the bark. When I was a young girl, that scared me a little, but my mother would always say the same thing. 'Opal, he's just sorting things out.' Now I do it, though I'm not always successful in my sorting. It does put the day's troubles in perspective, though."

She unfolds a napkin and spreads it on my chest.

"Quirting hasn't affected your memory, has it? You do remember that soup is better hot?"

I raise my spoon. My hand shakes.

"Unwise to offend the chef," I say.

Opal reads the paper on the couch while I eat. I don't stop until my spoon scrapes at nothing. It's the best tomato bisque I've ever tasted, and I say so.

Opal does not look up from the paper.

"I usually make it spicier, but I didn't want to give you a kick in the stomach too."

She picks the lamp up off the coffee table. She has a mirror in her other hand.

She hands me the mirror.

"Here."

I hold the mirror while she plays light over my face. My right cheek is the color of an inkwell. The bruise extends up to make a perfect ring around my eye.

"Women love a pirate," Opal says. "Through some miracle, the quirt didn't break the skin."

"Did the impact raise all these wrinkles?"

She smiles.

"No. They snuck up on us while we were sleeping."

I eat a second bowl of soup, trying to enjoy the sweet taste, but flares hiss like snakes, and the flashlight plays jumpily over the oak's dark base, wet in the dry chill, the pain rising again to pour into my heart. Even after all these years, there is still room.

When I ask Opal to reposition the bed, she does it without a word.

36

Opal fixes scrambled eggs and sausage for breakfast. As I eat, she says, "I apologize for forgetting. I should have asked if there is anyone you'd like to call."

It is the appropriately vague question for people our age.

"My wife passed away. I have no immediate family."

It sounds both abrupt and pathetic. I'm embarrassed.

"I'm sorry," I say.

"I'm sorry, and you can't apologize for life." She smiles. "You have no shortage of friends."

"What?"

"Messages on your phone," she says, and picks the phone up off the coffee table. "Fifteen of them. It says so right on the face. Is the phone new?"

"Yes."

She reads my face.

"You just press this button to listen to them," she says, handing me the phone. Reaching into the pocket of her denim jacket, she pulls out a white walkie-talkie.

"If you need anything, just talk into this. It's a baby monitor."

"Thank you."

She touches the green button in the center of the monitor.

"If you press this, I'll hear everything you say. When it's on," she points to a plastic dome in the upper right corner, "this light glows. Outside of phone calls, I'd prefer you left it on. Mostly so I can hear any confidences you might divulge in your sleep. Give my best to your friend."

A blood-red sunset stares at me from the face of the phone. The sales clerk had said there were thousands of choices. She could help me find one I liked. I told her a setting sun was fine.

I press Opal's button. The phone instructs me from there. It takes time. The messages get shorter and shorter. The last two are brusque.

I dial. The phone rings once.

"Why didn't you answer your phone?"

Surprise turns me a trifle defensive.

"Shouldn't you be at school?"

"It's Saturday. Why didn't you answer your phone?"

I look at the lightless baby monitor.

"I'm having trouble with the phone. Sometimes I lose it."

A partial truth does not add honesty to my inflection.

"You do not."

Don't lie to me again.

"Sarah says you're the most organized person she knows. She says you probably lay your clothes out for the week. She says you'd keep your letters ordered by date, if you ever got any letters. Sarah says you have to write letters to get letters."

Man, woman, and child, we should all count to ten. I almost smile.

"Do you think she'd want you telling me that?"

"I don't care." Children aren't perfect. I was a child. But if there is a God, His best work comes in small sizes. "I was *really* worried. My stomach hurts."

Each of us likes to think we're honest and good at heart, our lies white, protective, harmless. But in this we only lie to ourselves.

"I had a small accident."

"I knew it. You sound funny."

"I've got a frog in my throat."

This is true.

"You sound like you're talking with your mouth full."

"My tongue is a little swollen. And maybe my jaw."

"You're too old to get in fights."

"I was kicked by a horse. The horse didn't mean to kick me. I got in its way. It didn't kick me hard, but with a horse, even a soft kick is hard enough."

"What were you doing with a horse?"

"Standing too close."

"I mean it."

Are women born with a nose for nonsense?

"A man was hurting the horse. I tried to stop him, and the horse kicked me by accident. The doctor says I bruised my shoulder and my knee. So it's not bad at all. That's the truth."

"Why was the man hurting the horse?"

"I don't know."

"Was he a cowboy?"

"No."

"I didn't think so. Is someone taking care of you?"

"Yes. They just fixed me a delicious breakfast."

"Is *they* a man or a woman?"

"A woman."

Silence.

"Are you in a hospital?"

"No. I'm at a friend's house."

"I wish she was a man."

"She doesn't have my phone number," I say.

"She doesn't need it."

"Her name is Opal. You'd like her a lot. She has all kinds of animals. Horses, dogs, and a very loud cockatiel."

"You're trying to make me forget. What color is the cockatiel?"

"White." Like the lie. Not being able to get out of bed won't go over well. "With a bright yellow bill. His name is Einstein."

"I saw a cockatiel once at the zoo. It felt like someone was screaming inside my ear. How long will you be there?"

"A few days."

"That's okay, I guess. If you answer your phone."

Her mustering makes the world sing.

"Do you know what the sixth best thing is?" I ask.

"We're on seven."

"Okay. The seventh best thing."

"Tell me."

"The seventh best thing is we're friends."

"It has nothing to do with bullfrogs. I feel a little better now."

"I'm glad. Sad things are hard."

"Not the bullfrogs. I feel better because Opal is taking care of you."

A pause and the sound of something being placed down close to the phone.

"What was that?"

"The vase. There's two roses left."

I hang up with a bullfrog in my throat.

I wake in the night, soaked with sweat. I lie in the dark, still hearing the minute rustlings that herald death. But there is no thrust of steel, no shock of pain, no weight hauling down the arms of the survivor. I feel the cool towel on my forehead, but the whispered admonition is made indecipherable by the drumbeat in my head.

I didn't dream, but now I do.

The survivor isn't always the winner.

37

I sleep until late afternoon. I wake embarrassed.

Opal is reading in a wicker chair, glasses perched at the end of her nose.

She winks.

"Well. Rip Van Winkle returns."

"I've never slept so much."

"I'd say your body has experienced a bit of a shock. We're not twenty anymore."

"Sometimes that's a shock."

The sheets are soft and dry. My pajamas too. I flush like a school girl.

"I changed everything this morning. I apologize for the invasion of privacy, but just changing the linens would have left the job half done."

I stare into my lap.

"Thank you."

Her laugh is soft.

"You men are all the same. Shy until it doesn't suit you."

When I finally sneak a look, she has gone back to reading.

Opal makes crab cakes for dinner. She brings me a white linen bathrobe and a padded folding chair. Holding my elbow firmly, she steadies me while I put on the bathrobe. It rests with surprising weight across my shoulders.

We eat at the coffee table. There is a pillow on my chair. When I'm seated, Opal wedges another pillow behind my back. I squirm, trying to adjust the pillow.

One hand resting gently on my good shoulder, Opal repositions the pillow.

"Comfortable?"

"Yes. Thank you."

"The male patient. Conrad couldn't ask for help either."

She fusses with a place setting that requires no fussing.

The young doctor's comments, a hospital bed in a home. *My wife passed away. I have no family.* I despise my self-absorption.

"I'm sorry about your husband," I say. "He was lucky to have you."

She does not take her eyes off the napkin as she puts it in my lap.

"Life," she says. "There was nothing to be done about it."

"We can change the subject."

"It's all right. We might as well get everything out in the open. My husband had amyotrophic lateral sclerosis. Lou Gehrig's disease. Conrad preferred to call it that. He loved baseball. He played in college. He was good enough for a tryout with the White Sox."

"What position did he play?"

Pride lifted sixty years from her face.

"Shortstop. He moved so beautifully. We met in college. I knew nothing about baseball and cared even less. I went to the games just to watch him move. So effortless, like wind over ice." It is her turn to look at her lap. "If there is a God, he has a strange sense of humor. It embarrassed Conrad terribly that he was unable to account for himself."

The French doors bang open. An Australian shepherd trots directly to Opal's knee, but not before shooting me an intelligent glance.

"Hello, Keats." Opal scratches an ear. "He's used to having the run of the house." She lifts the dog's muzzle and gazes at him with helpless fondness. "Terribly spoiled, aren't you?" She looks at me. "I hope you don't mind. I thought it would be all right now."

"It's fine. I love animals."

"I already know that."

The crab cakes are just off his nose, but Keats ignores them.

"He possesses admirable restraint," I say.

"He's not much for seafood. His first owners fed him nothing but fish waste. I found him at the pound. Keats was Conrad's favorite poet. And now *you*," she scratches his chin, "are my favorite company." The scratching finds a particularly joyous spot. Nails click on the wood. "Ah, creature of simple, guiltless pleasures. I met Keats at the pound three days after Conrad passed away. I hadn't planned on an Australian shepherd. I was looking for a small dog. But the lady that operates the pound let him out, and I saw him run. That's all it took. I was a goner."

Opal rises quickly.

"I forgot the drinks."

She walks through the kitchen and into the darkness.

When she returns with the drinks, we eat in silence. I know she does not want company. I do the next best thing, for there is nothing worth saying.

38

When I wake on the third morning, a pile of neatly folded clothes rests at the foot of the bed. I dress quickly, one eye on the French doors. Keats watches from the kitchen, head cocked. The trousers and the light blue polo shirt are worn and comfortable. They fit as if they were tailored for me.

A comb and the hand mirror rest on the bedside table with a note. Already the bruises on my face are starting to break into patches and lighten. I find a bathroom just off the kitchen. I shave alongside framed photos of children, two boys and a girl dangling upside down on monkey bars, tomato-faced on a ski vacation, pretending to hook each other with fishing lines, holding beach balls in a backyard pool. I confess I look for photos of their parents, but there aren't any.

When Opal appears on the verandah, I am sitting on the couch. Keats bounds over and snuffles my trousers.

"You spruce up nicely," Opal says, but I notice she barely glances at me.

"I was hoping to fix you breakfast. I know where everything is."

"Mr. Whithouse. Have you been spying on me through the glass?"

"Only so that I may repay you, in very small fashion, for your kindness."

"Spying remains spying."

She has exchanged jeans and the denim jacket for a pleated plaid skirt and a white high-collared blouse. The collar is fixed at her throat by a broach, an oblong milky-white stone at its center.

"It's beautiful," I say, and this time I mean it.

"Thank you." She touches the broach reflexively. "Given you remain the patient, you're required to heed instructions. You're not allowed to fix breakfast this morning. You're not allowed to pay for breakfast either. If you make a public scene, you will be discharged from my care." She heads for the French doors. Over her shoulder, she says, "I prescribe the gravy and biscuits."

Opal drives a burgundy 1987 Ford pickup. As we bump down the dirt drive, I don't recognize anything. The driveway is nearly a mile long. I count fifteen horses, wet eyes watching us above the fence railing.

Just before we reach the road, Opal stops. A sleek brown roan lifts its muzzle from a mound of hay. Opal sticks her head out the window.

"Top of the morning, Satchel. I'd be obliged if you saved some of that for lunch."

The roan snorts and swings his head.

"Of course you won't," laughs Opal.

I watch the roan recede in the rearview mirror.

"He's a magnificent horse," says Opal, "but like most magnificent things, he's greedy and vain. He'll eat every last stitch of that hay and then move on to someone else's. I'd be better off feeding them dollar bills. Drought has sent the cost of hay through the roof. There are lots of recreational horse owners around here, and most of them are looking for a different form of recreation. It costs somewhere in the vicinity of twenty-five hundred dollars a year to feed one horse, and that's beyond a lot of folks' means. Lots of horses are starving."

Both windows are down. Opal's hair leaps about in the cross breeze. Plucking a brown ball cap off the dash, she pulls it low on her head.

"We're not special. It's the same in a lot of places. Drive the rural back roads, and you'll see skin-and-bones horses. Some people send their horses to slaughterhouses in Mexico, but around here, they send them to me. Mexican slaughterhouses are short on technology. Knives are jabbed into the horse's spine until it dies. It's a cruel end, but the truth is starving to death is probably worse."

She gives the windshield a small, pained smile.

"Coral islands don't birth the lushest pastures either."

The morning is hot and bright blue, identical to the one where I sat, Buddha-like, beneath a rearing horse.

Now that I am out in the world, I begin to return to it.

"Who helps you on the ranch?"

"We were ranchers, but the truth is I now run less of a ranch and more of a halfway house for animals. I had three regular hands who helped me—two now that you've rightly seen to the firing of one. Conrad and I had three children, but they all left as soon as they could. Followed you out to California. Land of milk and honey, though we all know it's pretty dry out there too. The weather's gone strange on us, and we're to blame. I'm not sure what's coming, but I worry for the children."

A dark green pickup approaches from the opposite direction. Opal holds up a finger. The expressionless man in the pickup does the same as he whizzes past.

"Lots of newcomers buying up land here, but there are still old timers around." She glances at the truck shrinking in the rearview mirror. "When William was sixteen, he had a fierce crush on me. Told me he couldn't live without me. Threatened to drown himself. Said he'd hold a rock, sink to the bottom of Pine Island Sound, and wait there until I fell in love with him. He told me the world would be our oyster, which around here really means something. Now he's mortgaged to the hilt and caring for a wife with dementia. I spoke to him in the grocery the other day, but I could tell all he wanted to do was get away."

She pushes at the bill of her cap.

"But what about you? How have you made your way in this world to date, Mr. Whithouse?"

I love her for leaving the world open-ended.

"I owned a hot dog company."

Again it chimes ridiculously in my ears.

"It's a shame horses don't eat hot dogs. We could partner up. What was the company called?"

"Sweet Thursday."

"A second chance," smiles Opal. "Very poetic, you and Mr. Steinbeck."

I stare hard over the hood, the asphalt whipping beneath us.

"You've read the book."

"Several times," says Opal. "I wonder how our literary giants would feel if they knew how we immortalize them. How did you get into the hot dog business?"

It's all the time I need to recover.

"Chance. I never went to college. I've often wished I had."

I don't know why I confide this. Perhaps I am still off balance.

"College isn't all it's trumped up to be," Opal says. "Look at us. I went to college and studied baseball. Now I'm ranching starving horses. You're an intelligent, self-made man traveling the country, going wherever the wind blows you."

"I wasn't intelligent. I was just focused."

"I admire perseverance far more than intelligence. One's a lot rarer than the other."

Another truck whips past with an exchange of fingers.

Opal says, "You know the red mangroves you see around here, the ones we haven't killed with runoff or torn up for development?"

I am familiar with mangroves. I nod.

"The Calusa Indians who settled here called the red mangroves 'the walking tree.' They slowly put down roots and keep advancing forward, one inch at a time. After a while, they've formed another island." She pats the steering wheel. "When I die, I'm having my ashes scattered in the mangroves so I can help them walk."

We pull into a small parking lot filled with pickups. The sign beside the road, little more than a mailbox, is familiar.

I laugh.

"Waterman's Galley."

"You've been here before?" Opal asks.

"Almost."

We take the last parking spot. Opal shuts off the engine.

"You sleeping in, we're lucky to get a spot. Angus serves a fine breakfast for a fair price. Most of the other restaurants on the island have turned boutique on us."

Paintings of lighthouses line the walls, and gray-haired men fill the tables. Everyone wears dusty jeans and cowboy boots. None of the coffee mugs match.

One black man works the grill. There are three waitresses.

As we make our way to a table, several men nod to Opal. One stands and wordlessly shakes her hand. They don't bother to hide their stares.

I hold her chair.

As she sits, she whispers, "This is more fun than I thought."

The waitress brings one menu and pours us waters. Pushing the menu to me, Opal raises her glass.

"Realize, too, that you still look like Jack Dempsey after his bout with Joe Louis."

The smell of coffee and bacon, the lighthouses, the roll of paper towels on the table, they are like a salve.

"I'm ready for a rematch," I say.

Opal tips her glass.

"To fighters. But if you're going to go the full fifteen, you'd better eat something first. You won't find anything here for more than seven dollars. That's why I'm treating. No point in protesting, so don't."

"I knew a man once who cooked at a restaurant just like this in Sharpes. Where I grew up. It was a long time ago."

"Might have been Angus. He's older than Lee County."

The three waitresses are at the counter. One drums her fingers. The cook sets steaming plates of scrambled eggs in front of the other two and turns back to the grill.

"Short-order cook is a synonym for magician," I say. "The man I knew turned out the best seafood he never tasted."

"How so?"

"He hated seafood. He ate the same three things—fried chicken, lima beans, and butterscotch pudding—every day. He hardly talked to anyone. My mother washed dishes in the restaurant. I'd come in sometimes at night to sit with her. He liked my mother. Eventually he warmed to me, in his fashion. When I finally worked up the nerve to ask him why he ate three things, he looked at me and said, 'I like 'em. Only a fool lets other folks' opinions decide what they do.'"

"A poor diet and fine advice."

"I wish I'd listened."

We are silent.

"Angus only talks about which waitress he's going to fire."

"My bet would be the drumming brunette."

"I won't bet against you."

Our waitress is a heavyset blonde with a perpetual smile. Opal orders pork chops and eggs. I ask for the full order of biscuits and gravy. The coffee is hot and strong.

Opal screws up her face.

"There's yogurt and granola on the menu now, on account of the snowbirds," she says.

I raise my mug.

"Here's to eating what we want."

"To butterscotch pudding," Opal says.

A trace of sadness passes across her face, the sort of look you see in airports on the faces of those left behind.

"And to Satchel Paige," I say. "Another sage."

Opal frames a game smile.

"Also Conrad's favorite player and my last remaining link to baseball. Too many steroid abusers these days."

Before I can stop myself, I lean forward and touch her hand. She starts, but she doesn't pull away.

"How old would you be if you didn't know how old you are?" I ask.

She doesn't say that's a silly question. Satchel Paige knew it wasn't.

"Forty-five, when I don't think. One hundred and forty-five when I do." The airport sadness creeps into her eyes again. "Sometimes you can live too long," she says.

Driving home, it sounds as if a bee is in the glove box.

Opal watches the road with amusement.

"You could answer it," she says. "It might be Louis's people calling about the rematch."

It's Sarah, breathless.

"Pogue. I'm so glad you answered. I was worried sick. Are you all right? Tesia *just* told me about your accident."

Our call is being monitored.

"I'm perfectly fine. Maybe a little stiff. Make that stiffer. No cause for worry."

"You were kicked by a horse."

"You of all people know how hardheaded I am."

Sarah's laugh bathes me in warmth.

"You have your wits. And someone's looking after you?"

"I'm in good hands. Her name is Opal." Opal lifts a finger. "She says hello."

"Tell her hello back. And tell her thank you."

"I will."

"Have you seen a doctor?"

"Yes. He came to the house. He said I'm not broken, just slightly bruised. A bit like yesterday's produce. All he prescribed was a little rest. I'm sorry for worrying you, Sarah."

It may be easier to swim alone.

Sarah says, "Hard up in a clinch, and no knife to cut the seizings."

Godfrey Bremser is in the truck, clasping my shoulder, pumping my hand, smiling the uncomfortable smile men smile when they brush against intimacy. *How old would you be if you didn't know how old you are?* Nineteen and smooth limbed and terrified enough to weep.

My shoulder throbs.

Silence in the truck, silence on the phone. We sit, three of us, together and alone. The leatherback is not the world's only mysterious creature.

I hear Sarah's voice. Godfrey Bremser dissolves, but I am still dry-mouthed.

"You don't need to apologize to me. You know I'm a worrier, whether you help me along or not. But I'm not worried about you anymore, though I am a trifle jealous of you and what you're doing. Carpe diem. Though I think you should quit equestrian camp."

"No more horse whispering for me."

Out of the corner of my eye, I see Opal grin.

"Apparently I'm out of time," says Sarah. "Let's both promise we won't worry any more than necessary."

"I promise."

I know it is a promise I cannot keep, but still the warm feeling folds over me like a winter blanket.

"Pogue!"

Tesia bursts on the line. She chatters without taking a breath, and I would not interrupt her for anything in the world, for her voice is a breakneck symphony, chord upon chord of infectious delight spilling from the phone, imbuing the air inside the cab with the hum of life. At one point, someone laughs, and I am not sure if it is Opal or me.

Tesia is still talking as we turn down the drive. She continues unabated as Opal shuts off the engine and wordlessly slips from the truck.

When Tesia finally hangs up, I step gingerly to the ground. The sudden silence is depressing. But when I close my eyes, the happy chattering rattles in my mind, and when I turn my face to the late morning sun, I feel it as a young boy on a riverbank feels the sun against his naked back.

Opal is in the kitchen putting away plates, Keats at her feet. They both give me an intelligent appraisal.

"Well," says Opal. "That was quite the conversation. I apologize, but there are only so many places to walk off to in the cab of a truck. I also believe the volume on your phone is turned up as loud as it goes."

I recall the salesgirl's tappings.

Sliding a last plate into place, Opal shuts the cabinet and smiles.

"Apparently, you've won a heart. Sending her roses was sweet. What was the occasion?"

Slow death.

"Celebration of life well lived."

"As it should be."

"They were bullfrogs."

I say it so it won't concern her, but I think of the turtles and their myriad ends. Why should the passing of any living thing be rendered trivial?

To defend their honor, I add, "Tesia loves bullfrogs."

"I'm a big fan already. How old is she?"

"Eight."

"And already with a suitor. If her fervor is any measure, your bouquet won't be her last." Opal runs a sponge along the edge of the sink. "Where does she live?"

"Cape Cod. Hyannisport. I'm going to meet her."

I say it slowly, as if trying the idea out.

"You've never met?"

"No."

"Well, apparently you were made for each other." Opal places the sponge in its dish. "I envy you," she says.

"For what?"

"For the chance to woo again."

In the afternoon, we drink homemade lemonade on the verandah. Opal has been out riding. Her jeans and boots are coated with coralline dust. Keats dozes fitfully at her feet. The ceiling fan spins hypnotically. Breakfast has exhausted me. We sit together on the couch, but I want to crawl into bed.

"If you don't mind my asking, who else did I meet on the phone this morning? Tesia's mother?"

Women are like poets, observers and filers away.

"Tesia's grandmother, Sarah. She lives with Tesia. Actually, it's her house. She's my wife's sister."

"Well, you can tell her I liked her just from the sound of her voice. Have you seen her recently?"

"No. Not for years."

Finishing her lemonade, Opal places it on the tray. Her eyes remain on the glass.

"I have come to the conclusion that it is a shame to wait for anything," she says.

"Wouldn't it be nice if wisdom came before age?"

"It might make things more confusing." Opal bestows a slight smile on the glass.

"Tesia is a beautiful name."

"I'm told it's too lady-like."

"I understand. I was going to be a fireman until my father informed me otherwise. He sat me on his lap, so very serious," her voice deepens, and she scowls, "'There's a reason they're called firemen.'"

"Now it's firefighter."

"Now it's too late. I often wonder how it might have been if I hadn't listened so much."

Opal's gaze goes to the bur oak.

"I have a fantasy," she says. "It's not too late for that, is it?"

I place two fingers gently on the underside of her wrist. Her pulse beats like a drum.

"No."

"It's easier to confide in a mysterious stranger."

I know her smile. It is the smile of a beauty queen in a cold basement, lost in yellowed clippings.

"Your doctor, Michael Sandoval, checks in on me twice a week. We sit on this couch, just like this, drinking lemonade. Sometimes I pretend he's come calling, and I'm young again. I've gotten so good at it there are times when I have to go into the kitchen to catch my breath." Her voice quiets. "I did it when Conrad was alive, laying right here in front of us."

Quickening of breath, blood risings, the odd weave of dreamy faintness and total absorption, the glorious ache of yearning, the blind rightness of it all. There are no words for this; even the greatest poets fail. Rapture brought to perfect pitch by the oblivious young becomes treasure turned over again and again by hands like husks.

Opal stands and picks up the tray.

"You'd think I was the one who'd been kicked by a horse," she says.

She is halfway to the kitchen when I find my tongue.

"We should all be kicked."

I say it with conviction, for more than anything, I want her to know she is not alone.

She turns slowly, and when she faces me, I see she is crying.

"Tomorrow's prescription calls for breakfast and a walk," she says. "It's poor nursing to just fatten you up."

In the evening, I go to the washroom to clean up for dinner. When I return to the verandah, a platter of cold cuts and a steaming mug sit on the coffee table.

I eat alone. The kitchen and the rest of the house are dark.

39

We have breakfast at Waterman's Galley again. Opal is animated, discussing everything from local land prices to a recent forecast of impending rain; perhaps this is why she told me to bring my windbreaker.

After breakfast, we drive to a marina at the edge of Pine Island Sound. Parking at the foot of the closest dock, she turns to me.

"Today's therapy includes a boat ride," she says.

A pontoon boat is tethered to the end of the pier. The pontoons and the canvas top are indigo blue. A sign running the length of the canvas top proclaims *Cayo Costa Star*.

A tall man with skin the color of teak stands on the bow. He helps us both on board.

"Top of the morning, Opal," he says.

"Good morning, Vince. This is Pogue Whithouse, the gentleman I told you about. The professional boxer in the midst of a comeback. I'm taking him out to Cayo Costa for a training walk." Leaning close to me, she whispers, "A fantasy."

Vince says, "Better luck next time around, Mr. Whithouse."

"I've decided not to take any more bouts with horses."

"Wise career decision," says Vince.

A family of four is already aboard, sitting together on one of the wood benches running the width of the boat. A boy about Tesia's age looks at me and slides close to his mother.

When we sit, Opal whispers, "Vince might ask us to disembark if you start scaring off the customers."

"He'll have to go a few rounds first."

Opal gives me an approving nod.

"Good. All I ask for is a fighter who bounces back."

Out on the Sound, the sky is a dome of blue. The wind, a docile exhale from the west, ruffles the water. Vince maintains a continuous patter of history, ecology, and meteorology, but I confess I don't listen. Beneath the water, my fondest and darkest memories vie.

We disembark at Cayo Costa. The family stays aboard.

"Pickup is at three, kids," Vince says, easing away from the dock. "Weather's supposed to be fine for the afternoon, but it's taking a turn this evening, so don't miss your ride."

"Neap tide today," says Opal. "We can always walk back."

Vince laughs.

"No scaring the locals into punctuality."

Opal leads us along the Pinewoods Trail, a tunnel of Australian pines rising high above a groundcover of sea grape. The trail is soft with needles. It is cool among the pines, but the wind carries the smell of brackish water and mud baking in the sun.

I walk with one foot in the present and one in the past.

"Perfect therapy," I say. "Thank you."

"I thought you'd like it. Conrad and I used to ride together on paths like this. He had his faults like any man, but he was a natural horseman. He never rode until we met, but he took to the saddle as easily as he moved to second base."

Even at a slow walk, it takes less than fifteen minutes to cross the island. When we reach the white sand beach fronting the Gulf of Mexico, I see the weather change is ahead of schedule. On the horizon, dark clouds spit rain curtains; a chill breeze, advance scout of the inevitable, licks our faces.

Opal inhales.

"My forecast is we'll get wet."

"When I was a boy, standing in the rain was one of my favorite things." I pause, still deciding, and then I speak to the onrushing clouds. "I have a fantasy," I say.

The woman beside me is quiet.

"When we were kids, we rode sea turtles in the Indian river. We built rafts and hooked the turtles with grappling hooks that we slipped under the lip of their shells. It didn't hurt them. In fact, I'm sure they liked it."

These first words, I have to think about them, but what follows comes rushing, not unlike the ride itself.

"We rode the raft one at a time. I loved being alone. Sometimes when the turtle pulled the raft, I'd close my eyes and listen to the water rush past. I'd pretend the water was singing, washing everything else away."

I search. I have never spoken the words.

"Most of the time, the turtles swam under the water, but sometimes they'd come to the surface. Their backs looked like huge lily pads." Happiness swells in my chest, a balloon wresting free of worldly bindings. "When they surfaced, I talked to them. I told them how beautiful they were, and I thanked them for making my world right. I was self-conscious and shy, but out on the river, it didn't matter. It was the only time I was completely at ease, though I didn't think about it like that at the time. And you know something else? I knew they heard me. It's why they stayed on the surface. And the singing water was their answer."

The first fat drops of rain begin to fall, distinct and cold.

Very quietly, Opal says, "And the fantasy?"

I believe she already knows, just as I believe she asks so that I might gain one more ounce of pleasure.

"I'll ride again."

Driven by the wind, the heavy raindrops sting slightly.

"We can stay here," says Opal.

When I look at her, I see her chin is tucked.

"This song is too cold," I say.

A row of cabins sits behind the low dunes. We reach the first cabin, clambering up the wood steps to the narrow porch as the sky bursts. We stand close beneath the sloped covering, elbows touching, the rain smashing mightily against the corrugated tin roof. The wind shifts, throwing rain onto the porch. We press up against the cabin so that the rain only touches the ends of our shoes.

We look out at the beach, alive with countless mushroom explosions.

Opal's elbow slides away, and warm lips touch my cheek.

When I turn, Opal is looking out at the beach with that half smile familiar to all men, the one that tells us women will always be the unsurpassed keepers of secrets.

Opal speaks to the sea.

"I didn't say whose therapy," she says.

In this dream, Abby walks along the beach, but she is not alone. I stand at the jungle's edge watching. Together, my wife and her companion crouch and patiently assemble the turtle bones. One by one, the completed skeletons rise from the sand and crawl into the sea. There are so many bones, but my wife and her companion work undaunted. I run down the beach, but no matter how fast I run, they remain at a distance. They walk slowly, holding hands. They do not turn at my shouts. They only crouch and work their miracle with their hands. I don't care about the resurrected turtles. I kick furiously at the ones that get in my way, shattering them. I cry out in frustration, unable to reach my wife and our child.

I wake to my own shout.

Opal's fingertips gently raise the hair off my forehead. The cool towel is like a mother's touch.

"It's all right. Another fever."

The cool weights my eyelids. Opal's fingers make gentle circles on my temples.

I struggle to mumble.

"I was dreaming about turtles."

"I dream about riding," she says.

In the morning, the fever is gone. Opal is business-like again. She makes no mention of the previous afternoon or the night. If I didn't know better, I'd think they were part of my dream.

We skip breakfast at Waterman's Gallery. Opal drives the pickup to a Publix Supermarket. Driving into town, she tells me Doctor Sandoval will be by in the afternoon to assess my recovery.

"You need a few things," she says, stepping from the cab.

She walks across the parking lot without a backward glance. I sit in the cab for a moment, mildly stung. Then I smile. We are not teenagers.

I find her in an aisle lined with cheeses and packaged meats. There are already items in the cart—a carton of fresh squeezed orange juice, a box of Ritz crackers, and a shiny silver thermos.

"That thermos is older than you are," Opal says. "It's not women who can't let go of things."

Pointless to protest, but I do.

"It still keeps coffee hot."

"Not anymore it doesn't."

She speaks over her shoulder, continuing down the aisle. Suddenly I wonder if, in the throes of fever, I said something hurtful.

I catch up to her as she bends at the end of the aisle.

"Look." She holds out the package. "They carry the finest brands." Opal rises up on her toes and kisses me on the lips. "Sweet Thursday. The common bonds of love and humanity, which make goodness and happiness possible. Steinbeck's greatest theme and our lunch."

I stare at the package in her hand, a dumbstruck stump.

Opal smiles at me.

"With butterscotch pudding," she says.

When we turn into the driveway, a half-dozen horses wait patiently against the fence. I see their ribs and the odd flatness of their rumps. Their faces are unreadable, but they watch the truck with a concentration that is absolute.

They stab them with knives.

The horses recede in the rearview mirror, still standing against the railing, waiting for time to run out.

On the night Abby died, the chief coroner watched me in the same fashion. He stood in his starched white smock, his face blank as Stonehenge. He looked like he'd been born in the jacket and the job.

We stood alone on his tile floor, breathing disinfectant.

"I am so very sorry," he said.

I could not look at him. I stared at a calendar with a picture of a single flower, the only color in the room.

He was a doctor. He knew all our secrets.

"Does anyone else know?" I asked.

"No."

"Thank you."

"It's a private matter," he said.

I thought we were done.

"Mr. Whithouse, I hope I am not overstepping my bounds, but there is something I feel I should share."

I looked at him now. My head felt like a great weight that would keep falling forward until it struck the floor.

"Yes," I said.

"I arrived on the scene before your wife died. Her injuries were," he paused, "traumatic. You should know she was in shock. She felt no pain." One hand smoothed an already crisp lapel. "She should have died instantly. Science can't tell us what kept her alive for so long. She fought for your child. I thought you should know."

Even after their throats are slit and their shells are smashed, the females continue up the beach, laying their eggs in pools of blood.

It is a miracle, this strength, silent and strong as a river running, the truth surpassing the wildest imaginings of Pliny.

After dinner, we sit in front of the fireplace in the den. Opal has placed a single red candle on the crosshatched brick. Its flame rises up without a wavering flicker, casting humble light.

We had vegetarian lasagna for dinner—penance, Opal says, for our hot dog lunch. I sliced vegetables beside her. I held the knife in my left hand. My right arm, no longer in the sling, only sparked once or twice as I positioned mushrooms, green peppers, and Vidalia onions on the cutting board.

The house sprawls like the ranch itself. It is the first time I have been beyond the kitchen. To reach the den, we walk through a spacious dining room, two chandeliers above a gleaming oak table, and then down a carpeted hallway past four bedrooms. I look straight ahead.

The den is at the end of the hall. Framed photographs line bookshelves and the fireplace mantle; family portraits and weddings, birthday parties, men standing beside tarpon and swordfish, laughing children squeezing squirming dogs, a baseball team, square shouldered and floppy pantsed, staring into the lens with stiff pride. An Opal I still recognize wraps a young girl in her arms.

The verandah was comfortable, a place for visitors and recovering patients. But this is a place of memory, a sanctuary for two, only one is gone.

After lunch, Michael Sandoval, pressing again with competent hands, pronounced me sufficiently healed.

Opal sits quietly on the couch, watching the frozen flame.

"I should leave tomorrow."

Opal doesn't respond. At first, I think she's lost in memories.

"Someone came today with a horse," she says. "A sweet-natured bay."

I heard the trailer, gravel crunching in the drive.

"You probably think I'm foolish. You probably think I can't take care of the horses I have, but I'm actually quite well off."

She smiles at the candle.

"Mother and father were married in Fort Lauderdale. On their wedding night, they walked to a hill behind their motel to watch the sunset. They saw this huge black ball rolling toward them. My mother said it nearly blotted out the sun. My father recognized it first. They ran for their room as fast as they could, the ball right behind them. My mother said she'd never heard my father laugh like that. I'm pretty sure those mosquitoes saw to my conception. Every year on their anniversary, wherever they were, they stood outside at dusk even if there wasn't a sunset they could see or a mosquito in sight. Then they'd run back inside, slower each year, and they'd fall into each other's arms."

She is wearing white cotton slacks. Her fingers pluck at a knee.

"People here hate mosquitoes. We've swatted them, poisoned them, screened them out, and cemented over their marshes, but they're still here. I appreciate that. Conrad did too. Our children never shared our appreciation. They ran, and they just kept going."

Her eyes walk over the photographs for another moment.

"I digress." Sitting up straight, she smoothes both knees. "I say I'm well off because I am. I pay for the horses and their feed by selling off pieces of land. Developers are paying ridiculous prices, even when they're forced to wait until the owner seeds the mangroves. I know my children will sell the land anyhow. I'm saving enough for them. They have their own lives now and their own debts. After he contracted Lou Gehrig's disease, Conrad would say to me, 'Promise me you'll never sell this land. Children need a place where they can lie on their backs and look up at the sky.' But my life is filled with horses now, not children."

She looks at me. I know what the kind gray eyes want. It's easy because I don't have to lie.

"He would understand."

"I don't want to disappoint him."

"He would be proud of you."

A draft issues from somewhere, palming the candle flame on its side.

"I lie awake at night," Opal says, "wondering what I'm trying to accomplish. And the honest truth is I don't really care much for any of it anymore. This house, this island, this ranch, not even the starving horses. There are days when I feel like I'm just passing time, waiting to die." A finger hooks a silver bracelet. "You never think about things ending, but they do. There's a last time they'll ride on your knee, or turn a double play, or take you in their arms. But you don't know it then. You just assume there will be another moment. And then it's over. No more moments."

"Your accomplishments are all around you."

"I suppose."

"I need to tell you something."

"You don't need to tell me anything."

"It's important. Part of my therapy."

I try to make the words light, but neither of us is fooled.

"Abby, my wife, died in a car accident. She was twenty-nine. She was driving too fast. The roads were icy. She hit a tree." Accident still didn't sound right. "We'd had a fight. I could have stopped her, but I didn't. I just watched her go. A moment."

"Don't."

Secrets are a terrible burden and pointless in the end. This woman struggling beside me had shown me kindness beyond measure.

"Abby would have admired what you're doing. She loved turtles the way you love horses. I fell in love with her the instant I saw her, but I know it wasn't the same for her. She was a scientist. She was curious about me at first. She gave me a chance, because I loved turtles too. I believe she came to love me. But then I forgot what was important. And now I can never forget."

I need to finish quickly.

"You loved a man, and he loved you. You raised a family. And now you're the pied piper, an equine godsend. You care, and caring is all that matters."

I hear the shifting of cotton.

Opal says, "Thank you for caring for me."

She leans forward, a cautious movement, like a child extending a finger toward a fire. There is no burning heat, only the scrape of dry lips as they find their place and then the faintest hint of green pepper.

We slip into bed wordlessly like husband and wife. I position myself so that she is comfortable, our sounds like a soft expiring. When we finish, we face each other silently, our pasts between us.

Opal touches my face.

"It's not part of the nursing manual," she says.

"I'm finished with manuals."

It's true. I am. The thought makes me bold.

We hold this kiss for a long time.

"Shocking," says Opal. "What will the neighbors think?"

"We are a lawless set of rascals."

When I wake in the morning, my clothes are folded at the end of the bed. An envelope rests on top of the clothes.

The small blue cooler on the Mustang's front seat doesn't surprise me either. I am surprised to see no horses, either from the drive or the road.

I make a stop before leaving town. The woman behind the mahogany desk is surprised at first, but once she ascertains my sanity, she takes care of things efficiently, assuring no property will leave Opal's hands again. What her children do is up to them.

I wait until I am halfway across the Everglades before I pull over in a dirt turnout.

I know the poem inside the envelope.

There's a sigh for yes, and a sigh for no,
And a sigh for I can't bear it!
Oh what can be done, shall we stay or run?
Oh cut the sweet apple and share it!

The note is brief.

I hope you'll forgive me this cowardly good-bye. Thank you for saving my horse. And thank you for giving me another moment.

I place Opal's note beside the photograph of the leatherback hatchling propped up on the console.

Maybe I am fooling myself. Maybe it's too little, too late. But it's also true that I'm not the same man I was a few weeks ago. The fresh voices of three women echo in my head, sharing this new world with me.

40

Driving into Sharpes is like turning into a dream. At first, I recognize nothing. The streets are new, slicing between a manicured maze of cookie-cutter homes and cubist condominiums. The downtown is unrecognizable too. There are art galleries and sidewalk cafes and fancy restaurants hidden behind tinted floor-to-ceiling glass, the dim forms of servers moving about like fish schooling just beneath the surface.

But as I find my way toward the river, familiar street names smile back at me, though now they are etched on oversized baby blue signs with a seashell logo. These streets are paved and narrower than the ones I remember, the familiar bends come quicker, and then I am driving beside the Indian River, my heart hammering, the dark blue water flickering in and out behind gated mansions.

The mansions are clasped in the green canopy I knew, but the mansions rule the riverbank now, complete with wrought iron gates that allow no access. I have not accounted for this. We see change all around us, but we keep sacred places in a compartment that never changes.

Walls butting one against the other, the mansions shout that I am on a fool's errand, but I have come this far, and it is greater foolishness to give in without trying. I fight off despair. Faux stone walls press right to the road. Even if I decide to try to find my way to the river through the few narrow bramble alleys between the homes, I will have to park in the middle of the street.

I drive slowly, passing from sunshine to shadow and back again, my will crumbling. I wave to a man standing at his mailbox. He returns a blank stare. I prepare to give up and turn away.

And then, easy as that, the phalanx of mansions falls away, and there is nothing but bright green grass and the river beyond, moving powerfully beneath the wide sky. I pull over and stare at the wood dock, blood hammering in my ears. For a moment, I'm certain my mind is playing its consummate trick, but if it is, my imagination has no equal, for when I step into the field, the grass gives lush way, and marshy river smell squishes up beneath me.

I nearly go to my knees, but I see a man making his way across the road toward me, and it is strange etiquette to greet someone on your knees, so I collect myself.

The man emerges from a wall of foliage on the opposite side of the road. Breaks in the foliage reveal the outline of a modest ranch home and, to one side, a series of rounded glass rooftops.

That the man chose greenery to ensure his privacy makes me like him already. That he ambles across the grass, fishing pole in hand, makes me want to throw my arms around him.

Relief and a bubbling touch of madness see me grin village-idiot wide as he draws near. Perhaps this is why he keeps his distance.

"Afternoon, sir," he says. He looks around, as if considering the day for the first time. "Classy vehicle you got there. Had one myself once, before greedy oil executives made it too pricey."

He's in his late fifties, but the slow amble did not mask the boyish spring in his step. He sports gray coveralls. His head is shaved to matching gray stubble. The coveralls are liberally spotted with dark stains that give off a smell I have nearly forgotten. I am afraid memory makes me sway even more.

He steps closer, considers reaching out but doesn't.

"You feelin' okay? Heat here can get to you if you're not used to it."

"I'm fine, thank you. I might have been behind the wheel a little too long. This land …"

His face goes hard.

"I'm not sellin'."

"I'm not buying," I say. "But if it's your land, I wonder if you would be kind enough to let me look at the river from your dock."

His jaw relaxes.

"You're the rare fellah who asks. Come on. It's nothin' fancy, but the whole damn lot's mine. Give you a personal tour. Name's Gray. Like the sky."

"Pogue Whithouse."

I will myself to walk.

"Excuse the smell," says Gray. "Raisin' oysters is dirty work. Neighbors don't like the smell of oysters much, but I'd guess the oysters don't feel much different about them."

It's as if the river is pouring down my throat. I focus, counting my steps to the dock. At the foot of the dock, two pilings rise from the muddy bank. They are weathered as rotted bones. I rest a hand against one of the pilings to steady myself. The wood is flesh soft.

"Rotted through, no doubt," says Gray, rubbing the stubble on his head. "I'm prone to old things, or, if you talk to my wife, plain lazy. S'pose I should replace the entire dock, but it still feels solid enough to me."

We walk over the planks. I step gingerly over the spots where flooring has gone missing.

"Everything else around here is too damn linear already," Gray says. "The world needs a few chipped teeth."

Halfway down the dock, two boys are fishing. They've used a gap in the planks to hang a six-pack of soda, filament line attached, in the river. They might be twelve or thirteen. One boy sits on an overturned bucket. The other, Orioles cap pulled down almost to the bridge of his nose, walks along the edge of the dock, his taut line making tight circles in the water.

When Gray grins, he looks twelve too. He plucks the boy's line with a finger.

"That means you got a bite."

The boy grunts.

"Just lettin' you know," says Gray. "Not sure if you can see anythin' from under there."

"I kin see."

"Where's your landing net, goober?"

"Ain't got one."

Gray winks at me.

"He didn't come down here to catch fish. He came down to go fishing."

Bending, Gray grabs the line and yanks. The jack, silver as a freshly minted dime, flies from the water and nearly strikes the boy across the shins. Boy and fish are equally surprised, but the jack recovers first. Snapping its tail against the planks, it performs two quick flops and plunks back in the water. The line goes taut and snaps.

"Catch 'n' release, you take the hook out first," Gray says.

"Jack's garbage fish," the boy mutters.

"You're only sayin' that cuz he got away. Not that I'm complainin'. One more for me."

We walk to the end of the dock. A rusted bucket sits beside a net and a mayonnaise jar.

"Owner's private box seat," says Gray. He leans his pole against a piling. "Given up on boats. Too goddamned expensive. Docks don't break down all the time. And when they do, you can just ignore 'em."

The river seems even wider than I remember. It stretches away like a dark blue prairie. A south wind sends white clouds scudding across the sky. The river gathers the sun and throws its heat against our faces.

Think I can swim across it?

I close my eyes, riding away on the flood, buffeted by storms. A knife and a tooth are swallowed again by indifferent waters.

"Fine day on the river. Welcome to Florida, Mr. Whithouse— least what's left of it. What brings you here from California? Ain't the fishin' any good out on the Left Coast?"

A school of mullet broils just off our feet, their thrashings making a sound like pebbles scattered on the water. They flash white just beneath the surface. It is my version of Christmas Eve snowfall.

"Open them up," I say softly, "and they're clean and white and sweet as can be."

Gray's eyes are on me.

"These fish, you catch 'em, their insides are black," he says. "River's polluted. Factories discharging effluent, and the damn Yankees coming down the Intracoastal in their Jewish canoes, dumping their shit along the way." For the first time, he smiles broadly. "But you're right, Mr. Whithouse. Ain't nothin' like smoked mullet. You get your mullet from the ocean, it's still like it was back when the river was clean."

His smile disappears. I follow his gaze to the middle of the river. A colossal yacht beats south, starboard side glinting in the sun.

"Headin' for Fort Ladydale. They'd lose their cobs if they had to come down by way of the Atlantic. The corps of engineers built this canal so they won't spill their martinis."

"Why isn't this land developed?"

"Because it's mine. I hope you were tellin' the truth back there. You don't look like a developer, but if you are, I don't care whose grandfather you are, you aren't welcome on this dock."

"I'm not buying anything."

"Good. Then we're both done repeatin' ourselves."

Gray flicks his wrist. Together we watch his line drop to the water, accompanied by Gray's hopeful whisper.

Reeling in slack, he says, "I'm sorry. It's just I'm plain worn down by the way things are headin', and bein' worn makes me rude. The South is a place. East, west, and north are nothin' but directions. But I fear one day it's all gonna be the same. Starbucks and Bubba Gump Shrimp, coast to coast." He flips a broken shell into the water with the toe of a boot. "Protectin' something special makes you feisty and a trifle paranoid too."

I am faltering in my purpose. I want to stand by this river forever, marinating in memories. My punishment and pleasure.

"May I ask another favor?"

"Long as it doesn't involve ceden' my fishin' hole."

Gray retrieves a shovel from his house. I wait at the foot of the dock. Behind me, the boy on the bucket gives a victorious yelp.

Holding up his fish, he shouts to Gray, "His bad luck ain't mine!"

"Them boys is fairly swimmin' in trophy fish," Gray says to me.

Beneath the crescent moon, I had paced off a straight line, thirty-five steps. Even then I knew enough to account for erosion and the occasional hurricane surge.

Toe to heel, heel to toe, slowly I step again. Gray walks beside me, shovel on his shoulder. I stop at thirty. My feet are bigger now.

Gray refuses to let me dig, just as he refuses to ask why he is digging. He digs three holes, each about two feet deep, before the shovel blade bites something hard.

"I'll be damned," he says.

He lays the shovel in the grass. On his knees, he carefully scoops the last dirt with his hands. The can is rusted, the Nescafe label long gone, but the plastic lid sits firm.

Gray keeps one hand on the can. My hands are shaking so badly we both know I will drop it.

He produces a smile I haven't seen before.

"Ready when you are," he says.

It takes me an embarrassingly long time to pry off the lid, for my fingers tremble too.

The can releases the cool of another time.

My fingertips touch the lanyard first. Sliding along the cracked leather, they touch cold stone. A firm hand grips my elbow.

I lift the talisman from the can.

Gray whistles.

"Beautiful."

He is right. The jade is spotted and dull, but the intricate carving remains lifelike to the finest detail.

I wipe it carefully with my shirt sleeve, and the past gleams.

I want to explain, but I can't speak.

Gray gently takes the can from my hand so that I can balance.

"Coffee's probably past its expiration date," he says. "Heard this was once a gathering spot, kids playin' in the river, spillin' a little blood, doin' what kids should do. You might like to know there's one or two of 'em still around. I like hearin' about the past, and they like talkin'. Claim they rode on the backs of turtles big as a Volkswagen bus."

He waits, but I cannot help this kind man. I have to turn away.

"Heard tell it was quite a ride," Gray says.

Like love, like loss.

Gray coughs.

"Unless you need me, I'd best be gettin' back to the oysters. Got anything else buried out here? The Hope Diamond? Jimmy Hoffa?"

"No."

I am embarrassed to find I have grabbed Gray's arm. I release him reluctantly.

"Thank you."

"If I recall correctly, I was a tad rude at the outset. I'm sorry. It's hard not to be judgmental. California and all."

"The South is a place."

My fist clenches the turtle as if it might swim away.

"I guess I don't need to worry about our world disappearing entirely," says Gray. "You're welcome back any time."

"I won't be back." It sounds all right. "I'm almost done with digging."

"Well then, that's fine."

Gray takes his slow steps. He turns back.

"Mr. Whithouse?"

"Yes."

"I want you to know I ain't ever sellin' this land."

Turning to the river, he gives a loud whistle.

"Ladies! Enough time on my dock today! Time to get!"

He turns back to me, but I cannot look at him.

"Don't want 'em fishin' the place out," he says. "Make yourself at home."

After the grumbling boys stalk past, I am alone. Palmed by insect hum and heat, I stand for a time, barely aware of my legs beneath me. But when I ask them to walk, they do, taking me out to the end of the dock.

I stare at the pendant in my hand, the hump of shell with its grid-work lines, the crosshatched neck, the graceful tapering of the flippers. It is the work of a gifted artisan.

When you are young, you believe secrets can be buried.

There is only one rightful place. I turn my hand over. The amulet floats for a moment before wobbling down into the darkness.

Some might pray to God. I cry and listen to the river sing.

41

Sarah prayed. Now and then, between poetry readings, she talked about prayer at the kitchen table. Snow drifting down like comfort, every flake different, she would ask me how I could doubt God's existence. She saw my lack of belief not as a fault but as a momentary setback. She never pressed like the Seventh-Day Adventists who came to my San Francisco door with their obstinate faces and their fifty-cent pamphlets. When she spoke of God, she spoke as softly and gently as the snowfall.

Sarah prayed fervent, well-meaning Episcopal prayers, but Ben still died on a July afternoon, within sight of the sailboats running before the Nantucket Sound breeze. He had taken a side job, applying his engineering skills as a repairman maintaining the rides for the carnival that came to town every summer. Fair skinned, he favored long sleeves. A sleeve caught in the chain of the Jet Flyer roller coaster. He rose sixty feet before the cloth tore loose.

I flew back from San Francisco unannounced. I hesitated right up to the front door, at the last debating my reflection in the arc of glass, but there are some things you cannot run from. From an upstairs window came the strains of a flute.

Sarah answered the door. She seemed neither happy nor angry. I knew her anchorless sway. She accepted my presence as she accepted the choice of flowers at the service. Time had seen her soften, the sharp angles rounded. Gray streaked her hair. Beyond that, she was unchanged, for this is another card in womanhood's repertoire of magic. Opening the door, she stepped into my arms without feeling. We did not hold each other long.

The Episcopal minister who buried Abby, now coming into the softness of middle age himself, performed the ceremony as I had known he would.

When it was done, Sarah and I stood again on the rise above the Bremser family plot. There were more headstones, set closer together. In 1975, the Vietnam War had only recently finished further seeding the grounds. The forest we had looked down on at Abby's funeral was gone, replaced by a sea of gray shingle rooftops making wavy rows along treeless streets.

"They call it Walden Pond," Sarah said. It was strange to hear bitterness in her voice. "Our next-door neighbor built the pond. It's cement, with an aerating system."

"It would be better if there were but one inhabitant to a square mile, as where I live," I said, but as soon as I finished, Henry David Thoreau's words drowned in the gray-roof sea.

"Thoreau would have stood his ground," Sarah said. "We should have stood our ground."

Three boys rode their bikes along the loopy roads. Even from a distance, I recognized the banana seats and the high handlebars.

"Ben took the job so we could send Cassandra to summer music school in Maine." She shrugged, as if memory were a bug ushered off her shoulder.

"How is Cassandra?"

"Six and without a father."

"I'd like to help."

I hated the sound.

"We don't need help. My parents can take care of us. We have lots of friends. Ben had insurance." Her voice caught. "He was a good provider."

I took her listless hand.

"If you will tell me why the fen appears impassable, I then will tell you why I think that I can get across it if I try."

Downy hairs rested above her lip.

"You sent that to me," I added. "During the war."

The hand withdrew.

"They're just words," she said.

Far away, voices shouted. The boys were up on their bikes, racing. They jerked the handlebars back and forth, scrubbing away their own speed.

"Why such a pointless life, Henry?"

"No," I said, and the fierce hiss of my voice shocked me.

Sarah regarded me as if I'd gone mad. Perhaps I had.

"You have to understand the difference," I said. "Death is senseless. But life is not. You and Cassandra, you are one in a thousand. You have to try."

"Abby's turtles." She didn't mean it to be cruel. "You and I, we win?"

"Yes. In life's fashion."

"Well, there's the rub."

The bike racers had stopped. They bent over their handlebars, legs spread, no doubt panting furiously, no doubt ignoring the gift of doing so.

"An amusement ride," Sarah said, and she began to cry.

She gave a hiccupping sob.

"I forced him to take the job," she said.

Before I left, I went to Abby's grave. It was covered in thick grass now. The green veldt shoved at the ceramic vase of lilacs, making it list. Bending, I straightened the vase. Thanks to horticultural advances, lilacs no longer experience an ephemeral season. The florist delivered a fresh vase twice a month. Abby could no longer protest the extravagance.

I wondered if the person who bent to place the flowers gave the delivery any thought.

Many things separate us, but the earth does so with an inarguable physicality. I had made love to the woman beneath my feet. She had possessed my heart.

Some things were still possible, some were not.

Someone coughed.

When I turned, the minister was wiping a broad, freckled forehead with a handkerchief.

"I wanted to tell you how sorry I am for your loss," he said.

He was, I could tell.

I said, "We always wish we could change things, don't we?"

"We do. But so many things are beyond us."

His burgundy vestments shone in the bright sunshine. By my figuring, he was no more than fifty, but he had lost most of his hair.

"The timing is inappropriate, but I know I'll have no other chance. I want to thank you for your ongoing support of the church."

"It's not a selfless enterprise."

He gave a bemused smile.

"The church has never declined offerings of that sort."

Are they schooled in wise irony and diplomatic grace, or do the skills just come naturally?

"You'll let me know if they need anything?" I asked.

"Of course."

He waited. His beaded forehead broadcast his discomfort.

Smiling, I said, "You have another question."

We had only spoken at length once, but I had come to like him. He had written me letters now, one every two months, for twenty-three years. The letters mentioned almost nothing of his life, but even letters written about someone else eventually reveal much about the writer. He had been meticulously diligent in keeping me informed, often with a dash of dry humor.

He dabbed his brow with a frayed handkerchief.

"And you have a keen sense of human frailty," he said. "You would have made a good priest, you know."

"It's too late for a career change."

"It's never too late in my vocation."

"Your question?"

"Right. Understand, I ask only because I care. Your life, I know it has been difficult, with substantial," he searched for the word,

Together We Jump

"burdens. I have also surmised that you are not," he hesitated again, "much of a churchgoer. I know you are only with us briefly, but if you feel the need to talk …"

"I've never been much for confessing."

I said it politely but with finality.

"Not confessing. More of an unburdening. It's something you might like to try at some point. It might help you reach some understanding."

I understood my sins far too well.

"Thank you. I won't forget your offer."

When he smiled, the piety left him, and he became more human.

"I suppose that's the best I could have hoped for."

The rest of the mourners had fled for their air-conditioned cars. He stood with his hands folded in front of him. I don't know why I asked. I was suddenly curious, and in all our letter exchanges, I had never asked before.

"Did you always want to be a priest?"

His smile spread.

"I go first?"

"Think of it more as an unburdening."

"I wanted to be a musician. I played jazz trumpet. Louis Armstrong, Dizzy Gillespie, Fats Navarro. If He will forgive me for this instant, they were my gods."

I remembered a letter noting Armstrong's passing.

"Do you still play?"

"Rarely. It makes quite a din in the rectory. Church architects have a thing for high ceilings. And church work occupies my time."

I remembered the music from the upstairs window.

"Cassandra still plays the flute," I said.

"Oh yes, she does." Each word an exclamation. The priestly smile gone, replaced by a dreamier version, spellbound by something floating through a smoky room. "She doesn't just play. She has a gift, a true gift, perhaps from God. I've attended every one of her recitals.

They are glorious. She is transported by music. Perhaps, you might say, swept away to a better place."

"I knew a boy who experienced that too."

"Was he a musician?"

"No."

"It is a gift that comes in many forms. Were you close?"

"Close enough to stand in his light."

"A gift in itself."

The manner in which he spoke told me he was no longer preaching.

After the minister departed, I stood alone with Abby. I don't believe the dead are listening, so I just stood in the sun thinking. Before I left, I bent to settle the flowers a last time. Rising, I reached out and steadied myself against her headstone. It was cold even in the heat.

If we are God's consummate accomplishment, why do we alone stand before a grave crippled by regret?

42

As an officer, the ferreting of the Japanese from their subterranean mazes was not meant for me, but I took my turn, squeezing through the black nightmare tunnels. This only caused my men to fear me more. In camp and on patrol, I felt their eyes on me. Perhaps they were right. Perhaps I was unhinged. I didn't know. I did know that a leader offers no explanation, and there was no simple explanation to offer.

And so, on another blast-furnace afternoon, the world hung with stench and blowflies, my men stood about a narrow opening we had found half hidden behind a jumble of rocks.

Flashlight in one hand, rifle in the other, I entertained a brief vision of Abby on our honeymoon night, and then I left the world behind.

The beginning of the passage allowed a few inches of clearance on either side of my shoulders, as if encouraging me down, but soon enough, it narrowed so that, even with my elbows tucked together in front of me, I was nearly wedged in place. Rocks snagged and tore my clothing. Sweat, salty and stinging, ran into my eyes. My chin bumped and scraped against limestone. I could not raise it.

The tunnel proceeded down at a steep angle. Pushing with the toes of my boots, fingertips straining in the dark for the first hint of cool, I inched forward. I could see nothing, not even my arms, but I did not turn the flashlight on, for if the tunnel ended in an inhabited cave, the beam would broadcast my coming. Leaving the flashlight off was a gamble too. Sometimes the Japanese burrowed up into the tunnels, waiting. I listened with every fiber, hearing nothing but my own screaming scrapings and raspings and the inexplicable notes of a show tune playing in my head. I tried to push the tune away—distraction meant death—but it continued to play. I resigned myself to terror's tricks.

My heart stopped with the first scent of cool. In the moment I realized the music wasn't in my head, the rock beneath my outstretched hands disappeared, and my surprised hands dropped both the flashlight and the rifle.

I followed them as fast as I could, pushing wildly with my feet and falling from the opening, scrabbling forward on my knees, hands sweeping the rock blindly, knowing these queer panting seconds were my last.

In the darkness, the sounds of Glenn Miller drifted. No one lifted the scratching needle.

My fingers touched steel. When I flicked on the flashlight, it was trained directly on the Japanese soldier, the phonograph beside him.

The slumped figure had disobeyed his emperor's decree to kill every last imperialist, but had I been the emperor, I would have forgiven him, for he was barely a boy. Perhaps at the last, his will had betrayed him. Now it fought to keep him alive. He had driven the bayonet into his chest with enough force to pin himself to the cave wall, but the slender fingers of a hand fretted with a trouser seam, and between scratchings, I heard faint inspiration.

Lifting the needle, I placed it at the beginning of the record. The boy's eyes looked to me as I sat beside him, but then they returned to whatever vision floated in the darkness. Bloody fingers tapped out a jittery rhythm. After a time, he laid his head against my shoulder, consenting to the unstitching in his chest.

There's gonna be a certain party
at the station
Satin and lace,

I used to call funny face.
she's gonna cry—until I tell her
that I'll never roam,
So Chattanooga Choo Choo won't
you choo choo me, home …

Together we listened. I stroked his hair, and when Glenn Miller's band struck a particularly joyous note, I pushed the bayonet home.

In their vast migrations, leatherback turtles follow no prescribed route. Each turtle charts its individual course. Able to shunt their blood to their core, and so adapt to waters warm and frigid, they are the closest thing the reptilian world has to warm blooded. They possess the highest red blood cell density of any reptile, a density hauntingly similar to that of mammals. The glands near the leatherback's eyes—the ones that filter and discharge salt in big goopy tears, allowing the turtle to drink saltwater without dehydrating—evolved from the glands that bathe our own eyes in salty fluid, adding a titrate more pain to our tears.

But they are not us. The deepest recorded leatherback dive is 3,900 feet: three-quarters of a mile. Imagine the silence and salve in a world we will never know. And always they swim, undaunted and without question, toward what they know is right, the past dissolving like bubbles in their wake.

But I know there is a connection between us. When the turtles made their languid bankings, turning toward us as we kicked out into the river, rising to the surface to expose their shells, both child and turtle felt it, as real as the current sweeping us both along.

Before you say my imagination has bested me, I will tell you that science—cold and analytic calculator—has noted this bond. One sleepless night, when we still lived in our apartment in Boston, I found one of Abby's notebooks on the kitchen table. Opening its weather-beaten cover, I read *Xica cmotomanoj*.

Abby's precise writing, the letters squared off as if chiseled, continued, documenting the ritual of the Seri people, fisherfolk who have lived for millennia in the Gulf of California, staunchly clinging to their language and culture in the face of modernity's tide.

The Seri sing, and the turtles come. More than two dozen scientists have seen it. Aiden tells me he knows a biologist, as skeptical as they come, who saw this with his own eyes. A fisherman took him, along with a tribal elder, out into the Sea of Cortez. The weather was miserable— windy, choppy, cold—weather that guaranteed no turtle sightings. The tribal elder, a woman, began to sing, and slowly the winds eased and the seas calmed, and turtles began rising to the surface. The biologist was so moved he wept, but the woman just shrugged. "We sing," she said, "and the turtles come."

Beneath this, my wife had made a last notation.

We are linked.

I would later come to know Aiden through his letters—the letters that would see the blood of my wife and our unborn child sink into the night ice, though I do not hold this against him, for it was my accident, and it no doubt broke his heart. But on this Boston night, that horror was ahead of me. Sitting at the table, reading the story again, it was Sean I thought of, my invincible brother, and I understood, as clearly as the Seri did, our connection to the sea turtle.

Xica cmotomanoj.

Vulnerable one.

43

"Georgia's gross."

"What do you mean?"

"It's a smelly swamp. With slugs."

At least I think she says *slugs*. The phone is so small in my hand, it's always sliding away. The ringing, sudden and unexpected, flusters me too, so that I often forget to hold it up to my good ear.

"Gross and stinky and filled with bugs," she adds, no doubt for clarification.

"I thought you liked bugs."

"Not when they're crawling in yuck."

Again I am missing something.

"You have marshes on Cape Cod," I say. "They have yuck and bugs."

"*Ours* don't smell like campground toilets."

Outside, the Georgia marshes scroll past, fields of wheat beneath threatening black clouds. It's true; the smell drifting through the Mustang's window is the sort that makes you check your feet. I roll up the squeaking window.

"See?"

Tesia triumphant.

"See what?"

"You rolled up your window. Georgia smells like wet manure. People in Georgia still use *outhouses*. Mom says that must give Dad hives. He uses lemon wipes on doorknobs."

White trash. Georgia's browbeating falls into place.

"Mom says she's gonna buy stock in disinfectant wipes. What's stock?"

"It has something to do with money, but it's pretty boring compared to bugs and bullfrogs."

"I know what Georgia's near."

Through the windshield, the world makes a flashbulb pop. Thirty minutes earlier, I crossed the St. Mary's River in a lightning storm that made the hairs on my forearm prickle. The drumming rain has stopped, but lightning still forks down, illuminating the world in horror film bursts. I wondered if cell phones conduct electricity.

"Pogue. You're supposed to guess."

"I'm sorry."

"You apologize too much."

"I'm sorry."

"Ha ha. Since you won't guess, I'll tell you. *Florida* is next to Georgia."

Abrupt silence. Apparently a new guessing game is on the table.

"And Florida smells like suntan lotion?"

"No. You *lived* in Florida. When *you* were a boy. Sarah said there were real Indians in Florida back then. Seminoles. I looked them up on the Internet. They weren't fierce like the Apaches." The disappointment is palpable. "They looked kind of tired and sad. Sarah said that Florida was a hard place before air-conditioning and mosquito spraying. I looked you up too. I got hot dogs."

What is astonishing to one generation is routine to the next. And so progress continues.

"I'm on the computer?"

"Everything's on Google. But only hot dogs for you."

My life in sum. It does not bother me. I don't want to share the rest with strangers.

"Sarah told me you don't talk much. She's right."

I wonder what else these two women have shared.

"Tell me something about you. Since I don't own a computer."

"Like what?"

"Tell me what you like. Besides bullfrogs."

"Baseball," she says, and I smile. "I don't play yet, but I'm already really good at wiffle ball. Sarah says I have a swing like butter. Next spring, I'm signing up for Little League. The boys in my class say girls can only play softball. I can't wait to hit a line drive into their teeth. I'm going to be the first girl to play professional baseball. I'm going to play for the Red Sox. Anybody can hit a ball as big as a grapefruit."

Somehow an indignant huff travels from Massachusetts to reside in my ear.

Lightning flashes, a lovely trident forking. Nature produces her miracles too. The air near a lightning strike is hotter than the sun.

"When the Red Sox come to California," I say, "I'll come see you play."

"You'll have to live a lot longer."

"I'll do my best."

"I also like brownies with Miracle Whip. I love animals. I have lots of friends, but Meghan Malloy is my best friend. I don't have brothers or sisters. My parents had me late in life. Mallory says I'm a mistake."

"Who is Mallory?"

"A know-it-all in my class."

"Someone who makes me as happy as you do isn't a mistake."

"That has nothing to do with being a mistake. It's about protection."

I move on.

"Do you like jewelry?"

"No. It gets stuck on things. A girl in our class got her bracelet caught in Mrs. Huber's paper shredder. I wish it had been Mallory, but it wasn't. It was Monique, and she's nice. Do you drive a fast car?"

"Pretty fast. It's called a Mustang."

"Cowboys ride Mustangs."

"They should name a car after bullfrogs."

"My dad bought a Corvette. I don't know what it's named after, but Mom says he bought it because he's a little boy who's afraid to grow old. I miss him. Mom says it's better the way it is. Dad wants to grow younger, and she's growing older, so they can't live together anymore. That's why we live with Sarah."

"Cassandra."

"You know my mom?"

"A little. Does your mom still play the flute?"

"She did when she was a girl, but she doesn't now. She gave her flutes away to our school music program. How do you know she played the flute?"

"Someone told me."

"It must have been a long time ago."

"It was."

"Well, I hope I don't grow old waiting for you to get here."

Thirty seconds later, the phone rings again. I nearly drive into the marsh trying to grab it off the passenger seat.

"I forgot," Tesia says. "I wanted to apologize."

"Apologize for what?"

"The last two roses. They died. It was my fault. I took them up to my room. I didn't know you had to change the water all the time. In one night, they turned all gross and smelly."

"Worse than Georgia?"

"Maybe."

"You shouldn't worry at all. Roses don't last long no matter how often you change the water."

"I couldn't save them."

I have no answer for this.

"I'm sorry for what I said about the marshes too. I'm sure Georgia's okay."

The marshes scroll past, spared of any feeling.

"Guess what," I say.

"What?"

"We both apologize too much."

There is a long silence before she speaks.

"That's why we're friends."

I cross the Altamaha River into Darien in the middle of the afternoon. I drive slowly across the two-lane bridge. In the thunderstorm's wake, steam tendrils rise from the river.

Downtown Darien is quiet again, this time under a bright sun. Square brick buildings still front the sidewalk in all their unremarkable glory, but their windows proclaim a town of commerce and life. Hank Sturm's Realty, Bobbie Joe's Hair Salon, Leander's Café, Chubby Chet's Smokehouse Bar B Que.

The white-steeple church still rises above the town. I park in front of it.

A lovely park rests behind the church. I walk among pines still limp from the rain and rows of mud-spattered daisies. The daisies are landscaped in perfect tiers like brightly dressed stadium spectators cheering my slow passing. It is hot, but already the Altamaha is stirring up its own breeze as rivers do. As I walk, I taste the first touch of cool.

Despite the glorious afternoon, the brick footpaths are empty. No one picnics on the grass. The playground, a colorful kaleidoscope of monkey bars and slides, yawns vacant.

A man shuffles toward me. He is my age, possibly even older. His snow-white hair is accentuated by ivory-black skin. In his determined march, he bends so far forward I can see the yarmulke bald spot atop his head.

Here is my zombie. It makes me smile.

When he shuffles within earshot, I say, "A fine afternoon for a walk."

Wrenching his gaze from his feet, he regards me impassively.

"Shouldn't be here," he says. "You'd best get."

He doesn't stop walking, but I do.

He barks again, without turning back.

"Don't say I didn't warn you."

A minute later, I hear the familiar chuck-chuck-chucking.

He waits for me, safely out of range. By the time I reach him, I am drenched.

"Guess you can skip the swim," he says.

His face remains stone, but the white eyebrows bump up and down.

I laugh, at the eyebrows, at the sprinklers, at myself.

"Who sets sprinklers for the middle of the afternoon?"

The eyebrows make a quick bob.

"No law says groundskeepers can't have a little fun."

How can we not see the truth when it's right in front of our eyes?

That evening, I take a walk among the pines. The wind blows their tops so that they form a lovely waving sea. I would like to walk with pleasant memories, but I don't.

Again my elbows and knees scrape across gravel as we roll in the dirt. Sean's fist drives into my side, but fury puts me beyond feeling. I hear my brother's grunt as I pin him beneath me, hear my gasps as I raise the impartial weight in my hand.

None of us ever spoke of it again. Sean had only two months' worth of chances, and my father was a close-mouthed man.

I can never be certain that, when my father grabbed me, I was not bringing the hammer down.

In the morning, buzzing summons me in the middle of shaving. I reach into my pocket. It amuses me how quickly I have succumbed to technology's summons.

Tesia speaks in a rapid-fire whisper.

"I knew you'd be awake. I can't talk long. I'm sitting in the car. Mom went back inside to turn off her curling iron. I'm not allowed to use my phone before school."

"Maybe you shouldn't be calling," I say, though we both know I don't mean it.

"Remember the bullfrogs?"

"Of course."

"For homework, Mrs. Huber told us to look up five interesting things about bullfrogs. Guess what? They can jump *six feet*. They jump up out of the water and swallow *flying* birds. They have *teeth*. Mrs. Huber never told us *that*."

"I'm sure she knew the bullfrogs wouldn't jump up and bite you."

"One time we had a substitute named Mrs. Hyanoora. She was a nice Japanese lady, but she went to the bathroom a thousand times. Every time she did, Junior DeSalis reached into the cage and yanked the bullfrogs' legs. I wish the frogs had bitten him."

"I know something about regular frogs."

"What?"

"In Japan, they're good luck."

"Maybe I can put that on my extra-credit list. I hope our bullfrogs are happy in heaven."

"I'll bet they're jumping sixty feet and picking bits of Junior DeSalis out of their teeth."

"That would be good. Mom's coming out the door."

"If she was a bullfrog, she'd be there already," I say, but the line is dead.

Presto, the day is fresh.

44

The eastern seaboard looms before me like a roadblock. Traveling no longer interests me. I have seen enough of my country. Shouldering only a mild twinge of guilt, I leave the back roads and join the dull, efficient rush of Interstate 95. That night, in a Savannah motel, I consult my map. On the TV, a newsman speaks of a crumbling economy and turmoil in the Middle East, but I barely listen. My eyes measure the coast. Three days of steady driving.

I remove the book from the satchel, the spine pliant from long use. It would be easy to buy a new copy, but I don't want one. There comes a time when holding something old is as pleasant as holding something young once was.

I read, but I am restless again. Steinbeck's words do not hold me. I put *Sweet Thursday* down and go outside.

The motel's security lights veil the stars. There is an empty field across the street. I walk out into the middle of the field and look up into the sky. The night is clear, a few bluish cloud tendrils, like ephemeral islands, backed by immense darkness. The stars waver. A bird calls hopefully, but no bird responds.

Our father fought in Germany in World War I. He never talked about his service, but I know he was shot once by a dumdum bullet. The Hague Convention didn't allow them, but there it was. The bullet entered his thigh cleanly and exited just below his butt, whisking a chunk of shredded flesh into the muddy night. The wound left a smooth, polished patch of skin. When he shaved in the mornings, Sean and I would stand silently in the open doorway, weaving and bobbing like boxers, trying to glimpse our reflections in his marble skin.

Our father never acknowledged us. He stood naked, tufts of hair in strange places, shaving precisely, while behind him his seed turned his sacrifice into a fun-house mirror.

The day he died, I asked him how he was shot. I did not know he was so close to death, but anyone could see his body was unraveling, and a fraction of his stubbornness unraveled alongside it, and I confess I took advantage of this. I had more important questions, but I knew there were answers even dying wouldn't unstitch.

He was tired and barely interested, but he answered. He remained brief to the end. He never saw the shooter. It was night. The rain came down in buckets. He could barely see his own hand. He had to give the sniper credit. After he was shot, he crawled into an empty foxhole. After a time, a French sniper joined him. The Frenchman gave him cognac from a canteen. When my father regained consciousness, he had been stripped of everything but his long underwear.

I waited, but there was nothing more.

I asked him if he bore either man any ill will.

My father looked up.

"People make mistakes," he said.

He looked very old, and this time he was, mouth again slack, skin sagging, the sunken cheeks beneath gray grizzle now fairly drowning in a latticework of broken veins.

There was no epiphany. I already knew what I had seen on the porch that afternoon when my father asked me to sit beside him, a glimpse of a mask dropping away.

We had both let Sean go.

"Dad," I said. "It's okay," but he was already asleep.

The nursing home called that night. They found him on the floor by the window. The nurse was matter-of-fact. I knew they weren't sad to see him go. He had shouted at everyone for almost everything, and once he had threatened to use the wrought iron door stopper to smash his TV when management ignored his requests to remove the TV from his room.

I hung up the phone and looked at my watch.

Nine twenty-five. Time to become a man.

I collected his belongings the next morning. Everything fit in one box—toiletries, a blanket our mother had made for him when he returned from the war, and a dozen books, among them, to my surprise, several dog-eared astronomy titles.

I had prepared myself for this, the last of my family passing, but I found it difficult to breathe. I went to open the window. A Dixie cup, half filled with water, balanced on the sill. A half-size lollipop, still perfectly round, rested in the water. After a lifetime of picking up discards, our father hated to waste anything.

I picked the cup up, intending to dump it in the bathroom sink, but my legs disobeyed me. I stood by the window, holding the cup. The sunlight turned its eggshell form translucent. In the silence of this stark room, our father's tongue had patiently sculpted the lollipop. I wondered what he had thought about as he stood at the window, rolling it around in his mouth. Our mother? Mrs. Cooper? The intractable nursing home management? His own stubborn inability to reprise his beliefs and accept the son he loved?

I would like to think in the end our father reached a semblance of peace. One never recovers from the loss of a child; this is unbearably true for a parent who believes he played a role. I sometimes wonder if he ever shared Sean's secret with Mrs. Cooper. It's possible. None of us is truly an island; even my stubborn father may have had a breaking point. I'll never know. But I'd like to think that he attained a measure of comfort and, at the last, he was focused only on the lollipop in his mouth, patiently whittling and studying the stars in the sky.

45

I follow the shortest course, but currents run with a mind of their own. Somewhere in the sprawl of northern Virginia, I find myself clasped in a river of traffic. Oakland's freeway looks like Opal's driveway in comparison. When I try to change lanes, people stare straight ahead and do not let me in. I mean to follow the Capital Beltway until it joins again with Interstate 95, but the metallic deluge forks off, and I fork off with it, flushed onto a surface road I do not know.

This road is smaller, so that our cars now crush together in trash compactor fashion. In the stop and go traffic, men in ties and women in business suits jerk their cars from lane to lane, talking on cell phones and sipping coffees. I wonder if they are talking to each other, relaying the merits of various lanes and keeping their advantage from me.

I am held captive in a middle lane. I wonder if I will just head in this unforeseen direction until the Mustang sputters out of gas. But then a great mall rises before me, an Oz-like assemblage of turreted and domed rooftops, and by some miracle, I insert myself into a turning lane, where a last rushing tendril of traffic spits me into a parking lot.

You take what fate provides. I'm hungry, and I need a place to spread out my map so I can find my way back to the interstate.

Inside the mall, the residents of northern Virginia have left their cars, but they retain their rush and their phones. They walk purposefully, heels clicking over mock granite floors polished to a boot shine. Music issues from somewhere and everywhere, but only a few feeble bars make themselves known above the chatter of conversation amplified by atrium echo.

There are dozens of restaurants, some with table space, but their open fronts are exposed to the din. In our land of plenty, the simple act of a quiet lunch is beyond reach.

I am about to turn back when I see the glass window hung with tatami matting. Inside it is dim and quiet, in part because glass and tatami provide insulation, in part because the dozen linen-draped tables are empty.

A discrete bell announces my entry. This is followed by brief murmuring from behind a silk screen at the restaurant's rear. The front of the screen is a brush painting depicting a samurai warrior kneeling before a small vase of flowers. The artist has painted the flowers so that they bend ever so slightly toward the reverential samurai.

A man emerges from behind the screen. He wears an immaculately pressed pinstripe suit. A small American flag is affixed to his lapel.

"They are yellow chrysanthemums but robbed of their yellow," he says. His slight smile mirrors his bow. "Perhaps you already know this, but the chrysanthemum appears on the Japanese imperial family's crest. For those of us deprived of royal blood, the chrysanthemum still adorns our passport."

"It's a beautiful painting."

Sumi-e, I want to add, *black ink painting*, but I don't.

"Yes." His hand sweeps the room. "Please, sir. As you can see, you may sit wherever you like."

I choose a table facing the screen. After being swept helplessly here, the humbled warrior is soothing.

"Will anyone be joining you?"

"No. I'm alone."

The man has a contagious smile.

"Sometimes it is better to enjoy a meal without distraction."

He places the menu in front of me. He does not remove the place setting across from me, and I am grateful. The settings are elegantly simple. Bowl, plate, and teacup are white porcelain, the rims traced in black.

"Lunch is not our busiest time. People are in a hurry, and our preparation takes time. Please let me know if you have any questions regarding the menu."

He disappears behind the screen. There is more murmuring. When he returns to take my order, there is a commotion behind the screen. The sound of breaking glass is followed by a pithy oath I recognize.

My host flushes.

"Please excuse me."

Returning to the edge of the screen, his voice is hushed, but the disgruntled voice behind the screen is not.

Returning, he says, "My apologies. My father is older now. Occasionally his hands betray him."

Occasionally.

"There is no need to apologize," I say. "It's a fate few of us escape."

"Yes."

While I eat, the figure behind the screen is still as a midnight pond. The sashimi and nigirizushi, the balled rice topped with the thinnest slice of freshwater eel, are delicious, the best I have ever tasted, and when my host returns, I tell him so. When he looks down, pretending to brush something from the back of his hand, I see his shirt cuffs are rolled back.

"It is nothing," he says. "I will tell the chef."

In the past, I would have said nothing, but in the past, I wouldn't have found myself lost and eating in a strange restaurant several thousand miles from home. I allow my new circumstances to whisk away my habits.

"Your father. May I ask his age?"

There is a moment's hesitation. For this I feel mildly guilty.

"Of course. This November, he will turn eighty-four. He is the father of five sons and three daughters. He also has thirteen grandchildren and five great-grandchildren."

The screen gives another slight bump.

"Fusei is a gift," I say, a trifle loudly.

The man's eyes assume the light of his smile.

"You are not our conventional customer."

"Everyone recognizes the gift of fatherhood."

It is impolite to pursue this further; unlike me, he exhibits restraint. But I have none. Suddenly I want to know about the man behind the screen. I discard propriety entirely.

"Your family owns this restaurant?"

"The restaurant belongs to my father. It is only my father and I. My brothers and sisters find the restaurant business unfulfilling. It was my father's dream to have a fine restaurant in America, but not everyone shares the same dreams."

"It is good of you to help him."

"It is good for me to help him. I enjoy his company. It is no sacrifice."

Before habit can return, I say, "With his permission, I would like to meet your father."

My host bends. By luck, he whispers in my good ear.

"Thank you. This will save him from knocking down the screen." Standing again, he says, "I will ask my father."

He disappears behind the screen. There is no murmuring.

The man in the wheelchair was a bull in his youth. He sits up straight, shoulders squared. He maneuvers the wheelchair with powerful forearms, but when he reaches the table, his head bows as delicately as the chrysanthemums. The fingertips gripping the end of the armrests are white, but I see how his hands still quiver, and I know his heart breaks with every broken glass.

I also know where the son received his bashful smile.

"I am Tomimatsu Ishikawa. The clumsy eavesdropper."

I stand. I consider bowing, but I extend a hand instead.

"I am Henry Whithouse. And I am flattered to think I might be so interesting."

His grip is powerful.

"It is true that at our age one becomes quite inquisitive," he says. "But it is also true that at our age, one quickly divines what is worth heeding."

"Please join me."

Now the father flushes.

"I do not wish to interrupt your meal."

"You would be providing both honor and favor. I'm traveling alone. It is not a recipe for good conversation."

"I am envious of your traveling."

"At the moment, I am lost in my own country."

Tomimatsu performs a dismissive shrug.

"At our age, who is not?"

Turning to his son, Tomimatsu speaks in Japanese. His son nods and disappears into the kitchen.

When the door closes, he says, "My son works very hard. In everything, he applies himself to the utmost. He has a master's degree in international relations from Georgetown University. He would prefer to apply that skill, but he stays here with me, applying his diligence to becoming a passable chef. As we both heard, my other children have gone their own way. I do not begrudge them this choice."

"Your son is an excellent chef."

"Thank you. There is always opportunity for improvement. Have you come far?"

"I drove from San Francisco."

"A long journey."

"My opportunities for travel are dwindling."

He holds up his hands. Deprived of the armrest, they shake like castanets.

"I can no longer drive." He smile is not one of disappointment. "Sometimes it is even difficult to press a glass against a screen. But I am grateful. At our age, the opportunity to have this conversation is a gift."

This conversation is amusing to both of us, like the subtle leanings and retractions before a first kiss, each of us waiting, helping the other along, until the proper opening presents itself.

"I fear infirmity has provided cowardice a convenient excuse," he adds.

"It took me fifty years to take this trip."

"You cannot discover any oceans unless you have the courage to lose sight of the shore."

"A Japanese philosopher?"

"A poster in the store next door."

We both laugh.

The kitchen door opens. The son places the first plate before me and then serves his father. Dark slices of tuna, glazed lightly with a seasoning, stand upright in precise rows.

"Like soldiers," Tomimatsu says, looking down into his lap. "The tuna is seared very briefly over a hot flame, marinated for a very short time in vinegar, then sliced thinly and lightly seasoned with ginger. The method of preparation originated in Tosa Province, but legend says a nineteenth-century samurai acquired the searing technique from Europeans in Nagasaki. So each of us needs the other."

The son has already disappeared into the kitchen.

"He is not nosey like his father. He keeps books in the kitchen. He reads everything, but he enjoys history most. Sometimes, though, I must correct his books. It is no fault of the authors. Many of them were born after the events they attempt to describe. To them, it is just a story. My son encourages me to write my own book, but the enterprise is vain. If I wrote such a book, no one would read it. I am an old man, uninteresting to anyone, though fascinating to myself."

"I would read it."

"I think you already know what I would write."

I answer quickly, out of respect and gratitude, but I also answer for my benefit too.

"I served in the Pacific. Marines. First division. Peleliu."

Tomimatsu lifts a shaking tuna soldier with his chopsticks, placing it on my plate.

"I also served in the Pacific, but our paths did not cross directly. I was chief engineer aboard the *Iro Maru*. She was a 14,000-ton tanker ship. The duties she performed are in the past now, but in the end, she was destroyed off Palau. Your pilots were unerring. The first bomb struck the engine room."

Our navy's planes rise again from the airstrip on Peleliu, their shells whistling into the jungle, scattering limbs and limestone.

"Everyone in the engine room was killed but me. I do not know why. Not one day passes where I do not see myself standing in my engine room. I am not the chief engineer. I am a boy staring stupidly at black smoke."

"We were raised to serve our countries," I say.

I am deeply sorry for many things I did in the name of country, and I am sorry for some of the things my country has done. But I served willingly.

Tomimatsu nods.

"You and I, we were born to another time. I confess there are times when I eavesdrop on other customers. Sometimes I think I am the only one listening. I do not know if my own sons and daughters know the meaning of service. They speak mostly of what they want, cars, homes, Christmas bonuses." He smiles. "Our ancestors did not celebrate Christmas. But my children do not see the past, nor do they see their talk as selfish. They simply see it as their moment in time."

I look toward the kitchen.

"One son understands service."

His chuckle is a deep rumble.

"Perhaps somewhere with him I made a mistake," he says. "But I did not intend to sit here and complain. I have had far more than my share of life's gifts. May I tell you a story?"

"I would enjoy that."

"It will be less tiring than reading an entire book."

He holds his hand patiently above the bowl until it assumes the required calm. He sips the tea quickly, placing it carefully back on the table.

"I did travel once. Fifteen years ago, I returned to Palau, before my body failed me. It was arranged that I would scuba dive down to my ship. But they did not tell me there would be a ceremony first. There were newspaper reporters and a television station on the boat. It was terribly embarrassing." His smile spreads slowly. "But water is the great divider and keeper of secrets. As soon as I sank below the surface, they were all gone; only the dive guide assigned to accompany me, for there is no telling what an old man might suddenly do ninety feet beneath the surface. But the guide understood. He swam behind me, keeping a distance.

"First I swam above my ship. It was so very strange. The bow was undamaged. On the deck, there was a pair of boots and ceramic sake bottles still corked. The bomb that finished us ripped a hole amidships, and so I was able to swim into the ship and, with some care, make my way to my engine room. Swimming toward the stern, I confess I was deeply afraid. So many memories. I did not know how I would react. I feared I might forget to breathe. I looked back several times to make sure my guide was near me. I considered turning back, but I knew I would never have the opportunity again."

He sat still, negotiating the dreamy interior again.

"The passage narrowed and grew dark. My dive light was on, but I did not need it. I knew every inch of my vessel. There was a gaping hole before me, and I saw my engine room. Everything was very still. The light coming through the destroyed deck made everything foggy blue. It was like coming alive in a dream. It was exactly as I remembered it, as if I were standing there again. Fifteen of my men were killed when the first bomb struck, but the *Iro Maru*, she was built to last. She burned for two days before she sank. She was not the only vessel sent to the bottom. The attack was a great success for America. My son's history books tell me the attack was called Operation Desecrate."

It is all about dominance, but some men will never be dominated.

Tomimatsu sits at the table, but he speaks to his dreams.

"I said a prayer for my comrades, but I was not sad. I was deeply happy to be there, to have the opportunity to remember and offer my respects, yes, but to grasp new memories too. As we ascended to the surface, rising slowly up the forward conning tower, I saw an anemone fixed to the tower. It was the purest white. Its tentacles moved in the current like flowing silk. I have never seen anything so beautiful. New life." He gives the slightest smile. "Had it not prophesied uproar, I would have gladly stayed there forever."

The door chimes. A couple stands blinking in the half light.

The bashful smile again.

"And so you are afforded escape from another drab story." Tomimatsu's hands drop to the wheels. "I must greet them. My son is a diligent worker, but he loses himself in his books."

"Thank you for the gift of your company," I say. "You are a fascinating old man."

Now the smile is broad as the man.

"Only because they are our stories."

I watch him seat the couple. He wheels into the kitchen, bumping through the door. The woman looks at her watch.

The son delivers menus and returns to me.

"Thank you for asking my father to join you. He enjoyed your company immensely."

"It was an honor to meet him." Time is short. "He is very proud of you."

It is pleasing to see him flush.

"My father is a remarkable man. A soldier and Hibakusha."

The word chills me.

The son is observant.

"He did not tell you."

"No."

"I am sorry. He said you discussed the war."

"We did. But we were interrupted." *Before the end.*

It is wrong to pursue such a private matter, but I have to know. I lower my voice.

"Your father, was he married before the war?"

"Yes. His wife and newborn daughter resided in Nagasaki. Eventually he remarried."

I understand now the gift of the anemone.

Hibakusha. Survivor of the bombing.

I return to the parking lot and slide behind the wheel. I sit silent but not still. My body shakes, and my hands are Tomimatsu's. Water sings to me, but the song is no lullaby.

I weep like a baby. I breathe in great shudders. I cry until I'm done. When I finish, I do what I should have done all along.

My finger is poised above the red button. It is Sarah I want.

It is Sarah who answers.

I hear my trembling breaths. I did not plan for it to be this way.

"I love you."

The male turtle waits offshore, but he probably doesn't know why.

The silence is not nearly as long as I expect.

"I know."

Is there nothing I cannot see?

"The poem," she says. "The one I marked and left for you in the kitchen."

"Lilacs."

"I pretended you wrote it to me."

What is love? What is fidelity? What is loyalty, courage, cruelty, hatred, misunderstanding, prejudice?

What is certain?

It is time to remember the good, and I do.

"Sweet is the breath of Morn," I say.

Sarah's laugh is soft as snowfall.

"I'd say it's closer to evening," she says, "but a fine evening it's turned out to be."

When I hang up, I feel the settling, a semblance of peace. But I am angry too, for the bridges I have not crossed have defined my life.

Many Hibakusha forged a new life. But I am no Tomimatsu Ishikawa, and that night, in another indifferent motel, the realization sees me cry again without restraint. Regret is the sharpest thorn. The pain we suffer is not in things beyond us. The pain is in realizing, too late, that these things were not beyond us at all.

46

This time, my phone rings before I shave. I look at the clock. Five forty-five.

There are never preliminaries.

"What happened?"

I smile.

"Is today a school day?"

"Yesssssss." The hissing word as muffled as the ones that follow. "Cut it out. What happened?"

"What do you mean what happened?"

"You called Sarah yesterday. What did you talk about?"

I think for a moment.

"Did she say?"

"No. That's why I'm asking you."

"We talked about poems."

"*Poems?*"

The word makes me feel good.

"Poems," I say. "Do you read poems?"

"Mom wakes me up in five minutes. Sarah went shopping yesterday."

For the first time, I am in control.

"Your grandmother isn't allowed to shop?" I tease.

"She doesn't *like* to shop. Not for herself. But she went shopping yesterday. Mom took her to the mall, and she bought a dress. I saw it. I made her take it out of the box when she got home. It's really pretty, all white, with a sash that goes around the waist. She bought a sun hat too. It's got a wide brim and a white rose sewn into the band, like those hats ladies wear in really old movies."

My spirits are rising as if they're in a high-speed elevator.

"They both sound beautiful."

"They are. But it's still weird."

"Sometimes old people do weird things."

"I know it's because you're coming. I hope you're going to dress nice."

"I am. I promise."

"A nice shirt with a collar. Maybe a pair of khaki pants. Like the models in Tommy Hilfiger."

"I can't be a model."

"I don't like models. Their faces are shiny like plastic dolls. Where are you?"

"I'm in Baltimore."

"Are you nervous?"

"Yes."

"Me too."

"Why should we be nervous if we're already friends?"

"Most friends have seen each other before. Can you throw?"

"Throw?"

"A wiffleball."

"I guess I can. I haven't thrown a ball in a long time."

"You'll have to warm up first. Sarah throws to me sometimes, but she's got a bad shoulder, and her aim isn't so great anymore. Don't tell her I said that."

"I won't. But I might not be any better."

"Everybody gets a tryout."

"Thank you," I say.

"For what?"

"For always making me smile."

"How far is Baltimore?"

"Not far at all," I say, and I almost laugh out loud.

"Good. And don't forget to comb your crazy hair."

In the evening, the phone rings again.

"Where are you?"

"Connecticut."

I say it with a trace of pride, but no one congratulates me.

"We've got a surprise for you. Sarah and I finished it today. It took a lot longer than we thought. But it was worth it. I did most of it myself."

"If you made it, I know I'll like it."

"You have to see it first."

I hear a single clack.

"What are you doing?"

"You hear it? Hold on. I'm putting the phone down."

What I hear over the next minute sounds like two people playing ping-pong very, very slowly.

When I'm sure she's forgotten, she picks up the phone.

"Batting practice," she says. "It's easier when I put the phone down. If I hold the phone, I have to make sure I don't throw the phone up in the air too. Take the baaaallll, throoooow it up." Now the recognizable clack. "You'd better have more than an aspirin tablet."

"What's an aspirin tablet?"

"A fastball. You'd better have more than one pitch. You know, slider, sinker, curve, knuckler, floater, bug. Actually, the last three are the same thing."

This clack is loud.

"Another souvenir for a lucky Bosox fan," I say.

"It doesn't matter."

"It doesn't matter?"

"Did you already forget about the surprise?"

47

The Hyannis shoreline is virtually the same. Money has its benefits, and privilege feels no onus to sell. The same homes sit back from the dunes, their shingles replaced, widow's peaks and porch balustrades repainted and repainted again, a faux addition or two. But the tidily aligned window rows still look out to Nantucket Sound, and on the putting green lawns, white Adirondack lawn chairs still rest alongside banks of flowers overhung with copper bird feeders.

The knoll on which Abby and I were married is gone. So is the hotel. The hill has been leveled for a parking lot whose asphalt is run through with sandy cracks, for the shoreline is fickle foundation at best.

The boy at the kiosk takes my money without a word. My reward is the last parking spot.

My mood mirrors the day, a postcard summer afternoon, the sky cloudless and deep blue. On the small strip of Quohog Beach, young women in beach chairs gossip with an eye on children running and splashing in blue-green shallows. My heart pounds so that I feel each beat. One of the mothers could be Cassandra; one of the racing children, Tesia.

But no one pays any attention to me as I walk slowly through the sand in my dress shoes. The simple act of walking across the sand is no longer thoughtless. But my heart races faster than the effort of walking merits.

Sun and storm have bleached and smoothed the rocks. When I walk onto the jetty, the gaps between the rocks are gone, filled in with cement. It's an easy walk to the end, even for an old man, but I wonder where the crabs have gone.

I close my eyes and turn my face to the sun, listening to the sounds of the world around me—the distant throb of the Nantucket ferry, the cries of gulls, the laughter of children, and the snapping of bedsheets in the crisp wind.

They are not bedsheets, of course. Opening my eyes, I watch a small armada of identical sailboats, cutting like ivory shards through the water. They lean in the same direction and jockey about, stealing as much wind as they can. I smile and nod to two girls, descendants of sea captains, refusing to acquiesce to convention or defeat. Both racing with the wind.

This time, it is not a good-bye. It is a dream remembered, a wedding procession for two beneath a full moon and the heavy damp of the sea. You cannot change the past, but there is a knife to cut the seizings, and I ask permission to do so.

I call from the parking lot.

"You're here!" Tesia yelps.

"Almost."

This is a white lie.

"When are you coming?"

"I should be there in about two hours."

"*Two hours?*"

"Maybe a little less."

"Not maybe."

"Your wish is my command."

"Why so long?"

I am running with the current now, the water funneling past, singing again.

"I've got some secrets too," I say, and this time I smile.

I thought I allowed for a substantial cushion of time, but it actually does take me two hours. Hyannis is much bigger than I imagined. There are floods of cars on Route 132 and floods of people in the Cape Cod Mall, glowering in long lines. But the line in the store I visit is shorter, and the teenage girl behind the counter sheds her apathy when I tell her what I am doing.

Driving to Sarah's, I roll all the windows down, but I still sweat. I'm glad the dress shirt is white. The thoughts that rush over me are as undisciplined as their coming. I pass loamy drives and cottages sequestered quietly amid pines, and kids riding bikes, their bare ribs shining in the sun. And then the Mustang is bumping up the sandy drive, lush spread of lawn on either side, and in the distance, I see the reeds that mark the edge of the pond. Through the windshield, the widow's peak juts into the sky like a fairytale castle turret, and as I come to stop in a cloud of hot silence, the screen door bangs open, and a small figure in a summer dress vaults over the porch and steps as if they don't exist. At the far end of the porch, another figure rises from the porch swing.

I remember how to get out of the car, but I forget everything else.

I am mildly surprised to see she has a shock of red hair, but it makes me smile to see her freckles, and I see where the yellow sash around her waist is smudged, and I already know there is dirt under her fingernails.

She runs across the grass and stops short. Two yards separate us. She quivers like a greyhound, but she holds her place.

Her eyes are as bold as I imagined. Together they roll toward her left ear.

"Sarah said not to tackle you."

"I'm so glad you're my friend."

I bend and spread my arms, absorbing the collision and the waft of baby powder.

From somewhere, I feel a vague tugging.

"Pogue," says Tesia firmly. "Start breathing."

48

Before dinner, we play wiffle ball. My tryout.
Stairs lead from the kitchen down to the garage. The garage is new, an addition. The garage door is already open, a blue plastic bat propped against the wall just inside the garage. Out in the drive, a blue bucket brims with wiffle balls.

"Blue's my good luck color," Tesia says, "but I won't need it."

Taking my hand, she leads me to the pitcher's mound. I toe the cardboard slab affixed to the drive with liberally scuffed duct tape. Ten yards from the pitcher's mound, home plate is drawn in front of the garage in blue chalk.

Tesia drags the bucket to the pitcher's mound. Returning to the garage, she closes the door. She picks up the bat and takes a scimitar swing.

"What's your lucky color?"

"Blue-green," I say.

"It won't help."

"We'll just see."

I pick a ball from the bucket and toss it casually in the air. Tesia raps the outside corner of the plate.

I conjure a man moving effortlessly to his left, fielding the short hop, and releasing the ball in the same uninterrupted motion, the throw like a tracer.

I am not Conrad. My first three pitches bounce off the gravel two feet in front of the plate. I can't remember the last time I threw a ball. My arm comes around as if my shoulder is weighted with gravel.

Tesia drops the bat to a drooping shoulder.

"Maybe we should just walk to the pond," she says.

"Not a chance. I'm finding my groove."

This time I perform a half wind-up—sometimes any change is good—pausing to glance back over my shoulder. Tesia leans over the plate, jaw set, bat spinning tight circles.

This pitch reaches the plate. The ball makes a pleasant whistling sound as it passes over my head and lands on the other side of a hedge forty feet away.

"Homer. Two to nothing."

"Two?"

"Who were you looking at over your shoulder?"

"Ah."

My pitches are big as pumpkins. Balls blaze past me like snowy meteors. I never find a groove, but I do find my competitive instincts. I throw as hard as I can, octogenarian aspirin tablets. Tesia redirects them into various bits of distant shrubbery. In fifteen minutes, we have emptied the bucket.

Tesia makes me sit in a fold-out chair. I watch her plunge into bushes, her dress snagging on branches. The sky is that soft blue that makes you want to rub up against it. Fireflies wink in front of the already dark bushes.

"Where did you learn to hit like that?"

"Baseball camp. Sarah signed me up. So I'll be ready for Little League." A ball sails twenty feet, bouncing off the rim of the bucket. The new Conrad. "Those boys will be sorry."

"Those boys and the Yankees."

It takes ten minutes to gather all the balls, with a few gone missing. Dropping the last ball in the bucket, she picks up the bat and leans over the plate.

"You want to bat?" she asks.

I wrest myself from the chair. My arm throbs.

"I'm not quitting until I strike you out."

"You'll have to stay up all night."

We go through two more buckets without the whiff of a strikeout. My tablet has become a creampuff. The fireflies wink mocking applause. The throbbing moves into my shoulder and neck. I do not want this moment to end.

A window slides up. Above us, Cassandra calls out, "Tesia, you and Mr. Whithouse need to come in. It's almost dark."

The smell of simmering meat and onions makes my mouth water.

Cassandra smiles down.

"I hope you like chili," she says.

"I'll eat anything to spare me further humiliation."

"We could turn the garage light on," Tesia says hopefully.

"*Young lady.*"

She drags the bucket to its assigned place outside the garage. Inside the garage, she leans the bat against the wall.

"You're different than Sarah said."

"How?"

"She said you never broke any rules or did anything surprising."

The mistakes you make are like a cold wind down a canyon that never ends.

"She was right."

I am so tired I wonder if I'm going to make it up the stairs.

Halfway up, Tesia turns back to me.

"I'm sorry about your wife."

"It's okay."

"How can it be okay?"

I watch her, this impossible gift in a summer dress, breathtaking and delicate.

"It has to be."

The bright kitchen makes us both wince. In the middle of the kitchen, an island is ringed with barstools. A steaming cup of coffee rests in front of a stool, a framed picture beside it.

Sarah sits on a stool across from mine. She holds a pencil, a folded newspaper in front of her.

"Black," she says.

"Thank you for remembering."

"I'm not a loose cannon yet. One reason I do the crossword puzzle every night."

Something jostles against me.

Tesia carefully positions the picture frame and steps back.

"It's your surprise," she says.

I pick it up with both hands. The frame is silver, without pattern. Beneath the glass, leaves are pasted on blue cardboard. Here and there, glue has oozed from beneath the leaves. The leaves are arranged in a not quite elliptical shape. Smaller leaves have been used to fashion what look like apostrophes. They sprout on either side of the ellipse.

It is like a form in the fog.

"You don't know what it is."

"It's lovely."

"That's not the answer. *Look*."

The leaves are brown. Despite the glue's best efforts, some cup up off the cardboard like supplicant hands.

Cassandra watches from the stove, stirring the bubbling chili. Sarah smiles, but no one offers help.

The disappointment on Tesia's face makes me founder even more.

Sarah taps the pencil to her forehead.

"Give him a minute, Tesia," she says. "He's a smart man. He surprised *you*."

Cassandra's and Tesia's gifts have already been delivered. I purchased Cassandra's present three days earlier, spotting it gleaming in the window of a disheveled store in Collingswood, New Jersey. The store was going out of business after forty years. When I asked the owner why, he said that children today wanted more excitement than musical instruments could produce. I knew a child who had felt differently.

Even from the kitchen, we can hear the bullfrogs trading croaks in Tesia's upstairs bedroom.

Tesia looks despondently at her watch.

"*Two* minutes," she says.

"Mr. Whithouse and I measure time differently," Sarah says.

I stare at the shape. I want nothing more than to recognize it. It is becoming familiar, so familiar it is like seeing a long-forgotten face on the street, knowing the face, wanting to call out, but the name floats just above your tongue. It comes to me.

I look into my coffee, but not quickly enough for a child's eyes.

Always from a great distance, I hear shouts of joy, the ringing of childish laughter from the riverbank. The river sings to them again, but not to me. The Florida sun shines. Sean stands in knee-deep water, checking the raft. He has done this countless times before, but this time I stand at the edge of the bank staring at my brother, carving his lily-white skin and the capable movements of his hands into my memory. Other kids mill about, talking excitedly, but I am alone. The edge of the bank feels like a precipice. My toes squeeze the mud. My heart squeezes in my chest.

"Pogue."

My brother holds out his hand. I reach out and take the talisman. Only at this moment do I realize that not once has my brother swum out to retrieve a raft.

Sean smiles as if we are the only two by the river.

"Our secret."

I can only nod.

Not until he pushes the raft into waist-deep water do I find my voice. He has already shimmied up onto the raft. He settles himself and begins kicking out into the river.

"Big as a pumpkin!" I shout. "In the Red Sea, they use leatherback shells as sailboats!"

There is a frantic edge to my shout. I am vaguely aware of shiftings and murmurings around me, but I have eyes only for my brother.

Gripping the raft, he looks back. I am not sure he sees me, but then he smiles again, and our eyes meet, and we both know Pliny was right.

He grins.

"Swim like a rifle shot and a leaf in a breeze," he says.

I know he can do neither, and I let him go. I do this because he is my fearless brother, and I know that even if I stop him now, there will be other opportunities. His feet churn the green water. I feel the smooth carving in my hand.

Perhaps in these more understanding times, things would have been different. But in the 1930s, homosexuality was not accepted, or, compromise, it was tacitly ignored. My brother knew this, just as he knew Matty Simpson's father would come, and our father would beat him once with his fists and forever after with a cold silence the world would echo. He could not accept this. Whether you call it bravery or cowardice is up to you.

I do know beyond doubt that the river was his kingdom and his salve, though every paradise has its dark side. I wonder what my brother thought of when he sat with his back to us before every ride, summoning his courage, pushing away his fear. *Do one thing every day that scares you.* It may have been punishment, or twisted atonement. He could have drowned on any summer day—a slip of the hand, an unexpected list of the raft—but he chose the day that he did.

I clenched the talisman and watched Sean kick out into the middle of the river.

Going to the bottom was a simple matter for someone who couldn't swim, but it was not enough for me. Even a confused boy, standing on a riverbank awash in adulation and grief and emotions he will never fathom, sees drowning as unheroic, perhaps even a coward's path. My brother deserved to go up in the flames of Vesuvius, and so he did. Shadows can be lies too.

I have kept his secret for a lifetime, though I believe our father knew there was no alligator, but few fathers have the courage to face the fact that they forced their child's end. I do not think less of our father for this. On many fronts, he was braver than most, but we all have bridges we will not cross, a fact I know all too well.

Should you ever find yourself on a raft moving through the water, pay close attention. The water moves past, but it also sweeps in from the left and the right, and sometimes it even flows in reverse, and sometimes it does all of this at once, so that, for a brief moment, the water gathers in one precise spot. In that moment, there is no song, only a stillness that is like an unalterable settling out.

I sip slowly, focusing on the dark wrinkling liquid, but still I see how Tesia smiles at Sarah, more secrets shared between the only members of the species willing to crawl ashore.

I put the cup down carefully.

"It's the best gift I've ever gotten."

"We know you love sea turtles," says Tesia proudly.

She still watches me. Children have not yet learned to turn away. My new outfit does not include a handkerchief.

"Guess what it's made of."

Leaves is too obvious.

"A hint?"

"The tenth good thing," she says.

She lets me struggle, but I know she will rescue me.

"The leaves are from the roses you sent."

My heart soars as I ride, the surging of eternity before me, and when the raft slips seamlessly beneath the river's surface, my companion's speed does not diminish. In the hazy green waters, other shapes swim. We move together but apart—Abby, Sean, my mother and father, the inquisitive Pliny, an old woman who knows how to be young, a young girl who can find ten good things and continue on.

When Tesia steps forward, I take her in my arms. But it is she who supports me, my favorite dream brought to life.

After Tesia has trudged grudgingly off to bed, Sarah and I sit on the porch swing, the book now closed between us. We hold hands. It seems quaint, like kissing Janie Clayton, but it is comfortable and very nice. Sarah's hand is soft and warm. If I close my eyes, it is Morn.

"You saved my poems," Sarah says.

A tropical breeze whispers in my head, riffling Peleliu's waiting waters.

"I had no choice."

Her laugh is as warm as her hand.

"You of all people know we make our own choices," she says.

Neither accolade nor epitaph.

"Do you remember Auden?" she asks.

'O plunge your hands in water
Plunge them in up to the wrist;
Stare, stare in the basin
And wonder what you've missed

I speak Auden's words slowly, letting them wander into the night. Beautiful things should not be rushed.

Beside me, Sarah watches them go.

"When I was young, I thought it was the saddest poem I had ever read," she says. "I thought it was only about missed opportunities. About things that might have been."

"And now?"

"Now I know there is always opportunity."

Her hand pulls away. The swing creaks as she stands.

"Let's walk," she says.

We walk along flagstones to the pond, passing through a tunnel in the reeds where someone has cut them back.

The dock is new, some kind of synthetic wood that gives way spongily beneath our feet. Every edge is ruler straight. It is not Gray's dock, but it is not Gray beside me in the moonlight.

"The South is a place," I say. "North, east, and west are just directions."

"Is that so?"

"A friend of mine said that. I used to believe him. But I don't anymore."

The moon is almost full and white bright, but the surface of the pond remains dark.

I envy Pliny. He blurred the line between fact and fiction until he believed his tales, but I was never so lucky. I know it was lonely for Sean at the last, with all the stars going out.

I stare at the dark water. Slowly they appear on the surface, lily pads scattered haphazardly.

We stand at the end of the dock like divers, our toes over the edge.

Sarah is smiling.

"In days gone by, our clothes would already be in a pile, and we'd be swimming," she says.

My shirt isn't quite off before she stops speaking, but it is close enough.

The night's cool is pleasing against my skin.

"*Mr. Whithouse*," says Sarah, but her fingers are not wagging reproach; they are working down the buttons of her dress.

On a quiet night, you can hear cotton fall.

We do not look at each other.

Off our toes, water bugs step jauntily across the water as if it were black marble. It is a sight to make Pliny rejoice, and it makes me smile wider.

"How do they do that?" asks Sarah.

"Miniature snowshoes."

"I like that," Sarah says, taking my hand.

"I'm afraid that's not enough."

It is a fine kiss, delicate as a water bug's tread.

"Do you do this with all the women you meet?"

I imagine us, ivory in the moonlight.

"Some," I say.

"Good."

I kiss her again, and there is nothing roguish about it.
The leatherback captains its own course.
"Deep?" I ask.
"Deep enough."
Together we jump.